Fortu

LEANNE BANKS
CINDY KIRK
MARIE FERRARELLA

MILLS &
BOON

First Published in Great Britain 2016
By Mills & Boon, an imprint of HarperCollins*Publishers*
1 London Bridge Street, London, SE1 9GF

FORTUNE'S HEART © 2017 Harlequin Books S. A.

Happy New Year, Baby Fortune!, *A Sweetheart For Jude Fortune* and *Lassoed By Fortune* were first published in Great Britain by Harlequin (UK) Limited.

Happy New Year, Baby Fortune! © 2014 Harlequin Books S. A.
A Sweetheart For Jude Fortune © 2014 Harlequin Books S. A.
Lassoed By Fortune © 2014 Harlequin Books S. A.

Special thanks and acknowledgement are given to Leanne Banks, Cindy Kirk and Marie Ferrarella for their contribution to *The Fortunes Of Texas: Welcome To Horseback Hollow* series.

ISBN: 978-0-263-92949-2

05-0117

HAPPY NEW YEAR, BABY FORTUNE!

BY
LEANNE BANKS

This book is dedicated to my husband, Tony,
for takeout and tolerance, super editors Gail Chasan
and Susan Litman,
and genius plotter Marcia Book Adirim.

Chapter One

Stacey Fortune Jones was sure she had the cutest date at the New Year's Eve wedding reception for her cousin Sawyer Fortune and his bride, Laurel Redmond.

"Your baby is just gorgeous," Sherry James, one of her neighbors, said as she patted Stacey's six-month-old daughter's arm. "She has the best smile."

"Thank you," Stacey said. Clothed in a red velvet dress with a lace headband, white tights and red shoes, her little Piper was a true head turner. Stacey had enjoyed getting Piper ready for her first big night out, and it seemed her daughter was having fun. Her big green gaze took in all the sights and sounds of the celebration, and she smiled easily with everyone who approached. "She's a sweet baby now that she's gotten through her colic."

Sherry made a sympathetic clucking noise. "Colic can be hard on both the baby and the parents."

Stacey gave a vague nod. "So true," she said. In Stacey's case, there was no need for the plural. There was no dad to help. He'd abandoned Stacey before Piper had even been born. Thank goodness her parents had let her move back in with them.

"Well, you've obviously done a great job with her. She's the belle of the ball tonight," Sherry said.

"Thank you," Stacey said again.

"Oh, my husband's calling me," Sherry said. "You take care, now."

Jiggling her daughter Piper on her hip, Stacey headed for an empty seat at a table to give her feet a rest. Looking around, she couldn't believe that an airplane hangar could be transformed into such a beautiful reception site. Miles of tulle and lights decorated the space, and buffet tables groaned with delicious food. The sounds of a great band and happy voices echoed throughout the building. The guests, dressed in their finest, added to a celebratory mood. This wedding was the event of the season for the citizens of the small town of Horseback Hollow, Texas. People would be talking about it for years to come.

Although some might consider the choice of an airplane hangar a strange place to hold a wedding, it suited the groom and bride, since this was where the two were running a flight school together. No one had thought Sawyer or Laurel would ever settle down, let alone with each other. But the two stubborn yet free-spirited people had come to the conclusion that they were perfect for each other.

Stacey watched the newly married couple dance together and couldn't help thinking about the wedding she had been planning with her ex, Joe. Sometimes she wondered if she had ever really known Joe at all, or if she had been in love with an illusion of the man she'd wanted him to be. Now she didn't know if she'd ever find the love she saw on the faces of the bride and groom. Even though the hangar was filled with family and friends, and her little Piper was in her arms, Stacey suddenly felt alone.

"Hey," a male voice said. "How's it going?"

Stacey blinked to find her longtime neighbor, Colton Foster, sitting beside her. She gave herself a mental shake and tried to pull herself out of her blue moment. Colton's sister, Rachel, was Stacey's best friend; but Stacey had been overwhelmed with taking care of Piper, so she hadn't seen him except in passing since the baby had been born.

She'd known the Foster family forever. Colton had graduated several years earlier from the same high school she'd attended. He'd always been quiet and hardworking. He was the firstborn and only son of the Fosters and had taken his responsibilities seriously.

Tonight he wore a dark suit along with a Stetson, but he usually dressed his tall, athletic body in jeans and work boots. He had brown eyes that seemed to see beneath the surface, brown wavy hair and a strong jaw. Stacey knew of several women who'd had crushes on him, but to Stacey, he would always be Rachel's older brother.

"Great," she said. "I'm doing great. Piper doesn't have colic anymore, so I've actually gotten a few nights of sleep. My parents adore her. My brothers and sister adore her. She's healthy and happy. Life couldn't be better," she insisted, willing herself to believe it.

Stacey searched Colton's face. She couldn't help wondering if he'd heard anything from Joe since he and her ex had been good friends. Colton had even been asked to be one of the groomsmen for Stacey and Joe's wedding. The question was on the tip of her tongue, but she swallowed it without asking. Did she really want to know? It wasn't as if she wanted him back. Still, Piper deserved to know her father, she thought. Stacey's stomach twisted as she met the gaze of her quiet neighbor. Maybe Stacey just wanted to hear that Joe was miserable without her.

The silence between them stretched. "She's a cute baby," Colton finally said.

Stacey smiled at her daughter. "Yes, she is. Someone even called her the belle of the ball," she said. "How are things with you?"

"Same as always," he said with a shrug. "Working a lot of hours to keep the ranch going."

Stacey searched for something else to say. The

gap in conversation between her and Colton felt so awkward. She couldn't remember ever feeling this uncomfortable with him. "I haven't gotten out very much since Piper was born, so it's been a while since I've seen a lot of people or been to such a big party."

He nodded. "Yeah. Rachel tells me she drops by your house every now and then. She's been keeping us updated on how you're doing."

"Rachel has always been a good friend. I don't know what I would have done without her when—" Stacey broke off, determined not to mention Joe's name aloud. She cleared her throat and decided to change the direction of the conversation. "Well, I'm glad you're doing well," she said, almost wishing he would leave. Maybe then she wouldn't feel so awkward.

Another silence stretched between them, and Stacey almost decided to leave despite the fact that Piper was half-asleep in her arms.

"It's a new year," Colton finally said. "A new year is always a good time for a fresh start. Are you planning to go back to work soon?"

Stacey sighed. "I'm not sure what to do now. I loved my job. I was a nurse at the hospital in Lubbock, but the idea of leaving Piper just tears me up. Even though my mother would babysit for me, it wouldn't be fair. My mother is busy enough without taking on the full care of a baby. Plus, I hate the idea of being so far away if Piper should need me."

"Is there anywhere else closer you could work?" he asked.

"I've thought about that, but as you know, the employment opportunities here in Horseback Hollow aren't great. There's no hospital here. It's frustrating because I don't want to be dependent on my parents. At the same time, I'm Piper's one and only parent, and I'm determined that she gets all the love she needs and deserves."

Colton studied Stacey for a long moment and realized that something about his younger sister's friend had changed. She used to be so happy and carefree. Now it seemed as if there was a shadow clouding the sunny optimism she'd always exhibited. He couldn't help feeling a hard stab of guilt. He wondered if the conversation he'd had with Joe over a year ago had influenced the man to propose to Stacey. Maybe he shouldn't have warned Joe that he might lose Stacey to someone else if he didn't put a ring on her finger. If they hadn't gotten engaged, maybe she wouldn't have gotten pregnant and Joe wouldn't have left her. After Joe had left Stacey pregnant with his child, Colton's opinion of his friend had plummeted. Now he wondered if Joe had just felt possessive about Stacey. He obviously hadn't loved her the way she deserved to be loved. Colton had always known Joe's home life hadn't been the best when he was growing up, but in Colton's mind, that was no excuse for how Joe had treated Stacey.

More than Stacey's outlook had changed, Colton noticed. She just seemed more grown-up. His gaze dipped to her body, and he couldn't help noticing she was curvier than she used to be. She'd filled out in all the right places. He glanced at her face and saw that her eyes seemed to contain a newfound knowledge.

Stacey had become a woman, he concluded. She was no longer the young girl who'd giggled constantly with his younger sister Rachel. He watched her lift a glass to her lips and take a sip of champagne, then slide her tongue over her lips.

The motion made his gut clench in an odd way. He wondered how her lips would feel against his. He wondered how her body would feel....

Shocked at the direction his mind was headed, Colton reined in his thoughts. This was *Stacey,* for Pete's sake. Not some random girl at a bar. He cleared his throat.

Stacey glanced around the room. "There are a *lot* of Fortunes. I'm still trying to keep all the names straight."

"That's for sure. Do you know all of them?" he asked.

Stacey shot him a sideways glance. "I've been introduced to all of them. I'm trying my best to remember their names. Between my mother, her brother James and her sister, Josephine, they have thirteen children."

Colton gave a low whistle. "That's a lot."

"And that doesn't include the wives. Just about

all of James Fortune's children have gotten married within the last year," she said.

"I'm curious. What made all of you take on the Fortune name?"

She shrugged. "We did it for Mom. I know it sounds weird, but for Mama, finding her birth family has been a big deal. Even though her adoptive parents loved and adored her, there were things about her past that seemed a big mystery because she knew she was adopted. I think that meeting her brother James and her sister, Josephine, makes her feel more complete. For my mom, taking on the Fortune name is a symbolic way of declaring her connection to the Fortune family. Most of us have added the Fortune name out of respect to her. My brother Liam is holding out, though."

"How does your father feel about it?"

"That's a good question," she said. "My father is very stoic. He hasn't said anything aloud, and he has loved my mother pretty much since the dawn of time, but I have a feeling he may not like the name change. I'm not sure he would ever say it, because he's supportive of my mom. He would always have her back, but I wouldn't blame him if this pinched his ego a little bit."

"Speaking of your Mama Jeanne," Colton said. "She's coming this way."

Stacey smiled. "Betcha she wants to show off her grandbaby. Watch and see."

Stacey's mother wore her snowy white hair on

the back of her head, and she sported a nice but not fancy dress. Jeanne Marie Fortune Jones was one of the most welcoming women Colton had ever met. Everyone in Horseback Hollow loved the nurturing woman. Jeanne extended her arms as she got close to Stacey and the baby. "Give me that little peanut," Mrs. Jones said. "It's time for me to give you a little break."

"She's been fine," Stacey said, handing over the baby to her mother. "I think she is half-asleep."

"Already? At her first party?" Mrs. Jones adjusted Piper's headband. "I need to introduce her to a few people before she totally zonks out." Mrs. Jones glanced at Colton. "Good to see you and your family here tonight. We're glad you could make it," she said.

"Wouldn't miss it," he said. "It was nice of you to make sure we were invited."

"Well, of course you're invited. You're like family to us. What do you think of little Piper here?" she asked, beaming with pride.

"She's a pretty little thing," Colton said, although babies made him a little uneasy. Seemed as if they could start screaming like wild banshees with no cause or warning.

"That she is," Mrs. Jones said. "I just want to make sure James and Josephine get to see her. You take a little break, Stacey."

Stacey nodded and smiled as her mother left. "Told you she wanted to show her off."

Colton glanced at Stacey's mother as she joined her Fortune siblings at a table and bounced the baby on her knee. The other woman, Josephine, smiled at the baby and jiggled the baby's hand.

Stacey smiled as she looked at her mother and her aunt and uncle. They were still learning about each other, but they were growing in love for each other, too.

"So, how does it feel to be a Fortune?" Colton asked.

"I don't know," Stacey said. "It may take some time to figure it out."

"Well, it must be nice not to have to worry about money anymore," he said.

Stacey shook her head and gave a short chuckle. "You must not have heard. My mother gave back the Fortune money. She didn't feel right about accepting it."

"Whoa," Colton said.

Stacey nodded. "Her brother James wanted to give her a lot of money. But she felt that money rightfully should go to his children. Mama doesn't want her relationship with James and the rest of the Fortunes tainted by her taking money from him."

Colton shook his head. "Your mama is an amazing woman. That was an honorable thing to do."

"I think so, too, but not everyone agrees with her decision," Stacey said. "For Mama's sake, I hope everything will turn out okay."

At that moment, Jeanne Fortune Jones was in heaven. Sharing her grandbaby with her newly discovered brother and sister, with family all around, Jeanne felt complete. Jeanne had always known she was adopted. Her parents had loved her as if they'd given birth to her, perhaps more. Yet even with all that love and adoration, something had been missing. Now she knew what it was—her brother and sister. Joined together in the womb as triplets, separated for most of their lives, the three of them were back together again. To Jeanne, it all seemed a beautiful circle of life.

Her often-stern-faced brother James cleared his throat. "Jeanne, I still wish you would accept the money I tried to give you earlier. It feels wrong. Won't you reconsider?"

Jeanne immediately shook her head. Her conviction was clear as crystal on this matter. Jeanne knew that James's children had turned their backs on him because they'd misunderstood James's attempted generosity toward Jeanne. Now, after months of an angry, silent divide, James and his family were being reunited. "Absolutely not. I refuse to be the cause of a rift between you and your children. Besides, you earned that money. I didn't have anything to do with it."

James sighed. "But I feel guilty that I have so much and you have so little."

Jeanne shook her head and smiled as she looked down at her sweet granddaughter. "I've been around long enough to know that there are all kinds of riches. I have a wonderful husband, loving children and this beautiful grandchild. And now I have the two of you. My life couldn't be happier. I feel like I'm the lucky one."

"Do the rest of your family members feel that way?" James asked doubtfully.

Jeanne thought of her son Christopher and his resentment. Chris just had some growing up to do. He would realize what was truly important in due time. At least, she hoped he would. "Mostly," she said. "Look at how most of my kids have accepted the Fortune name. They know I would do anything for them, and they would do anything for me."

Jeanne noticed her sister seemed quieter than usual. "Are you okay, Josephine? Is this party too much for you?"

Josephine shook her head. "No. It's a grand party. You Texans know how to pull out all the stops," she said in her lovely British accent.

Jeanne Marie studied her refined sister in her luxury designer clothing. Who would have ever thought that she, Jeanne Jones, could be related to a woman who had married into the British royal family?

The thought made her laugh. She and James and Josephine had been joined in the womb. That was the ultimate equality. But more important than that, Jeanne knew herself, her heart and her family. She was beyond happy with her life. She sensed, however, that James and Josephine might not be so happy with theirs, but she hoped she was wrong....

"All of my children are single. I hope they will

find love someday," Josephine murmured under her breath.

"Of course they will," Jeanne said, patting her sister's hand. "It just takes some time."

Josephine looked at Jeanne with a soft gaze. "I'm so glad we found each other."

Jeanne squeezed her sister's hand. "I am, too."

From across the room, Stacey enjoyed watching her mother with her siblings, but then she caught sight of her brother Chris striding toward her. His face looked like a thundercloud. "Uh-oh."

"I need to talk to you for a moment," Chris said, and gave Colton a short nod. "Excuse us."

Stacey lifted her lips in a smile that she suspected resembled more of a wince. "Excuse me," she said, and followed Christopher to a semiquiet corner of the airplane hangar.

"Do you see how chummy Mama Jeanne is being with James and Josephine? It makes me sick to my stomach to see her being so nice to them," he said.

"Well, of course she's being nice to them. She's thrilled she finally found out that she has brothers and a sister. You know Mama has always wondered about her birth family."

"That's not the point," Christopher said. "I don't understand how she is all right with the fact that her brothers James and John grew up with boatloads of money. And her sister, Josephine, was married to British royalty, for Pete's sake. It's not fair that they're so wealthy and she's had to watch every dime."

Chris had always been ambitious, pretty much since birth. The status quo wasn't going to be enough for him. Stacey had long known he wanted more for himself and the whole family. Chris and their father, Deke, had rubbed each other wrong on this subject on more than one occasion.

Stacey hated to see her brother so upset when she knew her mother was thrilled with the recent discovery of her siblings. "Mama's life hasn't been so bad. She has all of us kids and a great husband. They both have good health and would support each other through thick and thin." She couldn't help thinking about how Joe had left her high and dry once he'd learned she was pregnant. Her father wouldn't dream of doing anything like that to her mother.

Chris's eye twitched, and Stacey could tell he wasn't the least bit appeased. "It's still not fair. Tell the truth. Wouldn't it be nice if we didn't have to worry about money? Think about Piper. Wouldn't you like to know she would have everything she needs?"

"Piper will have everything she needs. Her life may not be filled with luxury, but she will get what she needs," Stacey insisted, feeling defensive because she wasn't making any money right now.

"Yeah, but you gotta admit things could be easier," he said.

Stacey sighed. "They could be," she admitted,

but shook her head. "But I can't let myself go there. I'm going to have to make my own way. There's no fairy tale happening for me."

"I'm not asking for a fairy tale. I'm just thinking Mom should at least get a piece of the pie," he said. "Seems to me that Mom's new brother and sister are greedy and selfish."

"It's not James Fortune's fault that we aren't getting any Fortune money. James gave her money, and Mama *chose* to give the money back. James may be a little stiff, but he seems nice enough. He really didn't even have to offer the money to Mama in the first place, but he did. I bet if any of us really needed financial help that he would be glad to help."

Chris tilted his head to one side in a thoughtful way, and Stacey could practically see the wheels turning in his mind. "You may have a point. I think I'll have a word with *Uncle* James."

Stacey opened her mouth to tell him to think it over before he approached their new relative, but he was gone before she could say a word. Stacey twisted her fingers together. She wished Chris wouldn't get so worked up about this, but she feared her discussion with him hadn't helped one bit.

Sighing, she glanced away and caught sight of the bride and groom, Laurel and Sawyer, snuggling in a corner, feeding each other bites of wedding cake. The sight was so romantic. She could tell by the expressions on their faces that they clearly adored each other. Her heart twisted. She wondered if anyone would ever look at her that way.

Stacey gave herself a hard mental shake and reminded herself that her priority was Piper now. She surveyed the room, looking for her baby, and saw that her new aunt Josephine was holding Piper in her arms. Mama Jeanne was sitting right beside her. Stacey knew her mother would guard the baby like a bear with its cub. Stacey told herself she had a lot to be grateful for with such a supportive family.

Feeling thirsty, she navigated her way through the crowd toward the fountain of punch and got a cup. She took several sips and glanced up. Her gaze met Colton's. He was looking at her with a strange expression on his face. She felt a little dip in her stomach. What was that? she wondered. Why was he looking at her that way? And why did her stomach feel funny? Maybe she'd better get a bite to eat.

She wandered to one of the food tables and nibbled on a few appetizers.

"Everything okay with Chris?" Colton asked from behind her.

She turned around and was grateful her stomach didn't do any more dipping. "I'm not sure. Chris has some things he needs to work out. I wish I could help him, but he can have a one-track mind sometimes. Unfortunately, I think this may be one of those times."

"You want me to talk to him?" he asked.

"He might listen to you more than he does me,

but I think this is something he's going to have to work out on his own," she said and rolled her eyes. "Brothers."

He chuckled and looked at the dance floor. "I'm not the best dancer in the world, but I can probably spin you around a few times without stepping on your feet. Do you want to dance?"

She blinked in surprise. Stacey couldn't remember the last time she'd danced except with Piper. His invitation made her feel almost like a real human being, more than a mother. She smiled. "I'd like that very much."

Stacey stepped into Colton's arms, and they danced a Western-style waltz to the romantic tune. Of course she would never have romantic feelings for Colton, but she couldn't help noticing his broad shoulders and how strong he felt. It was nice to be held, even if it was just as friends. Taking a deep breath, she caught the scent of his cologne and leather. Looking into his brown eyes, she thought she'd always liked the steadfast honesty in his gaze. Colton was Mr. Steady, all male and no nonsense. Looking closer, she observed, for the first time, though, that he had long eyelashes. She'd never noticed before. Maybe because she'd never been this close to him?

"What are you thinking?" he asked.

She felt a twinge of self-consciousness. "Nothing important."

"Then why are you staring at me? Do I have some food on my face?"

Her lips twitched, and she told herself to get over her self-consciousness. After all, this was Colton. He might as well be one of her brothers. "If you must know, Mr. Nosy, I was thinking that you have the longest eyelashes I've ever seen on a man. A lot of women would give their eyeteeth for your eyelashes."

Surprise flashed through his eyes, and he laughed. It was a strong, masculine, happy sound that made her smile. "That's a first."

"No one else has ever told you that?" she asked and narrowed her eyes in disbelief. Although Colton wasn't one to talk about his romantic life, and he certainly was no womanizer, she knew he'd spent time with more than a woman or two. "Can you honestly tell me no woman has ever complimented you on your long eyelashes?"

"Not that I can remember," he said, which sounded as if he was hedging to Stacey. He shrugged. "The ladies usually give me other kinds of compliments," he said in a low voice that bordered on sensual.

Surprise and something else rushed through Stacey. She had never thought of Colton in those terms, and she wasn't now, she told herself. "What kinds of compliments?" she couldn't resist asking.

"Oh, this and that."

Another nonanswer, she thought, her curiosity piqued.

The song drew to a close, and the bandleader

tapped on his microphone. "Ladies and gentlemen, we have less than a minute left to this year. It's time for the countdown."

A server delivered horns and noisemakers and confetti pops. Stacey absently accepted a noisemaker and confetti pop and looked around for her baby. "I wonder if Piper is still with Mama Jeanne," she murmured, then caught sight of her mother holding a noisemaker for the baby.

"…five…four…three…two…one," the bandleader said. "Happy New Year!"

Stacey met Colton's gaze while many couples kissed to welcome the New Year, and she felt a twist of self-consciousness. Maybe a hug would do.

Colton gave a shrug. "May as well join the crowd," he said, and lowered his head and kissed her just beside her lips. Closer to her mouth than her cheek, the sensation of the kiss sent a ripple of electricity throughout her body.

What in the world? she thought, staring up at him as he met her gaze.

"Happy New Year, Stacey."

Chapter Two

Colton couldn't get Stacey Fortune Jones off his mind.

Even now as he was taking inventory in one of the feed sheds with his dad, he wasn't paying full attention. He told himself it was because beneath Stacey's sunny smile, he sensed a deep sadness. That bothered him, especially since he wondered if he could have prevented it. He remembered the day he'd told his friend Joe, Stacey's ex, that Stacey was a special girl. If Joe didn't want to lose her, then he'd better put a ring on it. The very next day Joe had proposed, and Stacey had gone full speed ahead with the wedding plans. The result had been a disaster and Colton still blamed himself. If only he'd kept his mouth shut. He'd known Stacey was crazy about

Joe. Colton had thought Joe had just needed a little nudge. How wrong he'd been.

His father turned to him. "Did you input that last number I gave you?"

Colton bit the inside of his jaw. "Sorry. You mind repeating it?"

"What's wrong with you?" his father asked. "You seem as if you're a million miles away. Did you catch that virus that's going around?"

Colton shook his head, thinking the only virus he had caught was the guilt virus. He'd been fighting that one for a while now, and it had only gotten worse when he'd seen Stacey at the wedding. "No. I was just thinking about that extension course I'm taking and if we're going to want to spend the money on the improvements to the ranch that I've been learning about during my last lesson."

"Well, we've already got these e-tablet gizmos. Part of me likes that you're keeping us up to speed, but these e-tablets weren't cheap."

"Yes, I know," Colton said, his lips twitching in amusement. "You sure like playing solitaire on yours when you're not using it for work, don't you?"

His father shot him a mock glare, then made a sound somewhere between a cough and a chuckle. "All right, you've made your point. Let's get back to work, so you can take a break. You're acting like you need it."

"I don't—"

"Then what's the last number I gave you?" his father countered.

Colton frowned. "Okay, give me the number again," he said, but he sure didn't want a break. He needed to keep busy so he wouldn't be thinking about how he had contributed to ruining Stacey's life.

Despite his father's encouragement to take a break after doing inventory, Colton drove his truck out to check some fences that had been questionable in the past. Although January wasn't the busiest time for the ranch since the foals wouldn't come until spring, there was still plenty to do. Keeping the mamas healthy, safe and fed meant he had to stay on top of the condition of the fences and the pastures.

Colton checked several stretches of fence and only found one weak area. He made a note of it and returned to the family ranch. He'd been born and raised in the sprawling ranch house. After he'd turned twenty-five, they'd added an extra wing so that he could have some privacy. The fact that his room was farther from the center of the house usually worked for him, but there were times he just wanted his own place. Someday soon he would broach the subject with his father. Colton had a lot of money in the bank and in investments, so he could easily fund the purchase of a new home, but building Colton's home seemed like a matter of pride for Colton's father, Frank. All too aware of ranch finances, Colton didn't want to provide any extra strain. His father was still strong and healthy, but his back wasn't the best. Colton wanted to ease his burdens, not make them worse.

As he climbed the steps to the porch, he thought of Stacey again and made a decision. He was going to try to find a way to help bring back her sunny disposition. There had to be a way. Passing by the den, he saw his sister Rachel watching a reality matchmaker show on television. Those kinds of shows drove him crazy. He couldn't understand why Rachel watched them. The couples never ended up staying together. Obviously he didn't understand the female psyche.

Colton shrugged. Maybe he should pick Rachel's brain. Not only was she female, but she was also Stacey's best friend. Perhaps she could give him a few ideas. He grabbed a glass of water from the kitchen, then returned to the den and sank onto a chair.

"How's it going?" he asked when Rachel couldn't seem to tear her attention from the television show.

"Pretty good," she said, glancing at him. "I'm taking a little break from making lesson plans for student teaching. How about you?"

"Good," he said. "It's quiet. No trouble. Have you heard anything about Dad's back?"

"Not lately," she said. "I wish he would go to the doctor. I don't see how he's going to get better if he doesn't try to do anything about it."

"I try to keep him from doing things that might hurt him, but I can't be by his side every minute," he said.

"True," she said. "He's lucky you're around as

much as you are." She shot him a playful smile. "Colton, the saint."

"Yeah, right," he said in a dark voice. "Listen, I wanted to ask you something."

"What's that?" she asked, glancing back at the television. "Mom told me to tell you there's a potpie in the fridge if you want to heat it up for dinner."

"I'm not asking about dinner. I want to know what women want," he said.

She swiveled her head around to gape at him. "Well, that's a loaded question."

He lifted his shoulders. "Seems pretty straight-on to me. What do women want?"

Rachel laughed. "There's no one perfect answer. It depends on the woman." She looked at him with curiosity in her eyes. "Who do you have in mind?"

Colton resisted the urge to squirm under her inquisitive gaze. He'd rather die than admit he had Stacey on his mind. "Forget I said anything," he said and started to rise.

"Now, wait just a minute. You asked me a question. The least you can do is give me a chance to try to give you some suggestions." She looked at him suspiciously. "Although I can't help wondering who you're trying to please. And I don't have to tell you that nothing stays secret in Horseback Hollow for long."

"I know," he said.

Rachel sighed in frustration. "Well, there are the die-hard regulars," she said. "Roses and flowers."

Colton shook his head. "Nothing that obvious."

"Hmm," Rachel said. "The truth is that what most women want is a man who listens."

Colton frowned and shook his head. "That can't be it."

Rachel stared at him for a long moment. "I have an idea," she said, picking up her cell phone and dialing.

"What are you doing?" he asked, but his sister wasn't paying any attention to him.

"Stacey," Rachel said, sliding Colton a sly glance. "My brother needs a consultation. Can you come over?"

Colton nearly croaked. "Stacey?" he echoed.

Rachel nodded. "Great," she said into the phone. "See you in a few minutes." She disconnected the call and smiled at Colton. "This is great. You'll have advice from two women instead of just one."

Oh, Lord, what had he gotten himself into? "I think I'll heat up some of that potpie," Colton said, hatching an escape plan.

"Don't go too far. Stacey will be here soon," Rachel said, then shot him a crafty glance. "And don't take off for your bedroom. I know where to find you."

Colton stifled a groan. This was why he needed his own place. He was too accessible. Colton heated the potpie and returned to the den, telling himself he would set a mental time limit of fifteen minutes for the insanity about to ensue. He scarfed down as much food as possible during the next few moments.

A knock sounded at the door, but Stacey didn't wait for anyone to answer. She'd been bursting through that door as long as he could remember. "Hey, Rachel, I'm here," she called as she made her way to the den. Dressed in a winter-white coat, she carried her baby on her hip with ease. Piper wore a red coat and cap, and her cheeks were flushed with good health. She stared curiously around the room with her big, green eyes.

"Give me that sweet baby," Rachel said, rushing to reach for Piper.

Piper allowed herself to be taken from Stacey, but the baby watched to make sure her mama was in sight. Rachel unfastened the baby's coat and took off her cap.

Stacey shrugged out of her own coat and glanced from Rachel to Colton. "What's this about a consultation? Why on earth would Colton need a consultation from us?"

Rachel's face lit with mischief. "Colton asked me what women really want. We need to brainstorm Colton's love life."

Stacey looked at Colton in confusion. "I always thought Colton got along as well as he wanted to in that department. I've heard from a few girls who—" She cleared her throat. "Well, they seemed to like him just fine."

"Thank you, Stacey. I have gotten along just fine

in that department, despite my sister's opinion," he said in a dry voice.

Rachel jiggled the baby on her hip. "Well, this one must be different if you're asking *me* what women want," Rachel said.

Colton checked his watch. Thirteen minutes to go. This was going to feel like an eternity.

"Who is this girl?" Stacey asked, curiously gazing at Colton.

"He won't tell," Rachel answered for him.

Colton figured his sister was good for something.

"Well, what kind of woman is she? Country or city?" Stacey asked.

"If she's here, she's only one kind," Rachel said. "Country. We have no city to speak of."

"Hmm," Stacey said, and Colton again resisted the urge to squirm. "You could take her to dinner."

"Out of town," Rachel added. "People are so nosy here."

"Flowers would be good," Stacey said.

"He said flowers are too obvious," Rachel said.

Stacey frowned. "Too obvious?" she echoed.

"What if I just wanted to cheer her up?" Colton asked. "What if I don't necessarily want to date her?"

Rachel scowled. "Oh, that's a totally different matter. You don't want to be with her?"

Colton ground his teeth. "That's not the priority."

"So, you may want to be with her in the future?" Rachel asked.

"Let's deal with the present," he said in a grumbly voice.

"In that case—" Rachel said.

"Just visit her," Stacey said firmly. "And let her talk, maybe about what's been going on with her. Try and keep the conversation light. Nothing heavy."

"Small talk," Rachel said cheerfully.

Colton frowned. "What the hell is small talk besides weather?"

Both Stacey and Rachel laughed. "Nothing too deep," Rachel said. "You can even talk about clothing."

Colton scowled. "Clothing?" he echoed.

Stacey and Rachel exchanged an amused glance. "Work on it," Rachel said. "Read the paper. There may be something there you can chit-chat about."

"You could take her to get ice cream," Stacey said.

"In the winter?" Colton asked.

"I love ice cream any time of year," she confessed.

"If you really want to cheer up a woman, you could take a DVD of a chick flick and watch it with her," Rachel added.

Colton made a face. "If you say so," he said.

"Well, you asked," Rachel said with a bit of a testy tone. "Is this girl sick or just depressed? I know you said flowers are too obvious, but you could just happen to have some extra chocolates in your truck. Chocolate makes just about everything better."

"Except labor pains," Stacey said. "Chocolate doesn't help with labor pains."

Colton cleared his throat. He didn't like the direction this conversation was headed in. "I think I'm done with my dinner now."

"I'll take your plate," Rachel said. "You take Piper."

Colton pulled back.

Stacey shot him a look of surprise. "Oh, for goodness' sakes. You're not afraid of a baby, are you?"

"Of course I'm not afraid," he said, lying through his teeth. She was cute, but she was so *little*.

"Then, you can hold her," Rachel said, pushing Piper into his arms. "She's not radioactive."

Colton held the baby away from his body, staring into her face. She squirmed in his hands.

"You need to hold her closer," Stacey said. "She feels insecure in that position."

"I'm not gonna drop her," he said.

"I know that, but she doesn't," Stacey said.

He sat and gingerly set her on his lap, and she stopped wiggling.

Piper cooed at him, lifting her finger toward his face. She seemed to stare at his every feature. What amazing concentration she had. He inhaled and caught a whiff of sweet baby smell. Colton felt a strange sensation inside him, as if the baby was trying to communicate with him. She was a cute thing. He felt an odd protective feeling for the child even though Piper wasn't his. It was as if he was suddenly driven to keep her safe. At the same time, he was terrified she was going to start screaming any minute.

"You look so nervous, Colton. I can take her," Stacey said, lifting the baby from his arms.

Colton felt a huge sense of relief. At the same time, he wouldn't mind breathing in Piper's sweet scent again.

"So, did our advice help?" Stacey asked as she shifted Piper onto her hip.

Colton couldn't stop his gaze from flowing down her curvy body, then up again. A flash of what her nude body might look like slid through his brain. Colton gulped. Stacey—his sister's friend, the literal girl next door—was unbelievably sexy. Colton wondered if he was going insane.

"Isn't she sweet?" Stacey asked.

Colton lifted his head in a round nod. "Sweet," he said. *But frightening,* he thought, although he would never admit it in a million years. Colton was no baby expert, and he had no idea what to do with a tot like Piper. For that matter, he wasn't sure what to do with all the forbidden thoughts he was having about Stacey.

Later that night when Stacey had finally put Piper to sleep, she headed for her own bed after she'd washed her face and brushed her teeth. She couldn't shake the image of Colton holding Piper. The baby had taken to Colton almost immediately. He didn't know it, but Stacey did. Colton had looked wary about Piper, but the baby had clearly found him fascinating. She'd stared into his face as if she'd wanted to memorize every feature.

Stacey had found herself watching him more than she ever had in the past. Crazy, she told herself and closed her eyes and took several deep breaths. She counted backward from two hundred and finally fell asleep and into a vivid dream. Piper was crawling down the aisle of a chapel wearing her christening gown. Her sweet baby finally reached the altar, and Joe stood, with his back to Stacey.

"I do," Joe said.

Her heart pounding, Stacey tried to scream, but no sound came from her mouth. She felt utterly helpless.

"Joe," she whispered. "Joe…"

Stacey rushed toward the altar. "Joe," she called.

Stacey watched Joe bend over to pick up Piper. Her heart melted. Joe was going to love Piper. Her baby was finally going to have a daddy. It seemed to take hours, but Stacey finally reached her groom and touched his shoulder.

He turned, but her groom wasn't Joe.

It was Colton.

Alarm rushed through her.

Stacey awakened in a sweat. *Joe? Colton?* This couldn't be. "Colton," she whispered aloud and sat up in her bed. Why was she dreaming of Colton? Why was she even thinking of him? He was her neighbor, her best friend's brother. Ridiculous, she told herself. Beyond ridiculous. She shook her head and tried to push away the image of the tall, sexy cowboy.

Stacey forced herself to relax. She'd learned to seek sleep when her baby slept. Taking several deep breaths, she told herself not to think about Colton. She shouldn't think about his wide shoulders and his insanely curly, dark eyelashes. She shouldn't think about his strong jaw and great muscles and dependability. He was the kind of man who would always stand beside a friend and support him or her.

Colton was also a man who was clearly interested in another woman at the moment. Why else would he have sought Rachel's help about what women really want?

The reality of that made Stacey feel a little cranky, although, for the life of her, she couldn't say why.

"Go to sleep," she told herself. She would be so busy tomorrow with Piper that she would truly regret one minute of sleep she'd lose thinking about Colton.

The next day, just after Stacey put Piper down for her afternoon nap, she heard a knock at the front door. She knew that her mother had gone to a sewing circle meeting and her father was outside working, so she wanted to catch whoever was at the door before they awakened Piper. Heaven knew, Stacey cherished nap time.

She raced toward the front door and whisked it open. Colton stood on the front porch holding a pie. Surprise and pleasure rushed through her. "Well, hello to you. Come on inside."

"I can't stay long. My mother fixed a batch of

apple pies, and she thought your family might enjoy one," he said, following her.

"We certainly will. This will go great with the dinner I'm fixing tonight. Please, tell her I said thank you. Would you like some coffee?" she asked.

"No need," he said. "I really can't stay long. You're fixing dinner, you say? Do I smell pot roast?"

"You do," she said, and took the pie to the kitchen and quickly returned. "Since I'm not bringing home the bacon right now, I try to help around the house as much as possible. I fix dinner and clean while Piper naps. It's the least I can do. I'm also thinking about doing some after-school tutoring in math and science. I can have kids come here and Piper's not walking yet. I hear once the babies start walking, it's a whole different ballgame."

"I'm sure it is," he said.

Stacey looked up at Colton and noticed his eyelashes again. When had he become sexy-looking? she wondered. Although she'd certainly always known Colton was male, she just hadn't thought of him as a man. And she shouldn't be thinking that way now either.

The silence stretched between them, and Stacey felt heat rush to her face. "Are you sure I can't get you a cup of coffee? It's the least I can do with you bringing over a pie."

"Trust me. I didn't bake that pie," he said in a dry tone. "But I'll take a cup if you're insisting. I'll be working outside, and it won't hurt to get warmed up before I face the cold."

"Just a moment," she said, and returned to the kitchen to pour Colton's coffee. As she reentered the den, she gave him the cup. "Any problems or just the regular endless chores?"

He nodded. "I need to do a little work on some fences. My dad's back isn't what it used to be, so I try to tackle anything that may cause him pain."

"That's nice of you," she said. "He refuses to go to the doctor, doesn't he?"

Colton nodded again. "He doesn't believe in it. Says it's a waste of time and money. The last time he went to the doctor, he nearly died from a burst appendix. And we almost had to beat him into going."

"I remember when that happened," Stacey said. "It was a long time ago. I'm sure someone has told him that there have been huge advances made in medical science."

"All of us have told him that, but he'd rather eat nails than admit he's hurting."

"Maybe you can persuade him to go to the doctor if you take him out for lunch in Vicker's Corners sometime," she suggested.

"Possible," he said. "Rachel might have better luck with him than I would. He has always let her get away with murder."

Stacey laughed. "She would disagree and give you half a dozen examples of when she has gotten in trouble. But even I know he has been harder on you."

"Yeah," he said. "But I always felt as if I had good parents. I'm sure you feel the same way, too."

"True," she said. "My father can be a little remote sometimes, but he's as solid as they come. After I had Piper, both my parents insisted I come back here to live with them." A slice of guilt cut through her. "I just wish I could give Piper what I had growing up." She felt the surprising threat of moisture in her eyes and blinked furiously. "It just wasn't meant to be."

Colton squeezed her arm. "Don't be so hard on yourself. From where I sit, it looks as if you're doing a dang good job. That baby is surrounded by people who love her. That's more than a lot of kids can say."

The tight feeling in her chest eased just a little from his words of encouragement. "Thanks. I have my share of doubts."

"Well, stop your doubting. You've got a healthy baby, and she's doing great," he said. "Besides that, you've got a slice of Olive Foster's famous apple pie in your future tonight."

"The only way I'll get a slice is if I hide it until after the meal," she said.

"Well, that's a no-brainer," he said, and leaned toward her in a way that seemed much sexier than it should. "Hide the pie. Indulge yourself."

Stacey's heart raced at Colton's instruction. A naughty image of how she could indulge herself with Colton raced through her mind, but she immediately slammed the door on her thoughts. After all, the last time she'd indulged herself she'd gotten pregnant.

Chapter Three

"I'm sorry I can't go with you," Rachel said to Stacey on her cell phone. "My friend Abby called me at the last minute to babysit, and it's her anniversary."

"I understand. You and I can catch up later," Stacey said, even though she dreaded attending Ella Mae Jergen's baby shower. Ella Mae was married to a hotshot surgeon, and the couple owned houses in both Lubbock and in the next town past Horseback Hollow. Ella Mae was pregnant with her first baby. The shower was a big deal for Horseback Hollow because Ella Mae had been born and raised there and her parents still lived in town. The shower was being held in the Jergen's mansion in the next town. Stacey couldn't help feeling intimidated.

Ella Mae, however, had been supportive of Stacey and had attended the shower for Piper, so Stacey was determined to return the favor.

"What's wrong?" her mother asked as Stacey put a pot of beans on for dinner while she held Piper on her hip.

"Nothing," Stacey said.

"Doesn't sound like nothing to me," Jeanne said, and put a lid on the beans. "Let me hold my grandbaby."

All Stacey had to do was lean toward her mother, and Piper extended her chubby little arms to her Gabby. Stacey checked the chicken and vegetables. "Looking good," she murmured.

"You don't have to cook every night," her mother said as she clucked over Piper.

"I'm not contributing to the household with green stuff, so I want to contribute in other ways," Stacey said.

"I don't want you overdoing it," her mother said.

"I'm not. I'm young and healthy," she said.

"That sounds like something I said when I was younger," her mother said. "You still didn't answer my question about your conversation with Rachel."

Stacey sighed. "Ella Mae's baby shower is tonight."

A brief silence followed.

"Oh," her mother said, because she knew that the Jergens were wealthy and anything they did had to be, oh, so perfect. "Do you want me to go with you?"

Her mother's offer was so sweet that it brought

tears to her eyes. Stacey put down her spoon and went to her mother to hug her. "You're the best mother in the world. You know that, don't you?"

Jeanne gave Stacey a big squeeze, then pulled back with a soft chuckle. "What makes you say that?"

"Because you always do the right thing. I wonder if I can do half as many right things as you have," Stacey said, looking into her mother's eyes and wishing that just by looking, she could receive all of her mother's wisdom.

Her mother slid her hand around Stacey's shoulders and gave her another squeeze. "You're already doing the right thing. Look at this gorgeous, healthy baby. You're a wonderful mother."

"Thanks, Mom," Stacey said, feeling as if she'd just received the highest praise possible.

"You don't have to go to Ella Mae's baby shower. Just drop off a gift," her mother said.

"No," Stacey said with a firm shake of her head. "She came to my shower. I should go to hers."

Jeanne pressed her lips together. "If you're sure…"

"I am," Stacey said. "And you already said you don't mind watching Piper. Right?"

"Not at all," her mother said. "You don't ask me often enough. I love my little Piper girl."

Stacey's heart swelled with emotion. "I'm so blessed," she said.

"Yes, you are," her mother said. "Now go get ready for Ella Mae's shower. You hold your head high. Don't forget it. You've done the right thing, and you're a good mother. Just make sure you're the second one out the door."

Stacey looked at her mother in confusion. "Second one out the door?"

"I never told you this before, but if you ever go to a party that you don't want to attend, then you can be the second one to leave. You don't want to be the first, but being the second is fine," her mother said.

Another word of wisdom Stacey swore to remember. "I'll be watching for who leaves first."

"And if anyone starts making insinuating comments about Joe, then pull out Piper's baby pictures. That should shut them up right away."

Stacey smiled at her mother. "Thanks, Mom."

Stacey raced to her room to pull on a black dress and boots. She put on some lip gloss and concealer, then threw on a colorful scarf and her peacoat.

"See you later, Mom," she called, then headed for her Toyota. Thank goodness snow and sleet had stayed away from Horseback Hollow during the past week. She started her car and got to the end of the driveway before she realized she had forgotten the gift for Ella Mae's baby.

Stacey backtracked and collected the gift, then returned to her trusty car. She headed out of Horseback Hollow toward the next town, then took several turns down several back roads until she reached the gated driveway for Ella Mae's house. The gate lifted to allow her entrance, and Stacey rode down the paved drive to the front of the Jergen mansion.

The windows of the house were lit, and the front door was open. Stacey knew what she would find inside. A crystal chandelier and exquisite high-profile designer furniture and decor.

Stacey was accustomed to homemade decorations and freshly painted rooms. Mama Jeanne decorated her home with family photos and mementos. The Joneses' home was warm and welcoming, but furniture had been chosen for durability, not how pretty it was.

A man approached Stacey as she paused in the driveway. "May I park your car, ma'am?"

Stacey blinked. "Excuse me?"

"Yes, ma'am. I'm the valet for the evening," he said.

Stacey blinked again. Heaven help her. *Valet? Don't fight it,* she told herself. *Let him park the car.* She would have to park her own all the nights thereafter, and that was okay.

Stacey accepted a nonalcoholic basil-something cocktail. She would have preferred a beer. She joined in with the socializing and the games and predicted that Ella Mae would have a boy. Stacey suspected that Ella Mae's husband would want a boy right off the bat, so she hoped Ella would be able to seal the deal with a male child.

When it came time for the big reveal of the baby's sex, it was done via cake. Blue. Stacey had been correct. Everyone cheered.

Ella Mae circled the room with her posse and stopped to visit with Stacey.

"I'm so glad you could come," Ella Mae said. "I know you've been busy with your baby."

"So true," Stacey said. "You'll learn soon enough."

"Well, I'll have help," Ella Mae said. "I'll have a husband and a nanny."

Stacey lost her breath. She felt as if she'd been slapped. She took a careful breath and remembered what her mother had said. She pulled out her cell phone. "Have you seen my Piper? She's just gorgeous, don't you think?" she asked as she flipped through the photos.

"What a darling," one of Ella Mae's friends said. "She's beautiful."

Stacey nodded. "And good as gold."

A couple moments later Ella Mae and her pack moved on. Stacey watched the door and saw two guests leave. It was time for her to go. On the drive home she decided to stop at the Superette to pick up some bananas for Piper. Piper loved bananas. Luckily, the Superette had quite a few. Then she headed to the only bar in town, the Two Moon Saloon, with the intention of drinking half a beer. She would be fine driving after drinking a whole beer, but Stacey wouldn't risk anything. Since she'd become a mother, everything had changed. She couldn't take any chances.

She went to the bar and ordered a beer. The first time in nearly a year and a half. She took a sip and felt so guilty she asked for a glass of water. Sensing the gazes of several men on her, she sipped at her water and wondered if coming here had been a good idea after all.

The bartender put another beer in front of her. "The guy at the end of the bar bought this for you."

Stacey glanced down the bar but didn't recognize the man. "Oh, I can't accept it. I don't know him."

"I can't take it back," the bartender said.

Feeling extremely uncomfortable, Stacey took another sip of water and eyed the door.

"Fancy meeting you here," a familiar male voice said.

"Oh, thank goodness," she said, and stretched both of her hands toward Colton.

"Problem?" he asked, glancing down at her hands clutching his arm.

"I just went to Ella Mae Jergen's baby shower. She made a snarky comment about my missing baby daddy. I came here for a beer, but I couldn't make myself drink it. And some guy bought me another beer. Save me," she said.

Colton chuckled and gently extracted her fingers from his arm. "Hey, Phil, buy Stacey's admirer a beer on me."

"Thank you," she said. "I was just going to drink half a beer, but I felt guilty after the first sip. Do you know how long it's been since I had a drink at a bar?"

"Apparently too long," Colton said.

"Maybe," she said.

"You don't have to give up living just because you had a baby," he said.

She nodded, but she didn't really agree.

Colton lifted her chin with his finger. "Your life is not over. You can still have fun," he said.

"I have fun," she said, unable to resist the urge to squirm. "I have lots of fun with Piper."

Colton shot her a doubtful glance. "You need to start getting out more. And I don't mean baby showers."

Stacey lifted her eyebrows at Colton's suggestion. "You don't mean dating, do you?"

"You don't have to date. You just need to get out. You're acting—" He broke off.

Stacey frowned. "I'm acting how?"

Colton scrubbed his jaw. "I don't know how to say this."

"Well, spit it out," she said. "I want to know."

Colton sighed. "You're acting...old."

Stacey stared at him in disbelief. *"Old?"* she repeated. "I'm acting *old?*" She couldn't remember when she'd felt so insulted. "I'm only twenty-four. How can I be old?"

"I didn't say you *are* old," Colton said in a low voice. "I said you're *acting* old."

"Well, I have a baby now. I need to be responsible," she said.

"I agree, but you don't have to stop living your life," he said.

Stacey paused, thinking about what Colton had

told her. "You're Mr. Responsibility. I can't believe you're telling me to cut loose and be a wild woman."

"I didn't say you should be a wild woman. I just said you need to get out more," he said.

"Hmm," Stacey said. "I'm going to have to think about this." She paused. "I wonder who I could call if I decide to get out. If I decide I want to have half a beer."

"You can call me," Colton offered. "Remember, I'm Mr. Responsibility."

In her experience, Stacey knew that Colton *was* Mr. Responsibility. He always had been and she valued that quality in him now more than ever. But lately, when she looked at Colton, she couldn't seem to forget what it had felt like to dance in his arms on New Year's Eve. And that almost kiss they'd shared. Almost, but not quite. She wondered what a real kiss from him would feel like. Stacey almost wished he'd kiss her and she would be disappointed, so she could stop thinking about him so much.

The next day, Colton showed up unexpectedly at the Joneses' house. Stacey was happy to see him even though he seemed intent on asking her father's thoughts about some issue with the cattle. She brought Colton and her father some coffee. Colton tossed her a smile but kept talking with her father.

Stacey couldn't help feeling a little jealous of the time he was spending with her father. She knew Piper would awaken any moment, and her time would then be divided. *Hurry up, Dad.* But she knew the mental urging was useless. Her father was usually stone quiet, but when it came to talking about the ranch, once he got going, he didn't stop.

She checked her watch and felt her stomach clench as she waited for Piper to call out for her. Finally, her father took a potty break. *Hallelujah.*

"Better today?" Colton asked her as he headed for the door, where Stacey waited on the porch.

She nodded. "I guess so. Sorry if I freaked out on you last night."

"You didn't," he said. "It's like I said. You just need to get out more. I know your mama would be more than happy to watch Piper for you every now and then."

"I don't want to burden her," Stacey said as she stepped out of the front porch with him. "They've taken Piper and me in. I don't want to take advantage of them."

"You wouldn't ever do that," he said. "Listen, how about if I take you to the bar and grill in town? What's a good day for you?"

Surprise rippled through her. "Are you sure? I don't want to intrude on your, uh, relationship with your new girlfriend."

He hesitated a half beat. "She won't mind," he said. "When do you want to go?"

"I think Thursday may work. I'll have to ask Mama first. Can I get back to you?"

"Sure," he said, and squeezed her arm just like one of her brothers would. "Remember to smile."

She stared after him as he started to walk away. "Wait," she said, and he turned around. "Do I frown that much?"

He paused. "You used to seem a lot happier," Colton said. "I hate to see you so sad and burdened."

"My life is different now," she said.

"But is it sad?" he asked.

She took a deep breath and thought about his question. "Not really." She smiled. "I'll call you about dinner at the grill followed by a beer. I appreciate the pity date."

"It's no pity date," he said. "We've known each other a long time. We should be able to cheer each other up. You may have to do it for me sometime," he said.

"That's hard for me to imagine," she said.

"You never know," he said, and her father returned to the den, ready to talk ranching.

Stacey gazed at Colton. There was more to him than she'd ever thought. Stacey wondered what it would be like to go on a real date with Colton. She wondered how it would feel to be the object of his affection. Rolling her eyes at herself, she shook her head and went to the laundry room to wash another load of baby clothes.

The next day, Stacey played with Piper, after cleaning the house and fixing dinner. She couldn't help thinking about Colton's offer for an evening out.

It wouldn't be fancy, but it would be a relief. She debated calling him ten times over, then finally gave in. He didn't pick up, so she hung up. Five minutes later, she called again. He still didn't answer, but this time she left an answer.

A half hour later, he returned her call. "Hello?" she said as she stirred soup for dinner and held Piper on her hip.

"Need an escape?" Colton asked.

She gave a short laugh. "How did you know?"

"Saw the hang-up, then heard the desperation in your voice mail," he said.

"I'm not that desperate," she said, even though she really needed an evening out.

"I know. Everyone needs an escape hatch every now and then," he said.

"What's yours?" she asked.

"If I really want to get away, I can go into town or even Vicker's Corners," he said.

"But you don't have a baby," she said.

He chuckled. "That I don't," he said. "It won't be fancy. Tomorrow night okay? What time do you want me to pick you up?"

"Five-thirty," she said.

"Early night?"

She laughed. "These days I only do early nights," she said. "You have a problem with that?"

"None at all, I'll see you tomorrow at five-thirty." He chuckled. "Call me if you need to escape earlier."

Stacey couldn't help smiling. "I'll pace myself. Bye for now."

The following day, Stacey's afternoon fell apart. Piper woke up early from her nap, and Stacey feared she'd burned the baked spaghetti casserole. She was having a bad hair day, and Piper was so cranky, Stacey wasn't sure she should ask her mother to babysit for the evening.

"Are you teething, sweetie?" she asked Piper.

Piper's sweet face crumpled in pain. Stacey sighed. "Mama, she's so fussy. I'm not sure I should leave her with you."

Her mother extended her arms to Piper, but Piper turned away. "Oh, come on, you sugar," Jeanne said to Piper. "I'll take care of you. Rub your sore gums with something that will make you feel better."

"No rum," Stacey said.

"I wasn't thinking of rum," Mama Jeanne said with an innocent expression on her face.

"No whiskey," Stacey added.

"I would never numb a baby's gums with whiskey," her mother said. "But bourbon…"

Stacey sighed. "Let me find the Orajel. I should have given it to her earlier."

"You know what your doctors say. You need to stay on top of the pain. You've told me that too many times to count when my hip was hurting."

"You're right, Mama. I should have done better for Piper," she said, feeling guilty.

"Well, don't leap off a ledge. She's not suffering

that much," her mother said, snatching Piper from her arms. "Go put on some lipstick and blush. You look worn out."

Piper fussed and squabbled, but didn't quite cry. "You're sure you'll be okay?"

"I've had a lot more babies than you have, sweetheart," Jeanne said.

"I'm working hard to meet a high standard," Stacey muttered.

"Hold on there," her mother said, putting her hand on Stacey's arm. "You're a great mother. Don't let anyone tell you otherwise. I didn't have to take care of my babies by myself. I had your father to help me, and trust me, he walked the floor many times at night to comfort all of you."

"I just feel bad that Piper won't have the kind of mother and father I had," Stacey said.

"Piper's getting plenty of loving. Her mama needs to stop trying for sainthood. Enjoy your evening out. It will be good for you and your baby."

"If you say so," Stacey said.

"I do. Now, go put on some lipstick," she said.

"Colton won't care. He's just taking me out to be nice," Stacey said, halfway hoping her mother would deny it.

"Maybe so, but it will make you feel better. That's the important thing," her mother said.

"Right," Stacey said, and headed to her room to remake herself for a trip to the grill where she would eat a burger and fries. This was how her life had evolved. Her big exciting night within a month was a trip to the grill.

Pathetic, she thought, but couldn't deny she was just glad to get away from the ranch. She put on lipstick, a little blush and some mascara. At the last moment, she sprayed her wrists with perfume.

"Stacey," her mother called from down the hall. "Colton's here."

A rush of excitement raced through her, and she rushed down the hall. Colton stood there dressed in jeans, a coat and his Stetson. "Hi," he said. "You look nice."

"Colton is afraid of Piper," her mother announced.

"I'm not afraid of her," he corrected. "She just looks so happy in your arms that I don't want to disrupt her."

Stacey chuckled under her breath. "You can go after a bear on your ranch, but a baby brings you to your knees."

Colton scowled at her. "I can shoot a bear."

Both Stacey and her mother erupted with laughter. "We should give him a break," her mother said. "Y'all enjoy yourselves." She lowered her voice. "Drink a beer for me."

"Mama," Stacey said, shocked.

"Oh, stop. Even a mother of seven likes to kick up her heels every now and then. See you later," she said, and returned to the kitchen.

Stacey met Colton's gaze. "I never expected that."

"Me either," Colton said, then lifted his lips in a crafty grin. "But I liked it."

Colton helped her into his truck and drove into town. "So, have you figured out what you want on your burger? Cheese, onions, mustard…"

"Cheese, mustard, grilled onions and steak sauce," she said. "I don't need the whole burger. I want the bun and fixin's."

"And French fries?" he asked.

"Yes, indeed," she said.

"We can take the burger into the bar if you want your beer with your meal," he said.

"The bar is loud," she said. "I can have a soda or water with my burger. It will be nice to hear myself think."

"Does your baby scream that much?" he asked.

Stacey shook her head. "Piper's much better now that she's done with her colic. But now she's teething. I need to remember to soothe her gums. I forgot today."

"Must be hard. All that crying," he said.

"She sleeps well at night and usually takes a good long nap. I'm lucky she's not crawling right now. She's really a good baby, Colton. I could have it much harder," she said, wanting Colton to like Piper.

"Yeah," he said, but he didn't sound convinced.

"Is my Mama right? Are you afraid of Piper?" she asked in a singsong voice.

"I'm not afraid of a baby," he said, his tone cranky. "I just haven't been around babies very much."

Stacey backed off. She wanted the evening to be pleasant. "How do you like your burger?"

"As big as I can get it. Mustard, mayonnaise, onion, pickle, lettuce and tomato," he said.

"You can have half of mine," she offered.

"We'll see. Maybe your appetite will improve now that you're out of the pen," he said.

She laughed, but his teasing made her feel good. "You are so bad."

"And you are so glad," he said.

"Yeah," she said. She couldn't disagree.

Colton pulled into the parking lot of The Horseback Hollow Grill, and he helped her out of his truck. His gentlemanly manners made her feel younger and more desirable. They walked into the grill and had to wait a few minutes for a table. Maybe more than one person needed an escape tonight, Stacey thought.

They sat, ordered, and the server delivered their sodas. Stacey took a long, cool sip of her drink and closed her eyes. "Good," she said.

"Simple pleasures are the best," Colton said.

Stacey looked at Colton for a long moment and shrugged her shoulders. "So, talk to me about grown-up stuff."

His eyes rounded. "Grown-up stuff?" he echoed.

"Yes," she said. "Movies, politics, current events."

"Well, politicians are as crooked as ever. There are blizzards and tsunamis. Wait till summer and there will be hurricanes, mudslides and fires." He grimaced. "I hate to admit it, but I haven't seen a movie lately. Rachel is watching the reality shows. I watch a lot of the History Channel," he said.

"What about movies?" she asked. "Do you like James Bond?"

He nodded. "I did see the most recent one. Lots of action."

"And lots of violence," she said.

"Yeah, but the good guy wins."

"That's most important," she said, and the server delivered their meals.

"That was fast," she said.

"Burgers are what they are known for," Colton said, and took a big bite out of his.

Stacey took a bite of her own and closed her eyes to savor a burger someone else had cooked for her. "Perfect amount of mustard and steak sauce," she said. "But all I need is half."

"You sure about that?" Colton teased, taking another big bite.

"I'm sure," she said, and enjoyed several more bites of her burger. She ate a little more than half and stopped. "Oh, no. Now I'm full. How can I eat the fries? Let alone drink a beer?"

"You need to learn to pace yourself," Colton said as he stared at his fries.

Stacey liked the wicked glint in his eyes that belied his practical advice. "Maybe I should fix some fences. Maybe that would help my appetite," she said, unable to force herself to eat even one French fry.

"Relax. We can hit the bar in a few minutes. There's no rush. Rest your belly," he said.

Not the most romantic advice, but Stacey stretched and took a few deep breaths. "I may have to take lessons from you on pacing myself."

"I'm available for hamburger-eating pacing lessons," he said with a mischievous grin that made her stomach take an unexpected dip.

A few minutes later, Stacey gave up on her fries, and she and Colton walked to the connecting bar. Colton ordered a couple of beers, and Stacey took a sip. Country music was playing in the background. If she closed her eyes, she could almost time travel back to over a year ago when she and Joe had just gotten engaged. She'd been unbelievably happy. Her future had been so bright. She'd clearly been a big fool.

Stacey hiccupped. "Oh, my," she said and hiccupped again.

"Drink too fast?" he asked.

"I didn't think so," she said, but hiccupped again. "It's just been so long since I sat down and drank even half a beer."

"Maybe you need one of those sweet mixed drinks," he said. "I'm not sure the bartender here can do that for you."

"It depends on whether he has vodka or not. I'm pretty sure he doesn't keep cranberry juice on tap."

Colton laughed. "You're right about the cranberry juice. I see Greg Townsend over there. He's the president of the local ranchers' association. Do you mind if I have a word with him?"

"Please, go ahead," she said. "Let me catch my breath."

"I'll just be a minute," he said.

Stacey closed her eyes, took a breath and held it. She counted to ten. Memories of how foolish she'd been with Joe warred with her enjoyment of her evening with Colton.

"Can I buy you another beer?" an unfamiliar male voice asked.

Stacey opened her eyes to meet the gaze of a man she didn't know. "Excuse me?" she said. He was tall and wore a Stetson. He also had a beard. She wasn't a big fan of beards.

"Can I buy you another beer?" he repeated, extending his hand. "I'm Tom Garrison. I haven't seen you around here before. I work at the Jergen's ranch."

"Oh, I know the Jergens," she said and briefly shook his hand. "Well, I know Ella Mae."

"And you are?" he asked.

"Stacey," she said, suddenly noticing her hiccups had disappeared. "Stacey Jones. Stacey Fortune Jones," she added, because the Fortune part was still very new to her.

"A pleasure to meet you, Stacey Fortune Jones," he said. "I'm kinda new in town and a little lonely since it's winter. Maybe you could show me around."

"Oh," she said, shaking her head and feeling uncomfortable. "I'm super busy. I have a little baby."

She figured that would put him off. Most men were afraid of babies who weren't their own.

"I like babies," he said. "I'm good with them."

Stacey began to feel just a teensy bit nervous. She searched the room for Colton. "Good for you, but, like I said, I'm super busy."

"I don't see a ring on your finger. That must mean you're not taken," he said, moving closer.

"Well," she said, trying to shrink against her bar stool. She wished Colton would return. He would know how to take care of this pushy man. "Like I said, I'm extremely busy..."

"I could give you a good time," he said. "Make you laugh. Maybe more..."

"Or not," Colton said, suddenly appearing next to the pushy cowboy. "She's with me."

Stacey breathed a sigh of relief.

"She was sitting here all by herself when I saw her," Tom said.

"For all of two and a half minutes. Go stalk some-one else," Colton said. "Trust me, she's not your type."

"She's everybody's type," Tom grumbled, but walked away.

"Hmm," Colton said. "Can't leave you alone for even two minutes. There you go, seducing the new locals."

"I didn't seduce anyone," she protested. "I was just trying to get rid of my hiccups." She frowned. "I think my beer is flat."

"You want another one?"

"No. I just want to go home," she said and stood. "I'm glad you came back when you did. This was good enough for me. I won't be wondering how the other half lives. I'd rather eat a meal I've prepared and watch a good TV show." She met his gaze with a lopsided smile. "I'm getting old, aren't I? An old mama."

Colton shook his head. "Nah. You're just growing up. And you're the hot kind of mama, so keep up your guard."

Chapter Four

Colton wasn't sure his evening out with Stacey had been all that successful. She'd been quiet on the way home. He was bummed that he hadn't been able to cheer her up more. He wondered if he'd made things worse. He focused on his work at the ranch during the next couple of days and avoided the inquiring glances from the rest of his family.

As he drove home after a long day outdoors, his cell phone rang. It was Stacey. He immediately picked up. "Hey. What's up?"

"I'm trying to find Rachel," Stacey said. "I need her help."

"I'm just pulling into the drive. Let me see if I can find her and I'll call you back," he said.

Colton strode into the house and called for his sister. "Rachel," he called. "Rachel."

No answer. His parents didn't even respond.

He looked through the house and called a few more times. Sighing, he stabbed out Stacey's cell number. "Hey," he said. "No sign of Rachel or my parents."

"Darn," Stacey said. "My parents have gone to a town meeting."

"Oh, mine must have gone to the same meeting. This place is like a ghost house," he said and chuckled. "I think my voice may be echoing off the walls."

"Oh, bummer," Stacey said.

He heard the despair in her voice. "What's wrong?"

"Rachel was my last hope since my parents are out, and my sister Delaney isn't feeling well."

"Last hope for what?" he asked, pacing the hallway in his house.

"Well, you know my brother Toby took in three foster kids," she said. "He called me tonight and said the youngest is feeling bad. He has no experience with sick kids, so he asked me to come over and I said I would. But I don't want to expose Piper to anything. I don't want her to get sick."

"Yeah," Colton said. "That's rough."

She sighed. "I hate to leave Toby hanging. Would you mind watching her for a little while so I could help him out?"

Colton froze. The idea of taking care of a baby

terrified him. He could do a lot of things, but he had no experience with babies. But he couldn't leave Stacey in such a bind, could he? Well, darn. He inhaled. "Okay, I'll do it, but you need to give me lots of instructions. This isn't like roping a calf."

"She'll be easy. I promise. I'll write down lots of instructions and put them in the diaper bag," Stacey said. "I can't tell you how much I appreciate this."

"Yeah," Colton said, and headed back to his car. It occurred to him that he would rather get stomped by a bull than take care of a baby.

He drove his truck the short distance to the Joneses' ranch and pulled in front of the house. His family had celebrated with the Jones family many times. Their home was as familiar to him as his own.

But a baby wasn't familiar to him at all.

Colton ground his teeth, then forced himself to present a better attitude. He could handle this. He'd handled far more difficult situations. Piper was just a six-month-old baby. How hard could it be, he asked himself, but he was sweating despite the freezing temperature outside.

He stomped up the porch steps and lifted his hand to knock on the door, but it swung open before his knuckles hit wood. Stacey looked up at him with a hopeful expression on her face as she held her baby on her hip. "She should go to sleep soon," Stacey said. "She's just a little worked up tonight."

"Worked up," he repeated, feeling more uneasy.

Stacey fluttered her hands. "Oh, it won't last

long," she said. "She'll get tired. Let me grab my coat, and I'll be back before you know it."

She thrust Piper into his hands. He stared at the baby, and she stared back at him. Mistrust brewed from his side, and he saw the same mistrust in the baby's eyes. "What am I supposed to do with her?" he asked.

"Rock her, walk her. Feed her only if you're desperate because she's already been fed." Stacey buttoned a peacoat and handed him a diaper bag. "This is my complete bag of tricks," she said. "This will be a breeze. You're going to surprise yourself. Trust me. Thank you so much," she said, and rushed out the door.

Colton resisted the urge to renege. Barely. After Stacey was gone, he looked at Piper. She let out a little wail. Colton dived into the diaper bag, skipped everything and went straight for the bottle.

Piper sucked it down, then stared at him and gave a loud, powerful burp.

"Whoa," Colton said, backing away from the sound. "How'd you do that?"

Piper squirmed and fussed.

Colton bobbed up and down. "Hey. Your tummy's full. You should be better."

Piper whined in response.

Colton grimaced. He had been hoping food would be the quick fix. It usually was for him. He patted her back and continued to walk. Piper whined and occasionally wailed. Colton had no idea how to please the baby.

Oh, wait. Maybe she had a messy diaper.

Eewww, he thought. He didn't want to change a diaper. That was just too gross. But maybe that would turn the trick and the baby would stop fussing.

Groaning to himself, Colton went to the magic diaper bag and pulled out a diaper, a packet of wipes and a changing pad. "Okay. Okay," he said to Piper as he set her down on the pad. "Give me a break. This is my first time."

Piper stuck her fingers in her mouth and gazed up at him with inquisitive green eyes.

At least she wasn't crying, he thought and lifted her gown. "Okey, doke. We can do this," he said because some part of him remembered that he'd seen a few people talk to babies. It wasn't as if they understood. Maybe they just liked the sound of a human voice.

Who knew?

He looked at the diaper, and for the life of him, he couldn't figure out which was the front and the back.

Piper began to squirm and make noises. They weren't fussy, but they were getting close.

"I'm getting there," he promised. "Just give me a little extra time."

He pulled open the dry diaper, then carefully unfastened the baby's dirty diaper. Colton glimpsed a hideous combination of green, yellow and brown.

"Oh, Piper. How could you?"

The baby squirmed and almost seemed to smile. Heaven help him.

Colton pulled out a half dozen wipes and began rubbing her front and backside. Six wipes weren't enough, so he pulled out some more and cleaned her a little more. Afterward, he tossed some baby powder on her and put on the disposable diaper.

Sweat was dripping from his forehead. "There. We did it."

Piper began to fuss.

"Well, thanks for nothing," he said, picking up her and the dirty diaper. He wondered if there was a special hazardous-waste disposal container in the house for the baby's diapers. He didn't see one, so he tossed it in the kitchen trash and felt sorry for the poor fool who lifted the lid to take out the garbage.

He jiggled Piper, but she was still fussy. He wondered if he shouldn't have fed her. He cruised the hallways of the house. Piper never broke into a full cry, but he could tell she was right on the edge.

Desperate, he tried to sing. "Mamas, don't let your babies—"

Piper wailed.

"Not a good choice," he muttered and jiggled her even more. He walked and talked, since talking worked better than singing did. She calmed slightly, but he could tell she still wasn't happy. This female was definitely difficult to please.

After thirty minutes, she was still fussy and Colton was growing desperate. He headed for the magic diaper bag and sat down to dig through it. Piper sobbed loudly in his ear as he searched the bag.

"Give me a break," he said. "I'm trying." He dug his way all the way to the bottom and grabbed hold of a bottle. Pulling it out, he stared at a bottle labeled, "Last resort".

Colton was pretty sure he was at his last resort. He opened the bottle and found a wand. "Well, damn," he said, and began to blow bubbles.

Piper immediately quieted and stared at the bubbles.

Colton continued to blow, and Piper began to laugh. It was the most magical sound he'd ever heard. He blew the bubbles, and she giggled. Her reaction was addictive.

"Well, who would have known?" he muttered under his breath. Maybe everyone should come armed with a bottle of bubbles. He blew bubbles past the time he was tired from it, and Piper finally rested her head on his shoulder. Colton wasn't taking any chances, though, and he kept up his bubble blowing.

Finally, he glanced down and saw that Piper's eyes were closed—half moons with dark eyelashes fanned against her creamy skin. She was one beautiful kid, he thought. The spitting image of Stacey. He gently strolled through the hallways again.

Weariness rolled through him. He'd been up before dawn and trying to work through a mile-long list of chores his father shouldn't do. The sofa in the den beckoned him. He wondered if he could possibly sit down without waking Piper.

Colton decided to give it a shot. He slowly eased down onto the sofa. Piper squirmed, and he froze. *Don't wake up,* he prayed. He waited, then leaned back, inch by inch. "We're okay," he whispered. "We're both okay."

Colton relaxed against the side of the sofa and slinked down. He rested his head backward and moved the baby onto his chest. "Don't wake up." He rubbed her back until he fell asleep.

"Stick out your tongue, Kylie," Stacey said to her brother's youngest foster child.

Redheaded Kylie reluctantly stuck out her tongue. Stacey saw no signs of strep. "I'm sorry you feel bad, sweetie," she said.

"I can stick out my tongue," Kylie's older brother, Justin, said and fully extended his tongue from his mouth. The boy's expression had a disturbing resemblance to a rock singer.

"Not necessary, but thanks, sweetie," she said.

Stacey turned to her brother Toby. "Her temperature is normal, and her lymph nodes feel fine. I would give her some extra liquids and try to help her get some extra rest." She rubbed Kylie's arm. "Do you feel achy?" she asked.

Kylie shook her head. "No, but my head hurts."

"I'm so sorry," Stacey said. "I bet a cool washcloth would feel good. If she can't sleep, she can take some children's Tylenol. In the meantime, Kylie needs some rest, comfort and cuddling."

"Does that mean I get to use the remote for the TV?" Kylie asked.

Stacey laughed. "I think you are definitely due the remote."

"But I wanna see SpongeBob," Justin said.

"You can see SpongeBob anytime," Toby said, rubbing Justin's head. "Let's just pile on the couch and watch what Kylie wants to watch."

Her brothers sighed but scrambled onto the couch. "I hope it's not a princess movie," Brian, the eleven-year-old, said.

"I want *Monsters,*" Kylie said.

"Again?" Brian said in disgust.

"Kylie gets to choose tonight. If you don't like her choice, you can get ahead on your homework or read a book," Toby said.

Stacey did a double take. She still couldn't quite get used to seeing her bachelor brother turn into an instant dad by agreeing to take on these three kids. Then again, Toby had always had a generous heart, so she really shouldn't be surprised. Stacey knew he'd met the kids when he'd volunteered at the Y. When he'd learned their mother had died at an early age and that their father wasn't around, he'd tried to give them some extra encouragement. When their situation had gone from bad to worse and the aunt who'd been caring for them was forced into rehab,

Toby had stepped forward to take them into his house by becoming a foster dad.

"Well, I'd better head back to the house. I couldn't find anyone except Colton to take care of the baby while I was gone," she said, packing up her little medical bag.

"Colton?" Toby echoed, giving a startled laugh. "You asked Colton Foster to take care of Piper?"

Stacey lifted her hands. "He was my only choice. Everyone else was busy, and I didn't want to leave you in the lurch."

Toby sighed. "Well, tell him I said thank you. I'll feel better about Kylie now that you've checked her."

"You still need to keep an eye on her. You should check her temperature and symptoms in the morning. It's a shame the kids' regular doctor is out of town," she said. "I wish we had a clinic in Horseback Hollow. Maybe I could get a job there," she said. "That's wishful thinking," she murmured, then looked up at her brother and squeezed his arm. "Are you okay?"

"Yeah," Toby said, but raked his hand through his hair. "This situation definitely has its ups and down. It all goes along smoothly for a few days, then it seems like we hit a big bump in the road."

Stacey pulled on her coat and walked to the door. "Regrets?" she asked in a low voice.

Toby shook his head firmly. "I did the right thing, and they're good kids. They make me laugh every day."

"Well, I admire you, Toby. Not many men would

do what you've done," she said. Three kids, all red-heads with tons of energy.

"I think I'm getting a lot more out of this than I expected," he said.

She gave her brother a big hug. "Call me anytime, and bring the kids over to visit Piper. When they're well," she quickly added.

"I'll do that," he said and opened the door. "Drive safely," he instructed, protective as ever.

"Good night. Get that cool washcloth for Kylie. See if it helps," she called over her shoulder and got into her car.

Stacey drove toward her house, growing more nervous with each increasing mile she covered. It wasn't that Piper was a bad baby, but at times she could be demanding and very vocal. Stacey hoped the baby had calmed down enough to fall asleep. She supposed that if Colton had really needed anything, he would have called her. As she pulled in front of the house, the lights from inside welcomed her. She got out of the car, climbed the stairs and opened the door.

She paused for a long moment, listening for the sound of Piper. All she heard was quiet. Stacey breathed a sigh of relief. Piper must have fallen asleep. She was surprised the television wasn't on. She would have expected Colton to turn on a ball-game once he'd put Piper in her crib.

Stepping into the den, she caught sight of Colton napping on the sofa with Piper asleep on his chest. Her heart swelled with emotion. If that wasn't the sweetest sight she'd ever seen, she thought. Seeing her daughter being held by a good strong man reminded Stacey of everything Piper was missing on an everyday basis. Tears filled her eyes, and she blinked furiously to keep them at bay.

First things first, she thought. Get the baby to bed. She gingerly extracted Piper from Colton's chest, praying the baby wouldn't awaken. Then she tiptoed to the small nursery in the room next to hers and put Piper down in her crib. Piper gave a few wiggly moves, and Stacey held her breath. Then the baby sighed and went back to sleep.

Stacey returned to the den and touched Colton's shoulder. He didn't awaken. She gave him a gentle shake, then another. The man was dead to the world. He must be worn out, she thought. He'd probably put in a full day at the ranch, yet he'd still agreed to watch Piper for her.

A rush of sympathy flooded through her. Stacey had lived on a ranch long enough to know it involved hard backbreaking work and long hours. It wouldn't hurt him to rest a little longer, she thought, and pulled the blanket from the back of the sofa and put it over him.

Backing away, she pulled off her coat and hung it in the closet, then returned to the den. Sinking onto the chair across from the sofa, Stacey allowed herself the luxury of looking at Colton while he was unaware. She wondered why she'd never noticed how attractive he was before. Sure, she'd known him her entire life, but she wasn't blind.

He was as strong as they came. Broad shoulders and she'd bet he might even have a six-pack. She blushed at the direction her mind was headed. He had a bit of stubble on his chin. His hard masculinity was at such odds with those eyelashes, she thought.

She wondered what it would be like to sleep with him and wake up with him. Would he be grouchy or sweet in the morning? She wondered what kind of lover he would be. She'd only had one, Joe. Their lovemaking sessions had often felt rushed to her, and although it wasn't something she discussed, she'd never felt completely, well, satisfied after sex with Joe.

Stacey wondered if Colton was the kind of man to take his time with a woman. Although she hadn't paid much attention, she'd heard of more than one woman he'd left more than happy after a night together. Lately, she was becoming much more curious about Colton. She kept reminding herself that he was interested in someone else, but that didn't seem to take the edge off her…curiosity.

At that moment, she heard the front door open and her father talking to her mother. "That meeting went on forever," he grumbled.

"Everyone has a right to speak their mind," Jeanne said.

"Well, they could speak a little faster," he said, and closed the door firmly behind him.

Stacey saw Colton jolt awake at the sound. He glanced around. "What the—" He broke off and shook his head.

"Hi," she said.

"Hey," he said, rising quickly.

"Listen, thank you for taking care of Piper," she said, also getting to her feet.

"No problem," he said, rubbing his face. "I guess I'll head home—"

Her mother and father entered the den. "Well, hello there, Colton. It's good to see you."

"Colton agreed to watch Piper while I checked out Kylie for Toby. He said she wasn't feeling well and their doctor is out of town, so he wanted me to come over and make sure she was okay. She just had a headache. I think Toby may be a little nervous fostering those three kids. Can't say I blame him."

"I'm glad Kylie is okay. It sure was nice of you to come over here and look after Piper," Jeanne said.

"That, it was. She can run you ragged at bedtime," her father said sympathetically.

"Daddy," Stacey said in an accusing tone.

"But she's a cute one and we love her," her father added.

"Of course we do," her mother said. "Why don't you join us for some hot chocolate before you leave? I can have it ready in no time."

"You don't need to do that," Colton said, appearing a bit embarrassed.

"I want to," Jeanne said. "Now sit down and relax,

and I'll have that hot chocolate for you before you know it."

Colton sighed and sat down on the edge of the sofa. "Is there anyone who can say no to your mother?"

"Not for long," Stacey said, laughing. "How was Piper?"

Colton nodded. "She did fine," he said in a non-committal tone.

Stacey read between the lines. "She was a beast, wasn't she? I was afraid of that. Even though I'd fed her, she seemed unsettled." Stacey sighed. "I'm sorry."

"I wouldn't call her a beast," Colton said. "Now," he added and chuckled, "amazing how something so small can get you so twisted trying to get her to calm down."

"How did you get her calm?" she asked, curious.

"You mean after I gave her the bottle in your magic bag and changed the toxic dump of her diaper?" he asked.

"Oh," she said, cringing.

"Yeah, I might need to take the kitchen trash out tonight before I leave," he said.

Her mother entered the room with cups of hot chocolate filled with mini-marshmallows. "This will help you sleep better once you get home, Colton," she said.

"I think Piper may have worn him out, so he may not need any help falling asleep," Stacey said.

"Oh, dear," her mother said, wincing. "She's gotten so much better during the last month. Did she have a rough night?"

"I wonder if she sensed that I was in a tizzy about getting over to Toby's house," Stacey said.

"Well, I speak from experience. Babies can sense our moods. Especially their mom's moods. At the same time, she may have just had a little tummy ache. Can I get you something to eat, Colton?"

"No, I'm fine, Mrs. Jones. Mrs. Fortune Jones," he corrected.

Her mother smiled. "That was sweet," she said. "But you've known me long enough to call me Jeanne." Her mother looked at Stacey. "Now, what on earth made you think to call Colton to take care of Piper?"

"I was trying to reach Rachel and she didn't pick up. I was hoping Colton could reach her," Stacey said.

"Oh," her mother said with a glance that combined intuition and suspicion. "Colton was definitely the man of the hour tonight, wasn't he?"

Uncomfortable with her mother's almost knowing expression, Stacey cleared her throat. "Yes, he was."

Chapter Five

A couple days later, Colton went into town to get some special feed and pick up a few things from the Superette for his mom. He would almost swear his mother could sense when he was headed into town because she always seemed to have a list of items for him to pick up from the small grocery—well, the only grocery—in town.

Using the term town might have been an exaggeration. Colton may have lived his entire life in Horseback Hollow, but he'd traveled enough to know his birthplace was more about wide open spaces than tall buildings and city conveniences. The *town* was just two streets long.

Colton glanced at the list his mother had given him and picked up apples, bananas, onions, tomato sauce and pasta. He hoped that meant spaghetti was in his near future. He added a can of green beans to his basket.

"Hey. What are you doing here?" a familiar voice spoke up from behind him. He turned and saw Stacey standing in the aisle.

"Just picking up a few things," he said. "What about you?"

"Formula and baby food for Piper," she said. "I just took something to the post office for Mom."

She glanced at his food items. "Spaghetti," she said more than asked. "Are you cooking for someone special?"

Confused, he cocked his head to one side. "Someone special?"

"Don't be shy," she said with a coy smile. "Cooking for your lady friend. I have a great recipe for spaghetti sauce, but you need sausage and cheese," she said.

He shrugged. "I haven't ever fixed spaghetti before unless it was from a can."

"Well, you've got to do better than that for a woman. If you're cooking for two, you could add some delicious bread and salad and call it good," she said. "And something chocolate. Women love chocolate."

Colton opened his mouth to protest, but she didn't let him fit a word in edgewise.

"I could help you," she offered. "Why don't I give you a cooking lesson? If you're anything like my brothers, you've relied on your mother your entire life for your meals, so you never bothered to learn."

That was a little insulting, he thought. But true.

"You sure you won't tell me who you're cooking for?" she asked.

"My lips are sealed," he said. It was easy to keep that secret since his so-called lady love didn't exist.

She gave a little huffy sigh. "Okay, well, I can still give you a few tips on your cooking. Is tonight okay?"

"I guess," he said, trying to recall his parents' busy schedule. He thought they were playing bridge tonight.

"Okay, I'll see you around six, and I'll help you fix a spaghetti dinner that will wrap your lady friend around your little finger. Make sure you pick up some sausage and fresh Parmesan cheese. I'm assuming you already have beef," she said.

"Yeah," he said. He lived on a cattle ranch. He darned well should have beef.

"Okay. See you later," she said and strode away.

Colton stared after her, distracted by the wiggle in her walk and her cute backside. He gave himself a shake. Why had he agreed to a cooking lesson? Especially for the sake of his imaginary girlfriend? He swore under his breath. This was getting worse and worse.

Stacey paid at checkout and walked to her car with her purchases. She felt a little cranky and wasn't sure why. Climbing into her car, she started the engine and headed for her house. She turned on the radio to listen to a few tunes to cheer herself up. It didn't quite work, though. Seeing Colton at the Superette purchasing food to feed the woman he clearly had a crush on made her grind her teeth. It must be nice to have a man work that hard to please you, she thought. She wouldn't know because no man had ever tried that hard to make her happy.

Frowning, she tried to push aside her feelings. It wasn't as if she wanted Colton to be cooking for her. Even though she'd looked at him with a little lust the other night, she'd decided that was an aberration. She couldn't really believe that she wanted Colton. Stacey told herself she was just lonely for some attention. That had to be it.

She returned home and unloaded her car while Piper napped.

"Are you sure you're okay?" her mother asked. "You're awfully quiet."

"I'm fine. Do you mind watching Piper for a little while tonight?"

"Of course not. Do you have plans?"

"I, uh, offered to give Colton a cooking lesson. He said he's trying to cheer up an unnamed female," she confessed.

Her mother lifted her eyebrows. "Oh, my," she said. "How generous of you. You know Colton keeps such a low profile. It's easy to underestimate him as, well, a romantic possibility."

"Not really," Stacey said. "I've heard some rumors about girls that liked him just fine."

"Oh, really," her mother said and paused. "Well, I think you're very sweet to help him prepare a dinner for another woman."

"I'm not doing that," Stacey snapped, then deliberately took a breath. "I'm just giving him a cooking lesson. He's like all my brothers except Toby. He can't cook worth a darn because his mother has cooked for him his entire life."

Her mother tilted her head. "Are you criticizing me for cooking for my family?"

Stacey closed her eyes and smiled, shaking her head. She went to her mother and gave her a big hug. "Of course not. You're the best mother any of us could have. But you have to admit those boys like having their meals put in front of them."

"You're right about that," she said ruefully and returned Stacey's embrace.

Stacey's cell phone rang, and she pulled it out of her purse. She didn't recognize the number. "Stacey Fortune Jones," she answered.

"Stacey, this is Sawyer. We have a situation here at the flight school. We need your help."

Stacey's pulse picked up. "What's wrong?"

"There's been an accident. My pilot Orlando has been hurt. The paramedics are on the way, but it will take a while, and the doctor's not in town."

"Oh, that's right," she said, remembering the same doctor who took care of Toby's foster children covered the whole town. "I'll be right there," she said, and turned to her mother. "I have to go. There's been an emergency at the flight school."

"Oh, no," her mother said. "Is it serious?"

"I think so," Stacey said grimly as she ran to her room to grab her medical bag.

Pulling into the flight school, she stopped her car and ran toward the figures beside the burning plane. Stacey went into nurse mode when she assessed Orlando Mendoza. She checked his blood pressure and pulse and noted that the pilot kept going in and out of consciousness. He'd likely suffered a concussion, and she could see he'd sustained a compound fracture of his left leg and another fracture of his left arm, so she made a temporary brace for each to prevent unnecessary movement and loss of blood. Although she was able to stabilize him until the paramedics arrived, she couldn't be certain that he hadn't suffered internal injuries, as well.

Stacey watched the ambulance drive away from the airport, then returned home and took a quick shower. The entire time, she kept thinking about Orlando Mendoza. She'd wished she could do more for him, but it was a miracle he'd survived the crash. She checked in on Piper and her mother and answered Mama Jeanne's twenty questions about the accident. Unfortunately, Stacey wasn't sure how everything would turn out for Orlando. This was one more reason Stacey wished there was an emergency facility closer to Horseback Hollow. Her hair still wet, she put it on top of her head and headed out the door to go to the Fosters' house.

After driving the few minutes to the Fosters, Stacey raced to the porch and knocked on the front door. "I'm sorry I'm late," she said when Colton answered the door. "Did you hear about the accident at the flight school?"

He shook his head. "I just got in from the field. What happened?"

"One of the planes from the flight school went down and the pilot was injured. Orlando Mendoza. The paramedics were taking a while to get there, so Sawyer asked me to come and do what I could to stabilize him."

"Oh, man," Colton said. "You think he'll make it?"

"I don't know. He was unconscious most of the time and he had a badly broken arm and leg," she said, her mind flashing back to a visual of the man.

"Hmm," Colton said. "Listen, you look pretty upset. We don't have to do this cooking lesson."

She shook her head. "I can't do anything now for him except pray. I could really use a distraction."

Colton gave a slow nod. "Okay," he said with a lopsided grin. "If teaching me how to fix Stacey's spaghetti will distract you, then that's what we'll do."

"Fine," she said and headed for the kitchen. "Let's start with chopping that onion. Some key things you need to know about making spaghetti are that you shouldn't overcook the noodles and you should break up the meat before you put it in the pan. But don't overwork it," she instructed.

"I'm taking mental notes," he said.

"You won't just be taking mental notes," she said. "You'll be doing the work. You remember what you do more than you remember what someone says."

"That sounds like something my father would say," he said.

"It's actually something my father once said," she said, and met his gaze. "It must be a conspiracy."

He chuckled. "You must be right."

"Wash your hands," she said.

"Yes, Mama," he said.

She shot him a disapproving look.

"Whoa," he said, lifting his hand in mock self-protection. "You've got lasers shooting from your eyes."

"One of my superpowers. Let's get to work," she said. She noticed that Colton possessed a much better sense of humor than Joe had. Not that she was comparing.

Stacey felt overly aware of Colton's physical presence in the kitchen as they prepared the meal. His shoulders grazed hers. Her hip slid against his. She put her hand over his to show him how to chop the onion. She couldn't help noticing his hands. They were large, but there was nothing awkward about the way he used them. For an instant, she couldn't help thinking about how his hands would feel on her body. The image heated her from the inside out.

Stacey tried to ignore her feelings. She helped Colton drain the pasta, and he was just way too close. Way too strong. And she was way too curious. She looked directly into his brown eyes and glimpsed a spark that mirrored hers.

She could have, should have looked away, but she didn't.

His nostrils flared slightly, and she couldn't tell if he was having the same problem with curiosity and self-restraint that she was. "This looks good," he said.

"It should be," she said, and turned away to stir the sauce. "It's best to cook this a longer time, but thirty minutes will do if you're in a rush." She lifted a spoonful of sauce and blew on it for a few seconds. She took a tiny taste. "Yum."

She offered him a sample from the same spoon. Colton covered her hand with his to steady the spoon and took a taste. He nodded. "That's good. Hard to believe I fixed it," he said with a half grin.

"Yes, it is," she said, and threw back her head in a laugh. "I'm surprised at how well you do in the kitchen."

"You never knew a lot of things about me," he said.

Her stomach took a dip to her knees, and her sense of humor suddenly vanished. "That's very true. Maybe you could say the same about what you know about me."

"Maybe I could," he admitted and stepped closer to her.

In theory, Stacey could have turned away. In reality, she probably should have. But she was just too curious and too, well, warm. She wanted to feel Colton Foster's chest against hers. She wanted to feel his arms around her. She wanted to feel his lips on hers.

Stacey gave in to all her bad urges and flung herself into Colton's arms. His hard chest against her breasts felt so much better than she'd expected. His arms around her gave her a melting sensation. And his kiss made her want so much more. How could his mouth be both firm and sensual? How could such a little taste of him send her into a frenzy?

She opened her mouth, and he took her with a kiss that sent her upside down. She couldn't resist the urge to wiggle against him. Colton gave a low groan that made her burn. She felt his hand travel to the small of her back to pull her even closer. She was breathtakingly aware of his hard body from his chest all the way down to his thighs.

Oh, yes, she thought. *More, give me more.*

The force of her need bowled her over. Panic raced through her. This was Colton, and she was getting ready to make a fool of herself.

Stacey pulled back, knowing her face was flaming red. She was embarrassed all the way down to her toes. "Oops. I should go. I really should go," she managed and refused to meet Colton's gaze. She wondered how she would survive this, but couldn't focus on that. She grabbed her coat and ran out the door.

Stacey drove home with her window down so she could cool off. Despite that, when she walked in the door she still felt as if she were on fire. Fanning her face, she pulled off her coat and threw it on a hanger.

She gnawed the inside of her lip as she walked toward the kitchen. She needed a very, very cold glass of water. She just wasn't sure if she was going to drink it or pour it over her head.

"Stacey?" her mother called from the den. "Is that you?"

She took a deep breath and tried to compose herself. She walked to the doorway of the den. "It's me. How was Piper?"

"No trouble at all," her mother said. Her father was sitting next to her, dozing on the sofa. "She fell asleep like that," her mother said, snapping her fingers and smiling.

"I'm glad to hear that. Thank you again for looking after her," Stacey said.

"You know I will look after her anytime," her mother said.

"Yes, but I don't want to take advantage of you," Stacey said.

"It's not taking advantage," her mother insisted. "It's my pleasure. Besides, I know you would never take advantage of me. Enough about that." She waved her hand. "So, how did the cooking lesson with Colton go?"

Stacey forced a smile. "Great. I think he's ready to fix my super spaghetti recipe all by himself."

"Good for him," her mother said. "You're a sweet girl to help him do that for another woman. Colton's a good man. I might not be as generous as you are."

Stacey managed to laugh. "I've known Colton forever. He's just like a brother."

"But he's not really a brother," her mother said, then shrugged. "Doesn't matter. Can I fix you some hot chocolate?"

"No, thanks, Mama. I think water will do. I'm off to bed," Stacey said, and went to the kitchen to get that tall glass of ice water. Maybe she should get two.

The next day, Stacey prepared enough food for a month of meals. Thank goodness, the Jones family had a big roomy freezer.

Her brother Jude dropped by before dinner. "Wow," he said, when he looked at all the casserole dishes on top of the counter. "Are we feeding the entire town of Horseback Hollow?" he asked.

Stacey shot him a quelling glance. "This would feed far more than the township of Horseback Hollow. Technically, we don't even live in the township of Horseback Hollow."

Jude shrugged his shoulders. "True, so why did you cook so much?"

Stacey considered keeping her feelings to herself,

but if anyone should understand, it would be Jude. Everyone knew he fell in love or like at the drop of a hat. She'd always thought of him as a Romeo. "I'm cooking to distract myself from something that's bothering me. I have a crush on Colton Foster," she whispered.

Silence followed. "Colton Foster? When did this happen?"

"Recently," she said. "I didn't plan it. And I think he has feelings for another woman."

"Who?" Jude asked.

She shook her head. "I don't know. He's been cagey about it."

"You've talked to him about another woman and you still have a crush on him?" he asked in disbelief.

"It didn't happen exactly like that. Don't fuss at me," she said. "I thought you would understand."

"Hell, no," Jude said. "Don't jump into a new romance. It's not in your best interest."

She gave a double take at his advice. "Says the guy who falls in love or like at least once a month."

"I don't want you to get hurt. Colton's a good guy, but if he's involved with another girl…"

"I didn't say he was involved," she said. "He just said he wanted to make her happy."

Jude winced. "That's a big deal, Stacey. Guys don't talk about making a woman happy if they aren't already pretty committed."

"Thanks for the encouragement," she murmured as she bundled up another casserole for the freezer.

Jude squeezed her shoulder. "I'm just looking out for you."

She took a deep breath. "I know. It just seems ironic for you to be warning me away from my feelings for Colton."

"Maybe I'm changing in my old age," he said. "Or maybe I just don't want you to get hurt again."

Stacey thought about Joe and frowned. "I know it may sound crazy, but I feel as if my engagement to Joe was a lifetime ago."

"I still wouldn't mind kicking him into next week," he said. "He shouldn't have abandoned you."

"He couldn't handle the commitment," she said, and only felt a twinge of sadness over the situation. She had begun to realize that Joe's abandonment was his issue more than hers. "It's taken a while for me to realize this, but I wouldn't want him if he stayed with Piper and me out of obligation. At the same time, I feel terrible that Piper doesn't have the daddy she deserves. But the truth is, I'm not sure Joe deserves her."

Jude studied her for a long moment. "Dang, girl. You've grown up."

She smiled at her brother. "You think?"

"Yeah," he said, and waggled his finger at her. "Just don't go falling for the local cowboys. I don't want you to get hurt." His gaze slid to the pot on the stove. "Can you share any of that soup? The smell is killing me."

"That bad, huh?" she asked, smiling at his description.

"Have a little pity," he said.

"Tell the truth," she said. "When was the last time you prepared a full meal for yourself or anyone else?"

"Grilled cheese and canned soup count?"

She shook her head.

He sighed. "A long time."

"That's what I thought," she said. "Maybe you're due for a cooking lesson."

"I'll tell you a secret, Stacey. It's my goal to never need to cook for myself. That is the goal of most bachelors," he said.

"Well, at least you're honest," she said, and planted a kiss on his cheek. She fixed a large container of soup for him to take home. She spent the next hour storing meals. Piper awakened, and Stacey gave her a half bottle of baby food and her bottle. Afterward, it was time for baby calisthenics. Stacey set Piper on her belly and watched her do dry swimming. Piper grunted and groaned as she exercised.

When Piper's groans turned to cries, Stacey whisked her up in her arms and walked to the kitchen with her. Stacey finished wrapping up her meals for storage and put a few portions in the refrigerator. Her father was always grateful when she packed a lunch he could take outdoors.

Tucking Piper into a baby pack, Stacey began to clean the public areas of the house. She took care of the den, foyer and kitchen and began to feel tired. Pulling Piper from the sack, Stacey sank onto a chair in the den and told herself not to think about Colton.

Even her Romeo brother, Jude, had warned her away from her feelings. But Stacey couldn't keep her mind off of Colton. She wanted to be close to him. Very close.

She concentrated on rocking Piper, then burping her. Stacey knew she needed to focus on Piper. Her baby needed her love and devotion.

Unfortunately, Stacey was all too aware of her own needs. How was she supposed to make those needs disappear?

The next afternoon while her mother made some calls to her circle group, Stacey folded laundry in the den. Piper took a nap. Stacey did the hated job of folding sheets. Was there any good way of folding fitted sheets? With the television on a news show, she folded several linens.

A knock sounded at the door, and she rushed to keep whoever was on her porch from knocking again. She didn't want Piper waking from the noise. It was amazing how precious her child's sleep had become to her, she thought. She wondered if she should start putting a note on the front door when Piper was napping. Or would that be a bit too cranky?

Stacey opened the door and saw Colton on the porch. Her heart took a huge dip.

Colton removed his Stetson. "We need to talk."

Chapter Six

"I'm sorry. I shouldn't have taken advantage of you," Colton said.

Stacey felt her face heat with embarrassment and cringed. "Oh, no, I'm sorry. I shouldn't have interfered. I was supposed to be helping you with your girlfriend and ended up kissing you. I knew you had plans with her, but you and I got close and I stopped thinking about your girlfriend. I was just thinking about you and—"

"Stop," he said, and took her mouth in a kiss, then pulled back. "There is no girlfriend."

She stared at him in confusion. "No girlfriend?"

"No girlfriend," he repeated. "There is no one else I can think about right now. You're the only woman on my mind," he said.

Floored, Stacey could only gape at him. "I don't know what to say."

"You don't have to say anything. Just know that I didn't want to take advantage of you," he said and walked away.

Stacey gawked after him, wishing she could produce some magic words, but her tongue wouldn't even form basic syllables. "Colton," she finally managed, but he was already in his truck.

She was at a pure loss. He'd given her no chance to respond. How could she tell him how she really felt? How could she let him think their kiss was totally his fault? She raced to the back of the house and found her mother in between phone calls.

"Piper's asleep. Do you mind watching her for a while?" she asked.

"Not at all," her mother said. "Is there a problem?"

"I just need to go somewhere," she said, and didn't want to hang around long enough for her mother to question her further. Her mother was extremely intuitive. Stacey grabbed her purse, pulled on her coat and headed for her car. As she drove toward the Foster house, she tried to find the words to explain her feelings for Colton. She kept rehearsing several verbal scenarios, but none seemed adequate.

With no great plan in mind, she stomped up the steps to the Foster house and rapped on the door. A few seconds passed, and she knocked again.

The door whipped open and Colton looked at her. "What are you doing here?" he asked. "Listen, we don't have to talk about what happened again. I know you don't think of me that way," he said. "In a romantic way."

"Stop telling me what I think," Stacey said. She didn't know any other way to express her feelings for Colton except for kissing him, so that's what she did. She pulled him against her and kissed him as if her life depended on it.

Colton couldn't help but respond. He wrapped his arms around her and drew her to him. He clearly couldn't resist her. "You feel so good," he muttered. "Taste so good," he said, sliding his tongue past her lips.

Stacey felt herself heating up way too quickly. She wriggled against him, wanting to feel every bit of him. She wanted his skin against hers. She slid her hands up to the top of his head and continued to exchange open mouth kisses with him.

"I want you so much," she whispered.

"What do you want, Stacey?" he muttered.

"All of you. I want all of you," she said, her need escalating with each passing moment.

Colton's hands traveled to forbidden places. Her breasts and her read end. Beneath his touch, she felt herself swell like a sensual flower.

"Are you sure about this?" Colton asked, teasing her nipples to taut expectation.

"Yes, yes," she said, clawing at his chest. "I want you so much."

"Then you're gonna get me," he muttered and

pulled her up into his arms and carried her down the hallway. He took her into his bedroom and set her down on his bed.

"You're sure?" he asked a second time.

"More than sure," she said, and whipped off her shirt and bra. "Are you?" she asked, daring him.

One, two, three heartbeats vibrated through her, and Colton began to devour her with his hands and mouth. She had never felt such passion in her life. He made every inch of her body burn with desire and need for him. Stacey hadn't felt this alive in months…or ever.

She kissed his chest and belly…and lower. He groaned and took her with the same hunger.

"You taste so good," he said.

"So do you," she said, and pressed her mouth against his in a fully sexual kiss.

"I want to be inside you," he said, his tone desperate.

"I want you the same way," she said.

He pulled some protection from his bedside table, and finally, he pushed her legs apart and thrust inside her.

Stacey gasped.

"What?" he asked.

"You're just—" she said and broke off.

"I'm just what?" he asked, poised over her.

She took a deep breath and laughed breathlessly. "Big. You're big."

He shot her a sexy smile. "I'll try to make that work for you," he said, and began to move inside her.

They moved in a primitive rhythm that sent her twisting and climbing toward some new high she'd never experienced. She continued to slide against him, staring into his dark, sexy eyes.

When had Colton become so desirable to her? What did it matter? she asked herself and threw herself into making love to him. Stacey clung to his strong shoulders, and with every thrust, he took her higher and higher.

"You feel so good," he muttered. "So good."

Stacey felt herself clench and tremble. A climax wracked through her. She could hardly breathe from the strength of it.

Seconds later, she felt him follow after her, thrusting and stretching in a peak that clearly took him over the edge. He clutched her to him and gasped for breath.

Stacey clung to him with all her might. "Two words," she whispered. "Oh, wow."

He rolled over and pulled her on top of him. "When did you turn into the sexiest woman alive?"

Stacey laughed. "Me?"

"Yeah, you," he said, and kissed her again.

She sifted her fingers through his hair, enjoying every sensation that rippled through her. She loved the feeling of his skin against hers, his hard muscles. She slid her legs between his and savored his hard thighs. His lips were unbelievably sensual.

"I'm not sure how this happened," she said.

"Neither am I," he said. "But I'm glad it did."

They made love again until they were breathless. She wrapped her arms around him, shocked by how he'd made her feel. Stacey was in perfect bliss.

After that second time, Colton looked down at Stacey, all warm, sexy and satisfied in his bed, and felt a triple shot of terror. What the hell had he done? He hadn't just kissed his sister's best friend. He'd made love to her. Twice.

He held her tightly against him but was horrified by what he had done. "You're an amazing woman."

"You're a flatterer, but I'll take it," she said, cuddling against him.

"This is great, but I don't want us to have to make excuses to my family," he said.

A sliver of self-consciousness slid through her eyes. "Oh, good point," she said and bit her lip. She moved off of him, and he immediately regretted the absence of her body and sweetness.

Stacey quickly pulled on her clothes. "I should leave."

"Let me walk you to your car," he said, still full of questions and regrets. He pulled on his jeans and shirt.

Stacey grabbed her coat that had been left on the foyer floor. "I'm glad your mother didn't discover that," she said.

"We're talking about building a separate house, soon," he said.

"I understand the need for privacy," she said. "I don't have it. But I'm lucky to be able to live with my parents."

"I feel as if I should drive you home," he said, still upset with himself and overwhelmed by his feelings.

"I'm okay," she said, but she looked uncertain. The mood between them suddenly seemed awkward.

"Are you sure?" he asked.

She pressed her lips together in a closed-mouth smile. "Yes, I am," she said and shrugged. "I guess I'll see you around."

"Right." He nodded, thinking they had moved way too fast. Stacey had big responsibilities, and he might not be the right man to help her with them. He hadn't considered his previous experience with Piper a rousing success. "We'll talk later," he said, and helped her into her car.

"Yeah," she said, but didn't meet his gaze. She started her car and tore out of his driveway faster than a race car. He wondered if she regretted going to bed with him. He couldn't blame her. His parents' ranch wasn't exactly the most romantic environment.

Colton struggled with his own emotions over what they'd just done. They were friends, weren't they? If that was true, why had he wanted her so much? Why did he still want her? Whatever was happening between him and Stacey was complicated as hell.

* * *

Stacey forced herself not to look in her rearview mirror as she pulled away from the Foster ranch. She had clearly lost her mind, rushing back to tell Colton that she wanted him, too. Even though he'd said she'd been on his mind, it wasn't as if he'd said he wanted her in a forever way. She'd better not forget that. She'd been through a similar situation with Joe, although he'd given her an engagement ring. With Colton, he'd made no promises. He'd just taken what she'd eagerly offered, but afterward the expression on his face had been one of discomfort.

Buyer's remorse, she thought. He'd taken the goods, but now he wasn't sure he wanted them.

Pain twisted through her. She felt like a fool. Why had she believed Colton was different? She was all too familiar with this scenario. She'd been through it and lived to regret it during the past year of her life. When would she learn? she castigated herself. When would she stop throwing herself at men only to learn they only wanted her for a little while? Not forever. She wondered if she and Colton had just made a big mistake.

How could they go back to being friends now? Was that what he wanted? Humiliation flamed so hot it was as if a hole burned in her stomach. She pulled to a stop in front of her parents' home and shook her head at herself.

Glancing in the mirror, she saw that her hair was a mess, her lipstick smudged halfway across her face.

If her mother caught sight of her, she would know that Stacey hadn't just been running errands. Jeanne Fortune Jones was one of the most intuitive women on the earth, especially when it came to her children.

Stacey searched through her purse and found an elastic band but no brush. She raked her fingers through her hair and pulled it into the low messy bun she frequently wore. She pulled out a tissue and wiped the gloss off her face, then reapplied just a little to her lips. She checked the buttons on her coat, making sure they were properly fastened.

Holding her breath, she decided to make a dash through the foyer. "Well, there you are," her mother said from the kitchen. "I was starting to wonder where you'd gone so long."

"Sorry, Mom," Stacey said, pulling at the buttons on her coat. "I've got to use the bathroom or I'm going to burst. I'll be out in just a few," she said, and ran down the hall. She took her time, then hid out in her bedroom a little longer.

"Stacey, dinner's ready," her mother called.

Stacey cringed, then stiffened her spine. She could and should focus on Piper. As she stepped into the kitchen, she was relieved to see her brothers Liam and Jude sitting down to the table along with her father and mother. Her father and her brothers were too busy talking about the ranch to notice her. Her mother had put Piper in her high chair. As soon as Piper spotted Stacey, she lifted her hands and smiled in joy.

Even though the baby wasn't speaking yet, her nonverbal language soothed Stacey's heart, and she immediately picked up her baby. "Well, hello to you, Sweet Pea," she said, and sat down with Piper in her lap.

"She's never going to learn to be happy in her high chair if you don't leave her in there," Jeanne said.

"I'll put her in her seat in a couple minutes. How could I resist that smile?" Stacey asked.

"Your food will get cold," her mother warned.

Stacey shrugged. "I'm not that hungry."

Her brother Liam glanced at her. "In that case, I'll take Stacey's share."

Her mother shook her head. "You will not," she said. "Besides, there's plenty to go around. Stacey made this meat loaf yesterday, so she deserves a few bites."

"I hope you didn't mind putting it in the oven," Stacey said, rising to get some dry cereal for Piper.

"Not at all. You were just gone longer than I expected, so I started getting a little worried," she said, and Stacey felt the unasked question in her mother's voice.

She sighed, knowing she would have to fib, and heaven knew she wasn't any good at deception. "I ordered something for Piper, and I wanted to see if it had been delivered to the P.O. box yet. No luck, and there was a long line at the post office," she said. Part of her tale was true. She *had* ordered something for Piper, but it wasn't due for days. "Then I stopped by to visit Rachel, but she wasn't there. She had saved a recipe for homemade baby food I thought I might try. I guess the whole trip was a washout. Was Piper okay while I was gone?" Stacey sprinkled some cereal on the top of Piper's high chair, then set her child in the seat.

"An angel. She took a long nap and woke up in a quiet mood," her mother said, and finally took a bite of her own food. Her mother was usually the last to eat. "You need to sit down and eat," she told Stacey.

"I am," Stacey said and took her seat. She forced herself to take a bite.

"Did you happen to see Colton when you stopped by the Fosters'?" her mother asked as she took a sip of coffee.

Stacey's bite of meat loaf hung in her throat, and she coughed repeatedly.

"What's wrong with you? Are you choking?" her brother Jude asked, then thumped her on her back.

"Water," her mother said, standing up and leaning over the table to pick up Stacey's glass of water and press it into Stacey's hand.

Stacey took a few sips. Everyone looked at her expectantly. "Sorry," she said sheepishly. "I think I tried to breathe the meat loaf instead of eat it."

Liam chuckled. "Make sure you teach that little one over there a different technique."

"I will, smarty-pants," she said, and was determined to take the focus off herself. "The Winter Festival is right around the corner. I can't decide whether to bake apple/blueberry pies, chocolate pies or red velvet cupcakes."

"Apple/blueberry," her father said.

"Chocolate," Liam said.

"All three," Jude said.

Her mother laughed. "Aren't you glad you asked their opinions? Any of those sound good to me, but make sure you bake an extra one of whatever you end up making for us, or there's going to be a lot of complaining," Jeanne said, tilting her head toward her husband and sons.

Stacey smiled in relief. She would escape an inquisition this time.

The next few days, Stacey developed a plan for her tutoring service. She knew her strengths were math and science, so she decided to focus on those subjects as she contacted the local schools. She also sent an email to Rachel since she knew her friend was doing her student teaching this semester.

Her mother caught her reviewing a flyer at the kitchen table and gave a sound of surprise. "When did you decide to start tutoring?"

"I've been thinking about it for a while. Piper is older, but still manageable. I'm hoping to schedule the sessions during after-school hours. She takes a long afternoon nap, so I'd like to take advantage of that time and bring in a little bit of money."

Her mother frowned. "If you needed money, you

should have asked for it. Your father and I are happy to help you," she said, squeezing Stacey's shoulder.

Stacey's heart swelled at her mother's support. "You and Dad are already letting me stay here without paying rent. I don't like feeling as if I'm not contributing." She sighed. "I don't like feeling like a deadbeat."

Her mother sat down beside her. "Oh, sweetheart, you're no deadbeat. You fix the meals and do the laundry and cleaning here. For goodness' sakes, I barely have to lift a finger with all you do."

"Thanks, but—"

"No buts," Jeanne said. "We know that Joe hasn't offered any financial support, and he should have. At some point, you may have to confront him about that."

Stacey shook her head. "I hate the thought of it. He rejected both of us so thoroughly. I hate the thought of asking him for anything."

"But he *is* your baby's father," her mother said. "He has some responsibilities."

"I wish he wasn't Piper's father. I wish her father was someone more responsible, mature. Someone who adored her." A lump of emotion caught in her throat. "I wish—" she said, her voice breaking. She took a deep breath. "It doesn't matter what I wish. I'm probably never going to find anyone that loves me and Piper, and I need to stop whining about it. Piper and I are so blessed that my family loves us and supports us."

"Well, of course we love you," her mother said.

"But you're young, and you have a long life ahead of you. You'll find someone—"

"I don't think so," Stacey interrupted. "I can't count on that. I can't hope for it. I've just got to focus on doing the right thing for Piper, and I think tutoring is the right thing."

"If you're sure," her mother said. "And you know I'm happy to babysit for Piper anytime you need."

"Thank you, but I'm hoping I can do this while she's napping," Stacey said.

Her mother studied her for a long moment. "I worry that you don't get out with people your age very much. You and Rachel see each other now and then, but not that often. I wondered if you and Colton might be getting friendly."

"Oh, no. He was just trying to be nice and brotherly," she said, although her teeth ground together when she said it.

"If you say so," her mother said. "There's no reason you two can't enjoy each other as friends."

"Hmm. We'll see," Stacey said in a noncommittal voice. "At the moment, I need to make some copies of these posters and call in some favors from my teacher friends."

"All right. You sound like a busy girl. Are you still going to make desserts for the Winter Festival?" her mother asked.

"That's next week and I've already got it on my calendar," Stacey said. "I've got it under control."

Stacey did her best to stay busy during the next

days. She didn't want to think about Colton. She couldn't help feeling dumped. Thank goodness, no one except she and Colton knew what had happened between them. The longer the time passed, the more she knew, for certain, that now that he'd indulged his passion for her, he was done with her. She would have felt a bit more used if she didn't recall how much pleasure she'd experienced with him. Every once in a while, a stray image crossed her mind of the way he'd felt in her arms, the way he'd kissed and caressed her. Every time she had one of those thoughts she wanted to stomp it from her mind the same way she would stomp a spider. This was not the time for her to be thinking about her sexual needs.

Darn Colton Foster. Ever since Joe had abandoned her, Stacey had buried all her interest in sex. It hadn't been that difficult. But being around Colton had brought those emotions back to life, and these feelings were not convenient.

Not at all.

"Colton, I need you to take my pies to Dessert Booth number three-B at the Winter Festival tomorrow," Olive Foster said when he walked into the kitchen late Thursday evening.

Colton shook his head. "I've got a mile-long list of chores I have to do tomorrow. Maybe Rachel can do it."

"Rachel is student teaching. She can't do both,"

his mother said. "You'll only have to be there three hours."

"Three hours," he echoed, incredulous. "Why can't I just drop them off?"

"Because they need people to help work the booth," she said. "And I'm volunteering to help the handicapped at the festival."

"You may need to help Dad if he decides to do any of the chores I have planned for tomorrow," Colton grumbled.

His mother shot him a sharp look. "That's a terrible thing to say about your father."

"You know he has a problem with his back, even though he won't admit it," he said.

She sighed. "I'll guilt him into coming with me. That should keep him out of trouble."

"Kinda like you're guilting me into working a bake sale?" he returned.

"Colton, you are bordering on being disrespectful. What's wrong with you lately, anyway? You've been as grumbly as a bear with a sore paw. Are you having girl trouble?"

"Oh, for Pete's sake." Colton lifted his hand. This was not a conversation he wanted to have with his *mother*. "Just stop, Mom. I'll do the darn bake sale." Hell, he would do ten bake sales as long as he never had to discuss this subject with his mother again.

After lunch, the following day, Colton loaded up his truck with his mother's apple pies and drove to the Winter Festival. There was already a mile-long line of people waiting to get inside, but since he was a so-called vendor, he walked right in. It took him a while, but he finally found his assigned booth. He set the pies on the card table and turned around to get the second batch.

He was in such a hurry he nearly walked straight into someone just outside the booth.

"Don't," she said, and *she* sounded remarkably like Stacey. He should know since he'd been hearing her voice in his dreams every night. "Don't knock over the cupcakes," she said.

Colton grabbed two of the boxes that threatened to fall off the tower of desserts she carried and noticed Stacey was hauling Piper on her back at the same time she carried the desserts. "For Pete's sake, what are you doing?"

"I brought cupcakes and pies. I couldn't decide which to bake, so I made both," she said, striding toward the same booth where he just set down his mother's apple pies. Stacey frowned, then looked up at Colton. "What are you doing here?"

"My mother guilted me into bringing her pies and working this booth," he said.

"Well, that's just great," Stacey said, clearly disgusted. "Just great."

"Hey, my mother pushed me into this," he said. "Don't blame me."

"I'm not blaming you for bringing your mother's pies," she said, but he could hear she hadn't finished her sentence. There was more to it.

"You're blaming me for something," he said. "I can hear it in your voice."

"I'm blaming you for not calling me, Colton Foster. That was pretty rotten, unless you just wanted me for a quick roll in the hay," she said, and turned away from him.

Chapter Seven

Colton thought about responding to Stacey, but he couldn't find the right words. So he returned to his truck, swearing all the way as he hauled in the second load of pies. How could he explain himself? He wanted her, but he wanted to be sensible. With her history, he thought they should take their time. Plus, there was a baby involved. He didn't want to mess things up.

"Hey, Colton, you sure you don't want to share one of those pies with us while we wait out here in the cold?" a neighbor called from the crowd.

Colton paused only a half beat. "I don't have a fork handy for you," he said in return.

"I don't need a fork. I'll just eat with my hands. I love your mama's pies," the neighbor called back.

Colton chuckled despite his black mood and shook his head, walking to the dessert booth he would share with Stacey. His chuckle faded as he reentered the booth and set down the second haul of pies.

"You might want to put those on the table against the wall," she said as she arranged the desserts on the front table. "We don't want them to know we have a lot of them. They'll buy faster if they're afraid we'll run out."

"True," he said, and moved half the pies to the back table. "Are the cupcakes okay?"

"The frosting on two of them got smashed, but the rest are okay," she said.

"I can eat the damaged ones," he offered.

She shot him a disapproving glance. "We may have someone desperate enough to buy them," she said. "We're trying to make money for the mobile library, not stuff our faces."

"I wasn't suggesting we stuff *our* faces," Colton said. "I just wanted to stuff *mine*."

Stacey rolled her eyes and turned away, but Piper craned her head around to look at him. He couldn't deny she was cute. She batted her big eyes at him. Colton hid his face in a game of silent peekaboo.

After a few times of peekaboo, Piper let out a gurgling laugh. It was, Colton thought, one of the best sounds in the world. He played peekaboo again, and Piper let out a joyous shriek.

Stacey whipped around and glared at him. "What are you doing?"

"Nothing," he said. "Nothing."

"Hmm," she said in a short, disbelieving tone. "The attendees should be coming through soon." She turned her back to him again.

Piper looked at Colton, and he wiggled his fingers and smiled at her. She smiled coyly, then giggled.

Stacey glanced over her shoulder at Colton.

"What?" he asked.

She made a huffing sound and turned away to arrange a display of cupcakes. Colton couldn't help noticing Stacey's backside. He couldn't help remembering squeezing her curvy hips as he slid inside....

Colton felt his body instantly respond to the memory and visual. He shifted his stance and cleared his throat. "How have you been doing?"

Stacey immediately whipped around and stared at him with a wide-eyed gaze. "Since when?"

Colton shrugged. "Since last week."

"Oh, you mean since the day we had sex twice in your bed and you rushed me out the door because you didn't want your family asking questions and then chose not to call me. Even once."

Colton's gut twisted. Just in case he'd wondered, he now knew that Stacey had wanted him to call. He'd been unsure about how she'd felt since he'd taken her in his bed. Before, during and afterward, he'd wished that he could take her somewhere more private, but he'd been so hungry for her, and she'd seemed to feel the same way about him. Someone had to get control in this situation, although he was pretty sure he was nowhere near control. He didn't know if he could trust Stacey's feelings for him. To be honest, he wasn't sure if he was a rebound man for her.

"I wasn't sure you wanted me to call," he admitted.

She screwed up her face in a confused expression. "Why would you think that?"

"Well, you left pretty fast," he said.

"After you pushed me along," she said.

"I was trying to protect you," he said. "Did you really want to have to explain to anyone in my family why you were walking out of my bedroom with your hair all messed up and your coat on the floor in the hallway?"

Her hostility lowered a couple of notches. "I guess not," she said and paused. "But that still doesn't explain why you haven't called," she practically spat at him and turned around as the first attendees began to wander toward their booth.

After that, everything turned into a blur. It seemed that everyone who stopped at the booth wanted a pie or cupcake. The cupcakes went first because they were pretty and inexpensive. Every time Colton sold one of those cupcakes, he had to resist the urge to eat it. Red velvet with cream cheese frosting. His mouth watered. He kept hoping he could persuade Stacey to give him one of the defective cupcakes, but they were moving so quickly that he was losing hope. The booth was so tight she brushed against him every time she moved from the front to the back. He didn't know which was worse, the temptation of Stacey's body or of her red velvet cupcakes. Another brush of her sexy hips against his and his question was answered. He wanted Stacey a lot more than he wanted cupcakes.

"I need to ask a favor of you," she said, pulling at the straps of her baby carrier.

He shrugged. "What do you need?"

"To go to the bathroom. I'd prefer to go without Piper. Can you take her for a bit?" she asked.

"Sure," he said, feeling lame for not offering sooner. "Can I have one of those cupcakes in exchange? Half?" he added when he saw her frown. He needed some sort of consolation for how much he wanted her and couldn't have her, although he suspected a cupcake wasn't going to do the job.

"Half," she said, and eased the carrier from her shoulders. "You want to put her on your back?" she asked.

"That sounds good," he said, and turned around so she could help strap the carrier on him.

"I'll put her so she's facing away from you. That way she'll keep her fingers out of your hair. I'll be back soon," she said.

"We'll be here," he said.

Piper made an indistinguishable noise, but she didn't cry, so he figured he was good. He continued to sell pies and cupcakes, although the cupcakes were growing scarcer. "I need to put this cupcake in a protective place," he murmured and hid the treat behind his cup of coffee at the back table.

He smelled a peculiar odor, but was too busy to focus on it when a rush of attendees bought pies. Thank goodness, the pies were popular. Colton couldn't deny, however, that he was ready for this to be over. He'd rather be driving posts in dry ground than this.

Stacey returned, appearing breathless. "Sorry. The restroom was on the other side, and there was a line."

"There is always a line for the ladies room," he muttered and turned his back so Stacey could help disengage him from Piper.

"Oh, no," she said. "Oh, no."

"What's wrong?" he asked. "Is she okay? She's been quiet for a while."

"That's because she fell asleep," Stacey said.

"And that's bad because?" he asked.

"That's not the bad part," Stacey said. "Piper pooped all over your back."

"Oh, great," he muttered. Now he understood the source of the strange odor. "I'm glad someone feels better."

Colton and Stacey shut down the booth until the next volunteers were scheduled to appear. They were mostly sold out, anyway. Stacey helped Colton out of the baby holster, and she took Piper to the restroom while Colton headed home. This was one of the rare instances that Colton didn't have a fresh shirt in his car, so he drove with his windows open due to Piper's stink bomb.

He headed straight for the shower, stuffed the shirt in the washer on rinse, then fixed himself a bowl of soup from the Crock-Pot on the kitchen counter. Colton parked himself in a chair in the den to watch an action movie. He wanted to think about anything except Stacey and Piper, and it wasn't just because Piper had cut loose on him. He had been trying to dodge his feelings for Stacey since they'd been together, and seeing her today had felt like a slap in the face. Even though he saw his orderly life veering out of control when he was with her, he'd missed her terribly, and now he didn't know what to do.

A knock sounded, and Colton rose from his chair and opened the door. Stacey stood on the front porch holding a small covered plate. "I'm really sorry about what happened with Piper. It doesn't happen that often, but, well, babies can be messy. I kept back a couple of the cupcakes for you. I hope you'll accept them along with my apology."

His chest tightened at the kind gesture. "That was nice of you," he said. "Would you like to come in?"

She bit her lip. "I have Piper in the car."

He hesitated. "Bring her in. There's chicken noodle soup in the Crock-Pot. I'm just watching a movie."

"Are you sure?" she asked, her gaze searching his.

"Yeah, I'm sure," he said.

Stacey returned to the car and pulled Piper from

her car seat, along with a diaper bag. Colton rushed to take the bag for her. He wouldn't admit it aloud, but he was still a little gun-shy with the baby.

Stacey pulled a blanket from the diaper bag and spread it on the floor in the den while Colton ladled soup into a bowl for her and poured a glass of water. Colton returned to find the baby propped against some kind of pillow thing that kept her from falling over.

"Does she like that?" he asked.

"She can actually sit by herself, but she eventually topples. She didn't get much of a nap today, so I thought she could use a break," she said, and placed a couple of toys next to the tot. "I'm hoping for an early night."

"I'll say," he said, and set Stacey's soup on a tray on the end table.

"Thanks," she said, taking a seat on the sofa. She took a spoonful of soup. "This is good. It's nice eating someone else's food for a change."

"Yes, it is. That's probably why my mother does most of the cooking. She's good at it, so we just let her do it," he said.

"My brothers don't cook either. I got more interested in cooking when I went to nursing school," she said. "Then, after I got engaged, I wanted to take my mother's recipes with me when I got married. But that didn't work out," she said, and took another spoonful of soup.

An uncomfortable silence stretched between them.

"I'm sorry I didn't call," he finally admitted. "I wanted to." How could he tell Stacey that he feared he was a rebound man for her?

She looked up at him in surprise. "You did?"

"Of course I did," he said. "I didn't exactly hide how I felt with you when you were in my bed."

She looked away. "Well, I have a previous experience with someone who wanted to go to bed with me, but then left."

His gut clenched. "I don't want you to feel that way, but it just seemed as if everything was moving fast. It was out of control."

She nodded. "I wanted you, but I didn't want to want you."

"Exactly. I wasn't ready for what I was feeling," he said.

She gave another slow nod and took another sip of her soup. "Does that mean you want to forget what we did and go back to being friends?"

"That might be like trying to put the toothpaste back in the tube," he said. "I always want to be your friend, but I'd be lying if I said I don't want to be more."

Stacey met his gaze. "Then what do you want to do about it?"

The sexy challenge in her green eyes felt like a velvet punch in his gut. "Maybe we could spend some more time together. Go to Vicker's Corners, see a movie, take some walks when it's not freezing. Go for hot chocolate," he said, and wondered if she would find his suggestions lame.

She gave a slow smile. "That sounds nice, but people are gonna talk. I'm used to gossip, but you're not."

"I can handle it," he said defensively, although Colton had never liked people getting in his business. "I'm just probably not as nice about it as you are," he said and chuckled.

At that moment, he heard his parents walk through the front door. "Yoo-hoo," his mother called. "We're home."

Piper, who had been surprisingly quiet, looked up from playing with her toy.

Colton's mother and father came to a dead stop as they glanced into the den. "Hello, Mr. and Mrs. Foster," she said, rising from the sofa. Colton also rose. "I stopped by with a few of my red velvet cupcakes, and Colton offered me some of your delicious soup."

"Good for both of you. I'm glad Colton showed you some hospitality. Frank and I heard there was a mishap with the baby at the winter festival today, but couldn't get the details."

Stacey chuckled. "I'll let Colton fill you in on that. I should be getting Piper home."

"I'll just say I'll wash the shirt I wore today twice," he said.

His father gave a nod. "Been there, done that. It's good to see you and the baby, Stacey. I hope you don't mind if I get some of that soup."

"Not at all," Stacey said.

"Oops. Sounds as if there might have been a little mess," Colton's mother said. "Don't rush off," she said as Stacey put away Piper's baby paraphernalia. "Let me see that sweet little munchkin. She's growing like a weed."

Mrs. Foster extended her arms to the baby and smiled when Stacey handed Piper to her. "What a friendly little sweetheart. Your mother says she's sleeping through the night most of the time."

"That's right. We had a rough time the first few months, and she still has her moments. But don't we all?" Stacey said.

"I can tell you're a good mother. I always knew you would be. You just seem to roll with whatever comes your way. I know Rachel is going to be upset that she didn't get to see you and the baby," Mrs. Foster said. "Are you sure you can't stay?"

"I really should go," Stacey said. "I'm hoping for an early night. It's good to see you."

"Same here," his mother said, then plopped the baby in Colton's arms. "Here. You carry Piper out to the car. Stacey could probably use a little break from hauling around this little chunk of love after today."

Colton automatically stiffened but soldiered up. He couldn't disagree with his mother. After his limited experience with Piper, he was surprised Stacey wasn't exhausted all the time. From what he could tell, branding an entire herd of cattle would be easier than watching over a baby.

He carried Piper to the car and let Stacey fasten her into her safety seat. Piper fussed a little at the confinement. "You just better get used to this," Stacey said in a kind but matter-of-fact voice. "You'll be sitting in a safety seat every time you get in the car." She shook a toy connected to the front of the seat to distract the baby, and Piper quieted down.

"You're good with her. I'll say that much. She can be a handful," he said, shaking his head.

"She's curious and sweet, but you're right. She has her moments," Stacey said.

"That's when those bubbles come in handy," he said.

Stacey stared at him and smiled. "So you *did* use the bubbles that night you kept her for me?"

"Hey, I had to hit the ground running. That diaper bag is like a bag of tricks," he said.

"You almost sound as if you're still afraid of her," Stacey said. "My little Piper couldn't terrify a big, strong man like you, could she?"

"Of course not," he lied because the baby did have the ability to scare him more than a fright movie. "I'm just no baby expert like you are."

"Maybe she'll grow on you," Stacey said softly.

"Maybe," he said. Piper's mother was growing on him. He leaned toward Stacey and took her mouth in a lingering, sweet kiss that made something inside him fill up and want more at the same time. "I'm glad you came over. I'll call you."

"I'm going to be really upset if you don't," she warned.

He liked hearing that bit of testiness in her voice. It made him think she wanted him, too. "No problem," he said and kissed her again. He pulled back. "You're habit-forming."

"That's good to hear," she said. "I think your mother is watching from behind the curtains in the front room. She may ask questions. That's what mothers do."

"That's okay. I have the perfect answer," he said, putting his index finger under her chin.

"What's that?"

"Nunya. Nunya business," he said, and her laughter made it worth the inquisition he knew he would face when he went inside the house.

That night, Stacey slept better than she had in months, partly because Piper slept long and hard, and partly because being with Colton just made her feel better about life. He didn't have to do much. Just his presence made her feel calmer and more optimistic. She didn't want to overthink his effect on her. Stacey just wanted to enjoy it.

He called her on her cell the next morning, and she could tell he was outside and the wind was blowing. "Good mornin'," he said.

"Good morning to you. How long have you been out and about?" she asked as she toted Piper around the kitchen.

"Since a couple hours ago. You know the routine. I have to get up early in order the get the heavy chores done so my father doesn't hurt his back," he said.

"I wish you could talk him into seeing the doctor," she said. "It's as if he's in complete denial of this health problem."

"You're exactly right. He's in denial until he ends up in bed for a few days. Then he takes it slow. A few weeks after that, he thinks it'll never happen again. But enough of my crankiness. How would you like to go into town and get a burger at the grill? Early dinner?"

"That sounds like fun, but my parents are going to be at the winter festival all day, so I would have to bring Piper," she said. When he didn't immediately respond, she filled the gap of silence. "We can go another time. We don't have to go today."

"No," he said. "Let's take her with us. What time will work?"

"I'd like to get her back on schedule with her afternoon nap. Is four-thirty okay?"

"Sure. I'll pick you two ladies up at four-thirty. See you then," he said and disconnected the call.

Stacey felt a spurt of excitement and danced around the room with Piper. "We have a date."

She spent the morning entertaining Piper, then ran laundry and cooked a big pot of chili in the afternoon. She changed her clothes three times and might have changed them once more if Piper hadn't awakened. Her brother Jude must have smelled the chili from miles away because he stomped into the house an hour after she'd put it on the stove. Her brothers were at the family dinner table more often than not, despite the fact that they had their own places to live.

"Thank goodness there's food," he said. "I'm starving." He looked at Stacey and Piper and gave a double take. "You two look as if you're headed someplace special," he said.

Stacey resisted the urge to squirm. "Just going to the grill with a friend," she said.

"Rachel?" he asked as he grabbed a bowl from the cabinet.

She shook her head. "Nope. Do you mind setting that Crock-Pot on low and putting the lid on it if you leave before Mom and Dad get home? I think they should be here within a half hour," she said.

"Sure," he said and grabbed a spoon. "Any crackers or bread?"

"Crackers are in the cupboard." A knock sounded at the door, and her heart leaped with silly excitement. "Gotta go."

"Hey, you never said who is going with you to the grill," he said.

"That's right," she said, unable to stifle a little giggle. "I didn't. See you later," she said, and ran to the door and threw it open.

"Hi," she said, thinking it was ridiculous to be so excited about going to the grill in town. This proved the point that she really needed to get out more often.

"Hi to you and Miss Piper," he said. "You're both looking beautiful. You ready to go?"

"Thank you, and we are," she said.

"I'll carry Piper to the truck. I see you have the magic tricks bag," he said, gingerly taking the baby in his arms.

"It goes wherever Piper goes," she said. "Listen, do you mind if we take my car? I've already got the safety seat, and it'll be easier to keep it in there than switch it from my car to yours again."

"Good plan," he said. "It didn't occur to me."

"Probably because you haven't spent a lot of time with babies," she said.

"My mistake," Colton said. "The education of Colton Foster continues. I'll let you fasten her into that contraption," he said after he carefully set Piper into the seat.

As usual, Piper complained about the confinement, and Stacey distracted her. Within a couple moments the baby calmed.

"Have you ever tried to take her on a road trip?" he asked.

"Not unless you call the hour drive to Lubbock a road trip," she said. "She's really not a bad rider, but I wonder if she might get fed up with it after several hours. I have visions of throwing everything but the kitchen sink into the backseat to keep her amused."

"I think my parents must have done that when we took a trip to Dallas one time, although my Dad wouldn't put up with any foolishness when we got older."

"My father is the same way, maybe even more so," she said. "Deke Jones is a stand-up guy, but I have to admit that he didn't join me for any tea parties when I was a little girl. He was too busy for that."

"It's funny the things we remember. My mother showed up for most of my basketball games, but my father only came to a few each season. I always knew they both loved me, and that's what's important," he said.

"Very true," she said. "Now that I've had Piper, though, I find myself wishing she had everything I had growing up and more."

"Like what?" he asked.

"She has some of it," Stacey said. "A safe, warm home and family who love her, but—" She broke off, feeling self-conscious.

"But what?"

"Nothing," she said, feeling her face grow warm with embarrassment. "You'll think I'm crazy."

"No. I won't. Tell me."

Stacey smiled and shook her head. "I'm hoping I can talk one of her uncles into having a couple tea parties with her," she said. "I think it's good for little girls to have good men who are involved in their lives."

"I'm sure you're right about that," he said. "What do little girls eat at tea parties, anyway? I can't believe they like tea."

"Juice and cookies," she said.

"That's not all that bad," he said.

"No. It's the little chairs and pretending that makes it tough for a grown man," she said.

"Which of your brothers have you targeted for this?" he asked.

"I have a year or two before the parties will begin," Stacey said. "But I'm thinking Toby would be a natural. He's already a foster father. If not him, I may be able to con Jude into the job, especially if Piper serves something I've made."

"Sounds as if you're planning ahead," he said.

"Once I had Piper, I couldn't just think about the moment anymore. I had to think about the future, too."

"Is that why you seem sad sometimes?" he asked.

Stacey looked at him in surprise. "You think I seem sad?"

"Well, different. You used to seem happier," he said.

She thought about that for a moment. "I worry more," she confessed as he pulled into the small parking lot for The Horseback Hollow Grill.

He cut the engine and turned to her. "No worrying for the next couple of hours," he told her. "After all, you're about to eat a gourmet meal with the handsomest guy in Horseback Hollow," he joked.

Stacey smiled. The gourmet meal was a stretch,

but she was beginning to think that Colton was the best man in Horseback Hollow. She wondered why she'd never noticed until now.

Chapter Eight

"Oooh, what a cute baby," the server at The Grill said, then glanced at Stacey and Colton. "What a good-looking family. I bet you hear that all the time. I'm Maureen, and I'm new here in Horseback Hollow." Her gaze returned to Piper. "Look at that chin," she said, tickling it. "Just like Daddy's. Now, what can I get for you today?"

"Burger loaded and hot chocolate," Colton said. "What about you?" he asked Stacey.

"Grilled cheese and hot chocolate. Extra marshmallows please," she added.

"Will do," Maureen said and turned away.

"Sorry about that," Stacey said.

"Sorry about what?" he asked.

"That the waitress said Piper looked like you," she

said, feeling extremely awkward. She didn't want Colton to feel pushed into a relationship with either herself or Piper.

"She said we have the same chin," he said, rubbing his own chin and glancing at Piper. "I just didn't know I already had two."

Relief raced through her, and she swatted at him. "Stop that. She clearly only has one chin, but there's no denying those chipmunk cheeks. She looks as if she's packing a load of acorns." Stacey rubbed her daughter's cheek. "But you're gorgeous, anyway," she said.

"She is. She looks like you. Minus the chipmunk cheeks," he said.

"I'll take that as a compliment," Stacey said, and Maureen returned with their hot chocolate.

"Anything else I can get you?" she asked.

Colton glanced at Stacey. "We're good," she said.

Their food was served just moments later, and Stacey relished her grilled cheese sandwich. Although Piper was well-fortified with cereal on her high-chair tray, she watched every bite that Stacey took.

"She's getting more interested in food," Stacey said. "Especially whatever I'm eating."

"Can't blame her. What does she get? Dry cereal? She looks as if she wants to reach right over and grab the rest of your sandwich. You're clearly starving her."

"Right," Stacey said, shooting him a mock chastising look. "This is probably more than you want to know, but she's allowed to have strained and pureed fruits, vegetables and meats."

Colton made a face. "I didn't hear hamburger on that list."

"She doesn't have any teeth. She'd have to gum it," Stacey said.

A woman stopped by their table. "Why, Stacey Jones. I haven't seen you in ages."

Stacey recognized the woman as a member of her church. Stacey had missed quite a few Sundays since Piper had been born. Truth be told, she'd missed more than she'd attended since she'd gotten pregnant. "Mrs. Gordon, it's good to see you. How is your family?" Stacey asked as she stood and gave the woman a hug.

"We're hanging in there. My husband has had a terrible time with gout, but we keep plugging. Look at your baby. She's just gorgeous," Mrs. Gordon said, and glanced at Colton in confusion. "Colton Foster, right? For some reason, I thought your fiancé's name was Joe."

Stacey's stomach knotted. "He was. Joe moved to Dallas. But Piper is thriving, as you can see."

"Yes, she is. And how nice for both of you to have big, strong Colton around," Mrs. Gordon said in a coy voice.

"Hmm," Stacey said, so ready for the woman to move along. "Thank you for stopping by," she said. "And please give your husband my best."

She sank back onto her seat. "Why does everyone have to know everything about everyone around here?" she muttered and took a sip of her hot chocolate. She wondered how long she would be answering questions about Joe and why they weren't together. At this point, it looked like forever.

After they finished their meal, Colton drove Stacey and Piper back to Stacey's house. "You're awfully quiet," he said.

"I know I said that we have to expect people to talk here in Horseback Hollow because that's what they do, but I hate having to talk about Joe. People always look at me with pity. Poor Stacey. She couldn't keep her man," she said.

"Joe's leaving wasn't your fault. He couldn't handle the responsibility of a baby. He's the loser in this situation, not you," he said. "If you need another way of looking at it, aren't you glad that you and Piper aren't stuck with a man who doesn't love you? You deserve better than that."

"When he first left, I was in shock. I couldn't believe he would abandon his own child and me. It made me wonder if I ever really knew him," she said.

"Do you wish he would come back and the two of you could get back together?" Colton asked.

"I did for a while," she confessed. "It sounded like the perfect ending to a fairy tale that had gotten off track. But I don't know that I would ever be able to trust him again. I do know that I'm not the same woman who fell for him years ago. I just wish he wouldn't have rejected Piper. That's the worst part," she said.

Colton pulled the car to a stop in the Joneses' driveway. He leaned toward her. "I'm not sure this little outing cheered you up all that much."

She blinked at him. "I didn't know that was the purpose," she said. "I thought we just wanted to spend some time together. We did that with no meltdowns from Piper, and I had terrific hot chocolate and company."

"You're some kind of woman, Stacey, and don't you forget it," he said as he lowered his mouth to take hers in a delicious kiss.

Stacey felt her heart race. Her body immediately responded. His kiss triggered all sorts of forbidden emotions and sensations. She slid her hands beneath his jacket to pull him closer. He responded by nearly hauling her onto his lap.

"Damn this console," he muttered and kissed her again. He slid one of his hands from her waist upward to her breast.

Her nipples turned hard, and she felt her need for him pool in all her secret places. "Oh, Colton," she whispered and scrubbed at his chest, wishing she could feel his naked skin.

His kiss turned hot with want and need, and she strained toward him, her body and mind recalling how good he'd felt inside her. She wanted him that way again. Now.

The sound of Piper gurgling and talking her baby

language penetrated past the mist of arousal crowding her mind. Colton froze. Stacey did the same.

Frustration nicked through her. "This is hard," she said.

"In more ways than one," Colton said, his voice taut with forced denial. "Between you living with your parents and me living at the ranch, I feel like a randy teenager," he said and pulled back.

Stacey felt the same sense of dissatisfaction she heard in his voice. "What do you usually do? How do you usually handle things when you and a woman—" She broke off, wondering if she really wanted to know about Colton's previous partners.

"That's part of the reason I want a place of my own," Colton said. "Privacy. But I've felt as if I needed to keep an eye on my father, and I haven't wanted to tell my parents I want to build. The time is coming sooner than later, though. In the past, the women had their own places or we spent the night in Vicker's Corners."

"A whole night?" she echoed. "I'm trying to imagine spending the whole night away from home without a lot of questions." She sighed. "I wish this were easier."

He kissed her lightly on the mouth as if he didn't want to get anything started between them again. "Most good things don't come easy. Let me walk you and Piper to the door."

Stacey said good-night to Colton and walked

through the door. No sooner had she closed the door behind her than her brother Jude appeared.

"So, you went out with Colton again? Are you sure that's a good idea?"

Taken aback by his confrontational manner, she tilted her head at him. "I enjoyed Colton's company, a grilled cheese sandwich and hot chocolate. Is there anything wrong with that?"

"Well, not really," Jude said.

"We had a chaperone. Nothing naughty happened. Trust me, nothing naughty *can* happen," she grumbled.

"I just want you to be careful. I don't want to see you get hurt like you did with Joe," he said.

"Colton is nothing like Joe. Nothing," she said, and took Piper to the nursery. It was true that Colton was nothing like Joe, but Colton had never asked her to marry him. Stacey felt a stab of concern that Colton wasn't interested in being anybody's baby daddy, which also meant he wouldn't want to be Piper's daddy.

That night when she went to bed, it took her a long time to fall asleep.

Colton did a last check around the north pasture, then returned to the house. Grabbing a cup of decaf, he sank onto one of the recliners in the den. He halfway watched a basketball game through his drooping eyes. Feeling himself drift for a few moments, he awakened when his father walked into the room and got into the other recliner.

"Hey," Colton said.

His father nodded.

"You worn out from the second day of the winter festival?" Colton asked.

His father gave a heavy sigh. "Your mother insists on staying for the whole thing, and she wants me to stay with her."

"Your back okay?" Colton asked.

"A little sore. Nothing unusual," his dad said.

"Any time you want to go for lunch in Vicker's Corners, I'm glad to take you. There's a chiropractor there," he said.

"Chiropractor?" his father said. "Don't they crack your bones and put you in traction? Sounds as if that would make you worse."

"They make adjustments," Colton said. "They help get your back in alignment."

"Hmmph," his father said in disbelief. "Well, that's not why I came in here. Your mother wants me to talk to you."

"About what?" Colton asked, feeling curious and studying his father.

His father sighed. "It's about Stacey and her baby."

Colton frowned. "What about them?"

"Well, it's not really any of our business," his father began, and Colton immediately knew this wasn't a discussion he wanted to have with his father.

His father cleared his throat, obviously uncomfortable. "You need to be careful with Stacey," he said. "After what Joe did, she doesn't need anyone taking advantage of her."

Indignation rolled through him, and he pushed the recliner into the upright position. "I wouldn't take advantage of Stacey. What makes you think I would?"

"Well, you look as if you're getting, uh, friendly with her," he said. "I mean you look as if you want to be more than friends," he said, then rubbed his face with his hand. "Oh, for Pete's sake. Just treat her right. That's all I'm gonna say."

Colton met his father's gaze. "I'll treat her right. You and Mom don't need to worry."

"Good," his father said. "I'm glad that's over. Who's playing tonight, anyway?"

"The Bulls and Lakers," he said.

His father nodded. "Looks like a close game."

Colton didn't respond. His mind was too busy with his father's remarks. He resented the interference. He was a grown man. Colton stood. "I'm gonna hit the sack," he said. "Good night."

Colton headed down the hall and was intercepted by his sister, Rachel. In no mood for anyone else's comments, he lifted his hand. "Don't say a word," he said.

She frowned at him. "About what?"

"About Stacey and me," he said.

Her eyes widened in surprise. "Stacey and you?" she echoed. "What's going on? I've been crazy busy and haven't had a chance to talk with her for several days."

"Never mind," he said, and headed for his wing of the ranch.

Rachel bobbed along behind him. "Are you two seeing each other? That would be so cool," she said. "As long as you don't hurt her. You have to swear you won't hurt her, but I love the idea. I'll call her right now."

"She's got a little baby," Colton said. "She might be in bed trying to get some sleep."

Rachel's face fell. "True. Well, give me the scoop. When did this happen?"

"Rachel," he said as gently as he could, "it's none of your business."

The next morning, Stacey awakened with a different sense about herself and her life. She realized that in many ways she'd been hiding from the world, ashamed of how her relationship with Joe had ended, embarrassed that she and Piper had been dumped by him. The whole situation had made her feel like that mathematical expression *less than*.

She was ready to start reclaiming her life. Taking a quick shower and getting dressed, she fed Piper and dressed her in a cute outfit with stockings. She met her parents just as they were headed out the door to church.

Her mother looked at her in surprise. "Where are

you two going looking so spiffy? Is there a mother/baby beauty contest I haven't heard about?"

Stacey laughed in pleasure at the sweet way her mother had voiced her curiosity. "Piper and I are going to church this morning."

"Oh, my." Her mother covered her mouth and sniffed. "I've been waiting for this day."

"I hadn't turned into a total heathen," Stacey said.

"Oh, no. Not that," her mother said. "I'm just so proud of you and Piper. I want everyone to see what a good job you're doing with her. I think you will be an inspiration to many people."

"I don't know how inspiring I'll be if she starts screaming in church," Stacey muttered. "But I think it's time."

"Yes, it's time," her father said impatiently and pointed at his watch. "If we don't get moving we'll be late."

"You can sit with us," her mother said as they were hustled out of the house. "I'll be happy to take Piper out if she gets fussy."

"I'll take her out," her father said. "Especially if she starts fussing before the offertory."

"Deke," her mother said in disapproval. "Shame on you."

"What? I'm just being a nice granddaddy," he said and chuckled. He helped Jeanne into his truck, and Stacey tucked Piper into the car seat in her Toyota, then followed her parents to church.

She felt a twinge of nostalgia as she walked into

the small chapel her family had attended since before she was born. She'd celebrated so many holidays and Sundays in this place. As soon as she walked inside with Piper in her arms, she saw several familiar faces. She waved at each of her neighbors, then took her seat with her parents.

Piper did well until the minister began to speak. She got a little squirmy, but Stacey couldn't blame her. There'd been plenty of times she had gotten fidgety when a minister spoke. Despite her squirminess, Piper didn't let out a peep until the congregation sang a benediction.

"Good job," she said, praising the baby, and left the pew. Several people greeted her and made a fuss over Piper. There was no mention of Joe, but Stacey was prepared in case someone did. She made her way to the back of the church and found Rachel waiting for her with open arms.

"I decided to come to church at the last minute today. I'm so glad I did. Look at you and Miss Piper," she said, squeezing the baby's hand. "All dressed up for church. She must have done well during the service. I didn't hear her."

"She, ahem, *sang* during the benediction," Stacey said.

Rachel giggled. "Good for her. She'll be in the choir before you know it. Listen, I'm sorry I haven't been in touch with you. Changing careers to education and doing my student teaching has made me crazy. I had no idea how much time the lesson plans and parent meetings would take."

"No worries," Stacey said. "I know you've been busy."

"Not so busy that I should be the last to know that you are dating my brother," Rachel said.

Stacey groaned. "Oh, no. Not you, too. It seems as if everyone has an opinion about us seeing each other. And it's not as if either of us has any privacy where we live."

Rachel raised her eyebrows. "Privacy?" she echoed. "You want privacy with my brother?"

Stacey shook her head and waved her hand. "Forget I said anything."

"You sound like Colton," Rachel said. "He didn't want to talk about it either."

"Well, who wants to talk about a relationship when it's first starting? Who knows where this will go? Colton has a lot on his mind with your father's back problem. He keeps trying to talk your dad into seeing a doctor, but your father won't go. Colton says he's got to stay one step ahead of your dad to keep him from hurting himself."

Rachel nodded. "My father avoids doctors at nearly all cost."

"I think Colton wonders if you might be more successful with your father than he has been," Stacey said, hoping she'd managed to distract Rachel from her questions. "I need to get Piper home to change and feed her, so I need to head out to my car."

Rachel tagged along. "Well, just so you know, I'm all for this. Colton is a great guy, and you're the best friend I could ever have. He would be lucky to get you, and in a way, maybe you would be lucky to get him, too. Especially after Joe," she said.

"I don't want my relationship with Colton to have anything to do with Joe," Stacey said as she buckled the baby into her car seat. "I want to leave that behind."

"Kinda hard to do when Joe is Piper's father," Rachel said.

"He's been invisible for over a year. I need to move on," she said.

Rachel met her gaze and nodded. "Good for you. But when it comes to my brother, you need to know something," she said and lowered her voice. "He's slow at making the moves, so you may have to help him along."

Stacey bit her lip to keep from laughing at Rachel's warning. She couldn't help thinking of the scorching lovemaking she'd experienced with Colton. "I'll keep that in mind," she managed.

"Good," Rachel said. "I'll call you soon. Maybe I could babysit for you sometime."

"You may have a hard time squeezing me in with your student teaching," Stacey said.

"Maybe," Rachel conceded and gave Stacey a hug. "But I have three reasons to try to make that happen."

"Three?" Stacey said, hugging her in return.

"My brother, you and me. Wouldn't it be cool if you were both my best friend and sister-in-law?"

The possibility gave Stacey a jolt. "Oh, Rachel, don't go there. These are very early days."

"Well, it's not as if you haven't known each other forever."

"Yes, but I haven't always had a baby. I'm not at all sure Colton is ready to be a father to a child that isn't really his."

"He might need a little persuading, but I think it could be done." Rachel shivered. "It's too cold for me out here. I'll call you."

Stacey watched Rachel race to her car and tried to unhear the words she'd just heard, but it was like trying to unring a bell. What if she and Colton got married? Was it even a possibility? Her heart squeezed tight with a myriad of emotions. She closed her eyes and shook her head. She shouldn't even think about it.

The next day, Colton went into town to get some equipment to repair some fences and overheard a couple of workers talking about something happening at the bar.

"So, what's going on?" he asked.

"*Live* music at the Two Moon Saloon on Tuesday," the worker said.

"Really? I can't remember the last time there was live music at the bar," Colton mused.

"And I hear there might be dancing," the worker said. "I'm taking my girlfriend."

"Hmm," Colton said. He wondered if Stacey would be able to go on such short notice. On the way home, he called and left a message about the live music and continued on with his chores.

Stacey must have returned his call while he was out fixing a fence. Her mom would keep Piper. She sounded excited. He hoped that whoever was performing didn't bomb. The smile he heard in Stacey's voice did strange things to his gut. He felt a little lighter, a little less burdened as he pulled into the driveway to his house. His conversation with his father had kept him awake for an extra hour last night, but Colton knew he wanted to spend time with Stacey and she felt the same way about him. He knew his mother and father shouldn't be involved in this decision, and if they intervened again, he would have to speak his piece.

Colton stomped up the steps to the house with the winter wind whistling through his coat. He was dog-tired and all he wanted was a home-cooked meal. If that wasn't available, he would heat some canned soup and make a sandwich.

"Hiya," Rachel called as he passed the den. She appeared to be doing lesson plans or grading papers.

"How's it going?" he asked.

"I wish I'd earned my first degree in education. This is so time-consuming," she said.

"I'm not sure it changes much, sis," he said. "I

never hear teachers talking about how much extra time they have."

"True, I guess," she said. "But I like it, so maybe I won't notice the time."

He nodded. "I'm gonna get whatever is available in the kitchen."

"Wait," she said, scrambling to her feet. "I talked to Stacey at church yesterday," she said.

"Great," he said and moved toward the kitchen.

"I also talked to her today. Amazing what I can learn about my brother from his girlfriend," she said, following him.

He shot her a quelling glance.

"What I mean is I didn't realize how bad Dad's back is. Stacey said you've offered to take him to Vicker's Corners to see a doctor, but he won't do it," she said.

"That's right," he said, opening the fridge and hoping to find something wonderful. He spotted a small bowl of leftover beef stew and snatched it up.

"She also said that you thought Dad would be more likely to go with me to Vicker's Corners to see a doctor."

"Right again," he said. He put the stew in the microwave, then pulled some sliced ham, cheese and bread out of the fridge and went to the counter. "The trouble is you'd have to trick him."

Rachel frowned. "What do you mean?"

"You would need to make an appointment with him and find some other reason for him to go. You'd take him to lunch, then take him to a doctor's appointment and beg for forgiveness afterward. He would forgive you within twenty-four hours, less if he got some relief from his back pain."

Rachel's frown deepened. "That sounds like a lot of trickery," she said.

"As if you haven't done the same ten times over for less honorable reasons," he returned as he slapped the meat and cheese on the bread and slathered it with Dijon mustard.

"I wish Dad would be more reasonable about medical treatment," she muttered, crossing her arms over her chest.

"You and me both," he said, when the microwave beeped. He grabbed his bowl of stew and sandwich. He would worry about water later.

Rachel poured a glass of ice water and sat down at the kitchen table. She put the glass at the place opposite from her. "Well, sit down," she said, waving her hand. "We have to figure out exactly when and how I'll do this trickery."

"Dad is a sucker for his little girl. Just invite him to go to lunch with you, then take him to a doctor afterward," Colton said.

"Stacey and I didn't just talk about Dad," Rachel said.

A bite of sandwich lodged in Colton's throat. He coughed repeatedly and washed it down with a gulp of water. "Oh, really," he said in a deliberately noncommittal tone.

"Yes," Rachel said. "Stacey said the two of you could use some privacy. What do you say about that?"

"Privacy begins at home," Colton said.

Rachel made a face at him. "I'm trying to help."

"Then stay out of it," he said. "There's a baby involved. I don't want to be responsible for messing up that child's life. I'm taking it slow or not at all."

Chapter Nine

Colton sat across from Stacey in the Two Moon Saloon while a trio played. They might not win any awards, but folks got up to dance every now and then.

"This is fun," she said as she took a sip of her mixed drink.

Colton had smuggled in some cranberry juice for her to mix with vodka and ice. He'd known the bar wouldn't keep much juice on hand. If they did, their supply would quickly deplete on a busy night like tonight, with more women asking for mixed drinks instead of beer or straight liquor. It appeared many Horseback Hollow men had viewed the live music at the bar as a good date-night opportunity, so more women took part in drinks with their men.

"I'm glad you like it," he said, taking a long swallow from his beer.

"You don't like the group?" she asked.

"I like them fine," he said. "It's nice to hear some live music here for a change."

"I agree," she said, and the trio began to play a slow song. "Any chance you would dance with me?"

"Sure," he said, his body tightening at the sexy expression in her eyes.

Colton led her onto the tiny dance floor and pulled her against him. "You feel good," he whispered into her ear.

"You feel good, too," she said, and stretched her body so that it molded against his.

Colton couldn't help wishing they were both naked. Stacey was so sweet and inviting. He couldn't resist her. With every beat of the song, he felt the gentle friction of her feminine body against his. He grew harder with each touch.

She lifted her head, and it was the most natural thing in the world for him to take her mouth. She slid her sweet, silky tongue in his mouth, and his internal temperature turned hotter and hotter. He couldn't help but return her kiss.

His heart slamming against his chest, he squeezed her against him, and she stroked his jaw. The music ended, but he didn't want to release her.

She breathed against his throat, and it was all he could do not to lead her out of the bar and take her in his truck. He took a deep breath to pull himself under control. "I guess we should sit down now," he said in a low voice.

"I guess we should," she said, looking up at him with wanting for him in her eyes. "But that's not what I want."

"Me neither," he said. "It stinks."

She gave a slow smile that sizzled with sexuality. "Yes, it does," she said and pulled back.

Colton prayed that his arousal would calm down. He still wanted her, but his mind knew this wasn't the place or the time. They returned to the table and he took a drink of his beer while she took a sip of her cocktail.

She met his gaze with an alluring smile. "This makes me feel young again. Lately, I've been feeling kinda old and tired."

"You need to give yourself a break. Piper's got that kick of Fortune Jones in her. She's going to let you know when she wants something, and she'll try to make you race to get it for her."

Stacey lifted her eyebrows in surprise and took a sip of water. "What makes you say that? Are you implying that she's spoiled?"

"Not at all," Colton said. "I'm just saying she's—assertive. Isn't that what everyone is supposed to be these days?"

Stacey pressed her lips together, then let out a big laugh that filled him all the way up inside. "That sounds mighty close to calling my baby a brat."

"She's not a brat," Colton said. "Not yet."

Her eyebrows flew up to her hairline. "Not yet?" she echoed.

"Right," he said. "She's not even walking. She won't turn bratty until she's three."

Stacey gave a slow nod. "Good to know."

"Do you really disagree?" he asked.

"I just hope I do this parenting thing right. I don't want to be too harsh or too permissive. It's not as easy as it looks," she said.

"You're doing great," he said, and put his hand over hers.

"Thanks," she said, and her smile made his gut do strange things.

"Well, well," a male voice said. "A new couple. What would Joe say?"

Colton glanced up to see Billy Hall, Joe's best friend, sneering at Stacey and him.

"Hey, Billy. How are you doing?" Colton asked as politely as he could manage.

"I'm doing great. I just wonder what Joe would think if he found out one of his groomsmen was kissing his ex," Billy said.

"Joe is history," Stacey said. "He hasn't been around for over a year."

Billy pursed his lips. "Oooh, that's harsh. He might not like that."

"How would you know?" Colton asked.

"We talk every now and then," Billy said.

"You ever tell him what a useless piece he was to leave Stacey and his child?"

Billy gave an awkward shrug. "Well, no. He's my friend. I couldn't call him names." Billy paused. "But I could tell him his ex was taking revenge on him by getting involved with one of his best friends. How you like those leftovers?"

Without a pause, Colton rose and shook Billy hard.

Stunned, Billy stumbled backward. "What the—"

"Don't insult Stacey again," Colton said, clenching and unclenching his fist. "Ever."

"Hey, I was just taking up for Joe," Billy said.

"He doesn't need you to take up for him. He's doing fine," Colton said. "He isn't getting up in the middle of the night to take care of a baby. He's not giving Stacey one dime of support."

Billy's eyes widened, and he lifted his hands. "Okay, okay. I get your message." He turned toward Stacey. "Sorry," he said and walked away, wiggling his shoulders as if he were trying to straighten out his spine.

His heart still slamming against his rib cage, he sat down and took another long sip of beer. "Sorry about that," he said.

She pulled his hands into hers. "That was very nice of you. Not necessary, but—"

"Very necessary," he said. "You don't deserve that. Joe's not here. He hasn't done anything to redeem himself in this situation."

She lifted his hand to her lips and kissed it. "I'm not thinking about Joe anymore."

Colton felt a dozen emotions slamming through him, but the way she kissed his fist made his heart turn over like a tumbleweed. "You deserve better."

"I'm getting better," she told him.

They finished their drinks, and Colton drove Stacey home. What he wanted was to bring her to his bed and make love to her, but that wasn't going to happen tonight. He stopped the car and she immediately unfastened her seat belt and pulled his face toward hers. She took his mouth in a kiss that blasted through him like a ball of fire. Sweet Stacey had somehow turned into a sexy tigress, and he was reaping the benefit.

She slid her hands over his chest down to his abdomen and lower. Colton was torn between telling her to stop and begging her to continue. At the same time, his hands moved of their own volition to her breasts. With her coat open, he tugged at her sweater and slid his hands upward.

She continued kissing him, devouring him with her delicious mouth. She reached to unbuckle his belt at the same time the floodlights spilled over the front yard of her parents' home.

"Whoa," he said, stilling her hands even though he was dying for her to continue. He could just imagine her mother or father coming out for a friendly chat.

"What? Why?" she asked, looking at him with such a sensual, needy gaze that he could hardly stand it.

"Lights came on," he said gently and pulled her into an embrace.

Stacey gave a low growl of frustration. "This is ridiculous. We're adults, not teenagers."

His heart slamming into his chest at what felt like a hundred miles an hour, he took a deep breath. "I'll figure something out."

She sighed, then leaned her forehead against his chest. "Pretty crazy. Who would have thought I would be taking a cold shower because my best friend's brother is making me too hot?"

"You were hot before I came around," he said.

"You didn't notice before," she reminded him.

"I wasn't supposed to notice," he told her, rubbing her soft cheek with his hand. "You belonged to somebody else," he said, thinking of Joe. Joe, who hadn't stood by her when he should have.

After her date with Colton, Stacey felt as if she had a little more bounce in her step. Although she was still juggling her household commitments and taking care of Piper, she was thrilled to book her first tutoring session on Thursday afternoon. A mom with an elementary-school-age boy named Frasier brought her son to the ranch for Stacey to work some magic on him by helping him with math.

Stacey injected as much enthusiasm into the session as possible, but Frasier seemed quite listless. At one point he even laid his head down on the kitchen table. Concerned that he might be sick, Stacey mentioned the boy's condition to his mother. She felt a little guilty accepting the money from Frasier's parent, but made a mental note to perhaps give him an extended or free session in the future.

As soon as the boy left, Piper awakened from her nap. Stacey changed the baby, then carried her into the kitchen. "What a good girl to sleep all the way through my tutoring session. You're the best, aren't you?" she said to Piper as she gave her daughter a bottle. Piper sucked down her bottle in no time, and Stacey patted her back to help counter air bubbles.

"There my girls are," her mother said as she entered the house with bags of groceries. "Let me help you with those," Stacey said and pulled out a quilt for Piper. "Looks like you bought out the store."

Her mother laughed. "This was my big trip. I went to Vicker's Corners. Of course, if you add in gas, it may be a wash. But the grocery store there has a much better selection, and the prices are a little better."

Stacey rushed to her mother's sedan to help bring in the rest of the bags of groceries. "I see that you picked up some baby formula and baby food. I can reimburse you for that since I had my first tutoring session," Stacey said proudly.

Her mother smiled at her. "I forgot about that. How did it go?"

"Okay, except I hope that little boy wasn't sick. He sure didn't act like he felt well. I hope it will go better next time," she said.

"Oh, dear," her mother said. "I've heard there are a couple things going around. One is a quick but nasty stomach virus. Make sure you wash your hands."

"Good point. And I'll wipe down the table," she said. Stacey cleaned her hands and the table and helped put the groceries away as quickly as possible. She knew Piper would be wanting some food. Sure enough, just as Stacey unloaded the last bag, Piper let out a squawk.

"You go ahead and get her. I can take care of the rest," Mama Jeanne said.

Stacey put the baby in her high chair and pulled out a jar of pureed green beans. "Yum, yum," Stacey said. "Green vegetables."

Not Piper's favorite, but she must have been hungry because she eagerly consumed the first few bites. "She looks like a little bird when she eats from the spoon."

"She'll be reaching for that spoon any time now, and every mealtime will turn into a mess. Mark my words," her mother said.

"No problem. I'll just need a washcloth or paper towel. Oh, I meant to tell you that Piper and I will be riding with Colton to the Rothwell wedding on Saturday. The Rothwells are lucky that the Jergens offered them the use of their heated barn for their reception. I'm sure that's why they were able to invite so many people."

"Seems as if you and Colton are spending more and more time together," her mother said.

Stacey hesitated, then glanced at her mother. "You may as well offer your opinion on it, since everyone else has."

"Well, I wouldn't dream of interfering," her mother said. "Colton is a fine, fine young man. I just hope you two won't rush into, well, the physical aspect of a relationship. After all, you have a young baby."

Stacey gaped at her mother. "Mama, do you really think I would turn around and get pregnant again?"

"We're a very fertile family," her mother said. "Colton is likely quite the virile male and—"

Stacey covered her ears. "I don't want to discuss this anymore," she said. "It's not like Colton and I have lots of opportunities, between him living at his parents' house and me living at mine. Add in a baby and, oh, my gosh—"

"It's not that I don't approve of Colton because I very much do," her mother continued as if Stacey hadn't spoken. "I just don't want you to get into a situation where—"

"Stop," Stacey said. "Stop, stop, stop. Please."

Her mother pressed her lips together. "I like Colton," her mother said. "I like him better than I ever liked Joe. Your father does, too."

"Did you run into anyone interesting at the store?" Stacey asked because she had to change the subject, and it seemed that her mother knew everyone within a thirty-mile radius.

"As a matter of fact I did," her mother said. "Laurel Fortune was buying avocados in the produce department when I was there. She's such a sweet girl. Gave me a hug right away. I asked her how married life was, and she said the married part was great, but that she and Sawyer are very upset about the recent accident at their flight school."

"Oh, that's right. Did she say how Orlando is doing?" Stacey asked.

"He's still in the hospital, but they think he will recover. It may take a long time. She said how thankful she and Sawyer were that you were able to come and help stabilize Orlando until the paramedics arrived."

"I was glad I could help, but I was very concerned when I left," Stacey said.

"Don't dare tell anyone, but Laurel confided in me that the investigation has just started, but she and Sawyer are worried that it may not have been an accident."

Stacey gasped. "Oh, no. That would have been horrible. She thinks someone may have deliberately done something to cause the crash?"

"They don't know, but they're suspicious. Not everyone is happy about Fortunes coming to Horseback Hollow," her mother said, a worried expression on her face.

"Oh, that's ridiculous. It's not as if the Fortunes

are trying to take over the whole town. And why would they? They're all about making money, and there's not that much money to be made in Horseback Hollow."

"The Fortunes aren't all about money," her mother corrected her. "They've made the best from their opportunities and profited from them. Don't forget they are very active in charitable causes." Her mother took a breath. "And there's the fact that my brother James tried to give me a huge sum of money, although I probably shouldn't bring that up because the whole subject can get some people worked up."

Stacey couldn't help thinking of her brother Chris, who was still upset that her mother hadn't accepted the Fortune money; but she didn't say it aloud because she didn't want to add to her mother's misery.

"Stacey, are you angry that I turned down that money?" her mother asked in a quiet voice.

Surprised that her mother would ask her, Stacey shook her head. "You did what you thought was right. Do I wish I had the financial assurance to make sure that Piper will always have what she needs? Sure, but I know I can take care of that. Maybe not right now, but I'll make it happen. In the meantime, Piper and I both have something much more important than money. We have your love and support, and that's worth far more than money."

Her mother sniffed and walked across the room to hug her daughter. Stacey closed her eyes at the sensation of her mother's loving arms around her.

This, more than anything, was what she wanted to be able to give Piper the rest of her life.

"It makes me so proud to know what a good heart and soul you have. It makes me feel as if your father and I did something right," Jeanne said.

"Mama, I can assure you that I'll make plenty of mistakes, but you gave me a good heart and a strong sense of right and wrong. I also appreciate the value of hard work. Piper and I will be fine," she said, thrilled because she was finally starting to believe it.

Colton put on his tie and jacket and took one last glance in the mirror. This would be his first planned, semiformal evening with Stacey and Piper. He wanted it to go as well as possible. He hoped Piper was in a good mood because that could make a big difference.

He strode toward the front door.

"Woo-hoo, you look great," his mother called.

Colton smiled and turned to meet her gaze. "Thanks, Mom. You look great yourself."

"Well, thank you, sweetheart," she said, and moved toward him to give him a kiss on his cheek. "You going to pick up Stacey and her baby?"

"I am," he said. "I'll see you at the wedding and reception."

"You look good," his mother said. "She's a lucky girl."

"Thanks," he said. *I'm a lucky guy.*

He drove to the Joneses' ranch and knocked on

the door. He waited a couple moments, and Stacey finally answered the door.

"Sorry," she said. "I haven't been feeling great, and it took extra time to get Piper ready. The great news is she seems to be in a good mood."

"I'm all for Piper being in a good mood," he said, and studied Stacey for a moment. "You look a little pale. Are you sure you want to go?"

"I'm sure," she said. "This will pass. I probably haven't had enough water. I've been busy all day long."

"If you're sure," he said.

"I'm sure," she said and smiled. "Let's go."

Colton helped Stacey and Piper into Stacey's car, then got behind the wheel. He drove down the driveway of the Joneses' ranch and turned onto the main road. Stacey's silence bothered him. He drove a few miles down the road.

"I need you to stop," Stacey said. "I feel sick."

Colton immediately pulled to the side of the road. Stacey stumbled out of the car and got sick on the side of the road. He wasn't sure if he should comfort her or leave her alone. After a few moments, she got back in the car.

"I'm sorry, but I don't think I should go to the wedding. I think I caught a stomach virus from the little boy I was tutoring. Please take me back home," she said, and leaned her head against the headrest.

"Right away," he said, and made a gentle U-turn in the middle of the road. He took a quick glance at her and saw that she was taking deep breaths. He pushed the button to lower the passenger window.

"Thank you," she said.

Colton pulled into the driveway and stopped in front of the house. Stacey flew out of the car. "I'm sorry. I'll get Piper in a couple minutes," she said, and raced through the front door of the house.

Colton sat in the car, staring after her. Piper squirmed and cooed. It wasn't an unhappy sound, just an acknowledgment that the car had stopped. He took a deep breath but didn't glance back at the baby. He suspected that if he looked at her, she might start squawking.

He waited two more minutes, but there was no sign of Stacey. Well, darn, he was going to have to take Princess Piper inside. Stepping out of the driver's seat, he turned to the backseat and searched for the release of the safety seat. Piper squirmed, but she didn't yell at him. He finally found it and pulled her into his arms. Slamming the door behind him, he trudged up the steps to the house and walked inside to complete silence in the house.

Hearing the flush of a commode from the back of the house, he walked farther inside. "Stacey?" he called, once, twice, but there was no answer.

Colton sighed and looked at Piper. "Looks like it's me and you kid," he said. He suddenly realized he'd left the magic bag in the car and returned to retrieve it. The second time Colton entered the house, he decided not to call out to Stacey. She was clearly ill. That left him with one task, taking care of Piper.

"So, how's your diaper? Can you give me a little warning if you're going to do a complete blowout?" he said. "I'll need a whole box of those wipe things."

Piper looked at him and lifted her finger to his mouth.

"Is that your way of saying shut up? I thought women wanted men to talk more," he said.

Piper made garbled baby language, but it wasn't fussy, so Colton had hope. "You know, this isn't that much different than talking with most women. Most of the time I don't understand what they're saying."

Piper continued with her baby talk.

"I wonder if you know what you're saying," he said. "I should probably check your diaper, even though I don't want to."

Colton gave a peek and a touch. "Just wet," he said, excited in a way that he could never explain to a bunch of guys at the bar. "No poo. I can do this," he said, and put her down on the sofa and changed her diaper.

"Time for a bottle?" he asked and pulled one out of the magic bag.

Piper reached for it. He sank down on the couch while she sucked down the formula. When she was finished, she looked as if she were in a stupor. He propped her up on his leg. She let out a belch that would rival that of a trucker's.

"Whoa, that was impressive," he said and patted her on the back.

Piper let out another loud, extremely unfeminine belch.

"Way to go," he said.

Piper looked up at him and gave him a milky smile. That smile melted his heart. She was a sweetheart. In some dark part of his mind, he couldn't help wondering how Joe could have left her. How could he give up the opportunity to be a father to this sweet little girl?

Chapter Ten

Piper spit up a little on his suit's pant leg. Colton bit his lip, remembering the blowout at the festival. *Could be worse,* he thought, and removed his coat and tie. If Piper ruined his shirt, he could wash it. The tie and coat were more problematic. He lifted her in his arms and walked around the kitchen.

Colton wanted to check on Stacey, but he also wanted to give her some privacy. He'd had a couple stomach viruses in his life, and all he'd wanted to do was lie on the bathroom floor and pray for relief.

Piper began to babble again. Colton was just thanking his lucky stars that the sounds she was making were happy ones. "So, who do you like better? Spurs or Mavericks?"

Colton carried Piper around for a half an hour. It

seemed the easiest way to keep her happy. She grew drowsy in his arms, though, and he didn't know if he should put her down for the night. Plus, he was worried about Stacey. He meandered down the hallway to Stacey's room.

"Hey, Stacey," he said and tapped at the door. "Are you okay?"

"No," she called. "My stomach has been inhabited by an alien, and it has turned itself inside out."

He swallowed a grin. It must be a good sign that she could joke. "Can I do anything for you?"

"Just make sure Piper is taken care of if I croak," she said.

His heart squeezed tight. "Don't joke about that," he said.

Silence stretched between them. "I'm not gonna croak," she said. "I'm just gonna wish I could croak."

"Are you sure I can't get anything for you? Water? Soda?" he asked.

"Maybe some soda," she said. "Clear soda," she clarified.

"Done," he said and went to the kitchen. Juggling Piper from one arm to the other, he searched the refrigerator and found a can of seltzer. He poured it into a glass with ice and took it back to her bedroom.

"Got the soda," he said, knocking at the door.

A moment later, the door opened, and Stacey looked up at him as she propped herself against the doorjamb. He could honestly say she looked like death warmed over. She was pale, and her eyes were red-rimmed. "I can only take a sip," she said, and reached out to take a tiny drink.

"Are you sure you don't need to go to the hospital in Lubbock?" he asked. "You look pretty bad."

"I'm in the worst part of the virus," she said. "I just need to stay hydrated. One sip at a time." She closed her eyes. "I need to lie down. Can you watch Piper a little longer?"

"Yes, I just need to know—"

"Thanks," she said and shut the door.

Colton looked at the door for a long moment, then looked at Piper. Her eyes moved in a slow blink. "You look very sleepy," he said. "But I don't want you to wake up in the middle of the night. Maybe a late-night snack?"

He returned to the den and pulled out the magic bag. Rifling through it, he found a jar of peaches. "Sound good?" he said to her.

She drooped against his shoulder. Colton opened the jar and fed her while she rested in his arms. It required far more coordination than it took to wrestle a calf and brand it.

Piper scarfed down the pureed peaches and let out a hearty burp. Colton figured a poop was coming any moment. He felt a sudden surge of warmth on his legs. "Wait, wait, wait," he said, and lifted her up before she ruined his suit pants.

He laid her down on a blanket and grabbed the whole container of wipes. "I can do this," he said to himself. "I've done it before." Colton opened Piper's diaper and winced. Quickly, he cleaned her up and fastened her new diaper only to have her refill it.

"Oh, Lord, help me," he muttered and started cleaning her up again. Sprinkling powder on her, he fastened yet another diaper on her. Taking the little girl in his arms, Colton tossed the two dirty diapers into the kitchen can and walked toward the nursery.

Rummaging around the room, he found a gown. With some trouble, Colton removed Piper's shoes, tights and dress, then pulled on the gown. She whined at him several times.

"Cut me some slack. I haven't done this before," he said. He caught sight of some booties and pulled them on her feet. "Comfy?" he asked.

She wiggled and stared up at him. He stared back at her for a long moment and felt as if he was seeing the beginning and ending of the earth in her eyes. He couldn't look away.

Piper wiggled again, and he shook his head. He must have imagined that strange feeling, he thought. He picked her up and paced around the room. After a few moments, he decided to try out the rocking chair. He rocked her for several moments, then set her down in her crib on her back.

Bracing himself for her cry, he held his breath and waited. Colton counted to one hundred. No sound from Piper. He almost couldn't believe it.

Leaving the room and carefully closing the door behind him, he glanced back at Stacey's room. He wondered if he should check on her. Lost in a quandary, he stared at her door.

"Is there a problem?" Stacey's mother asked.

Colton nearly jumped out of his skin. He'd been so focused on Stacey and Piper he hadn't heard Stacey's parents enter the house. "Stacey got sick on the way to the wedding," he whispered, not wanting to awaken Piper. "We came back, but she was too sick to take care of the baby. I looked after Piper, and she's fallen asleep."

"If there's one thing I know, it's not to wake a sleeping baby," Jeanne said.

Colton smiled. "I'm with you on that, but I'm a little worried about Stacey. Would you mind checking on her?"

Jeanne disappeared into Stacey's room for a moment, then returned to the hallway. "She's falling asleep as we speak. I think the worst of the virus is past. I feel bad that this was her first experience tutoring."

"Knowing her, she won't quit," Colton said.

"Very true," Jeanne said to him and squeezed his arm. "Thank you for looking out for Stacey and Piper tonight."

"Piper was a breeze," Colton said. "I just wish I could have helped Stacey a little more."

"You helped her by taking care of Piper." Jeanne gave him a considering glance. "Looks like Piper may be getting used to you."

"I think I just got lucky with her tonight," Colton

said. "I always feel as if I'm spinning the roulette wheel with that little one."

"Don't underestimate yourself," Jeanne said.

"If you say so," he said. "You sure you don't want me to hang around a little longer in case you need an extra set of hands?" he asked, feeling oddly reluctant to leave Stacey and Piper.

"I'll be fine," she said and chuckled. "I had to juggle babies when they were sick many times when my children were young."

"I guess so," he said, and felt a little foolish. Of course Jeanne Fortune Jones knew what she was doing. The woman had seven children, after all. "I'll head on home, then. Tell Stacey to give me a call when she's feeling better."

"I'll do that," her mother said. "Thank you again for looking after both of them."

He nodded and collected his tie, jacket and hat. "Good night," he said, and headed toward his truck. Colton had an odd, empty, gnawing sensation in his gut as he drove home. He should have been relieved to hand over the reins of Piper and Stacey's care to Jeanne, but he wasn't. Taking care of a temperamental baby while Stacey was sick? It should have been one of the most miserable evenings of his life. He should have run screaming the second Stacey's mom came home. Instead, he'd taken to the task quickly—and more easily than he'd imagined possible. And walking away from Piper—and her beautiful mother—was getting tougher by the day.

Something was wrong, very wrong. He needed to rethink all this.

Over the next couple of days, Colton brooded over his relationship with Stacey. With everyone else voicing an opinion about it, he needed to figure out his own thoughts. In a different situation, in a different—bigger, more crowded—town, he and Stacey could allow their relationship to develop naturally with little intervention. Since, however, both of them lived at home with their families, it seemed they were overwhelmed by prying eyes. Colton had feelings for Stacey and Piper, stronger feelings than he wanted to have at the moment, but he wasn't sure what he should do about those feelings—or what he wanted to do about them. Colton wanted to take things slow. He wanted to be careful. There was a baby involved, for Pete's sake. At the same time, he wanted so badly to be with Stacey and Piper. And yet he couldn't stop thinking about Joe. Why had he abandoned Stacey and Piper? How could he have? Colton had known that Joe's father hadn't been around much, but surely that wouldn't have prevented Joe from being the husband and father Stacey and Piper needed.

The quandary frustrated him so much that he worked outside until it turned dark. Maybe if he wore himself out, he would fall asleep without thinking about Stacey and Piper. He walked into the house with two goals in mind, a meal followed by a shower, but he caught sight of his sister Rachel grading papers in the den.

"Oh, there you are," she called out to him, jumping up from the sofa. "I thought you might have fallen in a hole."

"No, but I've been digging a few," he said, and continued to the kitchen. He foraged through the refrigerator and found some leftover baked chicken and rice. "How's life as a student teacher?"

"Busy, busy. But not so busy that I can't offer to babysit so you and Stacey can have an evening out by yourselves," she said, and shot him a cheeky grin.

"That's nice of you," he said and heated his leftovers in the microwave. "I'll have to check with Stacey when she's feeling better."

"Oh, she's feeling better," Rachel said. "I talked to her today. She hasn't called you yet because she's embarrassed that she got sick and you had to take care of Piper."

"I didn't mind taking care of Piper. I was glad to do what I could to help Stacey when she felt so bad," he said impatiently.

"What's wrong with you?" Rachel asked. "You seem grumpy."

"I'm just tired," he said, pulling a mug from the cabinet. "I've been up since the crack of dawn, working outside in this wind."

"Hmm," she said, crossing her arms over her

chest. "Are you sure it isn't anything about Stacey? You're not leading her on, are you?"

Frustration ripped through him, and he slammed the cabinet door. Swearing under his breath, he shook his head. "That's part of the problem," he said. "Everyone is watching every move Stacey and I make. Everyone feels the need to offer an opinion. Did you ever think we don't need your opinion? Did you ever think we don't want to hear what you think?" he challenged his sister.

Rachel drew back, her eyes widened in surprise. "Why are you so touchy? I just said you shouldn't lead her on. You know that, too."

"Then why did you feel the need to tell me?" he asked. The microwave dinged, signaling his food was ready. He poured himself a cup of decaf and took his dinner to the table.

"I just thought I should make sure," she said. "Stacey has been through a hard time. You know what happened with Joe."

"I do," he said. "You think I should stop seeing her?"

Rachel blinked. "Well, no. Why would you say that?"

"Because it's starting to look as if everyone either wants me to make a lifetime commitment right off the bat or pull back. Those are two extreme choices, considering we just started seeing each other. I've never dated a woman with a child before. I don't know if I'm ready to be an instant father. I don't know that much about kids, let alone babies."

Rachel sank onto the kitchen chair across from him and sighed. "This kinda stinks for you," she said. "Everyone is so excited for Stacey to get involved with a man who would be both a good husband and father that they're jumping to conclusions. Do you wish you hadn't started seeing her?"

"No. I *do* wish everyone would stay out of our business, but I don't see how that's going to happen. I have feelings for Stacey, and for Piper, too, but I have to figure out how to slow this down and get it more under control," he said.

Rachel nodded. "I know control has always been important to you, but good luck with it. I hear it doesn't always work in the romance department. My offer to babysit Piper sometime still stands. Otherwise, I'll let you figure this out on your own."

After eating his dinner and taking a hot shower, Colton went to bed, but he still didn't sleep well. He tossed and turned, trying to figure out what he should do about Stacey.

It was so cold that by afternoon the next day, he decided not to torture himself by staying outside any longer and chose to work in one of the barns close to the house. Hearing the barn door swing open, he turned to see Stacey standing in the doorway holding Piper in one hand and a basket in the other.

His gut took an involuntary dip at the sight of them. Both pairs of eyes were trained on him expectantly. "Hey there," Stacey said, and lifted her lips in a hesitant smile. "Have you recovered from taking care of us on Saturday night?"

"I think the more important question is whether you've recovered. How are *you* feeling?" he asked.

"Much better. It was a twenty-four hour virus. I've been holding my breath because I was afraid either you or Piper might catch it. You haven't felt sick, have you?"

"No, but I'm lucky that way. I don't get sick very often," he said, thinking he might not have gotten the stomach virus, but he still felt as if he'd caught some sort of emotional virus that was keeping him bothered and interrupting his sleep.

"I'm glad to hear that," she said. "I wanted to thank you. Seems like I'm doing that a lot lately," she said and smiled again. "I made some chocolate-chip cupcakes for you. You seemed to like the other ones."

She lifted the basket toward him, and he moved forward to take it. "You didn't have to do that, but thank you."

"My pleasure," she said, and the silence stretched between them. He felt her searching his face, but he couldn't offer her any answers if he didn't have any answers for himself.

She cleared her throat. "Well, I guess I'll go now. Thank you again for taking care of us on Saturday."

"I'm glad I could help," he said, and watched her walk out the barn door. Part of him screamed that he should go after her. But Colton had no clue what he would say.

* * *

Stacey walked away from the Fosters' barn with a lump in her throat. She couldn't bear to return to her house right away, so she drove into town and wandered around the Superette with Piper perched on her hip. Stacey knew she'd gotten her hopes up about Colton, and she clearly shouldn't have.

She picked up a couple bananas for Piper and seriously checked out the chocolate bars.

"Oh, no," a female voice said from behind her. "I'm counting on the hope that I won't crave chocolate once I deliver this baby. You're scaring me, Stacey."

Stacey turned around to find Ella Mae Jergens looking at the candy-bar display. She smiled at the pregnant woman. "I've always loved chocolate," she said. "Pregnancy didn't make it any worse, so don't base your fear on me."

"You're so sweet," Ella Mae said. "I really have to watch my weight. I'm married to an important man, and there will always be women chasing after him."

Stacey felt sorry for Ella Mae if she thought her husband would stray due to a little pregnancy weight. "I'm sure he adores you and sees you as truly beautiful."

Ella Mae smiled. "You've always been a nice girl. I was glad to hear you've been spending time with Colton Foster. Other people have been saying the only reason you got involved with Colton was to get back at Joe, but I didn't believe them. You ignore those rumors and hold your head high, Stacey. You deserve a good man."

Stacey's heart tightened with distress. "What other people have been saying that?" she asked. The only time she'd heard the horrible rumor was from Billy, Joe's friend.

"Oh, I don't know," Ella Mae said. "I heard it from my mother, who heard it from someone else. You know how this town is. Any kind of gossip, true or false, spreads like wildfire. Don't pay any attention to it. It will pass. But I will get just one candy bar," she said, and grabbed one from the display. "Here comes my mother. I'm spending the day with her. Take care, now," Ella Mae said, and headed for the checkout.

Sick from Ella Mae's comments, Stacey put the bananas back and fled the store. Could the day get any worse?

After Stacey returned home, she couldn't muster much conversation. Her mother tried to make small talk as the two baked side by side in the kitchen, but Stacey just wasn't in the mood. She wondered if having to take care of Piper on Saturday night had pushed Colton over the edge. Even though he'd always been sweet to the baby, he wasn't her birth father. He may have looked at his experience Saturday night and feared for his future.

Or had he heard more about the nasty rumor that Ella Mae had repeated to Stacey? Stacey knew that people in Horseback Hollow liked to gossip, but she was sick over the latest outright lie that was spreading like fire.

"You're very quiet, Stacey," her mother said as Stacey washed some pots and pans. "Are you feeling ill again?"

"No, no. I'm fine," she said, and dried the lid to a pot.

"Is something bothering you? I talked with your father last night about your financial concerns and he doesn't want you worrying," she said. "If you need more money—"

"I don't," Stacey said. "I got another student lined up for tutoring this week, but I know I'm not going to be making a lot of money right now. I'll figure that out later."

Her mother nodded and spread out a dish towel on the counter to dry. "Okay. Is there anything else on your mind? You know you can talk to me."

Stacey inhaled and sighed. "I'm not sure this thing with Colton is going to work out," she confessed and fought the urge to cry. She wiped the already clean counter for the third time.

"Why not?" her mother asked. "Did you decide you don't have feelings for him?"

"Oh, no," Stacey said, and swallowed her deep disappointment. "I have feelings for him, but I just don't think Colton is ready to be a daddy."

"Well, you could have fooled me. You should have seen how he hovered over Piper on Saturday night," her mother said with a firm nod of her head.

"That was just one night, Mama," she said. "He may be thinking he's not ready to take us on a full-time basis," Stacey said. "I can't really blame him. A lot of men wouldn't want to father someone else's child."

"You can't possibly believe that," her mother said. "Colton Foster is a good man. He would always do what's right."

"But how is it right for him to take on the responsibility for a child that isn't his?" Stacey countered. "How is it fair?"

Her mother frowned. "I think you may be jumping the gun. You need to give Colton a little time."

"I'm trying not to pressure him, but everyone we run into seems to want to make a comment or give advice about us seeing each other. I don't know," she said, shrugging even though she was miserable. "Plus, I haven't told you, but there's a terrible rumor going around about us. Some people seem to think that the only reason I've started spending time with Colton is to get back at Joe."

"Well, that's a complete fabrication. How would Joe even know that you're seeing Colton since he hasn't bothered to check on you or his baby?" her mother asked, indignantly. "If I were a lesser person, I could wish some bad things on that boy. Leaving you in the lurch like that. With a note, no less. Thinking about it still makes my blood boil."

Stacey knotted her fingers together, then pulled

them apart and knotted them again. "This is turning into a big mess. I think I'd better give Colton some space."

Jeanne Marie Fortune Jones stepped in line at the tiny Horseback Hollow post office. Her mind hopped and skipped to different issues weighing on her—Stacey's romantic predicament and her troubled son Christopher—as she patiently waited her turn.

"Hello, Jeanne. Good to see you," Olive Foster said as she got in line behind her neighbor. "How are you?"

"Good, thank you. I see you have packages," Jeanne said. "Christmas gifts you need to return?"

Olive nodded. "I overdid it this year, and my husband, Frank, can be so hard to please," she said with a heavy sigh. "What about you?"

"I'm sending a letter to my—" She broke off and smiled. "My sister in England, and another to my brother James. I know everyone uses email these days, but I thought both of them might enjoy a letter."

"That's nice of you. Are you still getting used to being a Fortune?" Olive asked.

Jeanne nodded and stepped forward. "It's still hard to believe, but it's wonderful having brothers and a sister and all these new nieces and nephews."

"I think it's so sweet that your children added the Fortune name," Olive said. "It shows a lot of family unity."

"Not all of them have," Jeanne said, thinking of Liam. "But they're all adults and it would be wrong for me to push them. They should make this decision on their own. It's not a perfect situation, but I'm glad most of them are interested in getting to know their new family." Jeanne thought, too, of her son Chris and the resentment he held against the Fortunes and their wealth. She wished he could let go of his ill feelings, because she knew he would be much happier if he did.

"How is Stacey doing? I heard she got sick the other night," Olive said.

"Yes, she did, but she's much better now. Colton took care of the baby during the worst part of it. You've raised a fine young man."

Olive beamed with pride. "Thank you. We're very blessed with both our children," she said.

Jeanne hesitated, wondering if she should say anything else. "I know that Stacey has enjoyed spending time with him lately."

"Yes, we are pleased about that. Stacey's a wonderful young lady."

Silence stretched for a long moment between them. "Of course, I understand if things don't work out. They've just started seeing each other, and we don't know what will happen in the long run."

Olive looked pensive and stepped closer to Jeanne. "It's none of my business, but is something wrong between them?" she asked in a lowered voice. "Colton hasn't said a word about her the past few days, and he seems a bit withdrawn."

"Well, I have to confess I've been concerned lately, too. Even though I love Colton, I told Stacey to be careful about getting involved again. She didn't seem to appreciate me giving my opinion," Jeanne said. "It's hard to hold your tongue when you worry about your children."

"I know what you're saying. I hate to admit it, but I asked my husband to speak to Colton about spending time with Stacey. I wanted it made clear that he shouldn't take advantage of her." Olive winced. "I wonder if I should have kept my thoughts to myself."

"They're adults and very responsible," Jeanne said. "I'd hate to think I helped to mess up anything by sticking my nose in their business."

"Me, too," Olive said miserably. "I suppose it wouldn't help to bring it up to Colton in casual conversation."

"Probably not," Jeanne said.

Olive sighed. "I guess we'll just have to do what we should have done from the beginning. Be quiet and hope for the best."

Jeanne nodded in agreement, but she worried about her daughter. Stacey had already been hurt enough. "Please don't tell anyone, but someone has started a terrible rumor," she confided to Olive.

"About Stacey and Colton?" Olive asked in surprise.

"Yes. Someone, and we don't know who, has been

saying that the only reason Stacey has been spending time with Colton was to get back at Joe because he left her. The reason I'm telling you is because I want you to know that is absolutely not true. I think Stacey has fallen for your son, but she feels as if she needs to back off and give him some breathing room."

Olive frowned and shook her head. "Why is it that people find it necessary to gossip about people who are just trying to do their best? If someone is stupid enough to repeat that rumor to me, I'll set them straight. You can count on it."

Jeanne felt a surge of gratitude inside her at Olive's protectiveness of Stacey. "You've always been the best neighbors we could have. I would love it if we could be in-laws," Jeanne said. "I'll be saying my prayers and crossing my fingers that our children will work this out."

Chapter Eleven

Piper had lost her favorite binky. Or, *someone* had lost Piper's favorite pacifier. Perhaps her father's hunting dog had eaten it. The who didn't matter. The fact was that Stacey needed to get a replica of the favorite binky immediately. As Stacey headed out the door on a cold, rainy winter night, Jude called out, "Hey, do you mind picking up a burger for me from The Grill?"

"You just ate chicken potpie," she retorted, pulling up her hood.

"I'm still hungry," he said mournfully as he walked into the den with Piper in his arms.

Stacey couldn't turn him down. He was doing her a favor by pacing with Piper, who had been crying without stop for nearly an hour. With the windshield wipers whipping from side to side, Stacey drove to the Superette, praying that she would find the treasured binky. The rain spit in her face as she rushed through the door. She studied the poor selection of binkies and chose two—just in case—then checked out.

Next stop, The Grill. She went inside and placed the take-out order. Pacing the front of the restaurant, she heard the jukebox playing one of her favorite songs in the bar and peeked inside at what the other half were doing tonight.

She caught a quick glimpse of Colton nursing a beer and froze. He must have sensed her looking at him because he glanced up, and his gaze locked with hers. Wanting to avoid him, she pulled back inside and prayed Jude's burger would be ready soon. She haunted the cash register. *"Hurry, hurry,"* she whispered under her breath.

"Hey, what are you doing out on a wicked night like tonight?" Colton asked from behind her.

Stacey took a deep breath and turned around. "I could ask the same of you."

Colton shrugged. "Cabin fever. I just needed to get away from the house. What are you doing here?"

"Piper lost her favorite binky, and I had to try to find one like it. Jude asked me to pick up a burger for him. He's pacing with Piper, so it's the least I can do, even though he's already had dinner."

"You want to come in here while you wait?"

She shook her head. "No, thanks." She glanced

at the checkout, but there was no sign of her take-out order. "Listen, I just want you to know the rumors aren't true."

He frowned at her. "What rumors?" he asked.

"About me." She swallowed over the sudden lump that formed in her throat. She thought she'd gotten control of herself during the past few days. Why had that control evaporated so quickly? "There was a rumor that the only reason I got involved with you was to get back at Joe. I just need you to know that isn't true."

He stared at her in disbelief. "Who said that?"

"Well, I heard from someone who heard from someone from someone, so I don't know. It's just important to me that you know it's not—"

She broke off as an attractive brunette approached Colton from behind and looped her arms around him. "Hey, baby, where'd you go?"

Colton glanced at the woman in surprise. "I thought you were busy with someone else."

She shook her head and nuzzled him seductively. "I was just trying to get your attention."

Colton cleared his throat and looked at Stacey. "Uh, this is Mary," he said.

"Malia," the woman corrected with an indulgent grin. "He's so cute, isn't he?"

"Uh-huh," Stacey said.

"Maria is new in town," he said, still messing up the woman's name. "I just met her tonight."

Stacey couldn't believe her eyes. "Nice to meet

you, Malia. How did you end up in Horseback Hollow?"

"I needed to get off the grid. Violent ex," she said. "This seemed like a good choice."

"I hope it will work out for you," Stacey said, and finally Jude's order was delivered to the register. She was so relieved she nearly shouted. "Oh, there's my takeout. Have a nice evening. I need to get back home." She paid her bill and ran out the door to her car.

Just as she slid onto her seat, Colton caught the door before she could close it. "Hey, that wasn't what you think it was," he said, rain pouring down over his head and jacket.

"It's okay," she forced herself to say. "There are no strings between us. You can do what you want. Malia probably doesn't have any little kids."

"That's not what's important," he said.

"I'm not so sure about that, and I can't say I blame you. If I were a man, I might not want to take on the baggage of a baby that wasn't mine. I understand, Colton. I really do," she said, although she wished things could be different.

Colton shook his head, but she couldn't handle this discussion any longer. Her sadness overwhelmed her. "I need to go," she said, and pulled her car door shut.

Colton called himself ten times a fool during the next twelve hours. He could barely sleep when he thought of the injured expression on Stacey's face. He should have stopped her. He shouldn't have let her go. He should have told her how much he'd missed her and that he wanted to work things out with her. Instead, he'd stood in the rain trying to come to grips with the ridiculous rumor she'd relayed to him.

Colton spent the day working in the barn. The sound of silence, however, echoed inside his mind. Unable to bear the scrutiny of his family, he decided to go into town again and get a burger from The Grill. He didn't know where else to go. This was yet another time when he needed his own place.

After placing his order, Colton carried his burger and fries from the grill to the bar and ordered a beer, hoping he didn't run into Mary or whatever her name was. He stared up at the basketball game playing on the television while he ate his meal.

"Long time, Colton," a voice from his past said.

Colton glanced over his shoulder to see Joe Hitchens. He blinked. "Hey, Joe, what you doing here?"

"I decided to pay a visit from Dallas," Joe said. Colton noticed Joe was a little chubbier than when he'd left Horseback Hollow all those months ago.

"You left town kinda fast," Colton said.

Joe shrugged. "It was a rough time for me."

"For you," Colton said, beginning to seethe. "What about Stacey?"

"She was early enough along that she could have taken care of the pregnancy," Joe said.

"Taken care of the pregnancy?" Colton echoed.

"That's what she did. She delivered that baby and has taken care of her with no help from you."

"I meant," Joe said, lowering his voice, "she could have gotten rid of the pregnancy."

Colton gaped at the man in disbelief. "You mean get rid of Piper?"

"Is that what she named the baby? I heard it was a girl," Joe said.

"But you never bothered to call her or offer any kind of support," Colton said. He pushed aside his food. He had lost his appetite.

"She knew I didn't want a kid. She shouldn't have gotten pregnant," Joe said.

"As if you had nothing to do with it," Colton said, growing angrier with each passing second. "You bastard," he said, standing and punching Joe in the face.

Colton's knuckles throbbed, and Joe covered his face.

"What the—" Joe said. "You know what kind of father I had. I didn't ever want to be a father after the kind of example my dad set. He was gone more than he was with my mom and me."

"That's no excuse. You're the lowest of the low," Colton said in disgust. "I don't know how you can call yourself a man. We've been friends since high school, but I don't recognize you anymore. When did you turn yourself into the kind of person you've become?"

"You must have gotten pretty close to Stacey to be so defensive," Joe said. "Did you go to bed with her?"

It was all Colton could do to keep from hitting Joe again. "Go back to Dallas," he said. "You don't belong here."

"Who do you think you are? Dating my ex? Bros don't cheat on bros. You know the guy code," Joe said.

"What guy code? You haven't been here for over a year. What rights do you have?" Colton asked.

"That baby is mine. That woman was mine," Joe said.

"*Was* is the operative term. What do you know about Piper?" Colton demanded.

Joe narrowed his eyes, then shifted from one foot to the other. "Not much."

"Why are you even here now?" Colton asked. "You haven't been here for months, not even when your baby was born."

Silence stretched between them. "Someone told me you and Stacey had gotten involved," Joe confessed.

"You would come back into town for that, to stake your claim on a woman you ran out on, but not when the baby was born?" Colton asked, shaking his head. "Are you crazy?"

"I should have known you wouldn't understand." Joe rubbed at his cheek where Colton had punched him. "So, is the baby okay?" Joe asked reluctantly.

"She's as close to perfect as a baby can get. She's gorgeous. Big green eyes and blond hair just like Stacey. She's got a kick to her personality. If she doesn't like what you're doing, she'll let you know. But she's the sweetest thing in the world when she falls asleep on your shoulder. Makes you feel as if everything in the world is the way it should be."

Joe stared at Colton. "You love her. You love *my* daughter," he accused.

Colton met Joe's astonished gaze and nodded. "Yeah. I guess I do. I really do."

Joe raked his hand through his hair and shook his head. "I don't know what to say."

"I do," Colton said. "You need to man up or shut up. If you want Stacey and your daughter back, then you need to go tell her. I think Stacey deserves better than you, but there's more involved in this situation. There's Piper," Colton said. "I'll give you twenty-four hours."

Joe stared at him, clearly affronted. "Who are you to tell me I've got twenty-four hours?"

"I'm the man who has changed your baby's diaper, rocked her to sleep and had her poop down my back," Colton said. "Have you done any of that?"

Joe looked at him in hostile silence.

"That's right. You haven't. You've got twenty-four hours. Don't mess with me, Joe. I'm disgusted with you," Colton said, and tossed some cash on the counter and walked away.

The next twenty-four hours passed by in minute-by-minute increments. Colton thought about Stacey and Piper when he drove home, when he took his evening shower, when he brushed his teeth and when he tried to go to sleep. His attempt to sleep was completely futile.

When he got up in the morning, he didn't know how he was going to get through the day, so he did it the only way he knew how. Working. He worked clear through until six that evening. As he walked toward the house, he told himself that he only had an hour and a half to go.

"Hey, sweetheart," his mom said as he walked through the door. "You want some dinner?"

"I'm not that hungry," he muttered.

"Well, you should take in a little nourishment after spending all day outside," she said. "I fixed a pot roast. I think you'll like it."

Colton didn't protest as his mother fussed over him and urged him to take a seat at the kitchen table. In this situation, it was easier to acquiesce than fight her. His mother was clearly in supernurture mode. Colton took a few bites of pot roast and potatoes.

"You must be sick," his mother said. "You're not eating."

"The pot roast is great, but I have some things on my mind, Mom," he told her.

"What?" his mother said. "What's on your mind?"

"I don't want to talk about it," he said and rose from his chair.

"Is it Stacey Fortune Jones?" she asked.

The question stopped him in his tracks. "And what if it is?"

His mother sighed. "Give her the benefit of the doubt. Her mother says she has fallen for you. But don't tell her that I told you," his mother said.

His heart swelled at the possibility that Stacey could have *fallen* for him. He wondered when that had happened. He wondered *if* it had happened. "How do you know?"

"I met up with Jeanne the other day at the post office and we got to talking." His mother broke off and pressed her lips together. "But I'm not going to say anything else. I shouldn't interfere. This is between you and Stacey."

Colton stared at his mother in disbelief. "You give advice and opinions about everything, but now you're clamming up?"

His mother lifted her finger. "Colton, don't you bait me. I'm determined to do the right thing. You and Stacey need to figure out what's best for you," she said and turned away.

Colton, watching the clock every other minute, sighed and put his plate in the fridge to eat later. "Sorry, Mom. I'm just not hungry right now. I'll eat it for lunch tomorrow." Colton grabbed his coat and headed for his truck. Eighteen minutes to go.

He drove around for ten minutes.

Colton spotted a deer crossing the road in front of him and slowed down. The driver of a semi must have panicked, though. Colton tried to swerve out of the incoming path of the truck. But he was too late. The impact jolted him. He heard the sound of glass shattering. Pain seared through him, and everything went black.

Stacey put Piper down with ease and tossed a load of laundry into the washer for lack of anything else to do. She still couldn't get over seeing that other woman pawing Colton. He had appeared surprised, but perhaps that was because he hadn't expected the woman to follow him out of the grill. Stacey suspected Malia was everything Stacey wasn't. Employed, with no baby and no stretch marks. Malia had looked like a girl ready to have a good time, and now that Stacey was a mom, she had to think twice about throwing caution to the wind for the sake of a good time. She had to think about her little Piper.

Still, the image of Colton with Malia made her so edgy she felt as if her nerve endings were being rubbed raw with a wire brush. There wasn't anything she could do about it, she told herself. The fact that Colton hadn't tried to call her in nearly two days spoke volumes.

Stacey turned the television in her bedroom on low volume in hopes of distracting herself, but the reality show just irritated her even more. She brushed her teeth and dressed for bed, praying that she would get some relief with sleep. Just as she pulled back her covers and reached to turn out her lamp, her cell phone vibrated with an incoming call.

Spotting Rachel's number on the ID, Stacey debated letting it go to voice mail. She didn't want to discuss her feelings about Colton right now, especially with his sister. Sighing, she picked up, ready to say she didn't want to talk about Colton.

"Hey, Rachel," Stacey said. "What's up?"

"Oh, Stacey, it's terrible," Rachel said, nearly sobbing. "Colton has been in a bad accident. His truck was hit by a semi. The ambulance is taking him to the Lubbock General E.R."

Stacey's heart turned cold. She tried to make sense of what Rachel had told her. The only thing she knew for certain was that Colton had been hurt. "Do you know anything about his condition? Did they tell you anything?"

"All we know is that he's unconscious, and there may be internal injuries. Mom and Dad are driving to Lubbock in their car, and I'm going in mine. Stacey, I'm scared. I'm afraid I'm going to lose my brother."

For a moment, Stacey couldn't breathe. *She* was afraid of losing Colton, too. Even if they went back to being friends, Stacey didn't want to lose Colton. Just knowing he was alive on the earth gave her a good feeling inside her. He was a wonderful man, and the thought of not being able just to see him again made her feel like crying. Anxiety coursed through her. But some part of her professional training as a nurse kicked in.

"Don't give up yet," she said. "I'm sure he's getting good care."

"Oh, Stacey, I wish you could be here," Rachel said.

"I'm on my way," Stacey promised, even if she

had to drag Piper out of bed. She wanted to be there for Colton. She wanted to be there for his family.

Stacey changed into jeans and a sweater, then awakened her mother and told her the horrible news.

"Oh, no," Jeanne said. "That's terrible. Do you have any idea if they think he'll recover? Poor Olive and Frank must be beside themselves."

"I'd like to go to Lubbock to be with them. I'll take Piper with me, but—"

Her mother shook her head. "No. Absolutely not. I'll watch over her. You go ahead, but please be careful. And call us with any news."

Stacey gave her mother a hug and grabbed a bottle of water before she pulled on her coat and left the house. Driving through the night, she thought about all the times she'd spent with Colton. An image of him playing ball as a child flashed through her head. She remembered playing tag with Rachel, him and her brothers. Later on, when they'd become teenagers and she'd passed him in the hall, he'd never been too cool to wave to her as a younger student.

Now that she knew him as a man, her feelings were even stronger. Yes, he'd become the most sexy man in existence to her, but it was partly due to his tenderness and encouragement. It was partly due to the way that he tried so hard with Piper. How could she possibly resist Colton after all that?

She made the drive in record time and pulled into the parking lot at the hospital. She rushed inside to the E.R. but didn't see any Fosters. Her stomach dipped. She prayed that the worst hadn't happened. Stacey asked the registration desk about Colton, and a few moments later, she was ushered back to a waiting room.

Rachel rose and soared into Stacey's arms. "I'm so glad you're here."

Stacey couldn't help seeing Mr. and Mrs. Foster standing beside a row of chairs. Mrs. Foster's eyes were bloodshot from tears, and Mr. Foster looked dazed and shocked. Stacey's heart went out to them.

"Any news?" she asked.

"He's being examined. They said he's still unconscious," Rachel said, sniffing.

"They're looking after him," Stacey said, but she was so scared. She just couldn't show it. She turned toward Colton's parents and embraced Mrs. Foster.

"Oh, Stacey, I just want him to be okay," Mrs. Foster said.

Stacey squeezed Colton's mother tight. She wanted Colton to be all right, too. More than anything. She took a deep breath, knowing that waiting could be the worst. "Can I get coffee for any of you?"

Rachel and her parents shook their heads, all murmuring *no*.

The vigil began.

The minutes crept by slowly, feeling like days instead of hours. Stacey tried to make small talk but gave up after a half hour had passed. All of them were worried sick. Why hadn't a doctor or nurse entered the waiting room to speak to them?

Stacey was just about to prod someone at the emergency-room desk for details when a doctor walked in, still wearing his surgical scrubs. "Mr. and Mrs. Foster?" he said. "I'm Dr. McMillan. Your son took a hard hit. He has a concussion and some bad bruises. I have to say it's a miracle that your son didn't sustain more serious injuries. We'll keep him under observation until we're sure he's out of the woods from that concussion."

"Oh, stars," Mrs. Foster said, sinking onto a chair.

Stacey's heart was hammering in her head. "How much blood has he lost? Has he been conscious at all? Is there any lung damage? What about—"

"Whoa," the doctor said. "One at a time."

Stacey forced herself to pace her questions, and the doctor answered each one.

"When can the family see him?" she asked.

He glanced at his watch. "Let's give it another few moments," he warned.

The doctor left the room, and Rachel, wiping away the tears in her eyes, grabbed Stacey. "It sounds as if he's going to be okay," she said.

Stacey wanted to see Colton and touch him, check his stats to be sure, but she nodded. "It sounds very good."

Moments later, the Fosters were led back to see Colton in recovery. Stacey paced the waiting room, praying and wishing for Colton. Ten minutes later, a nurse appeared in the doorway. "Stacey, I understand you're Colton Foster's girlfriend. The rest of the family requested your presence."

Stacey nodded and followed the nurse to the recovery room. Colton was receiving fluids and oxygen. Her heart squeezed tight in fear. At the same time, she knew these measures were medically necessary.

"Why does he have all these tubes?" Mr. Foster asked, his face filled with fear.

Rachel reached for Stacey's hand.

"All these things are helping support Colton to recover from his injuries and the accident," Stacey said. "Soon enough, he won't be needing the line for fluids. Later, they'll only give him oxygen as needed. This is the worst, except for any bruising and swelling he may have. It looks like they're taking good care of him. That's what's important."

"Stacey, I'm so glad you're here," Rachel said.

"Me, too," Olive said and grabbed Stacey's hand.

Mr. Foster took a deep breath and looked at his son.

The three of them stood in the recovery area for several moments. "Even though Colton is unconscious, he can hear your voices, so talking is good for him."

Rachel immediately went to Colton's side and started chatting. Her voice suddenly broke. "I love you, big brother. Wake up soon," she said, and kissed him gently on his forehead.

His mother took a turn next. "I'm sorry I didn't

answer your questions tonight," she said and sniffed. "I love you. Everybody loves you."

His father stepped closer. "You're a good man. A good, strong man. Get better, son. We're here for you."

Stacey's throat tightened in a knot of emotion. She hated how much all of them were hurting. She didn't want to think about her own feelings. The three of them looked at her expectantly, as if they wanted her to speak to Colton, too.

Stacey slowly walked to Colton's side and gently touched his shoulder. "Hey, you. What are you doing playing chicken with semis?" She bit her lip. "We want you to get better, but don't work too hard at it. Let the medicine help you," she said.

Colton's eyelids fluttered. He opened his mouth and coughed. "Stacey? Stacey?"

Stunned that he would call her name, she leaned closer. "I'm here. I'm here. What do you need?"

"Joe?" he said.

She frowned. "Joe?"

"Did he come see you?"

Stacey figured Colton must be talking out of his head. "No. I haven't seen Joe," she said, but Colton had fallen asleep.

Chapter Twelve

Stacey sat by Colton's side for the next several hours. She urged Mr. and Mrs. Foster to return home, but Rachel insisted on staying. Colton awakened for short periods. Sometimes he blinked his eyes. He often asked questions as to why he was in the hospital. He asked again about Joe but fell back asleep.

"Why do you think he keeps asking about Joe?" Rachel asked.

"I have no idea," Stacey said. "Joe hasn't been in town for ages."

"Maybe he has amnesia. Maybe this is part of his concussion," Rachel suggested.

"I don't know," Stacey said. "If it keeps happening, maybe we should ask the doctor about it."

Colton's parents returned and shooed both Rachel and Stacey away to take a break. Gritty-eyed and tired, but mostly confident that Colton was on the road to recovery, Stacey returned home and fell into bed. When she awakened, it was early evening, and she checked on Colton via his parents. He'd been moved to a room and was doing much better.

Stacey sighed with relief and spent the rest of the afternoon taking care of Piper. Her daughter seemed thrilled to see her, which eased some of the upset and trauma she'd experienced during the past week. Rocking Piper to sleep was the purest form of therapy for Stacey. She kissed her sweet baby's head and put her to bed. Afterward Stacey updated her mother about Colton and his injuries. Thank goodness, her mother didn't ask any probing questions about Stacey's feelings about Colton. She went to bed, planning to visit Colton the next morning.

The next morning, Stacey dressed Piper in a cute pink outfit and made the hour-long trip to Lubbock. Piper snoozed on and off, and was so quiet Stacey had to check every now and then to make sure the baby was breathing. When they arrived at the hospital, Stacey changed Piper's diaper in the backseat of the car in the parking lot. The cold winter wind whipped around her. Piper's eyes widened like saucers from the chill.

"Wheee, that's breezy, isn't it?" she said, quickly

refastening Piper's pink outfit and pulling her baby up against her.

Stacey tucked Piper under her coat as she made her way to Colton's room, where his parents sat next to him.

"Hi," she said. "I thought you might enjoy some visitors."

Colton looked up, and, seeing Piper, he gave a groggy smile. "Hey, how's the little one doing?"

"Great. She barely made a peep on the way. An hour's drive. There's hope that she will be a good traveler."

"Joe didn't come to see you, did he?" Colton asked.

Stacey slid a questioning glance toward Colton's parents, but his mother just shook her head and rose. "Come on, Frank. Let's get some coffee."

"I just had coffee," Frank said.

"Well, I want some more," Olive said firmly.

Frank sighed and rose to his feet. "Thanks for coming," he said to Stacey and gave a little wave to Piper.

"You've mentioned Joe several times," Stacey said. "I thought it was a result of your concussion. Why do you keep talking about him? Did you have a hallucination?"

Colton gave a short laugh, then grabbed his bruised ribs. "No hallucination. He showed up at the bar the other day."

Shocked and confused, Stacey stared at Colton. "Joe? In Horseback Hollow? Are you sure?"

"Yeah, I punched him in the face," Colton said.

Stacey covered her mouth with her free hand. "Oh, my goodness. How did that happen?"

"Easy," Colton said. "He opened his mouth and started talking. I gave him twenty-four hours to go see you. Then, I told him I was taking my turn."

Stacey sank onto a chair, pulling Piper onto her lap. She shook her head but felt no sadness. "He never showed."

Colton took a deep breath and winced. "The night of the wreck, I was counting down the minutes to come see you."

Stacey's heart squeezed tight. "Oh, Colton, no." She rubbed her forehead. "That means you would have never had that accident if you had decided to stay home and wait until morning."

"I couldn't wait," Colton said. He closed his eyes. "I have a confession to make. Back before Joe proposed to you, I told him he needed to put a ring on your finger. You're a special girl, and someone was going to steal you away. He proposed to you the next day." Colton sighed, opening his eyes, his gaze full of regret. "I always felt guilty—that maybe you wouldn't have gotten pregnant if I hadn't given Joe that push."

Stacey blinked at the revelation. She felt a rush of emotions. All those months ago, Colton had been protective of her. What Colton told her just confirmed what she already knew. Joe had never truly loved her. He might not have wanted to lose her, but he hadn't loved her. "I hate that he had to be pushed along, and that I believed in him. I hate that he abandoned both Piper and me. But I could never regret having Piper. She's the light of my life."

"Yeah, but that doesn't change the fact that you've been through a terrible time because of Joe."

"Why did you give him twenty-four hours?" Stacey asked.

Colton shrugged his shoulders and winced slightly. He looked away, then back at her. "I'm in love with you. I don't know exactly when it happened or how. It just did. I fell in love with you. And Piper. Maybe I shouldn't have threatened Joe—"

"Stop," she said breathlessly and nearly fell out of the chair. "Did you just say you love me?"

He narrowed his eyes. "Yeah, I did."

"And Piper. You love her, too?"

"I do," he said, almost defiantly.

Stacey jumped from her chair and planted a kiss on his mouth. "I love you, too, Colton Foster. So very, very much."

He met her gaze. "Are you sure?"

"Very, very sure. I feel like the luckiest woman in the world. Say it again, please. Say you love me again so I can be sure. I feel like I dreamed it."

"I love you, Stacey Fortune Jones. I want you to be Stacey Fortune Jones Foster," he said.

Her heart stopped in her chest. "I feel as if I'm walking in a dream."

"I want to make your dreams come true as much as I possibly can," he said. "Even if that means sitting in tiny chairs I'm afraid of breaking for the sake of having a tea party with Piper."

Stacey's eyes filled with tears. "Oh, Colton."

Piper made a chirpy sound, and he turned to her. "I wanted to take this slow and be sensible, but life is too short. Stacey and Piper, will you marry me?"

"Yes, yes and yes," Stacey said and kissed Colton again.

His parents walked into the room. "Everything okay?" Mrs. Foster asked.

"Everything's great," Colton said. "Stacey, Piper and I are getting married."

"Well, thank goodness," his mother said, her voice full of relief and emotion. "We couldn't be happier."

"I guess we're going to have to build a house on the ranch for you three," Mr. Foster said. "We'll get started as soon as possible."

"Dad, I'd really like you to see a doctor about your back. I don't want you working on a house for me when you might hurt yourself."

His father frowned and shrugged. "Your sister's taking me for an appointment to see a doctor next week. I didn't want to do it, but she told me I owed it to you. I'm gonna hire a full-time hand and a few part-time guys, too. It's time. I've got more money in the bank than anyone knows, but don't spread that around. We'll get through. I just want you to get well."

Stacey squeezed one of Colton's hands. "This means you can concentrate on getting better," she said. "That's what we all want."

The next day, Colton arrived home from the hospital and was recovering by leaps and bounds. His doctor called him superhuman because he was healing so quickly. Stacey constantly chided him to take his time and rest, but she could see he found it hard not to forge into his regular routine. She visited him every day, and every day, it seemed as if their love for each other grew stronger.

A few days after that, Colton stood with her in the den of her parents' home. The room was usually a warm, welcoming place for family and visitors, but not today.

Today, the visitor was the biological father of her child. Stacey had fought the meeting with Joe, but Colton had insisted that she and Piper deserved some support from Joe. Stacey couldn't be less interested in seeing Joe. In many ways, she didn't want Piper exposed to such a man. She could only hope that someday he would grow up.

A knock sounded at the door, and she looked at

Colton. "You'll be okay," he said. "I'm here with you. You're just looking out for Piper. Remember that."

Stacey took a deep breath and answered the door to her former fiancé and Piper's biological father. He didn't look nearly as handsome as she remembered. She wondered how that had happened. "Hi, Joe. Come on inside," she said.

Joe entered with a slightly ill expression on his face. "Yeah, uh. I know I need to give you child support," he said. "I should have done it before, but I just couldn't face the idea that I had a child. I'll catch up," he promised.

"That's good," Stacey said. She wouldn't thank him. This was long overdue. "Do you want to see her?"

Joe took a deep breath. "Yeah. Yeah. I want to see her," he said as if he were facing the guillotine.

"I'll go get her," Stacey said, and collected Piper from her mother who was staying in the kitchen. Jeanne was still too angry with Joe to face him, and Stacey had made sure her father was working away from the house that day. She picked up her precious baby girl and carried her to the front foyer.

Joe stared at Piper for a long moment. "She's beautiful."

"Yes, she is and always has been," Stacey said. "I can't thank you for how you left us, but I can thank you for giving her to me."

Joe pursed his lips together in sadness. "I'd like to try to see her every now and then."

"I think she deserves that," Stacey said. "I think she deserves the best you can give her."

Joe gave a slow nod. "I don't know how to be a good father. I never had one. I'm gonna need some hints and nudges. My father was never there for me when I needed him. I was afraid I couldn't be a good father when you told me you were pregnant. That's why I told you that you should—" He cleared his throat. "I was wrong," he said in a gruff voice.

"You can put your meetings with Piper on your schedule on your smartphone calendar. You put your other appointments on there, don't you?" Colton asked.

"Yeah. I never thought of that," Joe said.

"You can start now, then," Colton said. "Input a date three weeks from today to call Stacey about when you can see Piper."

Joe pulled his cell phone from his pocket and tapped the information into his calendar. "Done. I'm sorry for the pain I've caused you, Stacey. But I'm going to try and—" Joe glanced at Colton. "It looks like you're in good hands now."

Stacey smiled. "Best hands ever," she said.

Ten days later, Rachel insisted on taking care of Piper for a full twenty-four-hour time period. Colton had completely recovered from the accident. He picked up Stacey and drove his new truck to Vicker's Corners so they could take a stroll downtown and spend the night at a bed-and-breakfast after dinner.

"It's perfect, but freezing," Stacey said, snuggling her gloved hands in his.

"It's the dead of winter," he said and looked down at her. "But I'm glad you think it's perfect."

"If I'm with you, it's perfect," she said. "And if you're recovering—"

"Mostly there," he said.

"But don't push it," she urged. "If you're recovering, that's perfect, too. Things could have been terribly different." Her heart caught at the thought of losing Colton, and her smile fell.

Colton caught her chin with his thumb. "Hey, no sad faces tonight. We're together and happy, right?"

Stacey nodded. "Yes, yes, yes."

"I like the sound of that word," he said with a sly, sexy look. "Let's have dinner," he said, and they stepped inside the restaurant.

The host led them to a table in front of a fireplace. "Oh, this is fabulous. I feel as if I'm in heaven."

"It gets better," he promised.

They ordered dinner and were served a delicious meal. Stacey savored every bite. She patted her belly toward the end of the dinner. "I don't think I can eat any more, but I would love some of that chocolate dessert."

"I'll get it to go," he said.

After he paid the check, they walked to their charming suite at the bed-and-breakfast. Stacey couldn't remember a more wonderful evening. With Piper in Rachel's care, and the full support of her family and Colton's, she couldn't feel happier to have such a special evening with Colton. A bottle of champagne welcomed them as they walked into the room. A gas fire flickered in the fireplace.

"Like it?" he asked.

"Oh, it's amazing," she said. "I love a gas fireplace. No work and all the pleasure."

"Does that mean you'd like that in my house plans?" he asked.

"I don't need a gas fireplace to be happy with you," she insisted.

"I've got a lot packed into my savings account, Stacey. Speak up about what you want," he said, putting his arm around her back.

"Okay," she whispered. "Gas fireplace and hot tub big enough for you and me."

Colton's eyes darkened with sensuality. "Sold. I like the way you think," he said, and took her mouth in a kiss.

With Colton holding her in his arms, she almost forgot about her surroundings. It was so good to hold him and kiss him. It was so good to be alone with him and to know he was healed from the accident.

Colton pulled back. "Let's have a glass of champagne," he said.

Stacey would rather have had a bucketful of Colton, but she went along with him. He pulled the champagne bottle from the ice and popped the cork. Grabbing a glass, he spilled the bubbly liquid into the flute and offered it to her. He poured a second flute for himself.

"To you," he said. "The woman I love. I've asked you once, but I want to do it the right way this time."

Colton knelt on one knee, and Stacey's breath hung in her throat. The past few weeks had caused such a roller coaster of emotions. She felt as if she were taking another heart-pounding turn on the ride. "What are you doing?"

He pulled a jeweler's box from his pants pocket and flipped it open to reveal a beautiful diamond ring. "Will you marry me?"

Stacey's heart squeezed so tight she could hardly speak. "Oh, yes, Colton. I can't believe how lucky I am."

Colton rose to his feet and kissed her again. "I feel the same way, Stacey Fortune Jones. I can't wait for you, Piper and me to start our lives together."

Stacey couldn't believe how her life had turned out. She was in love with the best man ever, and her daughter would have a daddy to show her the stuff of which a real man was made.

Stacey had never believed much in chance, but

she'd just received the best fortune ever in Colton Foster. Love forever. She'd come from a long line of lovers, and now she was getting her chance at the love of a lifetime.

* * * * *

A SWEETHEART FOR
JUDE FORTUNE

BY
CINDY KIRK

Cindy Kirk has loved to read for as long as she can remember. In first grade she received an award for reading one hundred books. As she grew up, summers were her favorite time of year. Nothing beat going to the library, then coming home and curling up in front of the window air conditioner with a good book. Often the novels she read would spur ideas, and she'd make up her own story (always with a happy ending). When she'd go to bed at night, instead of counting sheep she'd make up more stories in her head. Since selling her first story to Mills & Boon in 1999, Cindy has been forced to juggle her love of reading with her passion for creating stories of her own. . . but she doesn't mind. Writing for the Mills & Boon Cherish series is a dream come true. She only hopes you have as much fun reading her books as she has writing them!

Cindy invites you to visit her website, www.cindykirk.com.

To my longtime friend,
author Nancy Robards Thompson.
Here's to many, many more years of friendship!!

Chapter One

Standing on the sidewalk outside the Horseback Hollow Superette on a bright Friday morning, Gabriella Mendoza paused to read a text from her father, sent from his room in a rehabilitation center in Lubbock.

Bath@9. DON'T come b4 10.

Gabi sighed. Since it was barely eight-thirty, even if she chugged down the highway at the speed of a slug, she'd easily make the one-hour drive into the city before ten. This meant she needed to use this stop at the local convenience store to not only grab coffee, but kill time.

OK C U after 10, she texted back, then started toward the store known for carrying a little bit of everything. She was mentally calculating how much time she needed to waste when her phone pinged.

Gabi smiled. Though Orlando Mendoza had recently celebrated his sixtieth birthday, he texted with a fervor normally reserved for teenagers. She'd barely glanced at the incoming message when her forward progress came to a jarring halt.

"Whoa." The masculine voice held a hint of laughter. Large hands reached out to steady her when she stumbled.

Startled, Gabi jerked her head up and the unsteadiness returned full force. Even if his eyes hadn't been the color of the Texas sky, the blond-haired Adonis in worn Wranglers and a black Stetson would have caused any red-blooded woman's heart to race.

"Whoa," Gabi repeated.

He lifted his hands from her forearms, but the searing heat from his touch lingered. "Are you okay? I plowed right into you."

"Actually, I think it was me plowing into you." She flashed a quick, apologetic smile. "I'm one of the rare few who can't walk and read a text at the same time."

"Let's call it a draw." The cowboy offered up a lazy smile and rocked back on his heels. He made no move to step aside or walk away. It was as if he had all the time in the world to stand in the bright sunlight of this unseasonably warm day in late January and chat with a stranger.

And Gabi *was* a stranger, not only to him but to most of the two thousand residents living in this small North Texas town. Though she'd been living in her father's house in Horseback Hollow for the past couple weeks, she had yet to meet his neighbors. Since she'd arrived from her home in Miami, any free time had been spent at the hospital.

When she'd been notified the small plane her father had been flying had crashed, Gabi had hopped the first flight to Texas. With her mother dead and her brothers unable to make the trip for various reasons, she'd come alone.

Gabi hadn't minded the sacrifice. Her father had always been there for her. All she wanted was him to be independent once again. His transfer from the hospital to rehab yesterday had been a positive first step.

Hopefully with her father doing better, she'd have the opportunity to meet a few people in town. Like now, she could spend a few minutes flirting—er, becoming acquainted with—the handsome hunk who stood before her, without feeling she was neglecting her dad.

Unfortunately, before Gabi could formulate something smart and witty to say, his phone rang. The cowboy glanced at the screen, grimaced and answered.

"Have a fabulous day," she said softly, regretfully, wiggling her fingers goodbye.

He shot her a wink. Even as he listened intently, phone pressed to his ear, those clear blue eyes remained fixed on her. The scrutiny made her glad she'd taken a few extra minutes this morning to dab on some makeup and curl her hair instead of pulling it back like she'd been doing all week.

As Gabi entered the Superette, she almost called back that it had been nice to meet him. She stopped herself just in time.

They hadn't met, not really. They'd merely run into each other—literally—and exchanged a handful of words. She didn't even know his name. Of course, that didn't mean she hadn't liked what she'd seen, and it certainly didn't stop her from hoping he'd be there when she came out.

But, by the time she returned with a twenty-ounce cup of decaf in hand, he was gone. Heaving a sigh of regret, Gabi slid behind the wheel of her father's boat-of-a-Buick and turned toward the highway leading to Lubbock.

The car obediently settled into a smooth cruise, allowing her brain to shift to autopilot. She'd made this trip to see her father more times in the past few weeks than she could count.

When the landing gear on the plane he'd been flying had failed to engage, the experienced aviator had been forced to belly-land. Most of his injuries had been incurred when the plane broke apart on impact. She'd seen pictures of what was left of the Cessna.

What had the doctor said? *It was a miracle he'd survived.*

Gabi rolled up the window all the way, suddenly chilled to the bone. But she reminded herself that was the past.

Today was her father's first full day in the rehabilitation center and a cause for celebration.

By the time Gabi pulled into the parking lot of the facility, her mood was as sunny as the cloudless sky. She headed toward the front door of the facility with a bounce in her step.

Once inside, she quickly located the stairs. Seizing opportunities to exercise came so naturally Gabi never considered taking an elevator. She jogged up the steps two at a time, pleased her heart rate remained steady and her breath even.

Six years ago she hadn't been able to make it across even the smallest room without needing to sit down. Now her heart beat strong in a body as toned as an athlete's.

The walls lining the hallway leading toward her father's room were filled with pictures and inspiring stories of rehab center "alumni." With splashes of bright colors throughout and rooms with state-of-the-art equipment discreetly out of sight, the facility had a cheerful feel.

Doing her best to ignore the faint medicinal scent hanging in the air, Gabi stopped in front of room 325 and gently rapped her knuckles against the closed door.

"Come in," she heard her father say.

She paused. Did he realize it was her and not a nurse or therapist? Pushing the door open only a couple of inches, she paused. "It's Gabriella. Are you decent?"

Orlando Mendoza's deep, robust laugh was all the answer she needed. She pushed open the door and stepped inside.

Her father sat in a chair by the window, wearing a blue shirt with thin silver stripes and the navy pants she'd altered a couple days ago to accommodate his left leg cast. While the past few weeks had added extra streaks of silver to his salt-and-pepper hair, Orlando Mendoza remained a strikingly handsome man.

He lifted his right hand in greeting, drawing her attention to the cast that encased the arm. Seeing it brought back memories of the day in the intensive care waiting room when the doctor had sat down with her and detailed the injuries: fractured left leg and right arm, bruised kidneys, fractured rib, concussion.

But her father was tough. And determined. Perhaps it was the sight of him dressed in street clothes or the bright smile of greeting on his lips, but for the first time since the accident, Gabi truly believed he'd make it all the way back.

"Papi." She crossed the room, placing her coffee cup on a tray table before leaning down and wrapping her arms around him. "You look like yourself."

"As opposed to looking like someone else?" he asked with a teasing smile.

She laughed and pushed back to hold him at arm's length. If not for the arm and leg cast, Gabi could believe her father was simply enjoying a cup of coffee before heading to the Redmond Flight School where he worked. As a retired former air force pilot, flying had been his life for too many years to count.

When he'd gotten the opportunity two months ago to help run a flight school in Texas, he'd been as excited as a graduate landing his first job. While Gabi had been sad to see him leave Florida, she'd also been happy for him. The position was exactly what he'd been looking for since he'd retired from the air force.

And since the crime rate in the area of Miami where he lived had skyrocketed in recent years, she'd found comfort in the knowledge he was now in a small rural community.

"What are you thinking, *mija?*" her father probed, his tone gentle.

Gabi expelled a heavy sigh. "I thought you'd be safe in Horseback Hollow."

"He should have been."

Gabi turned toward the masculine voice to see her father's two bosses standing in the doorway. Sawyer Fortune had met her at the airport when she'd flown in from Miami after getting news of the accident. His new wife, Laurel, had remained by her father's side at the hospital.

In the difficult days that followed, they'd been her rock.

"Are you feeling up to company?" Laurel asked Orlando. She was a tall, pretty blonde with long hair pulled back in a ponytail. "If not, Sawyer and I can stop back later."

"You're not company." Orlando motioned them into the room and gestured to the small sitting area near his bed. "Please, sit."

After exchanging greetings and hugs, Gabi also took a seat and let her father direct the conversation. She could tell it made him feel good to have Sawyer and Laurel stop by on a workday to see him.

She sipped her coffee, offering a word now and then when appropriate. When the talk turned to sabotage, Gabi straightened in her seat. She fixed her gaze on Sawyer. "Are you saying someone deliberately messed with the landing gear?"

Sawyer raked a hand through his brown hair. Though it wasn't even noon, weariness clouded his eyes. He expelled a harsh breath. "We don't know for sure, not yet."

"Who would do such a thing?" Gabi's voice rose and broke. An accident was one thing, but for someone to deliberately set out to hurt her father… "He just moved here. He doesn't have enemies."

Laurel and Sawyer exchanged a glance.

Gabi's breath hitched. "Does he?"

"We don't think it's about him," Sawyer said finally. "The sheriff thinks someone may be out to get the Fortunes."

"*Your* family?" Gabi struggled to recall what she'd

heard about the Fortunes. *Wealthy* and *prominent* were the only words that came to mind. "Why?"

"Mija." The endearment slid off Orlando's lips as he reached over with his left hand and captured her fingers, giving them a squeeze. "The authorities are still investigating. All this is simply speculation."

The older man cast a sharp look in Sawyer's direction as if telling him there would be no more upsetting talk in front of his daughter.

Yet, it was Laurel, not Sawyer, who changed the subject. She shifted her attention to Gabi. "Now that you've had some time to settle in, what do you think of Horseback Hollow?"

"It's a nice town." Out of the corner of her eye Gabi saw her father nod approval. Even if she hadn't liked it here, she wouldn't have said otherwise. But she'd spoken the truth. Though she'd never considered herself a small-town girl, so far she was enjoying her stay. "I find it very peaceful."

Laurel smiled encouragingly. "Tell me what you've been doing to keep yourself busy."

"Well, I spend most of my days with Papi." Gabi slanted a glance and he smiled. "Since the weather has been unseasonably warm, I try to go for a run once I leave the hospital."

"To *try* isn't good enough. You mustn't neglect your exercise." Her father's voice brooked no argument. "It's essential."

Gabi bit back a sharp reply that would have been worthy of a brash fifteen-year-old rather than a mature woman of twenty-six. Instead she smiled. "I've gone for a run every day except the day I flew in."

"I always feel better when I exercise, too," Laurel agreed, a look of understanding in her eyes. "But I hope while you're here, you also take time to get acquainted with the people and the town."

The image of the man at the Superette flashed before Gabi. Yes, getting to know the cowboy would be a pleasure.

"I've gotten acquainted with you and your husband," Gabi said when she realized Laurel waited for an answer. "Now, when I return to Miami and Papi talks of Sawyer and Laurel, I'll know just who he means."

Sawyer inclined his head. "Are you planning on going back soon?"

"Not until my father is home and able to care for himself."

"You have a job," Orlando protested. "I won't put your position in jeopardy. Even the most understanding employer can lose patience when days turn into weeks."

"I took family medical leave," Gabi told her father for what felt like the zillionth time. "Staying isn't a problem."

"My daughter is a manager at Miami Trust." Pride filled Orlando's voice. "It's one of the largest banks in Florida."

"My boss was supportive of me coming." Gabi kept her tone soft and soothing. "You don't have to be concerned."

"I can't help but worry." Orlando lifted a shoulder in a shrug. "That's how I am."

It was true. Gabi remembered the lines that had seemed permanently etched between her father's brows when she'd gotten sick and needed surgery. Her mother's worry hadn't been as obvious, but Gabi knew they'd both spent many sleepless nights fearing for her life.

Impulsively Gabi leaned over and hugged her father. "That concern is one of the things I love about you."

Surprise flickered in his eyes. They'd had some battles in the past over what she'd termed his overprotectiveness, but once he'd moved to Texas, she discovered she rather missed having someone around who cared enough to worry.

Sawyer's phone trilled. He glanced down then rose to his feet with a look of regret. "I need to go."

"I appreciate you stopping by." Orlando's gaze shifted from Sawyer to Laurel. "Both of you."

"We want you back at the flight school." Laurel placed a hand on Orlando's shoulder, then bent and kissed his cheek. "It's not the same without you, O."

"Thanks for that." Orlando's cheeks turned a dusky pink before his tone turned brusque. "I'd walk you to the door but it took two nurses just to get me in the chair this morning."

Sawyer crossed the room to stand beside his employee. His eyes met the older man's dark brown eyes. "I promise you, if the plane *was* sabotaged, we'll get whoever was behind it."

"Thank you."

"Don't worry about your job," Sawyer told him. "It'll be there waiting for you. No matter how long you're off."

For a second, Gabi thought she saw the sheen of tears in her father's eyes, but when she looked again they were gone. She decided it must have simply been her imagination.

"I appreciate it" was all her father said.

Sawyer shifted those striking blue eyes in Gabi's direction. "I realize it's short notice but we're having a barbecue at the ranch tonight and—"

"We'd love to have you join us," his wife added with a bright smile. "I know you wanted to stay close while your father was in the hospital. Since he's now doing so well, I hope you'll consider coming this evening."

"Go," her father urged before Gabi could respond. "I'm planning on watching the ball game tonight."

"Sawyer's aunt and uncle as well as most of his cousins will be there." Laurel's tone turned persuasive. "They've lived in Horseback Hollow all their lives so if there's anything you want to know about the town or the area, they're the ones to ask."

Gabi couldn't imagine having too many questions about a town that was barely two blocks long.

"I can guarantee good food," Sawyer said when Gabi hesitated. "My aunt makes the best desserts, and she's promised to bring a couple of her specialties tonight."

"My Gabriella doesn't eat sweets." Orlando spoke before Gabi could respond. "It's not good for her. She—"

Gabi shot him a warning glance, and whatever else he'd been about to say died on his lips. Had she really missed his constant worry?

"Like everyone," Gabi said easily, "my goal is to eat healthy. That's not to say I don't enjoy a bite or two of something sweet occasionally."

Her father opened his mouth then shut it when she fixed her gaze on him.

"Please say you'll come." Laurel's eyes sparkled in her pretty face. "If only for a bite or two of Jeanne Marie's spectacular desserts."

Gabi considered. An honest-to-goodness Texas barbecue could be fun. God knew she was tired of hospital food. But this was her father's first night in rehab. How could she enjoy herself knowing he'd be sitting alone in his room watching a ball game by himself?

"There'll be lots of handsome men there." Laurel shot her a little wink.

As handsome as the man outside the coffee shop? Gabi wanted to ask. His eyes had been as blue as Sawyer's and, like her father's boss, the cowboy had a casual confidence she found appealing.

"Tonight at seven, O?" a man in a wheelchair called from the doorway.

"I'll meet you in the lounge," her father called back.

Gabi lifted a brow.

"The ball game," Orlando informed her. "Lloyd and I made plans to watch it together when we were sweating to the oldies in physical therapy this morning."

Gabi turned to find Laurel staring at her with an arched brow.

"Tell me when and where," Gabi told her. "I'll be there."

Chapter Two

As she turned off onto the lane leading to Sawyer and Laurel Fortune's ranch, excitement quivered in Gabi's belly. Her first Texas barbecue at a real ranch. She glanced down at her skirt and sweater, hoping she wouldn't find herself over- or underdressed.

Before Laurel left the rehabilitation center today, she'd assured her the barbecue would be casual. But Gabi had painfully discovered on several occasions that *casual* meant different things to different people.

Since her Florida attire was too lightweight for even a warmer-than-normal North Texas winter, she'd stopped in nearby Vicker's Corners on the way back from Lubbock. The small town, just down the road from Horseback Hollow, had a cute little downtown area filled with quaint shops. At a darling boutique that rivaled those in Miami for selection and price, Gabi picked up the skirt, sweater, tights and boots she wore tonight.

The shawl collar of her cherry-red sweater showed very little skin, which meant there was no possibility of her scar showing. She felt like a coward for caring what people thought, but since the horrible pool party incident several months back, she now kept it fully covered.

Gabi drove slowly down the gravel lane flanked by white fence and miles of pastureland. The fact that she hadn't yet spotted a single cow didn't surprise her. Sawyer had mentioned their ranch was basically a lot of land with a few horses. Laurel had laughingly added that bovines weren't their thing.

She wheeled the Buick between two dusty pickups and sat in the car for several seconds. Through one of the brightly lit windows, she caught a glimpse of Laurel, chatting with a guest, a glass of wine in her hand.

She liked Laurel. Liked her a lot. And Sawyer, as well.

Seeing how much her father mattered to them warmed her heart. Even knowing they shared Papi's passion for flying was a comfort.

After stepping from the large blue car, Gabi cinched the belt of the coat she'd picked up on her shopping trip today tightly around her. She wasn't sure what she was going to do with the pretty tweed once she returned home, but for tonight, with the wind holding a sharp bite, she was glad she had it.

Experiencing a sudden longing for palm trees and eighty-degree weather, Gabi sprinted to the porch and up the steps. She hunched her shoulders against the wind and punched the doorbell. She immediately shoved her hands into her pockets, regretting she hadn't thought to pick up a pair of gloves on her impromptu shopping trip.

Thankfully, the door opened before the chimes made it through a single stanza. Laurel stood in the doorway with her husband at her side, broad welcoming smiles on their lips. Gabi breathed a sigh of relief when she saw Sawyer wore jeans and a chambray shirt. Laurel's skirt and sweater mirrored Gabi's own attire.

"Come in," Sawyer urged, ushering her into the warmth. "It's freezing out there."

"I'm glad you made it." Her hostess took both of Gabi's hands and gave them a squeeze.

"Considering the weather, I wasn't sure you'd go through with the barbecue." Gabi resisted the urge to shiver. "I swear the temperature dropped twenty degrees in the past hour."

"We were forced to make a few adjustments." Laurel waited while Gabi handed her coat to a young woman dressed in black pants, white shirt and fire-engine-red cowboy boots. Then she looped her arm through Gabi's and ushered her farther into the house. "The barbecue is now indoors, centered around a crackling fire."

Happy to hear she wouldn't have to brave the wind and cold, Gabi took a moment to survey the interior of the large—and comfortably warm—house as they walked.

"You have a beautiful home." Gabi admired the open-beamed ceilings and dark shiny wood floors. Found the gilt Regency mirror above a Chippendale sideboard backed by timbered walls to be an appealing contrast.

"Thank you." Sawyer slipped an arm around his wife's waist. "We haven't lived here all that long, but it feels like home."

The words had barely left his lips when door chimes sounded. Laurel turned, but Sawyer gave her hand a squeeze. "Take care of Gabi. Introduce her around. I'll get the door."

"Don't worry about me—" Gabi began.

"It's my pleasure." Laurel sounded sincere. "We want you to have a good time this evening. You and your father are special to us."

Gabi let her gaze linger on the pretty, self-assured woman who'd been such a good friend to Papi. "I appreciate all you've done for him."

"Orlando is a great guy," Sawyer said, returning from the door.

"He's part of our family now," Laurel added.

"The Fortunes are a big family," Sawyer said. "But there's always room for one more good man."

Gabi blinked back unexpected tears. This connection

was what she hoped her father would find when he'd moved so far from family. She swallowed against the lump in her throat and glanced around the room. "Are there a lot of Fortunes here?"

"My aunt and uncle and their children—my cousins—are with us this evening," Sawyer responded, before he turned to respond to a young boy's tug on his sleeve.

A big family. Children. Gabi had once thought that would be part of her future. Until the doctor had sat her down and laid out the risks....

"Most of the guests are back here." Laurel led her to the edge of a great room.

The line of windows flanking the back of the home gave an open, airy feel to a room that was even more spacious than the one they'd passed. A buffet table topped with a red-and-white-checkered cloth along one wall drew her eye.

Mason jars tied with red bandannas sporting yellow daisies were strategically placed between platters of barbecue pork, smoked ham and Texas beef brisket. From where she stood, Gabi could see bowls of baked beans, black-eyed peas and Brunswick stew.

On the hearth of a massive stone fireplace, galvanized washtubs filled with ice, bottles of beer and cans of soda beckoned.

At the moment Gabi couldn't decide if she was more interested in eating, drinking or socializing. The food looked terrific, but the laughter and chatter filling the air called to her. As she swept the room with her gaze Gabi noted all ages were represented from a baby held in the arms of a pretty young woman with long, tousled blond hair to a man and woman who appeared to be in their sixties. She wondered if they were Sawyer's aunt and uncle.

Despite considering herself a fairly social creature, Gabi liked having Laurel at her side. The sight of so many loud and boisterous individuals in one room was a bit over-whelming.

A burst of laughter sounded by a bar set up in an alcove had Gabi turning toward the sound. Her breath caught in her throat.

It was him. Her handsome cowboy from the Superette.

He might be standing with his back partially to her, but she'd recognize the disheveled dark blond hair and mus-cular build anywhere. Even dressed simply in jeans and a long-sleeved Henley, he looked every bit as yummy as he had that morning.

As her gaze lingered, the air began to sizzle. As if slapped alongside the head by a ball of charged mole-cules, the cowboy broke off what he was saying and shifted his stance.

When his eyes met hers, everything in Gabi went weak. She barely heard what Laurel said. Something about in-troducing her around?

With great effort she pulled her attention away from those mesmerizing eyes. "I'd like that."

Would Laurel introduce her to *him?* If not, from the gleam of interest she'd seen in his eyes, she knew her mys-tery man would make sure their paths crossed this evening.

Their first stop was in front of an attractive older woman with pale blue eyes and long silver hair fastened in a low bun. Her turquoise jewelry accentuated the Southwestern flavor of the simple flowing dress she wore. Despite the fact she wore flats and Gabi's boots had three-inch heels, the woman was still several inches taller than her five-two.

The look in her eyes was kind, her smile warm, and Gabi liked her instantly.

"This is Sawyer's aunt, Jeanne Marie Fortune Jones," Laurel was saying, "and her husband, Deke."

Gabi widened her smile to include the rugged man with a thatch of thick gray hair.

As Laurel introduced her to the older couple, mentioning her connection to Orlando, the woman took her hand and pulled Gabi close.

"I'm so sorry about your father." Jeanne Marie's low soothing voice was a thick balm on Gabi's tattered spirit.

The solace she'd found in the woman's arms made Gabi realize just how much she missed her mother. Like Jeanne Marie, Luz Mendoza had been a demonstrative, affectionate woman who dispensed hugs freely and often.

"It's not right."

Gabi turned to Deke, surprised at the anger in his voice.

His eyes flashed. "Sabotage doesn't happen in this community."

"They don't know if it was sabotage. My father says the NTSB is still investigating." Gabi repeated what Orlando had told her. "It may have just been an unfortunate accident."

"More likely someone who doesn't like the Fortunes," Deke said loudly.

"Now you just hush." Jeanne Marie put a hand on her husband's arm. Her tone might be light but her eyes were steady and firm.

"Laurel mentioned your children are here tonight." Gabi spoke, eager to change the subject and ease the sudden tension in the air. "How many do you have?"

"Seven." A pretty young woman with a spray of freckles across her nose and tousled blond hair, who Gabi had noticed earlier, strolled up and answered for Jeanne Marie, then extended her hand.

"I'm number six, aka Stacey Fortune Jones." She gestured to the young woman next to her, so similar in appearance Gabi knew they must be sisters. "This is Delaney, the baby of the family."

Gabi introduced herself as Laurel stepped away to consult with the caterers and Jeanne Marie and Deke were pulled away by another couple.

"Stacey." Gabi tilted her head. "Are you by any chance the Stacey who administered first aid to my father after his accident?"

The woman nodded. "I stayed with him, did what I could until the rescue squad arrived."

Her father had called the nurse an angel sent from above. Gabi grasped Stacey's hands and emotion surged, clogging her throat. "From the bottom of my heart, thank you. We lost my mother a couple years ago. I—I don't know what I'd have done if I'd lost him, too."

Gabi's voice broke. She paused, took a steadying breath.

Stacey's eyes, as blue as her mother's, filled with understanding. "I was happy to help."

"Since my mother died it's just been me and my dad. My brothers aren't around much."

"Brothers?" Light danced in Delaney's pretty eyes. She stepped forward like a hound catching a scent. "How many do you have?"

"Four." Gabi counted them off on her fingers. "Matteo, Cisco, Alejandro and Joaquin."

"Older? Younger?" Delaney pressed.

"All older."

"We've got you beat." Delaney glanced at her sister. "We have *five* older brothers. Then our parents' luck changed."

"I broke the curse," Stacey said modestly.

"I arrived a year after Stace." Delaney flashed a smile. "They saved the best for last."

Gabi chuckled. "I always wanted a sister. Brothers can be nice but—"

"They can be a real pain," Stacey and Delaney said at the same time then laughed.

"Mine used to do all sorts of horrible things." Gabi

shuddered, remembering. "Matteo once dropped a frog down my shirt. And Joaquin put a snake in my bed."

"If you think that's bad—" Delaney went on to share some of the trials she'd endured at her brothers' hands with Stacey chiming in with another long-ago incident her sister had forgotten.

"The strange thing is, now that they're grown and gone, I miss them," Gabi said, feeling a bit melancholy.

"We don't have a chance to miss ours." Delaney expelled a long sigh. "They're all still around."

Across the room a baby's voice shrieked with the gurgling laughter of the very young.

Gabi pulled her brows together and fixed her gaze on Stacey. "Didn't I see you holding a baby earlier?"

Stacey smiled. "That's my little girl, Piper. Colton has her now."

"Her fiancé." Delaney emphasized the word, gesturing to where a slim man with brown eyes and brown hair stood, holding the baby and talking to Gabi's mystery man. "Isn't he handsome?"

Gabi pulled her gaze from the cowboy she'd begun to think of as hers to Stacey's fiancé. "He is a cutie."

"I think so." The older sister's red lips curved. "But then, I'm partial."

"Colton isn't just good-looking, he's super nice." Delaney shot her sister a warm smile of approval.

"Who's he speaking with?" Gabi asked in what she hoped was a casual tone.

"That's Jude." Delaney rolled her eyes. "One of our crosses to bear."

Gabi inclined her head.

"A brother," Stacey clarified. "Number three of our seven. I'll introduce you."

Before Gabi could respond, Stacey called out, "Colton. Jude. Over here."

The two men turned together. Gabi swore she saw a light flare in Jude's eyes. *Jude.* She rolled the name around on her tongue, liking the feel of it.

He crossed the room with a rolling, confident gait and a lazy smile on his lips.

"Hey, pretty lady," Jude said immediately upon reaching her side. "Can a cowboy buy you a drink?"

Delaney and Stacey looked at each other and burst into laughter.

"With lines like that, no wonder you're not dating anyone," Stacey teased.

Delaney made a gagging noise, worthy of any younger sister.

Jude ignored them both, keeping his eyes firmly focused on Gabi.

"I wouldn't mind a ginger ale," she told him.

"Be right back," he said with a wink.

"He's got you in his crosshairs." Delaney spoke in a theatrical whisper.

"Run," Stacey urged, her eyes dancing, "while you still have a chance."

Colton shook his head. "Women."

"Hey!" Stacey gave her fiancé a playful punch. "You've got two women in your life now, remember. Me and Piper?"

He brushed his lips across her cheek. "And I'm extremely glad of it."

Jude returned with a beer in one hand for himself and a ginger ale in the other for Gabi.

"Thank you." Gabi took the glass, her hand brushing his. Electricity traveled up her arm at the contact. But if he'd experienced a similar jolt, it didn't show.

Once again, Gabi suffered through introductions and expressions of sympathy for her father.

"I wouldn't have left him in the rehab center alone,"

Gabi explained, "but he's watching the ball game with another patient."

"I bet it makes him feel good to know you're out enjoying yourself." Colton looped an arm around his fiancée's shoulder when she moved to his side.

"I hope so," Gabi said, then made a fuss over Piper, rather than focusing on Jude, which is what she wanted to do. Though she was definitely in the mood for a little fun flirting, there was no need to be obvious.

She'd barely lifted Piper from Colton's arms when several more handsome cowboys stopped over. None of them made her pulse skip a beat like number three of seven but Galen, Liam, Toby and Christopher Fortune Jones were all fine specimens.

When Piper began to fuss, Gabi handed the baby to Stacey. Without missing a beat, Jude took Gabi's arm and announced he was giving her a grand tour of the buffet.

Before she knew what was happening, she was halfway across the room with the charming cowboy.

"A grand tour of the buffet?" Gabi slanted a playful glance in his direction. "Seriously?"

"Improv isn't my strength." Jude looked faintly embarrassed. "But sometimes there's only so much family a man can take. I'd like us to get better acquainted. We can't do that with everyone listening to our every word."

"Or your sister making gagging noises?"

He laughed. "That can be a deterrent."

"It's strange."

"What is?"

"Running into you this morning." She kept her tone light. "Now here."

"Fate," he said.

"Perhaps." She traced a finger around the rim of her glass and watched his eyes darken.

Without a word, he took her elbow, maneuvered her

around several older couples sharing appetizers and conversation.

By the time he spoke again, the darkness in his eyes had lifted. "How is your father?"

"Much better," she told him. "Thank you for asking."

"It was a sacrifice for you to come all the way to Texas to be with him."

It was a statement, not a question.

"Nothing could have kept me away."

"As it should be" was all he said.

The conversation shifted to her life in Miami. Gabi kept it brief when telling him about her job at the bank. Though she enjoyed her work, she'd learned real estate lending wasn't all that interesting to those outside of the industry. She sipped her ginger ale. "What is it you do, Jude?"

"I have a ranch not far from here." Jude took a pull from his beer. "I do whatever needs to be done."

Though he shrugged, the pride in his voice told her he was one of the lucky ones who'd found his passion.

She'd opened her mouth to ask about his duties when one of his brothers—Christopher?—walked by and deliberately pushed Jude against her.

Jude's arm shot out, slipping around her, steadying them both.

For a second Gabi thought she heard Christopher laugh, but then the outside world disappeared as she gazed into Jude's eyes.

"Sorry 'bout that," he said, his gaze never leaving hers.

She swallowed and found her voice. "I'm not."

He grinned. "Hell, I'm not, either."

Yet she noticed he took a step back.

Gabi tried to collect her rioting thoughts. *Say something,* she told herself, *get the conversation back on safe ground.* She found herself blurting out the first thing that came to mind. "You grew up in Horseback Hollow?"

"I did." A twinkle filled his eyes, as if he could read her mind and found her unsteadiness amusing.

"Do you plan to stay?" Her tone held a hint of coolness. Gabriella Mendoza drooled over no man, at least not so he could notice.

"I like it here." He took a barely perceptible step forward. "Lubbock is close and with the recent growth in Vicker's Corners, there's enough to do."

"I guess I'll have to take your word. I haven't had the chance to do much exploring."

"I'd be happy to show you around."

She gave a little laugh, took another sip of her drink. "I wasn't hinting for a tour guide."

"I know." His eyes met hers and then slid downward to linger on her mouth. "But since I'm already taking you on a tour of the buffet, why stop there? Let's take it a step further."

Gabi arched a brow, touched the tip of her tongue to her lips and watched his eyes change. "A step further?"

"Have dinner with me tomorrow night." Although his eyes burned, his smile was easy. "I'll introduce you to Horseback Hollow's culinary delights."

"I appreciate the offer." Gabi hesitated, sorely tempted. While it would be fun to spend time with Jude, the reason she was in Texas was to be with her father.

For a second the cowboy looked nonplussed. She guessed he wasn't used to being turned down. Not that she'd said no. She just hadn't said yes.

"You have to eat." His tone turned persuasive. "Surely you can spare an hour to become better acquainted with our town?"

With me.

Though he didn't say the words, Gabi knew what he was asking. She had to admit the short time she'd spent with Jude had only whet her appetite for more.

It wasn't as if she had to spend every waking second at her father's bedside, Gabi reminded herself. Taking a bit of time to get better acquainted with the town where her father lived *might* be a good idea.

But when she smiled and gave Jude Fortune Jones her answer, it wasn't getting acquainted with the town on her mind, it was getting better acquainted with her Texas cowboy.

Chapter Three

"**I**'m going to marry her," Jude told Liam, pointing across the room with his bottle of Dos Equis. "She's The One."

His older brother glanced out over the crowd, settling on...Delaney. "Uh, you're marrying our sister?"

"Not her." Jude spoke through gritted teeth. "The one next to her."

"The pretty Latina." Interest filled Liam's eyes. "She's a looker, all right. I wouldn't mind getting her between the sheets—"

Jude punched his brother in the shoulder. Hard. "Watch it. That's my future wife you're talking about."

Liam snorted. "Heard that one before."

"Heard what?" Sawyer sauntered up and handed Liam a beer.

"Jude says he's found The One." Liam laughed. "More like The One This Week."

Sawyer looked perplexed, but Jude saw no need to enlighten the cousin he'd only recently met. By the gleam in Liam's eyes, his brother didn't feel the same constraints.

"My brother here—" Liam gestured with his head toward Jude "—falls in love with every pretty filly that crosses his path. And just as quickly out of love. A guy could get whiplash watching him."

Obviously intrigued, Sawyer cocked his head. "Who is it this time?"

"Gabriella Mendoza." Jude let the name roll off his tongue. The name was as pretty as the woman. "I'm going to marry her."

"Ah, didn't the two of you just meet tonight?" Sawyer asked cautiously.

"Actually we ran into each other at the Superette this morning." Jude smiled, recalling how pretty she'd looked with the sun glinting off her walnut-colored hair. "Love at first sight."

"It's a little faster than normal," Liam informed Sawyer as if Jude wasn't standing right there. "I'm figuring it's the hearts and flowers in the air, what with Stacey getting engaged and Valentine's Day drawing near."

"Scoff all you want," Jude told his brother. "She's The One."

"She's a nice woman," Sawyer said cautiously. "And very attractive."

"I'm taking her to dinner tomorrow."

Surprise flicked across Sawyer's face. "You move fast."

"I figure why waste time?" Jude took a long pull of beer. "When you know what you want and you find it… you go after it."

Gabi spent most of the next morning at the rehabilitation hospital, observing her father's therapy sessions. With an arm broken on one side and a leg broken on the other, it was difficult for Orlando Mendoza to even get up from the chair much less manage what the nurses called his ADLs—activities of daily living.

But her dad was tough. A man didn't survive all those years as an air force pilot and raise five kids without survival instincts. Gabi had lunch with him in the dining room down the hall from his room. Apparently the nurses believed in keeping the patients out of their rooms as much as possible.

"This is tasty." Gabi glanced down at the grilled chicken breast, brown rice and asparagus spears.

"It's exactly what you should be eating." Orlando spoke in the fatherly tone he took on when he was poised to lecture. "I hope you didn't have alcohol last night."

Gabi thought of the blended margaritas, the fine wine, even the bottles of Dos Equis. She shook her head. "You know I don't drink."

"You had a cup of coffee with you when you came yesterday."

"It was decaffeinated." Gabi held on to her growing frustration with both hands, reminding herself that her dad had a lot of time to worry. Even when he'd been busy, worrying about her and her health had been his favorite pastime.

"Oh," he said. "Good."

"I know how to take care of myself, Papi." She kept her tone gentle as she brought her hand to her chest. "This heart was a precious gift. I don't take it for granted."

"You were so sick." Her father's dark eyes took on a distant look. "Your mamma and I thought we were going to lose you. Barely more than a baby and we thought we would lose you."

Those dark days had occurred when Gabi was nineteen, hardly a baby by anyone's standards, unless by overprotective parents.

"You always pushed yourself too hard." He shook his head. "I told you many times to slow down but you wouldn't listen."

"It was a *virus*. From the stomach flu," Gabi reminded him. "It didn't have a thing to do with my college schedule or my extracurricular activities."

The virus had attacked her heart. She thought she was on the road to recovery after a particularly bad few days of a GI bug that was making its way across campus until she became short of breath. The next day she landed in the ICU.

She almost died. That's what her parents told her. The doctors said her heart was so badly damaged a transplant was her only hope. Because of her grave physical condition she'd moved to the top of the transplant list.

Miraculously a heart had come her way. Now a heart that had once beat in another young person's chest pumped in hers. She meant it when she told her father she didn't take it for granted. Not for one second. When her cardiologist had told her no drinking, smoking or caffeine, she'd listened.

She knew other transplant patients who rebelled against the restrictions, but Gabi felt best when she ate right, exercised and followed doctor's orders. Still, her parents worried. Now that it was just her father, he worried double.

"I love you, *mija.*"

The emotion so evident in his voice, in his eyes, melted away the annoyance. "Ditto. Now, if you're not going to eat that green Jell-O, hand it over."

Her father laughed and pushed the gelatin in front of her. "Hopefully they'll have red this evening. That's my favorite. And yours, if I remember correctly."

Gabi paused, a forkful of chicken hovering just outside her mouth. "About tonight. I plan to stay most of the day, but I won't be eating dinner with you."

Her father lowered his glass of milk.

"I'm going to check out The Horseback Hollow Grill this evening," she told him.

"I've eaten at The Grill," Orlando said slowly.

"What's it like?" Gabi kept her tone light and offhand.

"Like King's," he said, referring to a hamburger and hot dog place not far from his home in Miami. "Their specialty is grilled cheese sandwiches. I like them with jalapenos."

"Guess what I'm wearing will be good enough." Gabi

glanced down at her jeans and sweater. As her father continued to stare, she forced a chuckle. "I'm excited about the prospect of becoming better acquainted with Horseback Hollow. That way, when I go back to Miami and you talk about different places, I can visualize them."

The tight set to her father's shoulders eased. "That makes sense. But eating alone can't be fun for you."

"Don't tell me you haven't eaten alone since moving here?"

"I have," he grudgingly admitted. "Perhaps Laurel could—"

"Laurel is busy with her new husband and the flight school." Gabi spoke quickly before her father could pull out his phone and call his boss. She lowered her fork to the plate. "Besides, I'm not going alone. Jude Fortune Jones, Sawyer's cousin, generously offered to show me around town."

For several long seconds, accompanied by the thumping of her heart, Orlando said nothing. He chewed, swallowed then took another sip of milk. "I've met Jude."

Gabi lifted a brow. "And?"

"He appears to be very popular with the ladies."

The sharp stab of jealousy that struck Gabi took her by surprise. But she merely smiled. "Good. Then he should be an excellent dinner companion."

"I don't want you getting involved with him."

Her father's vehemence surprised Gabi. "Why? Is there something you haven't told me?"

"You have a job in Miami. A good one."

"That's true," Gabi agreed. "And once you're better, I'll be returning to that good job. In the meantime, I'd like to do a little exploring. With someone local."

Gabi finished her lunch and stayed for several more hours, watching her father work with the physical therapist on transferring from the bed to the chair. She listened as the occupational therapist showed him ways to use his left hand to do everything from getting toothpaste on his toothbrush to slipping on a shirt.

By the time the OT left, her father's eyes were drooping and his primary nurse suggested a nap.

"I'll be back after dinner." Gabi brushed a kiss across his leathery cheek and felt a surge of love.

"Lloyd and I have a date to play poker," he told her. "There's no need to drive back tonight. Enjoy your evening."

"Are you sure?"

"You spent all day here," he said. "Besides, I need to win some money off Lloyd, and I can't do that with someone breathing over my shoulder."

Gabi smiled. "Okay, then."

"Don't have the grilled cheese." This time the fatherly tone brooked no argument. "Too much fat in it."

Gabi simply smiled, gave a little wave and left him to his nap.

The knock on the front door of her father's small home sounded at precisely 6:00 p.m.

Gabi smiled. Apparently, the man was not only pretty to look at, but punctual, as well. *Popular with the ladies.* Some of her pleasure dimmed before she shoved the thought aside.

It didn't matter to her if Jude dated a different woman every night. This was simply dinner and conversation. She didn't expect more. Didn't want more.

When the knock sounded again, she sauntered across the room. After glancing through the peephole, she pulled the door open.

"I appreciate a man who's on time." With a welcoming smile she waved him inside.

Dressed simply in jeans, chambray shirt and a battered

leather jacket, he whipped off his Stetson when he stepped through the doorway then thrust out one hand. "These are for you."

"Thank you." She glanced down at the bouquet he offered. Startled surprise quickly gave way to sweet pleasure. "Daisies are one of my favorite flowers. Have a seat. I want to put them in water before we leave."

She took the flowers into the small kitchen at the back of the house. Instead of sitting in the living room as she'd directed, he followed her.

"Nice place."

Gabi tried to see it through his eyes. White painted cupboards, grey Formica countertops, speckled linoleum flooring. Perfect, if a person was into retro decor. "My father feels at home here," she said. "Our home in Miami was bigger, but since it's just him, he doesn't need much space."

"The fact it's not large and all on one level should make it easier for him when he comes home."

"Good point." She rummaged through the cupboards, finally pulling out a red vase. "This will be perfect."

Her mother had collected red glass, and this little cylindrical vase had been a favorite. She quickly filled it with water then took a second to arrange the flowers.

"You have a knack," Jude commented from where he stood with his back resting against the doorjamb. "My mother does, too. If it were me, I'd stuff them into a vase and call it good."

Gabi took a step back and gazed in satisfaction at the arrangement. "They're too pretty to treat in that manner."

"They're pretty." Jude's husky voice did strange things to her insides. "But not as pretty as you."

She smiled. Oh, yes, he was a smooth one.

"Do I need a coat?" she asked, looking at his leather jacket.

"It's in the forties, so I say definitely." He paused. "Do you have one?"

"I didn't," she told him. "There was no need in Miami. But I went shopping recently in Vicker's Corners and picked one up."

In fact, that's where she'd purchased the crimson sweater and black pants she wore now. From all signs, the small town in between Horseback Hollow and Lubbock was experiencing a growth spurt. She'd seen signs advertising new condominiums and touting luxury estates for sale.

"What'd you think of VC?" he asked as they moved to the living room, where she retrieved her coat from the postage-stamp-size closet.

"I liked it." She thought of the cute little business district with all the eclectic shops lining the main street. "But Horseback Hollow is nice, too."

"If I had to compare the two—" with well-practiced ease, Jude took the coat from her hands and held it up "—I'd say Horseback Hollow is the Jones family while Vicker's Corners is more like their gentrified relatives."

"Would those gentrified relatives be the Fortunes?" Gabi tried to ignore the brush of his knuckles against the side of her neck as he helped her slip on the coat.

"Bingo."

"Your mother recently found out she was related to the Fortunes, isn't that right?" Gabi tried to remember what her father had said, but the comment had been something he'd tossed out in passing and she hadn't given it much thought.

"That's right." He waited for her to pick up her purse then opened the front door and stepped to the side.

Good-looking. Manners. A powerful combination.

As she passed him, Gabi caught a faint whiff of his cologne. First he brought her flowers, now he wore the scent that had tantalized and enticed her last night. Jude Fortune would be a difficult man to resist.

Which she would, but that didn't mean she couldn't enjoy his company and the way he smelled. "You added Fortune to your name."

"My mother asked." Jude lifted one shoulder in a shrug. "She doesn't ask for much."

Gabi walked by his side to the truck parked in the driveway and tilted her head, thinking of her father. "What did your dad think? Mine is so proud of the Mendoza name that I can't imagine him being happy if any of my brothers decided to make a change."

Jude waited to answer until she stepped inside the truck. "Like most of us, he finds it difficult to deny her anything."

As he rounded the front of the massive vehicle, then got behind the wheel, Gabi thought of her mother. Her dad had loved his wife totally, completely. If there had been something important her mother had asked of him, he'd have gone along.

Jude slanted a sideways look. "Red is definitely your color."

A ripple of pleasure passed over Gabi. "I like your style, Jude."

He grinned and backed the truck out of the driveway. "Tell me about Gabriella."

On the short drive to the café, Gabi filled him in. She talked about her brothers and what it was like growing up as the youngest and the only girl. When he pressed for more, she told him she'd had a love for the business world since she'd opened her first lemonade stand at age five and made ten dollars.

"It didn't sink in until years later that my only customers had been relatives and close neighbors." Gabi chuckled. "I thought it was this great spiel I had going that drew them in."

"You enjoy your job."

"I do. Though the banking industry has taken some hits, the one I work for has done well." Gabi rolled her window partially down and let the fresh air waft into the cab of the truck. "It smells so fresh here."

"I bet this has been a bit of culture shock for you."

"Since I haven't seen a bodega or a palm tree in weeks, I'd say that's an accurate statement." Gabi wondered how she could feel so relaxed around a man she'd just met. She'd been on plenty of first dates, and they were usually awkward, tense affairs. "Still, something about this place feels like home. I had difficulty understanding when my father told me how much he liked it here. Now it makes sense."

Jude wheeled the truck into an angled parking spot and cut the engine. "I hope dinner tonight only solidifies that impression."

Seconds later, Gabi stood in the doorway of The Horseback Hollow Grill, affectionately called The Grill by locals, and felt the first twinge of unease. Although clean, the tiled flooring had more than a few cracks. Artificial flowers in hammered coffee pots sat on tables. The tables reminded Gabi of the type you'd see in old-time diners, rounded edges encased in silver metal.

Jude inhaled deeply. "It always smells good in here."

Gabi could almost see onion rings swimming in a grease pool and hamburgers being flipped on the grill. Her head may have told her to run to the nearest deli for a turkey sandwich on whole wheat—hold the mayo—but her stomach had other ideas. It growled. Loudly.

Jude grinned. "Someone is ready to eat."

"I may be a little hungry" was all Gabi said as the hostess directed them to a booth by the front window.

"I can vouch for the burgers." Jude waited until she'd slid into the booth before taking a seat opposite her. "Half pound of pure Angus. My sisters are especially fond of the grilled cheese sandwich, which is a specialty."

Because of her heart, Gabi limited the amount of red meat she consumed as well as avoiding fried foods. She could already see there wasn't much on the menu that would get a cardiologist's seal of approval. Tonight she'd simply have to wing it.

Jude kept the conversation light and entertaining until the pretty blonde waitress arrived to take their orders. He seemed oblivious to the young woman's attempts to flirt. Fixing his eyes on Gabi's, he smiled. "Have you decided?"

"I'll have the hamburger." Gabi shifted her gaze to the blonde. "Well-done, please. May I substitute a salad for the fries?"

When the woman nodded, Gabi smiled. "Vinegar and oil for the dressing, on the side."

Jude ordered the hamburger and fries. When the waitress left, he told Gabi, "You can have some of my fries. They're the best."

"I might take you up on that offer," she said, relieved to have made it through the ordering without a lot of explanation. Though she wasn't ashamed of having had the transplant, she'd noticed that people often treated her differently once they knew. "I told you everything about me on the drive over. Now it's your turn to dish."

"I hardly think you told me everything," he said, "in a five-minute drive."

Though his tone was teasing, Gabi froze. She hadn't thought her father had mentioned the transplant to anyone, but she didn't know that for sure. "What did I leave out?"

"You didn't say anything about a man in your life." He took the iced tea the waitress gave him while Gabi slipped a straw into her ice water.

"That's because there is no man in my life," Gabi said honestly.

"I find that difficult to believe."

"It's true." Gabi thought back to Tony, the IT manager from the bank, and the horrified look on his face when he'd seen her scar. She shrugged. "Work takes most of my time."

"Their loss is my gain." Jude reached across the table and took her hand, bringing it to his lips. The feel of his mouth against her skin brought a rush of desire as unexpected as it was pleasant.

Gabi wasn't a neophyte, though she was hardly experienced, either. During her twenty-six years she'd only had two lovers: her high school boyfriend on prom night and a fellow business student in college.

The prom night had been a disaster. A car was not the place for lovemaking.

The relationship with her college boyfriend had taken place over most of her freshman year. He'd been fairly experienced, but looking back, Gabi could see now that he'd been more concerned with his own pleasure than with hers. Still, she'd enjoyed their time together and had believed he cared about her.

Then she'd gotten sick. He'd come a couple of times to the hospital, but by the time she was feeling better, he was out of her life.

"Tell me about Jude." Gabi fought to keep her voice steady, no easy task since her body had begun to vibrate.

"Not much to tell." He lowered her hand to the table and casually laced his fingers through hers. "I got my BA from Tech and I've worked on the ranch since I was old enough to hop on a horse."

"Have you ever thought of moving away? Trying something new?"

His blue eyes grew thoughtful. "A few times. But like my daddy, I love what I do. I like the variety and being my own boss. Horseback Hollow might be small, but it's a cohesive community and Lubbock is just down the road. Vicker's Corners is even closer."

"Sounds like we've both chosen the right path…for us." He continued to hold her hand, and the feel of his warm skin against hers sent her thoughts careening down a road she had no intention of traveling. Gabi was relieved when the waitress appeared with a mountain of food and he sat back.

"Oh, my." She gazed at a burger as big as her plate and a salad big enough for three to share.

Jude grinned. "I told you the food here is the best."

Gabi carefully considered for a moment then removed the hamburger from the sesame bun.

"Wimp." Jude stopped, looked stricken. "Sorry."

"No worries." Waving a dismissive hand, Gabi stole one of his fries. "I simply prefer to enjoy the meat."

In the end, she ate half of her burger and a third of the salad and sat back, satisfied.

"They have great sundaes here." Jude spoke in a persuasive tone when the waitress had cleared their plates.

Though she wouldn't mind having a spoonful, she doubted her stomach could handle even one more bite. "I'm so full you're going to have to roll me out of here as it is. But, if you'd like dessert, go ahead."

"I've had enough to eat," he said. "But I wouldn't mind taking a walk. Are those boots you're wearing—"

"They're very comfortable." Gabi brightened at the realization Jude didn't seem in any hurry to have the evening end. "I'd love some fresh air."

Gabi pulled out her wallet to pay her share of the tab, but Jude had already handed the waitress several bills and told the blonde to keep the change.

"I can pay for my own."

"You could." He slid from the booth. "But tonight is my treat."

Gabi slipped out from her side, and when she stood, he was right there, holding out the coat that she'd hung on a metal hook at the edge of the booth.

He took her arm as they stepped out into the cool night air. They walked down the sidewalk, the full moon hanging like a large golden orb in the clear sky overhead.

"Thank you for the dinner," Gabi said again.

"You didn't eat much."

"It was good." She gazed into his eyes and had to resist the urge to reach up on her tiptoes and plant a kiss on those full lips. "I enjoyed it."

His eyes locked on hers. She saw them darken. Held her breath as he took a step forward and lowered his head to hers.

Chapter Four

Jude slipped his arms around Gabi's slender frame and watched her eyes close. His mouth skimmed the edge of her jaw, testing the sweetness of her skin. He nuzzled her neck then found himself shoved off balance from behind.

Irritation spiked. Jude whirled. If Chris was screwing with him again, his brother wouldn't find him so understanding this time.

"Sorry 'bout that, dude," the young shaggy-haired cowboy called over his shoulder as he lurched down the sidewalk, laughing with his friends, all three men obviously intoxicated.

When Jude turned to Gabi, he discovered she'd taken a step back. Just a small one, but enough to tell him the moment had passed. Still, the heat simmering in the air practically guaranteed there'd be another moment, another opportunity, before the night ended.

"There are so many out tonight." Gabi gestured toward the business district. People stood in front of the Superette, the saloon and The Grill. They talked, flirted, and one couple kissed as if no one else in the world existed.

The same way he'd felt only moments ago, Jude realized.

"I didn't know this many people lived in Horseback Hollow," Gabi said.

"It's Saturday night and unseasonably warm." Jude

raised a hand in greeting to several ranch hands then refocused on Gabi's beautiful face. "Most of the cowboys from nearby ranches come into town to eat, drink and dance."

Her eyes went round as quarters. "Dancing? Really? Where?"

"The Two Moon Saloon," Jude said, mentioning the business adjacent to The Grill. "The owners bring in bands on Saturday nights. In fact—" he glanced at his phone "—the party should be getting started anytime now."

"I like to dance." A wistful look crossed Gabi's face. "Salsa mainly."

"We mostly two-step around here."

She inclined her head, her brown eyes thoughtful. "Is it difficult to two-step?"

The way she looked at him told Jude she could be persuaded to prolong the date…if dancing was part of the package.

"Naw." He took her arm. "Easy. Want to give it a try?"

After a second's hesitation, she nodded. "Sure. Sounds like fun."

He looped an arm companionably around her shoulders as they walked. "Have I told you I like a woman with an adventurous spirit?"

Gabi simply laughed, the moon scattering light on the dark hair that hung past her shoulders.

As Jude expected, the place was packed. He'd hoped to find a quiet table in a corner where he and Gabi could be alone when they weren't on the dance floor. But the second he walked in and saw friends and relatives scattered throughout the bar, he knew there would be no alone time. Not this evening.

They ended up at a table with two of his brothers and several ranch hands. When one of the cowboys kept talking to Gabi, Jude gave the guy a dark glance, making it clear the lady was with him.

But was she? Though Gabi didn't flirt with the other men, she also didn't cling to him. It was almost as if they *were* buddies, out for a night on the town together.

If that's the way she wanted it, he'd be her buddy. In time, they'd be more. He hadn't been kidding when he'd told Liam and Sawyer she was The One. The moment she'd run into him, he recognized her as the woman he'd been waiting for his whole life. Corny, but true.

When the band began to play a current country classic, he grabbed her hand and pulled her to the dance floor. As predicted she picked up the steps easily. Two quick. Two slow.

"You're doing great. That's it." Approval mixed with the encouragement in his tone. "Let your feet glide."

Gabi had a natural sense of rhythm. Her lithe but curvy body surprised him with some great moves within the simple step. As they danced, her cheeks flushed with color and her smile flashed often.

The band took a brief break, and he and Gabi were on their way back to the table when they ran across Sawyer and Laurel. While Gabi chatted with them, Jude excused himself.

When he returned, her head jerked up at the Richie Ray tune that the band had begun to play.

"That's salsa music." Delight filled her eyes even as they narrowed suspiciously. "Did you have anything to do with this?"

"Do you want to stand here and talk?" he asked then held out a hand. "Or shall we dance?"

"You can salsa?" Delight filled her voice.

In answer, he led her to the dance floor and proceeded to show her some of his moves.

The night passed quickly. Jude couldn't remember the last time he'd had so much fun or danced to so many songs.

By the time she grabbed his arm and pulled him from the dance floor, his breath came in short puffs.

Gabi's own breath wasn't all that steady. "I think I'm going to call it a night."

Her cheeks were pink and her lips reminded Jude of a plump, ripe strawberry from his mother's summer garden. She looked so pretty, and he wanted her so badly that he almost kissed her right then, in front of half the citizens of Horseback Hollow.

Then he remembered what Sawyer had said about her father being overprotective. If Jude Fortune Jones kissed Orlando Mendoza's daughter on the dance floor of the Two Moon Saloon, news would be all over town by morning.

And even some sixty miles away in Lubbock, before Orlando finished his breakfast, someone would mention the incident to him. There was no reason to get the man stirred up when he was trying to recover. Besides, the way Jude saw it, what happened between him and Gabi was personal. That's how he preferred to keep it. For now.

Gabi paused at the edge of the dance floor, leaning close to ensure he could hear her over the twang of the steel guitar. "My father's house isn't far so—"

"Hey, Jude." A leggy redhead he'd dated last summer sidled up to him, her fingers traveling up his sleeve. "I got the band to promise they'd do the electric slide next. Told them it's our song."

"Sorry, Lissa." He put his hand on the small of Gabi's back. "We were just leaving."

Gabi opened her mouth as if to protest, but he closed it with a brief, hard kiss.

His pretty Latina's long lashes fluttered, and when he pulled back, she appeared slightly dazed.

"Oh." Lissa frowned, her gaze shifting between Jude and Gabi. "I saw you dancing, but I didn't realize you two were together, together."

"We are. Great seeing you, Lis." Without giving the red-head a chance to respond to his pronouncement, he took Gabi's arm and propelled her out the front door.

Once they reached the sidewalk, Gabi dug in her heels. "Stay. Dance with your friend. My father's house isn't far. I can walk myself home."

"Not alone."

The flat quality to his voice must have raised red flags. Concern filled her eyes. "Isn't it safe?"

"It's not that." No matter how much Jude wanted her to stay with him and not take off on her own, he refused to lie. "You'd be perfectly safe. The fact is, I'm not nearly ready for the night to end."

"Oh," she said, then again. "Oh."

"Unless this is your way of saying it's been fun but it's time for me to get lost?"

Gabi slowly shook her head and the tight knot in his belly dissolved. She rested her hand on his biceps. "I enjoy being with you."

"Good." He tucked her fingers more firmly around his arm.

In no particular hurry, they strolled down the sidewalk, soon exchanging the noise and lights of the downtown district for an occasional barking dog. Still warm from the dancing, Jude let his coat hang open.

Gabi kept hers firmly cinched around her waist. Thin blood from the hot Florida weather, he decided.

Jude gently locked his fingers with hers. Their hands swung slightly between them as they walked. For a second, he could see his parents strolling down the lane in the evening after supper, holding hands in companionable silence.

He and his siblings had thought it strange. For the first time, though, he understood that contentment. Feeling the warmth of Gabi's hand against his, seeing her face bathed in moonlight, he was happy sharing this moment with her, simply being with her.

They were almost to her father's house when out of the corner of his eyes, he saw her lips twitch. "Something funny?"

"Just remembering my high school days." She gave his hand a squeeze and smiled. "Back then my father would be waiting up for me with the porch light blazing."

Her dad didn't sound much different than the fathers of some of the girls he'd dated in high school. "I bet he'd miraculously appear on the porch just as you and your guy reached the steps."

Your guy.

Jude didn't like the sound of that, then reminded himself that while someone else may have been the first to kiss her, to caress, to make love with her...he would be the last.

"He wouldn't immediately appear." Gabi offered a wry smile. "Once the car hit the driveway, I had, oh, thirty seconds to get inside before the light began to flash. If I ignored that warning, he'd come outside."

"Half a minute doesn't give much chance to say goodnight," Jude observed.

"Any good-night kissing had to be done before I got home." Gabi grinned then sobered. "Not that I dated all that much."

"That surprises me."

"Why?"

"You're pretty," he said honestly, knowing the word didn't do justice to her beauty. Long, dark, wavy hair and big brown eyes. A slim, compact body with curves in all the right places. A smile that arrowed straight to his heart. "I'd have thought the boys would be flocking around."

"Two words." She exhaled a sigh and wiggled four fingers. "Older brothers."

Jude thought of Stacey and Delaney. He and his brothers had considered it their mission to protect their sisters from predatory males. "I can relate."

"I bet you can." Gabi rolled her eyes. "Because of my brothers and my dad, most guys ended up dropping me off in front of our house and speeding away."

Cowards, Jude thought with disgust. "I'd have insisted on walking you to the door."

"Then you're one in a million, Jude."

"I'm happy you recognize my worth." He shot her a wink as they climbed the stairs of her father's porch. "Seriously, my brothers and I were taught it was our responsibility to see our dates safely to the door."

When she stopped and turned back to him without opening the door, Jude's heart slammed against his ribs. Stealing a quick kiss in the saloon was one thing. But with those unreadable dark eyes staring up at him now…

Jude had been dating since he was fifteen. So why did he feel as unsure as he had when he'd been about to kiss a girl for the first time? It made no sense. Other than Gabi was different and he didn't want to screw up.

The air grew thick, so thick he had difficulty breathing. The world around them faded away. All that existed was her. All that mattered was her.

Take it slow. Don't rush her.

The warning in his head stemmed from good, cold logic. She wasn't going anywhere, at least not soon. Her father had only recently been moved to rehab. They had plenty of time to build a relationship. For her to see, to accept, to embrace that he was her future husband.

Yes, he decided, he should take a step back. He'd been impulsive in the saloon. He needed to keep his desire for her under tighter control. There would be other opportunities, other nights for another kiss. A lifetime.

Dropping hands to his side, Jude kept his gaze on her

eyes and away from those luscious lips. "I had a good time tonight."

Something that looked like disappointment flashed in her eyes. Her brows pulled together. "Do you have something against kissing?"

He stared, nonplussed. "No. Do you?"

"Not if I like the guy." She gave him a long stare that fried every brain cell he possessed. "Not if he likes me."

"I like you." The second the words left his lips, Jude realized he *had* reverted back to his teenage self. Except he'd never been this lame.

"Happy to hear it." Her arms wound around his neck. "For a second I wondered if I'd lost my appeal."

"Oh, darlin'." Jude wanted so much to pull her close, to fit her hips against his. He settled for resting his hands on her shoulders. "That's never going to happen. But I don't want to rush you."

"You kissed me in the saloon," she reminded him.

"Impulse." He shook his head. "Not very gentlemanly."

"I believe—" She brought a finger to her lips and pretended to consider. "No, I'm certain. Being a gentleman is highly overrated."

Jude brushed a strand of hair back from her cheek with the back of his hand. "I doubt Orlando Mendoza would agree with that sentiment."

She laughed, a silver tinkle of a sound that relaxed the tight muscles in his shoulders.

"True." She gazed up at him from beneath lowered lashes. "But he's not here, is he? Besides, I make my own decisions."

She was right. What her father wanted didn't matter. With the moon illuminating her face, her eyes shining, all that mattered was her and him and the moment.

Jude lowered his mouth and touched her lips with his. She tasted like spearmint candy. He loved spearmint. He moved his hands down her arms then settled them on her waist.

"I like you, Gabi." He let the word hum between them. Her brown eyes darkened to black in the dimness, but he didn't need light to read her expression. Leaning over, he kissed the base of her jaw.

She brushed her lips against his cheek.

"I like you a lot," he murmured, twining strands of her hair loosely around his fingers.

"Jude." She spoke his name then paused, as if not sure what she wanted to say.

When her gaze met his, their eye contact turned into something more, a tangible connection between the two of them. Time seemed to stretch and extend.

Then she ran her hands up the front of his coat and leaned toward him.

He made a sound low in his throat then folded her more fully into his arms, anchoring her against his chest as his mouth covered hers. His hand flattened on her lower back, drawing her more tightly against the length of him.

He loved the way she smelled, an intoxicatingly sweet mixture of perfume and soap. Loved the way she tasted. Spearmint.

"You are beautiful," he whispered into her ear right before he took the lobe between his teeth.

Shivers rippled across her skin.

"You're soft," he continued as he kissed her below her ear, then down her throat.

"The scent of you drives me wild."

The honking of a car horn and wild teenage laughter with a loud male voice yelling, "Get a room," had Gabi jumping back and Jude stifling a curse.

They'd already been interrupted a couple of times this evening. Enough, Jude thought, was enough. But he

reined in his irritation as the night took on a sudden chill.
"Gabi—"

"The porch light has flickered," she said with a rueful
smile. "It's time for me to go inside."

Damn.

Jude shot a murderous glance at the disappearing tail-
lights. Then he staunched the emotion and met her gaze.
"I want to see you again."

"It's a small town," she said in a tone he found a little
too cavalier. "It's inevitable."

He put his hands on her shoulders. Firmly met her gaze.
"I want to see you again."

Her cheeks went a little pink. "I don't do casual affairs,
Jude. I won't be in town long enough for anything more."

Jude wasn't interested in a casual affair, either. He
wanted the more, would have the more, but it was much
too early for that discussion.

"I enjoy spending time with you," he said again, firmly.
What had his father once told him, *Begin as you mean to
go on?* "I'll be calling, asking to see you again."

To seal the promise, he kissed her again.

Chapter Five

Gabi swore her lips still tingled when she arrived at the rehabilitation center the next day to see her father. The newspaper lay on a dining room table when she walked in.

Her breath hitched when he gave her a big smile. Love flowed through her. Though she adored her brothers, they'd been a unit of four. She'd spent most of her time with her mother. And when her father was home, she'd been a daddy's girl.

"You're looking chipper." Gabi slid into the chair on the other side of the table.

"I could say the same about you." He studied her thoughtfully. "You've got color in your cheeks."

"I've been spending more time outdoors," Gabi admitted, thinking of the early-morning run she'd taken as the sun painted the sky shades of pink and orange. "Though I've had to bundle up. It's definitely not as warm as Miami."

Her father laughed. "Not yet anyway, but I hear it's supposed to hit sixty today, which is really good for this time of year."

"Actually, I like the cooler weather. And Horseback Hollow is a great little community," she told him. "I understand now why you're so happy here."

"I wasn't sure you'd be able to see it." Orlando appeared

pleased by her admission. "There's not much for young folks to do."

"I enjoyed the barbecue Friday night." Gabi decided to avoid any talk of last night's activities with Jude. "I got to know Sawyer and Laurel better. Deke and Jeanne Marie seem like very nice people."

"Their daughter Stacey is the one who stayed with me until the rescue squad got there."

"I remembered you telling me that and made sure to thank her."

"Good girl." He gave an approving nod then his gaze grew shrewd. "You haven't mentioned how your date went last night."

"It wasn't a date." Gabi resisted the urge to squirm in her seat. She could have cheered when her tone came out casual and offhand as she'd intended. "We went to dinner at The Grill then did a little dancing at the Two Moon Saloon."

Her father took a sip of coffee, inclined his head. "Dinner. Dancing. Sounds like a date to me."

"We had a nice evening." Gabi lifted one shoulder, flashed a smile. "I learned how to two-step."

The nurse came in before Orlando could begin a full interrogation. By the time the RN finished checking his vital signs and administering his medications, the talk turned to family. Apparently Gabi's brother Cisco had called that morning, and he and Orlando had enjoyed a lengthy and pleasant conversation.

"Stacey and I were chatting about older brothers at the barbecue," Gabi said, then wondered if bringing up the Fortune Jones family was a mistake. "I believe she and Delaney had it worse. They had five older brothers. I just had four."

"Your mother loved her boys." A smile lifted Orlando's

lips ever so slightly. "But she cried with happiness when she finally had a daughter."

Gabi's heart swelled. "I miss her."

"I do, too." He reached over and patted her hand. "It can't be easy for you now, being the only woman in a family of men."

"It's not that—" Gabi's phone began to play a catchy Latin tune. She shot an apologetic look at her father. "Sorry. I thought I'd put it on vibrate."

"Get it," Orlando urged. "It may be important."

Without even glancing at the readout, she answered the call. "This is Gabi."

"Good morning, Gabi. This is Jude." The rich baritone sent a flood of warmth surging through her veins. "How's your day going?"

"It's good." Before she could check her reaction, her voice took on a slightly breathless quality. "I ran four miles this morning, did some housework, and now I'm going to have lunch with my father."

"How's he doing?"

Gabi slanted a glance at her father and found him unabashedly staring. In spite of his injuries, he looked strong enough to hop into a plane and soar into the wild blue yonder. Or stride onto a porch and stand between her and anyone of the opposite sex. "Better every day."

"Glad to hear it." Jude paused. "I won't keep you, but I plan to inspect the fence on the southern border of our property tomorrow. I'd like your company. We can take the horses out. The weather is supposed to be good."

When Jude had called her adventurous, Gabi considered that to be the supreme compliment. She'd been given a second chance at life. She was determined to embrace that life, to live to the fullest each and every day.

"Well, ah—" Gabi glanced at her father. Still staring. "I've never ridden a horse before."

"No worries." Jude chuckled. "We have a mare, Sweet Betsy, who's so gentle a two-year-old would be safe on her. I'll have her saddled and ready for you. Is nine too early for you?"

Gabi considered her father's schedule. Most of his therapies were in the morning when he was fully rested. If she and Jude were back by noon—and she couldn't think why they wouldn't be—she could come straight to the hospital and have lunch with her father.

"Nine works."

"I'll be by your house at—"

"There's no reason for you to drive into town to pick me up," Gabi told him. "I'll meet you at your place at nine."

"Actually, why don't we meet at my parents' ranch?"

"Sounds good." Gabi found herself smiling as she ended the call. She'd always wanted to ride a horse. It looked like now she was going to have that chance.

"You're riding a horse?"

Gabi's back automatically stiffened at the disapproval in her father's tone. For a second, she'd been so caught up in making plans she'd forgotten he was sitting there, sucking in every word.

"It should be fun." When the scowl on her father's face deepened, she added, "I bet most of the women around here ride."

"You're not from this area," he said pointedly. "And you have to be extra careful."

Gabi told herself not to go there, to simply let the subject drop. But her mouth seemed determined to open and get her into trouble. "Are you worried I'll fall? If you are, don't give it a second thought. Jude plans to saddle up Sweet Betsy for me. Supposedly this horse is so mild-mannered a two-year-old could ride her."

"Yes, I'm worried about you on a horse. You're a city

girl." Her father spoke through gritted teeth. "But I'm even more worried about you falling for a man like Jude."

Gabi counted to five. Lifted a brow. "A man like Jude?"

"He's got a rep."

Without taking her eyes off her father, she leaned back in her chair, forced a casualness at odds with her hammering heart. "Tell me more."

"He likes women," Orlando said as if that explained it all.

"I'd say that's a good thing."

Her father made an impatient gesture with his good hand. "From what I've heard he goes from woman to woman, doesn't stick."

A knife sliced into her belly and twisted. Jealousy, she realized. Ridiculous, considering she and the handsome cowboy had only recently met.

"Why would that be a problem?" Gabi lifted a brow. "I live in Miami and I'm not looking to relocate."

"I don't want to see you hurt."

The look in his eyes was one of love, and Gabi felt her irritation subside. "Papi." She covered his hand with hers. "Jude is simply being nice, showing me around the area. He's not looking for anything more than companionship. I'm not looking for more, either."

Her father narrowed his gaze. "Does he know of your condition?"

The quick, hot surge of temper took Gabi by surprise. "I don't have a *condition*," she snapped. "I've had a heart transplant. I'm all better now."

Or close enough. She was down to only two meds.

Not surprisingly, Orlando didn't back down. "Does he know?"

"This may surprise you, but I don't shout my medical history from the rooftops of every town I visit." Gabi pushed back her chair with a clatter and rose to her feet. "I'd appreciate it if you didn't, either."

She bent, kissed his leathery cheek and spoke briskly. Lunch would have to wait for another time. "I'll be back in a couple of hours. I'm going to run some errands, pick up a few things while I'm here in Lubbock."

"I love you, Gabriella." He grabbed her hand before she could move away. "Sometimes my love makes me a little overprotective."

"A *little?*" She paused. Sighed. "I love you, Papi, but you need to remember I'm a grown woman. I handle my own affairs."

"But your heart—"

"My heart—" Gabi spoke slowly and distinctly so there could be no misunderstanding "—is strong and healthy and all mine. You don't have to worry about me giving it away to a stranger and getting hurt."

The truth was she didn't plan on giving her heart away to any man. Not even one who was handsome as sin and wore a black Stetson.

Jude ran into Sawyer in Vicker's Corners, just as he finished loading supplies in the back of his pickup. When his cousin crossed the street, Jude shut the tailgate and lifted a hand in greeting.

"Looks like you're going to be busy." Sawyer gestured with his head toward the truck. "Don't you know Sunday is the day of rest?"

"Not on a ranch." Jude kept his smile easy. Although he didn't know Sawyer well, so far he liked what he'd seen. He appreciated the way Sawyer and his wife had looked out for Gabi's father. How a boss treated those who worked for him said a lot.

"Past lunchtime. Have you eaten?"

Jude took off his Stetson and raked a hand through his hair. "Not yet. It's been one of those days."

"Me, either." Sawyer gestured toward a family-style restaurant on the corner. "Got time to grab a quick burger?"

Though there was plenty of work waiting for him back at the ranch, Jude didn't hesitate. A man had to eat, after all.

Because it was nearly two, the after-church crowd had cleared out long ago and the only people in the place were a couple of grizzled old cowboys playing checkers at a corner table.

The hostess led them to a table by the window.

"How's Orlando?" he asked, after Arlene, a retired schoolteacher-turned-waitress, had taken their order and brought the drinks.

"You'd know better than me." Sawyer leaned back and relaxed against the vinyl seat, downing a good portion of his iced tea in one gulp. "I was surprised to see you with Gabi last night."

Jude smiled and changed the subject. "How's the accident investigation coming? Is sabotage still on the table?"

Jude had heard all about the anonymous letters received at the post office. Letters alluding that what happened to Orlando could happen again if the Fortunes didn't pull up stakes in Horseback Hollow. He was grateful neither his brothers nor the ranch hands had brought up the letters at the bar when he'd been with Gabi.

Sawyer waited to answer until the waitress had set the food in front of them and was out of earshot. "The NTSB is still investigating. Until they file their report we won't know for sure."

Jude hefted the massive burger. "What's your take?"

Sawyer dipped a French fry into a puddle of ketchup. "I don't think so, but being part of a famous family does open you up to all sorts of things."

"That sucks."

"Sometimes." A speculative look crossed Sawyer's face. "Are you sorry you became a Fortune?"

Jude shifted uncomfortably in his seat, but Sawyer had always been honest with him. He could be no less. "It takes more than DNA to make people family."

"True enough." Sawyer popped a fry into his mouth. "Though I have to say when I saw you, I recognized you as a Fortune immediately."

Jude grinned and simply shrugged. No use denying it. Everyone commented on the physical resemblance between Jude and his cousin.

"Your brother Christopher doesn't seem to be having any problem adjusting to his new family," Sawyer said in a casual tone that Jude guessed was anything but casual.

"That so?"

Sawyer added more salt to his fries. "He's considering a move to Red Rock."

Jude kept his face expressionless. "First I heard."

The thought that Chris would leave Horseback Hollow to hook up with the Fortunes didn't shock Jude. Not as much as if Sawyer had told him one of his other brothers was considering the possibility.

At twenty-six, Chris was the youngest of the five boys and the only one who'd never taken to life on the ranch. From the time he'd been a little boy, he and their father had been at odds. If their dad said something was black, Chris would insist it was white.

Still, Jude had to wonder what his little brother was up to....

Jude shoved the speculation aside. He had no doubt he'd find out soon enough what Chris had up his sleeve.

"Back to Orlando." Jude took a drink of cola. "I know he's worked for you the past couple of months. Has he said much about his daughter?"

A trace of a smile lifted Sawyer's lips. "You mean about your future wife?"

"Scoff all you want." Jude met Sawyer's mocking gaze with a steady one of his own. "When Gabi is walking down the aisle straight toward me, you'll be eating those words."

"Okay, okay." Sawyer took another bite of burger. "I'm sure you know more than me. She's one of five kids. The mother died several years back. O is very protective of her, so watch your step."

Jude's fingers tightened around the glass of cola. "Watch my step?"

The words were so cold frost could have formed on them.

His cousin waved a dismissive hand, his fingers holding a French fry. "You know what I mean."

"I would never take advantage of Gabi." The words were said slowly, concisely and with an edge even Sawyer couldn't fail to notice. "I care about her too much."

"Good. Then Orlando won't be a problem."

Jude wasn't sure about that, but right now it didn't matter. His focus was on Gabi, on getting to know her and having her get to know him. Not everyone fell in love at first sight.

Until Gabi got to know him she couldn't love him. And love was essential if they were going to have a long and happy life together.

Chapter Six

Gabi decided riding Sweet Betsy was very much like sitting in a rocking chair. The chestnut-colored mare had one speed and that was slow. Nothing interested her, not the rabbits hopping across the field nor the cattle grazing nearby.

Wherever Jude's stallion went, the mare was content to go. Jude had smiled approvingly at Gabi's jeans, boots and long-sleeved shirt with a jacket for the ride. Because the sun shone bright, he'd plopped a hat on her head.

She was grateful to have it. The sky was blue without a trace of clouds. A slight breeze added to the pleasantness of the day.

Though there wasn't a palm tree in sight, Gabi found the openness of the landscape appealing. Just like the man at her side. Gabi slanted a sideways glance at the handsome cowboy, with the roll of wire hooked to his saddle.

"Do you like banana bread?" Jude asked when they drew close to a large pond.

It was an odd question, but Gabi answered truthfully. "Who doesn't?"

"My mother made some this morning, and I brought a few slices with me." Jude shot her a wink and slipped off the back of his horse with an ease Gabi envied. "I could be persuaded to share."

"I'll start working on appealing to your altruistic side,"

Gabi declared. "Once I quit gazing longingly at terra firma."

Taking hold of the chestnut's reins, he assisted Gabi off the horse. She stood there for a moment, her hands resting on his muscular forearms.

"It feels odd," she murmured.

He grinned. "Being on solid ground again?"

"No." Gabi cast a wary glance at the pond where their horses now stood drinking. "Being this close to water and not being on alert."

Jude cocked his head.

"Back home, when you see water that isn't the ocean, you think snakes and alligators."

The look he shot her was clearly skeptical. "You're making that up."

"I'm not," she insisted. "The church I attend in Miami has a couple of lakes on their property. They got rid of the gators once but had to bring them back. Know why?"

"No clue."

"The snake population exploded. They even got into the building."

He gave a disbelieving snort.

"Honest to God." She swiped a finger across her heart. "We brought the alligators back to keep the snakes under control. And not just any snakes, water moccasins, the deadliest of all."

Jude shook his head. "You like living in such a place?"

"It's been my home for as long as I can remember," she said simply. "But it doesn't feel that way so much since my mom died and my dad moved away."

A wave of sadness washed over her at the realization that her father's departure had changed everything. In an attempt to shake off the unwanted melancholy, she performed a couple of stretches then shook out her hands, which had been holding the reins in a death grip. By the time she straightened, her mood had lightened.

"I could have been a Texan," she announced.

If Jude was surprised by the out-of-the-blue pronouncement, it didn't show. "Could have been? Or could be?"

"Could have been," she repeated. "My father and his brothers were born in Texas, but relocated to Florida when they were young."

He slapped his hat against his dusty jeans. "That explains it."

She lifted a brow.

"You're a natural on a horse," he told her. "You're a born cowgirl."

Gabi laughed.

The sound made Jude smile. She captivated him. As she had from the first moment he'd seen her.

"Where's my banana bread?" Gabi asked.

"I thought you were going to persuade me to share."

She stared at him for a long moment, a speculative gleam in her eyes. "What's it going to take?"

He simply smiled, enjoying the game.

"A little buttering up?"

He grimaced. "That makes me sound like a tub of popcorn at the movie theater."

She fisted her hands on her hips, considered. After a second, she took a step closer, slid her hands up his chest to the lapels of his shirt. "Oh, Jude," she simpered. "You're so handsome."

He cocked his head and stared pityingly at her.

She dropped her hands, frowned. "You're right, way too cliché."

"But you're on the right track," he admitted, making her smile.

"Okay." She took a deep breath, let it out slowly then tipped her head and gazed up at him through lowered lashes. Her voice became a sultry purr. "Have I told you that I absolutely adore your muscles?"

He appeared to consider then shook his head. "I don't believe you have."

"I do," she said, all wide-eyed and innocent. "I know some women go for the starving-poet look. You know—guys with that long shaggy hair and not a manly muscle in sight."

"I take it you're not one of them."

Gabi trailed a finger across his biceps, a hint of a smile curving her lips upward when the muscle jumped. "I prefer men who look like men. I like them gentle but strong. You know—the kind of man a woman can depend on."

She stopped, as if she'd taken it further than she'd intended. But Jude liked knowing that she found him attractive, that his body appealed to her. And since they were exchanging confidences...

"Have I told you the kind of woman who appeals to me?"

Gabi shook her head, a cautious look in her eyes.

"Short women with dark hair?"

"Not just any short woman with dark hair." He took a step closer. "You."

She inched back. "Ah, that's sweet."

"I mean it." He took her face in his hands and gave her a smile so warm it made something inside her ache. "I've dated women of all shapes and sizes and found many of them attractive. But none compare to you."

She feigned a look of mild interest. "Tell me more, smooth-talking cowboy."

"I speak the truth."

"Yeah, right."

"Seriously, I love the way your hair shines like dark walnut in the sun." He touched those silky strands as he spoke, marveling at the softness. "Your eyes remind me of the finest Venezuelan chocolate."

"They don't make chocolate in Venezuela."

He smiled. "They do. My mother received some as a gift for Christmas from Sawyer. I remember the rich, dark color. It was the first thing I thought of when I saw your eyes."

She blinked. "Well, thank you."

"And your body." His gaze slid up and down from the cowboy hat to the tips of her dusty boots. "You're small and muscular, but you have curves in all the right places. When you're against me we fit together perfectly. You fit me perfectly."

"If you were the one trying to convince me to give you a piece of banana bread, it'd already be on your plate."

Jude let his gaze linger on her lips. "I'm not hungry for banana bread."

Her dark eyes sparkled in the sunlight. She moistened her lips with the tip of her tongue.

"I admit I'm tempted to kiss you," she said in that sultry tone he found so incredibly sexy, "but I'm not into public displays of affection."

Confused, Jude glanced around to see who was riding up. But he saw only cows and pastureland. "We're the only ones here."

Gabi gestured with her head toward the herd of longhorns eyeing them suspiciously from behind a string of fence.

He grinned and shook his head. "They don't count."

"Maybe." When she looked like she might be thinking of making a run for it, Jude grabbed her hand and tugged her to him.

"Not so fast, darlin'," he said in a deep voice with the faintest hint of a Texas drawl. "First things first."

Gabi stood so close he could see the flecks of gold in the rich brown depths of her eyes.

"Oh, that's right." She gave a throaty laugh and batted those long lashes. "You owe me a slice of banana bread."

"I want to kiss you." His gaze met hers. "And you want to kiss me."

"I guess we might as well go ahead and lock lips." Though Gabi's voice had a slightly bored edge, the flicker of desire in her eyes gave her away. "It's not like we have anything better to do."

"We could eat the banana bread." He trailed kisses up her neck.

She arched back, giving him full access to her throat. "Too many fat grams."

He nibbled on her ear, inhaling the light floral scent of her perfume. "We'll stick with this, then."

"I thought you were going to kiss me." Her breath came in little puffs.

"I think that's what I'm doing," he said, nipping her shoulder through the fabric.

When his hands began to slide slowly upward, Gabi inhaled sharply, her body quivering.

"You haven't come close to my mouth," she said in a breathless tone.

"I'll be getting there, darlin', don't you worry."

When his mouth reached the V of her shirt and his tongue made contact with the hollow of her throat, she gasped.

He'd never seen a woman keep herself so covered up. But Jude had to admit it was enticing. He couldn't wait to catch his first glimpse of the curves underneath all that fabric.

His hand slid up to cover her high firm breast, teasing the nipple through the thin cotton of the shirt. Her breath caught then released with an involuntary sound.

As he continued to lift, support and stroke her yielding flesh with his fingers, he closed his lips over hers, softly at first then slowly increasing the pressure. Soon he found himself kissing her as if she was water and he'd been in a desert. Which, in a way, was true.

Before her, there had been nothing. She filled him in a way no other woman had done. This was his future wife in his arms.

Her body hummed beneath his touch. The surprised wonder in her eyes when he hit a sensitive spot told him she didn't have a lot of experience. This was fine with him. But it meant he needed to go slow.

Going slow became increasingly difficult. The taste of her aroused him. Hunger struck against equal hunger, creating fire. As they continued to kiss, as he caressed her, the fire became an inferno. He cupped her and she whimpered, pressing up against his hand.

If Jude was only thinking of himself, he'd take the blanket off his saddle roll, shuck his clothes—and hers—and be rolling around on the ground in seconds. But he wanted the first time they made love to be special.

She melted against him, allowing his tongue to slip inside, just as he wanted to slip inside her.

As if reading his mind, she shifted slightly, opening her stance. They came together perfectly—two halves finally made whole—only separated by clothing.

When she began to shimmy against him, Jude had to fight to hold on to control.

Up. Down. Up. Down.

Her throaty cries made his blood burn hot.

Up. Down.

He envisioned her—wet, slick and ready beneath the denim.

Her breath came in little moans. Or were those sounds

from his own throat? Could a man die from raw need? At the moment it seemed highly probable.

The sun burned hot overhead but Jude barely noticed. All he knew was Gabi and the feel of her soft body against the hard length of him.

Tension filled every muscle. He couldn't get enough of her. He dug his fingers into her hips and increased the rhythm. Faster. Her frantic response urged him faster still.

She strained toward him, reaching, needing, wanting.

Seconds later, her body convulsed in release. She cried out, pressing hard against him, her eyes going blind. Still he continued. Up. Down. Slowly now—gentling the contact until the last bit of pleasure had been wrung from her body.

Until she went limp and collapsed in his arms with a shudder.

Once Gabi's brain became capable of forming a coherent thought, she realized anything she'd experienced before had only been a pale imitation of the real thing. She hadn't even gotten naked yet, but she'd experienced more passion and felt more satisfaction than she ever had before.

While Gabi had enjoyed her previous sexual encounters, she'd never been swept away in the moment. Yet, only a few seconds earlier, she'd been willing to do anything to ensure Jude kept touching her, kissing her.

She now stood cosseted in his arms, sated and content. A slight breeze ruffled her hair as she rested her head against his chest and listened to the comforting beat of his heart.

Gabi inhaled deeply. She loved the way he smelled— a woodsy mixture of cologne and soap and maleness that kept heat percolating low in her belly.

Jude's lips brushed the top of her head. "You," he said, "are amazing."

The feeling beneath his gentle tone and the answering emotion it aroused sent red flags popping up. How could she feel so close to a man she barely knew? Things were moving too fast and in a direction she couldn't afford to go.

If it was only the physical aspect drawing her to Jude, she'd be safe. But Jude Fortune Jones was the total package. Which was why it made sense to put a little distance between them. But when Gabi moved slightly back, he tugged her close.

Her fingers itched to reach between them, unzip his jeans and give him all the pleasure he'd so generously given to her. Then round two could begin, only this time sans clothing.

The mere thought of his talented fingers and mouth on her bare skin sent anticipation coursing up her spine and heat pooling between her thighs.

She'd let it go this far. What would be wrong with taking it all the way?

Yet, even as temptation beckoned, there were things they needed to settle first. She could be Jude's friend and even entertain the possibility of a friends-with-benefits relationship while she was in Horseback Hollow.

But she couldn't become involved in a serious relationship or plan a life with him. Not with her future so tenuous.

She'd witnessed firsthand the toll that losing her mom had taken on her father. It wouldn't be fair to fall in love, marry and knowingly put a man she loved in that same situation.

Though Gabi had done well since her surgery, she knew that could change without warning. She'd seen that happen with Mary and Kate, a couple of her transplant buddies.

While she may have told her father she was "all better" and didn't have a "condition," she knew she'd always be a heart patient. She'd always be on antirejection medication. And she'd always be at an increased risk of a health crisis that could take her life.

Of course, she might be making a big deal over nothing. Not all men who pursued a woman did it with a serious relationship or marriage in mind. If Jude was indeed a man who "liked the ladies," a few weeks of fun and sex before she returned to Florida could be all he was after.

If she knew that was his mindset, Gabi would rip off his clothes and have her way with him right now. Even the knowledge that the cows would get an eyeful wouldn't slow her down.

But what was going through his head was a mystery, so Gabi determinedly stepped from his arms and pretended sudden interest in straightening her clothing.

When she looked up, his blue eyes, so often filled with good humor, reminded her of a stormy windswept sea. The expression on his face was serious as his eyes searched hers. "Are we good?"

It didn't take a rocket scientist to realize he wanted to know if their momentary interlude had screwed things up between them.

Easy-breezy, she told herself and smiled. "Stellar."

The tenseness eased from his shoulders, but a hint of worry remained in his eyes.

"The air between us was hot enough to combust." Jude shoved his hands into the pockets of his jeans. "I hadn't planned—"

"On a make-out session in front of the bovines?"

Jude laughed then cocked his head. "We could take it to the next level and really give them something to look at this time."

His wicked smile tempted, but she shook her head.

"You have to check on the fence," she reminded him,

keeping her tone light, fighting for casual. "Besides, I'm in the mood to ride."

It sounded plausible. Practical. Believable.

If she could have kept her eyes from straying to the bulge below his belt buckle. *If* her breath hadn't hitched.

She heard him chuckle, jerked her head up.

The stormy eyes now held laughter and what she recognized as the hot glint of desire.

"A horse." She moved quickly to Sweet Betsy's side even as the image of *her* riding *him* painted bold, fiery strokes across her brain. "I want to ride a horse."

The knowing look in his eyes told her he wasn't fooled. "Need any help mounting the...horse?"

Gabi's throat went dry as dust. If he touched her now...

"Got it covered," she managed to croak before pulling herself up onto the mare with the ease of an experienced rider.

In seconds Jude was on the stallion. He shifted a bit as if trying to find a comfortable position.

Though it wasn't at all charitable, especially in light of how generous he'd been with her, Gabi stifled a snicker.

Instead of giving the horse a light tap of his heel, Jude stared with those enigmatic blue eyes, his gaze lingering on her mouth.

Gabi licked the lips that were now as dry as her throat.

As if satisfied, his molten gaze dropped to her chest. Her breasts had begun to tingle when his gaze lowered again.

One look was all it took. A river of heat rushed through her to settle at the apex of her thighs. She squirmed, trying to find a position that didn't intensify the ache between her legs.

The smile Jude shot her stopped just short of a smirk.

Then he pressed his lower legs against the horse and took off across the field toward the fence line.

Now he wasn't the only one who wanted, the only one left with unrequited yearnings. As he disappeared over the ridge, Gabi realized with a pang that letting him ride away was exactly what she'd soon face.

But not today. Not yet.

She pressed her heels into Sweet Betsy's sides and raced after him.

Chapter Seven

Gabi and Sweet Betsy reached the big red barn shortly before eleven. After the ranch hands took the horses, Jude invited Gabi into the house. He promised coffee to go with the slices of banana bread they had yet to eat.

A desire to stay warred with Gabi's need to leave and make sense of what had happened today. She was relieved she could honestly say her father expected her to join him for both lunch and dinner.

Disappointment skittered across Jude's face, but he walked her to the Buick like a gentleman, their interlocked fingers swinging easily between them.

The simple act only intensified the conflicting emotions battling inside her. She wanted to see Jude again, wanted to touch and be touched by him. But considering the intensity of the emotions and desires he engendered, being close didn't seem wise.

She worried this was all a game to him. Yet, wasn't that what she wanted? She felt dizzy as possibilities spun and swirled in her head. Could she do easy-breezy with no strings? Did she have a choice?

Thankfully she had the hour drive to Lubbock to think, to plan, to decide where they went from here.

But when she tried to slip behind the wheel of the Le-Sabre, Jude blocked her with his arm, a pleasant smile on his lips, a watchful look in his eyes. "I want to see you again."

"I'm sure you will." She lifted a shoulder, not wanting to commit to any course of action until she'd thought things through. "Horseback Hollow is a small town. Our paths can't help but cross."

Confusion blanketed his face. It was obviously not the response he'd expected. "Are you angry with me about something?"

"No." She briefly rested a hand on his arm. "I like you, Jude. What woman wouldn't? You're a handsome, sexy cowboy."

To her surprise, he didn't appear particularly pleased by the compliment.

"That liking goes both ways." He spoke cautiously as if feeling his way over unfamiliar terrain. "But I think there's more between us than sexual attraction."

A chill traveled up Gabi's spine. "More?"

"Friendship for starters."

He looked sincere, even sounded sincere. But her antennae were quivering. "Friendship is all there can be."

Jude rocked back on his heels, shoved his hands into his pockets. After a moment, a boyish grin tipped his lips. "Would that friendship be served with or without benefits?"

When she didn't immediately answer, he continued, the words coming fast. "I'm open to either possibility. If you want sex to be a part of the friendship, great. If you prefer to keep it at a good-night kiss, that's fine, too. If you don't want any physical contact—" a pained look crossed his face "—I'll respect your wishes."

"That seems a bit extreme." Gabi laughed. Then, without a thought for the wisdom of her actions, she brought her mouth to his in a light kiss. "Thanks for a wonderful morning."

As she slid behind the wheel, his eyes met hers. "Are you free tonight? After the dinner with your dad?"

Jude reminded her of a tenacious terrier. The voice of

reason in her head urged her not to make any commitment to see him again until she'd had time to think.

Stall. That would be the smart thing to do. She'd tell him she had plans for later tonight. She'd—

"What do you have in mind?" The question slipped past her lips before she could stop it.

His slow smile did funny things to her insides. "Do you know how to play poker?"

"I'm proficient." She quirked her lips in what her father called her Mona Lisa smile.

"Some guys and I get together once a month for Texas Hold 'Em," she heard him say. "I'd like you to fill in. Ryan's wife had a baby last week, so we're a man short."

"In case you haven't noticed—" she gazed at him through lowered lashes "—I'm a girl."

"Oh, darlin'—" Jude took off his hat and swiped his brow in an exaggerated move "—believe me, I've noticed."

Gabi laughed, as pleased by the easy camaraderie as she was flattered by the sexual overtones.

"Do you play for money?" Even as she asked, she told herself this wasn't a date they were discussing. It was simply cards. She'd been on a tight budget since coming to Horseback Hollow and could stand to pull in some extra cash.

"Fifty is the buy-in." He brushed a strand of hair back from her face. "I can front you the—"

"Not necessary."

Hope flashed in those brilliant blue eyes. "Does this mean you'll come?"

With poker on the agenda? Gabi grinned. "Wild horses couldn't keep me away."

Gabi's car had barely disappeared down the lane when Jude's mother appeared on the porch and invited him inside. Over thick slices of banana bread and strong black coffee, Jude mentioned Gabi would be filling in for Ryan tonight.

Jeanne Marie cocked her head. "I don't recall you ever inviting a woman to play before."

Jude paid close attention to the bread he was slathering with butter. "With Ryan sitting out, we're one short."

His mother topped off his coffee then resumed her seat across the table. "One of your brothers could have taken his place."

Breaking off a piece of bread, Jude shook his head. "I look at their ugly faces enough during the day."

"You like this young woman." A smile blossomed on Jeanne Marie's lips. "*Really* like her."

Denying it would be pointless. Hadn't he already declared his feelings to his family at the barbecue? He only hoped his *friend* Gabi didn't hear he loved her from one of his relatives before she was ready to accept they were meant to be together forever. "I knew Gabi was The One from the first moment I saw her."

Unlike Liam, Jeanne Marie didn't scoff. Instead her eyes turned dreamy. "It was that way between your father and me. Forty years of marriage later, we're more in love than ever."

"Gabi just wants to be friends." Jude decided he might as well lay it all out. But simply speaking the words brought back the confusion.

His mother cut her slice of banana bread precisely in half then picked up the small square, her blue eyes fixed firmly on him. "How do you feel about that?"

"It's okay." Jude shifted his gaze away, knowing his mother would be able to read the truth in his eyes. "For now."

There was no way he was telling his mother that Gabi thought he was sexy. That while all signs indicated she'd be amenable to a friends-with-benefits arrangement, she didn't appear to want more. At least not from him.

The bottom line—she'd sleep with him, but not love him. *That* was a kick in the ass.

"She's being smart." Jeanne Marie punctuated the words with a decisive nod. "The best relationships are built on a firm foundation of friendship and mutual respect. Love won't survive the ups and downs of life without a sturdy base."

Jude took a bite of bread, chewed, considered.

"You thought you were in love before," his mother gently pointed out. "Those relationships didn't last."

"This is different," he insisted. "Gabi is different."

"She very well may be." The matter-of-fact manner was as much a part of Jeanne Marie as her wide-brimmed summer gardening hats. "If she is, if what you feel for her *is* the real thing, becoming friends will only strengthen the bond between you. That's a good thing."

Jude took a drink of his rapidly cooling coffee, considered what he'd do if Gabi refused to move past the friendship stage. There was no alternative. If that happened, he'd simply find a way to change her mind.

"Honey, if the two of you are meant to be together, it will happen," his mother assured him, her voice softening. "In the meantime, inviting her to your home tonight was a smart move."

Startled, Jude inclined his head.

Jeanne Marie's smile widened. "Believe me. How a woman plays poker can tell you a lot about her."

During the drive back from Lubbock, Gabi had come to a decision. While in Horseback Hollow she'd accept Jude's friendship. "Benefits" might eventually be part of that friendship, but not until she knew Jude better and he knew her.

While a serious relationship with marriage in mind might not be possible, that didn't mean she'd cast aside her moral compass and sleep with someone she didn't know and trust. Easy-breezy, yes. But only with a healthy dose of true friendship and mutual respect tossed into the mix.

The niggling thought that Jude couldn't truly know her until she told him about the transplant was shoved aside as she considered what to wear for an evening of poker. When she played with her brothers, it was comfort clothes; yoga pants and a T-shirt. But then, she'd never cared about impressing them.

By the time the pile of clothes on her bed outnumbered those in her closet, Gabi had settled on tan pants and a royal-blue cotton sweater. Dangly earrings with brightly colored stones added a festive touch.

Since the other players were men, Gabi figured the refreshments would be salty snacks and beer. Before she left the house, she stashed a couple of bottles of water and a bag of baby carrots into her favorite grocery bag.

If the guys commented on her healthy snacks or the fact she wasn't drinking alcohol, she'd tell them she was staying sharp so she could take their money.

Her painted lips curved. The men would soon discover that wasn't far from the truth. From the time she'd been little more than a child, her analytical mind had embraced numbers and probabilities. When she reached middle school, her father reluctantly admitted he had nothing more to teach her about the game of poker. It was around that same time that her brothers began to refuse to play cards with her if money was involved.

Gabi wondered how Jude would react when he lost. Her father said you could learn a lot about a man playing cards with him, *especially* if you beat him. Which meant she was going to know Jude Fortune Jones a whole lot better by the end of the evening.

After parking in front of his home, Gabi sat for a minute. She let her gaze linger on the old farmhouse that Jude called home. The one-and-a-half-story white clapboard structure had a fresh coat of paint, a new green roof and a gorgeous wraparound porch. Half-moon pieces of stained glass over the front windows gleamed in the yard light's glow.

The warm, friendly aura emanating from the structure enveloped her when she finally stepped onto the porch and rang the bell.

When the door opened, Gabi's smile froze. Instead of Jude, his father stood in the doorway, tall and broad-shouldered in a Western shirt and jeans.

"The token female has arrived," Deke called over his shoulder, then flashed Gabi a grin and motioned her inside. "I bet you've come hoping to clean the boys and me out of our hard-earned cash."

"Ah, I guess that's the plan." Gabi roused herself from her stunned stupor. "It's good to see you again, Mr. Fortune Jones."

A pained expression skittered across his face. It was gone so quickly, Gabi wondered if she'd imagined it.

"Deke, please." He reached around her and pulled the door shut. "If you're going to make a valiant attempt to take my money, we might as well be on a first name basis."

Gabi had liked Jude's father from the moment she met him. There was no subterfuge in the man, none of the posturing so prevalent in South Beach men. Just like his son, what you saw in the rugged rancher was what you got.

"I thought I heard the door." Jude appeared in the doorway, looking positively delectable in worn jeans and a long-sleeved T-shirt the color of oatmeal. "Hey."

"Hey back at you." Gabi glanced around, taking in the ceilings with rough-sawn cedar beams, the cream-colored plastered walls and the textured rag rug on the shiny hardwood floor. On one side of the living room, plaid fabrics on wing chairs and an old deacon's bench added color and warmth. The other side of the room held a table surrounded by Windsor chairs. "You have a lovely home."

"Thank you." Jude took Gabi's hands and gave them a squeeze. His eyes never left her face. "It's good to see you."

The warmth of his gaze chased away the last remnants of the chill from the outside wind. "I'm happy to fill in."

"I was looking forward to winning some money this evening." Deke's deep voice pulled Gabi's attention back to him. "Until my son told me you're a cardsharp and I'll be lucky to have my pants when I walk out the door."

Gabi felt her cheeks pink. She shot Jude a censuring look. "I don't know where he got that idea."

"I recognized the gleam in your eyes." Jude's teasing tone made it hard for her to hold on to her irritation. "But win or lose, you're still my girl."

Jude moved to her side, and for a second Gabi feared he meant to kiss her, right in front of his father. Instead he extended his hand. "May I take your coat?"

Feeling foolish, Gabi shrugged off the jacket. She glanced around. "Have the other players arrived?"

"Dustin and Rowdy showed up about ten minutes ago." Deke's easy manner reminded her of his son. "They're in the kitchen trying to wheedle Jeanne Marie out of another brownie."

"Your mother is here?" Gabi glanced at Jude. She thought she'd known what to expect this evening. Now she was thoroughly confused. "Is she filling in, too?"

"My parents came for dinner." Jude paused. "I'd have asked you to join us but you mentioned you had plans with your father."

"You fixed dinner for them." Gabi widened her eyes. "I'm impressed."

Deke gave a snort of laughter.

Jude shot a quick glance at his father, whose grin only widened. After placing her coat in the closet, he ushered Gabi into the living room. "My mother likes to make sure my kitchen gets some use."

Deke nudged Jude with his elbow. "What the boy is trying to say is Jeanne Marie made the meal."

"The *boy* is a man." A muscle in Jude's jaw jumped. "And I can speak for myself."

His father only chuckled.

"Coming over and insisting on fixing a meal is something my mama would have done." Gabi's voice softened the way it always did when she thought of her mother. "She loved to putter in the kitchen."

Deke's eyes turned dark with sympathy. "I heard you lost her several years back."

"What doesn't kill you makes you stronger." Gabi forced a lightness to her tone she didn't feel, then sighed. "Or so everyone says."

"I told you she wouldn't give us another one," a male voice groused.

"She might have if you hadn't—" The dark-haired man stopped speaking when he saw Gabi. "Well, hel-lo, pretty lady."

Jude placed a proprietary hand on Gabi's arm as the two men trooped into the room, cowboy boots clicking on the hardwood.

"Dustin, Rowdy, this is Gabriella Mendoza," Jude began.

"Gabi, please," she said quickly.

"She's filling in for Ryan this evening," Jude said, then continued with the introductions.

"Pleased to meet you." Dustin, sandy-haired with a broad smile and a baby face, pumped her hand.

Rowdy had a shock of dark hair and a gap-toothed grin. His gaze settled appreciatively on Gabi. "You're much better-looking than Ryan. If we're voting, I say he's out, you're in."

"If I take your money, you might not feel the same way," Gabi teased back.

They spent the next few minutes bonding over light banter about poker prowess. Jude had just finished explaining that his father was filling in for Liam, who'd come down with the flu, when Jeanne Marie appeared in the doorway.

"Gabriella." Jude's mother smiled broadly. "I thought that must be you at the door. You simply have to try one of my chocolate hazelnut cheesecake brownies."

Gabi hesitated.

"If she doesn't want it, can I have it?" Rowdy's question earned a scowl from Dustin, who obviously also had his eye on the sweet treat.

"She wants it." Jeanne Marie crossed the room and extended the plate holding a large chocolate square to Gabi. Though he was at least fifteen hundred miles away, Gabi swore she heard her cardiologist gasp when her gaze settled on the decadent brownie.

"My mother's brownies are legendary in this area," Jude told Gabi.

Not seeing another option, Gabi graciously accepted the treat. Before she could succumb to temptation, she broke off a bite-size piece then let Dustin and Rowdy devour the rest.

As the savory blend of chocolate, cream cheese and the faint hint of Nutella melted against her tongue, Gabi nearly moaned aloud. She found herself wishing she'd broken off a bigger piece. "That was simply heavenly."

"Won a purple ribbon at the State Fair in Dallas." Jude's mother smiled indulgently as the ranch hands once again began to pester her for more then disappeared into the kitchen when Jude announced it was time for the game to begin.

While Jude teased Gabi about not giving him any of her

brownie, everyone took seats around the table. Deke picked up a deck of cards and began to shuffle. Dustin collected the money from all the players while Rowdy divvied out the brightly colored chips.

Ignoring the bowls of snack food already on the table, Gabi slipped carrots and bottles of water from her bag. When the urge to munch hit, she'd be ready. For now, her focus shifted to the cards she'd been dealt. Gabi fingered the slick surfaces and experienced a familiar thrill.

It quickly became obvious to Jude that Gabi not only knew how to play, but play well. He could tell she'd grown up around men by the easy way she teased the others at the table.

Dustin and Rowdy treated her like a sister, not a woman they'd like to date. If they had, he'd have had to make it even clearer that *his friend,* Gabriella Mendoza, was off-limits.

The final hand was dealt, and Jude stifled a low whistle when he set his gaze on his hand. *Three aces.* Smug satisfaction settled over him even as he kept his face impassive.

Rowdy dropped out first, then Dustin. His father held on a little longer before folding.

Gabi chewed her bottom lip, a clear indication she wasn't nearly as confident of the cards in her hand as she appeared. Still, with a toss of her head, she shoved all her chips into the center of the table. "I call and raise you."

It took everything Jude had to keep a grin from his lips. If she thought she could bluff a master like him, she was mistaken.

Once his chips were in the center of the table, he laid down his cards, fanning them out. "Three aces."

He started to pull in the pot, when he felt her hand on his sleeve.

"You haven't seen my cards." Her voice held cool amusement.

Dustin and Rowdy glanced at each other. Deke took a long pull of beer.

Dustin grinned. "This is going to be good."

"Show us what you got, honey," Rowdy said with a wink.

With great precision, Gabi laid out her cards. "I believe a straight beats three of a kind?"

Though she posed it as a question and her innocent expression gave nothing away, Jude wasn't fooled. He'd been taken by a master.

Dustin whooped. "It's your pot, Ga-bri-ella."

Jude cocked his head. "How long did you say you'd been playing?"

Gabi shrugged and pulled the chips to her. "Since I was, oh, eight or nine. My father says I have a knack."

"We've been snookered." Rowdy choked back a laugh before pushing his chair aside with a clatter.

Gabi looked startled when Dustin and Deke also rose to their feet. "You're leaving?"

"Gotta get a little shut-eye. Sun will be up before we know it." Dustin's gaze locked on Gabi's. "Come back and play anytime."

"It was a pleasure meeting you, Miss Gabi." Rowdy tipped his hat then shifted his gaze to Deke. "See you in the mornin', boss man."

Deke patted her on the shoulder. "It was a pleasure, little lady."

Gabi rose to her feet. "It was nice meeting you both. And seeing you again, Mr. Fortune Jo—"

She stopped at the look on his face. "Ah, Deke."

While the older man headed to the kitchen to fetch Jeanne Marie, Gabi walked the two cowboys to the door, the men in a jovial mood despite leaving with empty pockets.

Once the two cowboys were in their vehicles and she

and Jude were cleaning up, he cast a sideways glance at her and made a confession. "When I saw you chewing your lip, I was certain you were bluffing."

She couldn't quite suppress a smile as she pocketed her winnings and put the chips back in the carrier.

"That was deliberate?"

Gabi laughed. "I love a good game of cards."

Was that what he'd been meant to learn this evening? That she was not only pretty, fun and sexy as hell, but possessed a mind that would constantly challenge him?

Though at the moment it was her pretty face and those full, pouty lips that called to him. He tugged her close, pleased when she melted against him. His mouth had just begun its exploration when the kitchen door swung open.

"I heard the vehicles leave—" Jeanne Marie, with her husband behind her, came to an abrupt halt in the doorway. One brow winged up.

Gabi shoved tousled hair back from her face and flushed. "I was just leaving."

Deke's gaze shifted from his wife to Gabi and Jude. "What's up?"

Ignoring her son's dark look, Jeanne Marie smiled at her husband. "I interrupted your son saying good-night to Gabi."

"Don't hurry off on our account," Deke told Gabi. "Jeanne Marie and I are heading home."

"I really have to go." Two bright dots of pink colored Gabi's cheeks.

"Don't forget this." Jeanne Marie crossed the room and lifted the market bag with a bold paisley print from the floor. "This one has to be yours. My son doesn't own anything this stylish."

During the course of the evening Jude had watched Gabi pull bottles of water and baby carrots from the brightly colored sack. Because he sensed drawing attention to her choice of snacks might bring her some good-natured ribbing from Rowdy and Dustin, he'd kept silent.

"Thank you." When Gabi slipped the now-perfectly folded bag into her purse, Jude realized she really did mean to leave before they had a chance to say good-night properly.

"Stay a little longer," Jude said in his most persuasive tone.

She may have shaken her head, but he found himself encouraged by the regret he saw in her eyes. "I promised to have breakfast with my father tomorrow morning. That means getting up extra early."

"How is Orlando doing?" Jeanne Marie asked over her shoulder as she retrieved her and Deke's coats from the closet.

"Better." Relief skittered across Gabi's face. "The orthopedic surgeon will be stopping by tomorrow. We're hoping to learn when he'll get a walking boot."

"Once that happens—" Deke pointed a finger "—you're going to have your hands full keeping him down."

Gabi smiled. "That's a problem I'd love to have."

"I'll be in Lubbock tomorrow, both at the hospital and the rehab center," Jeanne Marie announced as she slipped on her coat. "Do you think your father would like company?"

"You're going to the hospital?" Concern sharpened Jude's voice. "Why?"

"No worries." Jeanne Marie patted her son's arm in motherly reassurance. "I'm simply filling in for Halcion. She's visiting her new grandbaby in Arizona."

Gabi inclined her head. "Halcion?"

"One of my mother's many friends," Jude responded before Jeanne Marie had a chance to open her mouth. "Hal grew up in Horseback Hollow, but moved to Lubbock several years ago."

"She and Abe volunteer at the hospital and rehab center every week," Jeanne Marie explained.

"How nice that she and her husband—"

Deke gave a snort of laughter.

"Abe is her golden retriever," Jude clarified, shooting his father a dark look.

"He's a certified therapy dog," Jeanne Marie added. "The animal has a real talent for bringing comfort to the patients."

"I've heard of therapy dogs." Interest sparked in Gabi's eyes. "But I've never seen one in action."

Jeanne Marie looped her arm through Gabi's and gave it a squeeze. "Looks like tomorrow may be your chance."

Chapter Eight

As oatmeal went, the sticky substance in the bowl in front of Gabi fell into the pitiful range. The golden raisins and walnut topping, however, were excellent.

Her father looked up from his poached egg and toast. "How's your cereal?"

"Good." Gabi took a big bite, forced it down with a sip of juice when it attempted to stick. "The doctor seemed pleased by your progress."

"I'm doing *splendidly*." Orlando rolled his eyes at the word the surgeon had used more than once during his early-morning visit. "What he doesn't get is that until he gives the okay to put weight on this leg, I'm not going to be able to take care of myself."

They'd both hoped a walking boot would be prescribed, but the doctor had only said *soon*.

"Give it time, Papi. It hasn't been all that long." Even as she spoke the words, Gabi knew that to her active, vibrant father the weeks since the accident had been an eternity.

"Feels like forever." Orlando stared glumly down at his rubbery egg.

"When I spoke with Jeanne Marie last night, she mentioned coming by today." Gabi hoped the news of an unexpected visitor would lift her father's mood.

Orlando looked up, more curious than enthused. "Why?"

"Her friend, Halcion, is out of town, so Jeanne Marie is making the rounds with Hal's therapy dog."

Gabi handed the half-finished bowl of oatmeal to a nursing assistant picking up the dishes.

"Dogs come through here all the time," her father informed her. "I may know this woman's animal."

"Abe is a golden retriever."

"The dogs I've seen have all been small." Orlando stabbed the egg with his fork then looked up. "You spoke with Jeanne Marie last night? After you left here?"

"I played poker at Jude's house. Jeanne Marie and Deke were there, too," she added quickly.

Still, her father's lips pressed together. "Hadn't you already spent the better part of yesterday morning with the boy?"

The trail ride. It seemed so long ago. And it was the last thing she wanted to think about when her father's gaze was trained on her like a hawk assessing his prey.

She snatched a grape from a bowl on her father's tray and popped it into her mouth. "Jude needed a sub for poker and it sounded like fun. I cleaned them out."

Pride replaced the concern in her father's eyes. For a second he appeared to forget his worry over the time she was spending with Jude. "You surprised them."

"They didn't have a clue until it was over." Gabi discussed the hands played and how she'd won the last pot with a straight. "The weird thing is they want me back."

"They?" Orlando lifted a brow. "Or Jude?"

"Since the group only meets once a month, it's probably not going to happen. I'm sure I'll be back in Florida by the time they get together again." Gabi forged ahead, not giving her father a chance to comment. "By the way, I discovered Jeanne Marie is big on volunteering. I have to say her enthusiasm made me feel like a slug. I realized all I've done for the past couple years is work."

"You have an important job," Orlando reminded her. "It's understandable that you've focused your energies there."

Gabi couldn't argue. Her duties at the bank did keep her busy. But everyone had *some* free time. "Mom always made it a point to volunteer. I remember going with her when she delivered Meals on Wheels."

"Your mama—" a look of pride crossed his face "—she cared about people."

"I want to be that kind of person," Gabi said with a fervor that surprised her. "I've been blessed in so many ways. I want to give back."

"When you return to Miami—"

"I'm not going to wait that long, Papi." Gabi stuck out her chin. "I want to start now."

He didn't attempt to dissuade her, merely looked curious. "What do you have in mind?"

"I'm not sure yet where I want to volunteer." Gabi pulled her brows together. "But I sense an opportunity is right around the corn—"

"Is this a private conversation or may I join you?" Jeanne Marie stood in the doorway to the dining area, a huge smile on her face.

The older woman's silvery-gray hair was pulled back in a bun. Today, she wore a flowing burgundy skirt and a gauzy cotton top with burgundy splashes. Next to her a gorgeous golden retriever stood, resplendent in a red vest.

"Jeanne Marie, I'm so happy you stopped by." Gabi pushed back her chair and crossed the room to crouch by the animal. "I take it this handsome boy is Abe."

Gabi chuckled when the retriever sat and held out a paw for her to shake.

"Good-looking animal," Orlando concurred.

"You like dogs?" Jeanne Marie asked him.

"I do." Orlando straightened in his seat, his military

posture reminding Gabi of all the years he'd spent in the air force. "Luz and I were both big dog lovers."

Jeanne Marie strolled to Orlando's side, the dog trotting obediently by her side. The look on the older woman's face was kind. "Luz was your wife?"

Without warning, Orlando's eyes grew misty. "Thirty-eight years we were together before God called her home."

"I can't imagine losing Deke." Jeanne Marie pulled back a chair and took a seat. The dog inched close to Orlando.

His hand dropped, and automatically he began to stroke the dog's soft golden coat. Gabi watched in amazement as the tension around her father's eyes eased.

"My husband and I have been married forty years," Jeanne Marie confided before launching into a lengthy anecdote about life in the seventies.

Gabi listened with half an ear until she heard Jeanne Marie mention her name.

"I'm enjoying this conversation so much, I wonder if you could take Abe around for me? That way your father and I can visit a little while longer."

Gabi offered a tentative smile. "I'd be happy to help. But I'm not sure of the protocol."

Jeanne Marie explained the steps, beginning with checking in at the assigned nurses' station for a list of patients open to a therapy dog visit.

"Abe is well trained," Jeanne Marie added after she finished her instructions. "Just follow his lead. And have fun."

Gabi took the dog's leash and headed down the hall toward the only nurses' station not crossed off on Jeanne Marie's list. The pleasure Gabi got at the mere thought of performing this simple act of kindness only reinforced that changes needed to be made when she returned to Miami.

Miami. The city had always been home. She liked it there. Who wouldn't? Great weather. Fabulous beaches. Not to mention an impressive nightlife. Horseback Hollow had a different feel. Warm. Homey. Of course, that could simply be because this was where her father lived now.

Still, the thought that Gabriella Mendoza might possibly be a small-town girl at heart, made her smile.

The dark-headed nurse at the circular station greeted Gabi warmly and Abe by name. She gestured down the hall toward rooms in the hospital part of the structure.

"Leslie will be transferred to the Texas Medical Center in Houston tomorrow," the RN told her. "Her parents are busy making arrangements. The girl loves animals, and I know she'd appreciate company."

The "girl" in room 202 appeared to be in her early twenties. She had muddy-brown hair cut in a chin-length bob and big blue eyes. She could have been any one of the college students Gabi saw on the streets of Lubbock except for the unhealthy yellowish tinge to her skin and fluid-filled bags under her round doll eyes. But she brightened when she saw Abe.

"Hi, Leslie. I'm Gabi. This is Abe." Gabi paused in the doorway and gestured to the retriever, whose tail swished slowly side to side. "Is it okay if we come in and visit?"

"I'd like that." The girl put down the magazine she'd been reading and smiled.

"Sucks to be in the hospital." Gabi took a seat in the chair next to the bed while Abe stood close, staring up at Leslie with his big brown eyes.

Eyes which slowly closed in doggy-bliss when Leslie began to scratch the top of his head.

"I'm being transferred to Houston tomorrow," Leslie told Gabi. "I've moved up on the liver transplant list, and we need to be ready."

Gabi had been too sick to remember much about the days preceding her own transplant. "That's fabulous news. Shouldn't you be out celebrating?"

The girl choked out a laugh. It died in her throat as the door opened behind Gabi.

"Jude." Pleasure lit Leslie's tired eyes.

Gabi swiveled in her seat. Her heart skipped a beat at the sight of the rugged cowboy standing in the doorway, hat in hand.

"I didn't realize you had company." Though he spoke to Leslie, his gaze remained on Gabi.

"These two are the latest." Leslie smiled at Gabi and Abe then motioned Jude inside with a hand that trembled slightly. "Delaney and Stacey were here earlier."

"My dad mentioned something about them driving to Lubbock this morning." Jude moved to pat the top of Abe's head before shooting Gabi a questioning glance.

"Your mother was having a nice conversation with my dad and she asked me to make the rounds with Abe." Gabi gestured to the girl whose now-obviously curious gaze shifted between her and Jude. "Leslie and I were just getting acquainted. How do you know each other?"

"My dad works for Jude's father," Leslie explained before Jude could respond. "He's one of the foremen."

"Bill is a stand-up guy," Jude told Gabi then turned to Leslie. "I hear you're planning a trip to Houston."

"Tomorrow," Leslie said with a weary smile.

"Big day." Jude leaned over the bed and gave the girl's hand a squeeze. "You should be resting."

"I suppose." Leslie shifted a wistful gaze to Abe. "I hope they have therapy dogs at the transplant center."

"It was nice meeting you, Leslie." Gabi rose to her feet. "I'll be thinking of you."

"Thanks." The girl shifted her gaze to Jude. "I'm glad you stopped by."

"Hey, you guys are practically family." Jude's eyes were a deep, intense blue as he gazed down at the too-thin girl. "Take care, Leslie. Good luck."

Jude followed Gabi and Abe out of the room and pulled the door shut behind him. He scrubbed a hand over his face. "You should have seen her a couple years ago. So much energy. Full of life."

"She'll be that way again." Gabi rested a hand on his arm. "They've made great strides in organ transplantation in the past decade."

"Won't she have to take all sorts of drugs?"

"I'm sure they'll be some antirejection meds she'll have to take." Gabi kept her tone even. "It's a small price to pay for having the rest of her life."

Jude shrugged then refocused on her. "How many more patients do you have to visit?"

"Actually, Leslie was our only one on this unit." Gabi didn't bother to hide her disappointment. "We're on our way back to my dad's room now."

"I'll walk with you," Jude said.

"It was nice of you to stop by and see Leslie."

"I've known her since she was born," Jude explained. "She and my sisters used to play dolls on the front porch."

As they paused in the narrow hallway to let a gurney transporting a patient pass, Gabi reached down to stroke the dog's head.

Jude smiled. "Looks like you and Abe have bonded."

"I like dogs." Gabi let her fingers slide through the silky golden fur and felt the stirrings of regret. "Unfortunately my condo doesn't allow pets."

"You could move."

"I could. My lease is up next month." Gabi considered the possibility for a moment then shook her head. "It wouldn't be fair. I work too many hours. Dogs need someone around, at least a good share of the time."

"I grew up with dogs." Jude placed his hand against the small of her back as they crossed the hall connecting the hospital with the rehab center. "They were never allowed in the house. My dad is old school. According to him, animals belong outside."

"As long as they have food, water and a warm place to go to when the weather turns bad, they probably love having the freedom to roam." Gabi thought of the wide-open spaces she'd seen during her ride on Sweet Betsy. "It amazes me how a person can go for miles in the countryside without seeing another soul."

Jude cast a sideways glance. "That worked in our favor yesterday."

"About that." Gabi took his arm then glanced around to make sure no one was close enough to hear. "Things got a bit out of hand."

He didn't say anything but his eyes searched hers. "I thought you enjoyed the…experience?"

"I did." Gabi lowered her voice as they strolled past a busy therapy area and tried to ignore the heat creeping up her neck. "I've been giving a lot of thought to what occurred and what comes next."

His blue eyes turned wary when she tugged him to a little alcove with two spice-colored chairs and a table topped with several current magazines. "Let's sit for a second."

Once seated, Jude stretched his long legs out in front of him and crossed his ankles. To a casual onlooker, he'd appear relaxed, a handsome cowboy in scuffed brown boots and worn jeans. But Gabi had begun to know his face. The tight set to his jaw belied the relaxed demeanor.

She took a deep breath. "The bottom line is I can't sleep with you until I know you better," she blurted out. "Until you know me."

Something she couldn't quite identify flickered in his molten blue eyes.

"Casual sex with someone who is little more than a stranger may work for some women." She spoke quickly, fighting the urge to babble. "Not for me."

"I don't want you to consider me a stranger, Gabi." His gaze searched hers. "Not knowing each other well is an easy enough problem to fix. All we need to do is spend more time together. Unless you have plans with your father, we can start tonight."

"My dad mentioned yesterday they were having a John Wayne movie marathon tonight." Gabi laughed. "Thankfully my presence is not required."

"Perfect," Jude said. "I have something in mind you'll really like."

"What is it?"

"An event that will give you the opportunity to become better acquainted with the community and with me." He leaned over and, before she could protest, kissed her soundly. "Trust me. We won't be strangers for long."

Jude pulled up in front of Gabi's house shortly before six but didn't immediately get out of the truck. He thought about his earlier conversation with Gabi and his mother's comments about friendship being the framework of a long and happy marriage.

Tonight he and Gabi would work on building that foundation. Because he wasn't certain how long she'd be in Horseback Hollow, Jude was determined to make the most of every second with her.

The problem was he didn't feel all that upbeat tonight.

That afternoon, while moving cattle, his father had mentioned that a longtime neighbor, Roy Lerdahl—who'd been diagnosed with ALS last fall—had made the decision to sell his spread.

The land, which had been in the Lerdahl family for generations, would be auctioned off next month to the highest bidder. Jude had known Roy all his life, had gone to school with his children, apparently none of whom had an interest in ranching.

It didn't seem fair that Roy had to give up his spread. Not fair that one of the strongest—and best—men Jude knew had to face such a devastating disease.

Bad things shouldn't happen to such a good person. Anger surged, and Jude gave Gabi's door a hard punch.

"Coming." He heard her cheery voice through the thick wood.

The door opened, and Gabi stood there, a breath of fresh air and just what he needed after a hard day. She wore a flowing skirt in her trademark red and a white shirt with those little holes in it. Eyelet, his mother called it. She'd left her dark hair down, falling in gentle waves past her shoulders.

The smile on her lips faded when she saw him. "What's wrong?"

Jude whipped off his hat, raked a hand through his hair. "Crappy day."

"Come in." She took his hand, pulled him into the living room then over to the sofa, where she sat beside him. "Tell me what's wrong."

Something in her eyes said she wasn't being polite, that she really did want to know. So he told her. About growing up and seeing his father and Roy as larger-than-life. Strong, solid men who could handle anything the elements threw at them.

His disbelief when he'd heard Roy's diagnosis. And his grief and profound sadness as he watched a man he'd come to consider a friend deteriorate before his eyes. "Dad says Roy's ranch will go up for auction next month. Roy and his wife will move to an apartment in Lubbock."

"I'm sorry." Gabi leaned her head against his shoulder and her hand curled around his.

"It's just not fair." The words burst from Jude's lips like a bullet. "Roy is one of the best men I know. He doesn't deserve this."

"No, he doesn't." Sadness filled Gabi's eyes.

"Do you believe these…trials in life…are random happenings? You know, good or bad luck, or do you think there's some meaning behind them?"

"I don't have the answer." Gabi expelled a long breath. "I wish I did. When my mother was diagnosed I railed against God. How could this happen to such a good, kind, caring woman? Why not to some serial killer?"

"Exactly," Jude agreed.

"Some people say these trials in life are supposed to make you stronger." For a second Gabi's eyes took on a distant glow, then she blinked. "I say, these are lessons most of us could learn without being hit over the head and pummeled into the ground."

Jude briefly closed his eyes. "I feel so helpless. I want to help Roy but there isn't anything I can do."

"You can continue to be his friend," Gabi said softly. "You can visit him in Lubbock even when it's uncomfortable for you. Let him know he hasn't been forgotten. Sometimes when things happen, friends step away because they're not sure what to say or do. Just being there will mean a lot."

The words struck a chord in Jude's heart. "You're right. That's something I can do, something I *will* do."

"He's lucky to have you for a friend."

"Actually, he's more my dad's—"

"No," Gabi said firmly. "He's your friend, too."

"Yeah." Jude cleared the emotion from his throat. "He's my friend."

Jude slipped his arm around her shoulder, and Gabi laid her head against his chest. He pressed a kiss against her dark hair, and some of the heaviness gripping his chest lifted.

"We don't have to go out tonight," she whispered. "We can just hang out here."

"We could," he said, "but I want to show you a slice of small-town life."

"Slice of small-town life. How poetic."

He felt her smile against his shirtfront.

"Tell me, does this slice include food?" she asked. "I'm starving."

"It certainly does." He stroked her hair with the palm of his hand. "I'm taking you to an old-fashioned soup supper."

She lifted her head. "Soup supper?"

God, she was beautiful.

"All kinds of homemade soups as well as breads and desserts."

"How often are these soup suppers held?"

"Usually they have them when they need to raise money for some community cause. The one tonight is to fund a high school band trip."

Gabi straightened, shifted on the couch to face him. "Were you ever in the band?"

Had she realized that this easy conversation continued to help him relax? Or was she simply interested?

Jude shook his head. "Back then I was big into sports—football, basketball and baseball. How about you?"

"I was in the band." Her lips curved. "I attended a large high school. The band was like a big family. It gave me a real sense of belonging."

"I bet I can guess what you played." Jude cocked his head and thought for a minute. "Flute."

"What makes you think I played the flute?"

"That's what my sisters played."

"Actually I played the trumpet."

He narrowed his gaze. "You're kidding me."

"I'm not." She grinned. "My parents bought a trumpet for my brother Cisco, but he gave it up almost immediately. They didn't want to waste it, so when I told them I wanted to play an instrument, that was my only choice."

Jude pictured her with a trumpet against those full lips and felt a stirring of desire. "How'd you like it?"

"It was good." She gave a little laugh. "All my fellow trumpet players were boys."

"Sounds like you had fun in high school."

"I did," she said. "I was constantly on the run. My father was always telling me to slow down."

"Let me guess.... You didn't."

"No." A shadow crossed her face. "I didn't. What about you?"

Jude smiled. "I enjoyed high school. The sports. The parties."

"The girls," she added.

"There were a few," he admitted.

"Quite a few would be my guess."

"I imagine you had more than a few boyfriends."

"Not as many as you'd think. Four older brothers," she reminded him.

"That's right." He thought for a moment. "Of all the guys you've dated, who was the biggest disappointment?"

When her smile faded, he wished he could pull back the question.

"There was a guy I dated in college," she said finally. "I was going through a rough period and he just…disappeared. That's why I know that Roy will appreciate your visits."

"Jerk." Jude spat the word. "If he was here, I'd punch him for you."

"Not worth it." Her gaze met his. "If I'd stayed with him, I wouldn't be here now."

He closed his hand over hers, interlocked their fingers. "Then I'm grateful."

"Is there someone I need to punch for you?" she asked with a light, teasing smile.

"I've dated lots of women," Jude admitted. "But no one

who got close enough to hurt me. There wasn't anyone who captured my heart."

He brought her hand to his lips. "Until you."

Chapter Nine

Though Jude had been mesmerized by Gabi since that first intoxicating glance outside the Superette, his feelings had begun to grow roots and deepen. Granted, just looking at her now brought to mind tangled sheets and sweaty limbs. But he found the woman beneath the beautiful and sexy exterior equally compelling.

Gabi hadn't even laughed when he told her his surprise date was attending a soup supper with a couple hundred of his closest friends. He took her arm as they navigated the gravel of the church parking lot. "In a small town, events like these soup suppers are part of who we are and the life we live."

"You like Horseback Hollow."

"I do." Jude glanced at the small church with its doors propped open in welcome. "I went away to college, enjoyed the clubs and nightlife then came back. This is home."

"That's how I used to feel about Miami," Gabi said with a sigh.

"Past tense?"

He slowed his pace while lifting a hand in greeting to a harried-looking couple hurrying after three towheaded boys streaking up the church steps.

"My brothers got busy with their own lives. Friends married and left Florida." Gabi expelled a ragged breath. "My mother died."

"And your father moved halfway across the country."

She nodded, bit her lip. "I was happy for him. Thrilled he'd found a job that was such a perfect fit. But—"

"You were alone."

"That was when I realized it's a close network of family and friends that gives you that warm, contented feeling, not a city." Gabi paused at the foot of the concrete steps leading up into the church then glanced down the block to the heart of the small, sleepy town. "I can see why you love it here."

"Could *you* love it here?" It was something he needed to know. "Could you see yourself moving to a place like this?"

Gabi didn't appear to find the question strange. "I've actually given that some thought."

"And?" Though a hard knot had formed in Jude's gut, his voice remained steady.

"I believe I could," she said.

He expelled the breath he didn't realize he'd been holding. "Good."

Gabi lifted a brow.

"I'm sure your dad would like having you nearby." He gave her hand a squeeze. "I would, too."

She flushed and started up the steps. "It's not like I'm ready to quit my job and pack my bags."

"But it's a possibility," Jude said as they reached the open doors. "Down the road."

"Yes," she said. "A possibility."

Jude smiled. For now, that was good enough.

"Do you think people will find it odd we're here together?" Gabi's brows knit together in a slight frown. She stood beside Jude at the entrance to the large social hall in the church basement. "I hope they don't think we're a couple."

Jude knew that was exactly what everyone would think, and it was okay with him. "It's hard to control impressions," he said lightly, then changed the subject. "Wait until you taste the soup."

"If it tastes half as good as it smells in here, it's bound to be wonderful." She glanced around the crowded room and her eyes widened. "Look, there's Dustin and Rowdy."

The two cowboys, dressed in jeans, boots and Western-style shirts stood blatantly flirting with two young women in their twenties, one of whom Jude had dated last year.

"Are those their girlfriends?"

"I believe they're just friends." Jude smiled slightly when the brunette, Tiffany, glanced in their direction. She tossed her head and placed a hand on Dustin's arm.

Catching sight of them, Rowdy waved.

"We should say hello." Without warning, Gabi began weaving her way through the crowd. He caught up with her just as she reached the foursome.

Jude made quick work of the introductions.

Caroline, blonde and perky, asked about Gabi's father and her life in Miami.

Tiffany's cool gaze continued to shift between him and Gabi until there was a lull in the conversation.

"So." Tiff's shrewd blue eyes narrowed on Gabi. "I take it you're Jude's new flavor-of-the-day?"

Gabi's lips quirked upward. "Flavor-of-the-day?"

"Okay, maybe not the day." Tiffany's laugh held an edge. The schoolteacher slanted a glance in Jude's direction, brought a finger to her lips. "How long does it usually take for you to get tired of a current squeeze? Days? Weeks? If I remember correctly, we lasted a whole month."

When Jude scowled and shot her a warning glance, Tiffany responded with a sugary-sweet smile. He thought things were cool between them, that she appreciated him being up-front and honest when he'd felt ready to move on. Apparently he'd been wrong.

"Actually, Jude and I are simply friends," Gabi responded before he found his voice. "He's been kind enough to introduce me to the community while I'm in Horseback Hollow seeing to my father's recovery. Everyone has been extremely nice. It's easy for me to understand why my father likes living here so much."

Tiffany had the decency to look slightly abashed.

"Come on, Tiff." Caroline grabbed her friend's arm. "I want to get some of Mrs. Hansen's pasta fagioli soup before it's all gone."

"Rowdy and I'll come with you." Dustin cast an apologetic look in Jude's direction before the foursome disappeared into the crowd.

Gabi turned to Jude. Instead of jealousy, a teasing glint sparkled in her brown eyes. "Flavor-of-the-day? You never mentioned you were running an ice-cream shop of women."

"I'm not." Jude shoved his hands into his pockets. "Tiff's obviously out of sorts this evening and not making sense."

"The two of you dated."

Though it was said as a statement, not a question, Jude felt obliged to respond.

"For a short time." He rocked back on his heels. "Last fall."

"It ended badly?"

"I didn't think so," Jude said honestly. "We went out for several weeks. The initial attraction faded quickly."

"You broke up with her."

"I told her it wasn't working for me." He hadn't wanted to leave Tiff hanging, so he'd been honest. After a moment of silence, he cleared his throat. "Does it bother you?"

She met his gaze. "That you used to date her?"

He nodded.

"Not at all." She waved a hand in the air. "Why should it?"

He didn't care for the flippancy of Gabi's response or the way she appeared to take Tiffany's comments in stride. Other women would have been all over him, crazy jealous.

Maybe she simply didn't care enough to be jealous. The thought stabbed like a rusty spur.

"The flavor-of-the-day thing, though," she continued, bringing a finger to her lips. "That's intriguing."

"I don't know where she got that—"

"If you were a flavor of ice cream—" a thoughtful look crossed her face "—what would you be?"

"What's your favorite flavor?"

"Rocky Road." For a second a dreamy look filled her eyes. "I don't have it often now, but when I was younger, I could eat a big bowl of it all by myself."

"Then I'm Rocky Road." Jude wiggled his brows, a trick he'd perfected when he was thirteen and hadn't much cause to use since. "That makes me your favorite."

She laughed softly, patted his cheek. He waited for her to ask what his favorite ice cream was, but instead her gaze focused across the room on the long tables holding numerous slow cookers. "Let's check out the soups."

Squelching his disappointment, Jude strolled with her to inspect the selections.

After a few minutes of sampling and deliberation, he chose a spicy Tex-Mex chili that made his tongue sizzle. Gabi picked a sedate tomato-based soup loaded with vegetables.

While their selections were being dished up, Jude whirled at a sudden slap on the back. The tall man with a receding hairline paused only long enough for Jude to introduce him to Gabi.

"I played football with him in high school," Jude told

Gabi as his former classmate hurried off. "He's married now with four kids."

A look he couldn't decipher crossed Gabi's face.

"You need to quit slacking," she told him, sounding surprisingly serious. "Go forth and find yourself a nice woman. Settle down. Populate the earth."

"Don't worry about me. Once I go down that road, I'll make up for lost time." Jude grinned. "And have a lot of fun doing it."

Gabi took her bowl of soup from an older woman with a helmet of gray hair while Jude grabbed his from the woman's twin, then led Gabi to a nearby table.

"You want kids?" she asked in an offhand tone.

"Sure." He shrugged. "Don't you?"

She dipped her spoon into the soup. "When I was growing up, our neighborhood was filled with large families. I can remember telling my mother once that I wanted a dozen children."

"Whoa," he said.

"I don't feel that way anymore."

"Thank God." He pretended to wipe sweat off his brow.

She gave him a little smile and picked up her whole-grain roll. As he buttered his jalapeno corn bread, Jude's spirits lifted. Other than the incident with Tiff, this was turning out to be a good night.

He'd learned Gabi would consider moving to Horseback Hollow and that she wanted children. On those two matters, they were completely in sync.

At the sound of a banjo tuning up, Jude shifted in his chair toward the stage. A grizzled old man and a teenage boy were setting up. "Looks like we're in for a concert tonight. I hope you like bluegrass."

The boy took out a banjo while the white-bearded man, who Jude recognized as the boy's grandfather, pulled out a mandolin.

It wasn't long until music filled the hall. Gabi was soon tapping her foot and clapping with the rest of the crowd. When they finished their set, she cheered loudly. "They're good."

"Local talent." He nudged her elbow with his. "I bet you don't hear that kind of music much in Miami."

"Definitely not," she admitted.

The tension he'd seen on her face earlier had disappeared. Jude thought about taking her hand but held off. He might end up pushing her away with such a public display of affection. That was definitely not part of his plan.

He'd found the right woman. He was ready to settle down. And once he convinced Gabi he was the right man for her, they could live happily ever after.

Gabi strolled into the rehab center bright and early the next morning, anticipation quickening her steps. Before she left for Lubbock, she'd received a text from her father telling her he had a big surprise.

She couldn't wait to see what had him using three exclamation points. Hopefully the surprise was bigger and better than simply a decent bowl of oatmeal.

When she reached the dining room, she spotted her father at a table by the window. Gabi started to lift her hand in greeting then rushed across the room.

"When did they put that on?" she asked, gesturing to the walking boot.

"The doctor came by at the crack of dawn and gave the okay." Orlando's smile flashed then disappeared. "It hurts like a—" He paused, appeared to consider his words. "It's very uncomfortable when I put weight on the foot."

"The therapist is going to work with him later today on using a platform walker." Obviously overhearing the conversation, Carla, her father's pretty, red-haired primary nurse, stopped beside the table.

Gabi had spoken with Carla many times about her father's progress, and she'd always been helpful. The RN never acted as if her questions were an imposition. In fact, several times their conversations had ventured into the personal realm. Gabi knew Carla had grown up in Horseback Hollow and still lived there, commuting every day to her job in Lubbock.

"Won't using a walker be hard with his broken arm?" Gabi kept her tone offhand, not wanting to worry her father.

"It's more difficult," the nurse agreed, then smiled at Orlando. "But the type of walker the doctor has prescribed is designed specifically for a person in his situation."

Gabi glanced at her father then back at Carla. "That's good news."

She found the nurse staring. "Didn't I see you last night at the soup supper? You were there with Jude Fortune Jones."

Out of the corner of her eye, Gabi saw her father lower the cup of coffee and fix his gaze on her.

Busted.

Gabi nodded, smiled brightly. "Wasn't the soup spectacular? And I loved the entertainment."

"That was my grandpa and brother." The nurse turned toward Orlando. "Bluegrass music. Derek plays the banjo and my grandfather is a whiz on the mandolin."

"I'm sorry I missed it." Orlando sipped his coffee, the look in his eyes telling Gabi once they were alone she had some explaining to do.

The phone in the nurse's pocket buzzed. She pulled it out and glanced at the readout. "I'll be back in a few minutes with your medications."

"No hurry." Orlando waved a dismissive hand. "My daughter and I have a few things to discuss."

The minute the nurse was out of earshot, her father met her gaze. "You were with him again."

His tone was as flat as his eyes.

"It was a fundraiser for a high school band trip." Gabi could have cheered when her voice came out casual and offhand, just as she'd intended. "Soup, bread and desserts. All for a five-dollar donation."

"I don't have a problem with you supporting local youth groups," Orlando said pointedly. "I do have an issue with you spending every free moment with that cowboy."

"I don't see why." Gabi pressed down her irritation. "Jude is a nice guy from a well-respected family."

"He's using you."

"As we haven't had sex, I don't see how."

Orlando winced. "Gabriella."

"Let's call a spade a spade, Papi. You think all Jude wants is to get me into bed, and obviously you believe I'm so weak I'll do it just because he pays me a few compliments."

"Mija—"

"That attitude is as insulting to me as it is to him." Gabi lifted her chin.

"You forget, I raised four boys. I know what men—"

"You also raised one daughter. One who makes her own decisions."

"I know—"

"Apparently you don't or there wouldn't be a reason to have this discussion." Gabi took a deep breath and reminded herself she'd made her point. There was no need to beat it into the ground.

Seeing the distress on her father's face, her anger dissipated. She placed a gentle hand on his arm. "I can take care of myself. Don't worry about me."

Orlando smiled. "Asking a father not to worry about his little girl is like asking the sun not to rise in the morning."

"Please. Try." Gabi bent over, kissed his cheek. "I'll stay for your therapy this morning then I'm heading back to Horseback Hollow."

Orlando opened his mouth. Shut it.

"Not to see Jude," she said, answering his unspoken question. "To speak with Jeanne Marie and find out where I can put my talents to work in the community."

Jude spent the better part of the morning helping his father put out hay for the cattle and inspect the property's perimeter. When he returned to the house for some fencing, his heart stopped at the sight of Gabi's car in the driveway.

Though Gabi had appeared to enjoy his company at the soup supper, when he'd tried to set up another date, she'd been evasive. Which didn't make sense, considering their earlier discussion.

Still, he'd been encouraged by the heat of the kiss they'd shared as well as the progress they'd made in getting better acquainted.

Jude glanced down at his jeans. Though his mother didn't like dusty work clothes in her parlor, this time it couldn't be helped. Still, he stomped off most of the dirt from his shoes and swatted his pants with his hat before stepping inside.

The second he opened the front door, Jude heard the sound of feminine laughter. He stuck his head around the corner. "You're having a party and didn't invite me?"

Jeanne Marie chuckled. "You're always welcome, honey. Is your daddy with you?"

Jude shook his head. "He's still out."

"Well, come and sit down. We're having tea and cream puffs."

His mother might be having cream puffs. The one on the tiny plate in front of Gabi had barely been touched.

But then Jude had noticed his future wife wasn't much for sweets.

"It's nice to see you again, Miss Mendoza." Jude flashed a smile and, despite his polite words, took a seat right next to her on the sofa.

"My goodness, Jude, give the girl some room. There's plenty of space on that sofa."

Winking at Gabi, Jude made a great show of scooting over…just a little.

"Would you like a cream—" his mother began.

"This will work." Lifting the one off Gabi's plate, he took a big bite then had to reach for a napkin as the filling exploded.

"I declare, Gabi's going to think you were raised by wolves." His mother slapped at his sleeve. "That was hers."

"I don't mind, Jeanne Marie." Gabi sounded as if she was trying to swallow a laugh. "While the cream puff is delicious, one bite was perfect."

"If you decide you'd like another one, let me know." Jeanne Marie shot Jude a narrowed, glinting glance. "Later, you and I will have a talk about manners."

Jude offered his mother a conciliatory smile. "Don't let me interrupt your conversation."

"You already have," his mother said with an exasperated sigh, then lifted her teacup and studied Gabi over the rim. "Do any of the volunteer opportunities we've discussed interest you?"

Gabi's expression turned thoughtful. Jude thought she looked especially pretty today in a bright yellow sweater the color of the sun.

Then there were those gorgeous eyes—large, dark brown and full of secrets. Jude could stare at her all day. But not with his mother gazing at him, a bemused look on her lips.

"I'd like to do something with Texas No-Kill," Gabi

said after a long moment. "Do what I can to solicit more foster families for the animals."

Jude decided his mother must have told Gabi how the no-kill animal shelter, located between Horseback Hollow and Vicker's Corners, had been struggling. Delbert Knolls, the volunteer director, had recently left the organization because of declining health.

"How do you propose to do that?" Jude asked.

"I haven't seen the place. Or spoken with the people involved with it." Gabi lifted a shoulder in a slight shrug. "Until I have, it'd be presumptuous of me to offer any suggestions."

Beautiful and smart, Jude thought.

"I can introduce you to Steve Watkins," he told her. "He's a local banker who has temporarily taken the reins of the shelter until someone agrees to manage it permanently."

"That's sweet of you, Jude." Jeanne Marie beamed at her son. "I didn't realize you were interested in volunteer work."

"On the contrary." Jude shifted his gaze and fixed it on Gabi. "I'm very interested."

Chapter Ten

Gabi strolled with Jude toward the café where they would meet the acting director of the no-kill animal shelter. She tried to stay focused on the upcoming meeting, but her thoughts kept drifting to the handsome man beside her.

Jude's dark blond hair gleamed in the streetlight's glow. Since the afternoon, he'd showered, shaved and splashed on cologne; a subtle enticing scent that tempted her to lean close. Tonight he wasn't wearing his trademark Stetson or his Tony Lama boots. A darn shame because she found the cowboy look appealing.

But he looked sexy as sin in dark pants and a black sweater. A far cry from the dusty jeans and muddy boots he'd worn into Jeanne Marie's parlor.

He'd certainly earned his mother's wrath for coming into the house in his work clothes. Though Jeanne Marie hadn't said anything with "company" present, Gabi had overheard the older woman's sharp words to her son when she'd slipped back into the house to retrieve the purse she'd forgotten.

Jeanne Marie's terse comments reminded Gabi of her mother's futile attempts to civilize her four brothers. It often seemed to her as if the boys acted up just to see Luz's fiery temper flare. Gabi's lips curved. Unless you'd been the one on the receiving end of her mother's temper, the show had always been entertaining....

"Something funny?"

"I was thinking of my mother." Gabi's smile inched wider. "My brothers were always pushing her buttons. I really believe they enjoyed getting her riled up."

"Probably." Something in his grin told her he and his brothers had done the same. "I suppose you were a little angel."

"Always."

"I have a thing for angels." Jude slung an arm around her shoulder. "Especially those fluffy wings. So sexy. Perhaps you can show me yours…later?"

A giggle bubbled out from Gabi's throat. Though *giggling* wasn't something she'd done since high school, it fit her upbeat mood. If they weren't on a public street, she'd plant a big kiss right on Jude's mouth just, well, because she was so happy. Being here. With him.

But kissing Jude on Horseback Hollow's Main Street in full view of the citizenry wouldn't be wise. Gabi took a deep breath, forcing her eyes—and her thoughts—from his mouth. "Tell me about Mr. Watkins."

Thankfully, Jude didn't seem to find the question odd.

"His family owns several banks in the area." His hand slid down to link fingers with her.

Gabi wished they could keep on walking, just the two of them. Talk and laugh and get to know each other better under the light of a full moon. But they had a meeting to attend. One she'd requested. "Has he always been interested in animal welfare?"

"You can ask Steve yourself." Jude gestured with one hand. "That's him now, getting out of the BMW roadster."

"Looks like we're both early." The stocky man lifted a hand in greeting. He had stylishly cut short dark hair and direct hazel eyes. Several inches shorter than Jude, he carried himself with a quiet confidence. He extended a hand. "Steve Watkins. You must be Gabriella."

His handshake was firm, his gaze admiring.

"It's a pleasure to meet you." Gabi pretended not to notice he held her hand several seconds longer than necessary. "Please, call me Gabi."

"I'm sorry about what happened to your father." Steve cast a sideways glance at Jude. "Are they still thinking the accident may be retaliation against the Fortunes?"

"Possibly." Although Jude's back stiffened, his tone remained even. "According to Sawyer, we won't know if there was tampering with the landing gear until the NTSB finishes their investigation."

Steve shifted his attention back to Gabi. "How's your father?"

"He's making solid progress," she told him. "He got a walking boot today,"

"That's good news." Steve opened the door to the café then stepped back to let Gabi pass. "My brother had to wear one of those boots after he fractured his ankle last year. It took him a while to adjust, but it made a big difference in his mobility."

The waitress led them to a corner table. As soon as they ordered, Steve began to pump Gabi for personal information. When he discovered she was in the banking industry, he positively beamed.

"You can have your cattle and horses, Jude." Steve shot Gabi a conspiratorial smile. "This woman and I know the thrill that comes from seeing a spike in closed-end agreements."

A muscle in Jude's jaw jumped. "There's a lot more to running a successful ranch than tending livestock."

"Of course," Steve said dismissively then refocused on Gabi. "So you're interested in volunteering at the animal shelter."

"I am. But I'm only here until my father is back on his

feet." Gabi wanted to be completely up-front. "The way he's progressing, that might not be very much longer."

Talk of the shelter filled the conversation while she ate her salad and the men chowed down on burgers. Steve explained the challenges faced by the no-kill shelter. Jude not only provided history on the shelter's early days from information gleaned from his parents, but indicated he had an interest in volunteering.

"I hate to cut this short but I have a board meeting tonight." Steve leaned forward, closing the distance across the table between him and Gabi. "I'm free tomorrow. We could grab something to eat, discuss the various volunteer jobs in more depth once you've had a chance to think about them overnight."

"Gabi and I have dinner plans tomorrow," Jude answered before she could respond. "But we would be available later in the evening."

Steve inclined his head slightly at Jude's emphasis on *we.*

"Gabi and I are dating," Jude confirmed, dipping a French fry into a mound of ketchup. "We're practically going steady."

Gabi dropped her fork to her plate with a clatter.

Steve only laughed. "Message received loud and clear."

"Eight o'clock work for you?" Jude asked Gabi.

Gabi merely smiled and gave a jerky nod.

"It's a plan." Steve's phone gave a little beep. He glanced at the readout and grimaced. "Sorry. I need to head out."

When they reached the sidewalk, Steve paused, focused those hazel eyes on Gabi. "We're always looking for qualified people for management positions in our banks. If you decide to stay in this area, I'd be interested in discussing various opportunities we might have for you."

"Thank you," she said. "I'll keep that in mind."

"That went well." Jude reached around her to open the truck door.

"Which part? The part where you told Steve we had plans for tomorrow night when we didn't? Or when you took a time machine back fifty years and said we were *going steady?*" She paused for a breath, not certain if she should be irritated or flattered. "Or perhaps you're referring to when you decided to volunteer so I won't be alone with him?"

"I'm not sure what you mean." Jude's innocent expression didn't fool her in the least. "Hearing you and Steve talk, I was seized with the volunteer spirit."

"Let me make one thing clear." Her gaze met his. "If I wanted to meet with Steve alone, if I wanted to go out with him, I would."

His smile turned sheepish. "I guess I overstepped."

"By about a mile."

He took a deep breath, let it out slowly. "I'm sorry, Gabi."

"Apology accepted." Impulsively, she looped her arm through his. "Yet, I have to say I'm glad you volunteered."

Startled surprise crossed his face. "You are?"

"Certainly." Gabi gazed up at him through lowered lashes. "Volunteers are always needed to clean cages."

"Remind me again why you're cooking tonight," Gabi asked, munching on a piece of celery. "And why it had to be at my dad's place instead of your own?"

"A change of scene is always good." He took a sip of the sparkling grape juice he'd brought with him and continued to stir the contents of the bowl in front of him. "Besides, if I made dinner at my place, the stove might convulse at being used twice in one week."

Gabi laughed. "We could have gone out."

"I'm more than capable of preparing a meal," he said, then winked. "For my steady girl."

"Until I'm wearing your class ring on a chain around my neck—" she leaned over and kissed him "—we're not going steady."

The look of pleasure on his face made her smile.

"What are you making?" She moved to the counter by the stove, where he was blending a baking mix with some milk. On the stove ground beef, onion and four cans of vegetables had just come to a boil.

"Dumplings." He swatted her hand away when she reached for the mixing spoon. "Every bit as good as Martha Stewart's."

While she watched, he spooned the mixture over the stew, then reduced the heat and covered the pot.

"Should be done in twenty."

Jude looked so proud of himself that Gabi took a step forward and slid her arms around his waist. "You're quite a guy, Jude."

"Took you a while to notice."

"Oh, I noticed right away." She gazed up at him. "What I didn't expect was that you'd continue to impress me."

"Oh, darlin', I'm just getting started." His head jerked up. "Perfect. They're playing our song."

Gabi cocked her head and listened intently. Jude had brought his iPad with him. Before he'd started dinner, they'd enjoyed a glass of sparkling grape juice while music from his playlist created a warm, intimate atmosphere in the living room.

But from where she stood in the kitchen, she couldn't hear the tune now playing. "What song is it?"

"Hold on." Jude dashed from the room and a second later the melodious tones of Adele could be clearly heard.

"It's our song," he said with satisfaction when he strolled back into the kitchen.

Gabi recognized the artist but not the tune. "Does 'our song' have a title?"

"'Crazy for You.'" Jude held out his hands. "May I have this dance?"

"You're crazy."

"I'm crazy...for you." His arms were strong and sure as he maneuvered her into the living room, where the coffee table had been mysteriously moved to the side, creating a small dance space in the center of the room.

Resting her head against his broad chest, cosseted in his arms, Gabi felt as if she could face anything...as long as Jude was with her.

As they swayed to the bluesy melody, she let the world and any worries slip away. When "their" song ended, an equally romantic one took its place.

"Do your brothers know you have Neil Sedaka on your playlist?" Gabi tilted her head back to meet his gaze.

Jude winced.

"It'll be our secret," she whispered loudly, and he grinned.

His arms tightened around her. "I'm glad you let me come over tonight."

She lifted a brow. "Did I have a choice?"

"You always have a choice." Jude's lips brushed her hair. "To leave. To stay."

Gabi's heart wrenched. If only that were true. The transplant had given her life, but had taken some choices out of her hands. Her relationship with Jude would have to stay casual. It wouldn't be fair for her to pursue a future with him while having such an uncertain future. But for tonight she was going to pretend she was a twenty-five-year-old woman with her life stretched out before her and not a care in the world.

"We dance as if we've been doing it our whole lives," he murmured.

"For a guy who breaks horses and herds cattle, you're surprisingly light on your feet."

"My grandmother loved ballroom dancing." The deep voice against her ear sent a shiver of desire coursing up her spine. "She passed that love on to my mother. My dad isn't the dancing type. So when we got old enough—"

"Jeanne Marie taught you to dance."

He chuckled and looked faintly embarrassed. "Let's just say she tried her best."

"You know how I told you my father taught me the ins and outs of poker?" With a laugh she shook her head. "What I didn't tell you was Mama didn't like that one bit."

Gabi's mother had been a definite force to be reckoned with in their household. Luz Mendoza had been a fiery, determined woman with a big heart.

"You miss her." Jude's soft voice encouraged confidences.

Initially prepared to change the subject, Gabi reminded herself—again—that talking about things that mattered was the only way she and Jude would get to know each other.

"She was my best friend," Gabi said simply, meeting his gaze. "I could go to her with my worries and know she'd understand. We were two women surrounded by a sea of testosterone."

His eyes searched hers as they swayed to a Michael Bublé classic. "How did she die?"

"Cancer." The word was bitter on her tongue. "We had time to say our goodbyes. I guess that was something...."

His hand tightened on hers. "I'm sorry."

"Yeah, me, too." Gabi fought the dark cloud trying to settle over her by reminding herself she'd been lucky to have such a mother. Not to mention a very happy childhood.

Until my freshman year in college. An unexpected chill stole over her and she shivered.

"Don't tell me you're cold." He rubbed his hands up and down her arms.

The ding from the stove made any response unnecessary.

"I've wowed you with my dancing prowess." Jude tugged her to the already-set table. "Now prepare to be impressed by my superb culinary skills."

A half hour later, Gabi had to admit that Jude's "Rush Hour Stew" was delicious. Best of all, the no-salt-added vegetables fulfilled her daily vitamin requirements.

"I didn't think about dessert," he admitted.

"That's okay." She took a sip of the ice-cold skim milk she'd chosen to drink with her meal. "I'm not much for sweets."

"I've noticed." Jude smiled lazily. "You're extremely health conscious."

He'd given her the perfect opportunity to tell him about her transplant. They were alone, relaxed, and there was plenty of time before their meeting with Steve. Gabi wasn't sure why she'd held back the information. After all, it couldn't remain a secret forever. "I believe in taking care of my body. I—"

Her phone rang. She stifled a curse.

"Ignore it," Jude urged.

"I can't." She pushed up from the table and retrieved her cell phone from the counter. "It might be the rehab center."

She glanced at the unfamiliar number on the readout and her stomach contracted.

"This is Gabriella Mendoza." She listened for a moment and felt the knot in her stomach melt away. "No. I don't mind. I can stop by the shelter tomorrow and speak with the supervisor."

"Who was it?" Jude asked when she slipped the phone into her pocket.

"Steve." Gabi shrugged. "Tonight's meeting is off. Something came up."

"You don't seem upset."

"That's because I'm not. Now we don't have to rush off to meet with him." Gabi glanced at the table and the sink filled with dirty dishes. "Since you cooked, I'll clean up."

"Hold off for a minute." Jude sprang to his feet and held out a hand. "Since we have time, sit on the sofa with me. Take a few minutes to relax."

"Relax?" His innocent expression didn't fool her a bit. "You want to just…relax?"

Jude held up his hands, palms out. "If you find me irresistible and choose to kiss me, well, that's your choice."

Gabi laughed and shook her head. The guy was likable. Not to mention…irresistible.

For that reason alone she should package up the last of the stew and send him on his way. But the second the thought of fleeing crossed her mind, she squelched it. Wasn't this closeness what she'd wanted? Hadn't she told him they had to be friends before she could sleep with him?

Now that she found herself flooded with feelings of… friendship, sending him away made no sense at all. "Let me at least clear the table. Then we can relax."

To her surprise, Jude pitched in without being asked. It was another positive factoid to add to her growing Jude Fortune Jones book of knowledge. "You'll make some woman a good husband."

"Glad to know I've impressed you again," he said, an engaging twinkle in his eyes.

"Since I'll be leaving town shortly, if any woman needs someone to vouch for your positive attributes, you can give them my number." The simple realization that the woman who would one day capture Jude's heart wouldn't be her brought a sharp, slicing pain.

"I appreciate the offer, darlin'—" The words flowed easily from his lips. "But I'm not looking at other women."

"Maybe not right now," she said lightly. "But you will be eventually."

His eyes met hers and Gabi's heart gave three hard thumps.

Jude opened his mouth, closed it without speaking then drew her to the sofa. When they were settled, he looped an arm around Gabi's shoulder, his gaze focused on her mouth. "I have a question for you."

"Yes." She flashed a smile. "You may now kiss me."

"Ah, great, but that wasn't my question." The normally confident cowboy looked oddly flustered. "Friday is Valentine's Day."

"Really?" The knowledge made her feel slightly ill. When she'd taken her leave from the bank, she'd calculated that between vacation and sick days she had enough time built up to take her to the middle of February. Which meant she'd receive one more paycheck before the money stopped....

"Do you have plans?"

"Pardon?"

"Plans. Do you have plans for dinner on Valentine's Day?"

"I hadn't given it much thought." Gabi gave a little laugh. "I'll probably do something really romantic, like pig out with my dad on red Jell-O in the rehab dining room, then come home and go to bed. What about you?"

"While your current plan sounds like tons of fun, I have an alternative suggestion." He toyed with a piece of her hair, sliding the silky strands between his fingers. "Though it's hard to compete with Jell-O."

"Almost impossible," she conceded, a smile hovering at the corners of her lips. "Cherry is my absolute favorite."

"There's a new restaurant in Vicker's Corners," Jude said casually. "They have a diverse menu, so you should be able to find something you like, though I doubt red Jell-O is on the menu."

They exchanged a smile.

"There's a small dance floor," he continued in a persuasive tone, "which would give us a chance to show off the moves we perfected this evening."

Gabi tried to ignore the heavy pounding of her heart. In her mind, she'd always thought of Valentine's Day as a special day—one for couples in love, or who were thinking about being in love. Perhaps she should add couples considering *making love* to the list. Regardless, she found herself oddly touched by the offer. "Are you asking me out on a real date, Mr. Fortune Jones?"

"We've been on dates before." He lifted a fist, counting off the events by raising a finger. "The barbecue."

"That wasn't a date," she scoffed. "That was the night we were introduced."

He simply smiled and continued. "The trail ride. The poker game. The soup supper. After tonight's meal, I'll have to move to my other hand."

"Those weren't dates," she argued.

"Semantics." Jude's fingers closed around hers. "Say you'll come. You know we'll have a great time. We always do."

Gabi brought a finger to her lips. "I'd need to speak with my dad first to make sure he hasn't made any plans that involve me. Since I can't say yes right now, if you want to ask someone else—"

"There isn't anyone but you." He trailed a finger down her cheek, his blue eyes focused intently on her.

Gabi's breath caught in her throat.

"I want you," he said in a soft, low tone as his hand slid over hers, engulfing it with gentle pressure. He planted a kiss to the side of her lips, his mouth warm against her skin. "Only you."

His arms were around her, clasping her against a wall of muscle before he focused on scattering little love bites along her jaw. "The fact that you're always so covered drives me wild."

She laid her lips against his cheek, found the slightly rough texture arousing. "Oh, Jude."

His fingers raked through her hair, and his lips pressed to hers in an intoxicatingly sweet kiss that seemed to last forever. Yet, not nearly long enough.

She wrapped her arms around his shoulders, wanting the closeness, the connection, to continue.

As if he understood, Jude took it slow, his mouth moving from her lips then back again in unhurried caresses that only stoked the fire flowing through her veins.

His hands roamed then lingered over her breasts, his fingers teasing her nipples to points through the thin cotton of her shirt and bra.

Gabi's breath quickened as the kisses and touching continued—soft, urgent, relentless. Her control became a thin thread stretched further by each kiss, each touch, each caress. When his tongue swept her lips and slipped inside, the last strand snapped.

A moan escaped her lips. A desperate ache rose low in her belly. She pressed against him, offering herself to him, wanting him to give her the same pleasure he'd given her by the pond.

She gasped in protest when he pulled back without warning and strode to the window. Gabi watched in stunned disbelief as he pushed back the curtains and stared out into the darkness, his hands braced on the windowsill.

Gabi would have moved to him, but her trembling knees wouldn't support her. "What's wrong?"

He turned, his eyes dark.

"I want you, Gabi. I've never wanted anyone more." Jude rubbed his neck and scowled. "But not here. Not in your father's house. I can't make love to his daughter under his roof while he's in the hospital."

She supposed she could have denied they were on the verge of making love, told him there was nothing wrong with kissing on the living room sofa. But the raw need that still held her in its grip told a different story.

So Gabi didn't argue. She let him take her hand and even gave him one quick kiss before he walked out the door. The ache she felt when he got in his truck and drove off was only a prelude, she realized, to the devastation she would feel when he walked out of her life for good.

Chapter Eleven

After receiving her father's reluctant blessing and leaving the rehab center at two, Gabi spent the rest of Friday afternoon getting ready for her date with Jude. It had been a long time since she'd indulged herself, so she took a long bath then brought out her favorite pear-scented lotion. She smoothed it over her body, the pads of her fingers tracing the raised scar than ran down the front of her chest, between her breasts.

My battle scar, she thought to herself, then sent up a prayer of thanks to the young man who'd died and whose family had generously donated his organs.

The heart that now beat strong and sure had been a great gift, one she didn't take for granted. Though she knew the scar wasn't pretty, she still didn't understand the horrified looks on the faces of those at the pool party, and the memory still stung every time she caught her reflection.

Their reaction made her wonder what Jude would think when he saw it. Would he be shocked? Disgusted? Or would he view the scar as she did, as a symbol of a life-giving act?

She didn't need to worry about that now, because she didn't plan on letting him see it. Not yet. Perhaps never. Even if things went as she anticipated tonight and they made love, she could hide it by insisting the room be dark. If he felt the ridges of the scar on her skin, she'd simply tell him she had heart surgery. In a few weeks, she'd return to Miami and her life there.

Instead of excitement, the thought of leaving made her sad. She liked Horseback Hollow. The people were friendly and the pace suited her. She wished she could be here when the flowers were in bloom and the leaves had sprouted on the trees.

Gabi imagined herself attending parties, barbecues and picnics. It wouldn't be long before she knew everyone in town and they knew her.

If she and her father were in the same town, she could meet him for lunch, or invite him over for the evening. She and Jude…

Like a movie in slow motion, images played in her mind. She and Jude riding horses across windblown pastures, swaying to romantic songs with melodies that wrapped around them like a pretty ribbon, walking down Main Street with fingers entwined…

Stop, she told herself, *stop the madness.*

For too many reasons to count there could be no her and Jude. Whatever was between them was transient. Which made the possibility of her staying in Horseback Hollow simply wishful thinking.

If Gabi made the small Texas town her home, she'd have to sit back while Jude met another woman, fell in love and raised children. Despite wanting what was best for him, she couldn't bear to watch the man she loved build a life with someone else.

Man she *loved?*

Gabi's heart stuttered. She couldn't be in love with Jude. Love took time to develop—months, often years.

She respected Jude, admired his caring, compassionate nature and enjoyed spending time with him. She…

Gabi sighed. What was the point in lying to herself? She loved him. But the fact that he now had her heart changed nothing. The doctor had warned her it wouldn't be wise for her to bear children. Nor could she guarantee, despite her best efforts, she'd stay healthy. Heck, she couldn't guarantee she'd be around to celebrate a single anniversary.

She knew her father believed she should tell Jude about the transplant. But the way she viewed the situation, it didn't make sense to put a damper on their impending fling with all the heavy medical talk and questions that were bound to ensue. And Gabi certainly didn't want Jude to begin treating her with kid gloves, as if she was fragile.

Still, she didn't like keeping this from him....

When sadness tried to gain a foothold, Gabi firmly reminded herself this was a day for love and romance. Though she might not be able to profess her love, she could show Jude how she felt. Tonight, if everything went as anticipated...she'd give him her body as she'd given him her heart.

Her lips quirked upward. Before she took off her clothes, she had to put some on. Since she hadn't been sure how dressy the café would be, Gabi had checked the internet. Thankfully, the management of The Garden appeared firmly grounded in the twenty-first century. She found pictures—both interior and exterior—and a menu online.

The only comparison between this place and The Horseback Hollow Grill appeared to be that they were both eating establishments in the state of Texas.

The place looked decidedly upscale, so Gabi decided on a red lace dress with the high neckline she'd purchased in an after-Christmas sale. Expert use of the curling iron turned her normally wavy hair into a mass of tumbled curls. Lipstick, the same shade as her dress, was carefully applied.

Gabi was happy she'd gone to the extra effort when she opened the door and saw Jude. The man looked positively scrumptious in a suit, a crisp white shirt open at the neck and sleek black oxfords.

"These are for you." He offered her a florist's box tied with a white ribbon with silver threads.

When she opened it, Gabi found two dozen red roses nestled inside. Their fragrant scent filled the room.

"They're lovely." Gabi swallowed past the lump in her throat. "Thank you. Let me put them in water."

She quickly arranged the flowers in a cut-crystal vase and gave them one last look before she got into his truck and they drove to Vicker's Corners.

Jude laughed when Gabi mimed her dad's reaction to the rehab center's plans to show a romantic comedy in the lounge that evening.

"The male patients threatened to boycott," Gabi informed Jude.

He turned off the highway toward Vicker's Corners. "Were their demands met?"

"They most certainly were." Gabi grinned. "The very romantic *Live Free or Die Hard* will now be on the screen this evening."

Jude chuckled and slowed when they reached the town's quaint business district. The sidewalks were filled with couples enjoying the warm evening. "I'll drop you off at the café then look for a parking space."

"Absolutely not." Gabi's tone brooked no argument. "It's a beautiful evening. I'd enjoy a stroll."

He stopped the truck and waited for a car to back out of a parking spot. "Are you certain you'll be okay walking several blocks?"

She gave him a long, penetrating look.

Turning the wheel sharply, he commandeered the vacated space and grinned. "Message received loud and clear."

"I've been walking in heels most of my life," Gabi said

when he helped her out of the truck, pleased when she saw his gaze linger on her legs.

The look he shot her three-inch heels was clearly disbelieving.

"I could run a marathon in these shoes," she insisted.

"I'm not saying a word." Jude smiled, a boyish sort of smile that sent her stomach into flips and melted her heart.

The antique streetlights were on, lending a golden glow to the night. Laughter and what sounded like a mix between rock and country music spilled out to the street from several drinking establishments.

"I heard on the radio the area hit record highs today," Gabi said conversationally as they walked down the street.

"A perfect evening." He leaned over and kissed her cheek. "With the perfect woman."

Gabi laughed self-consciously. "I'm hardly perfect."

"C'mon." He put a hand protectively around her waist when they were forced to navigate through a crowd of casually dressed couples on the sidewalk outside a Tex-Mex cantina. "You even eat right."

"That's something everyone should do," she pointed out.

"I try," Jude admitted. "But it's my fondness for sweets that gets me in trouble. My mother had to put a padlock on the cookie jar when I was growing up."

Gabi shot him a look telling him she knew full well that was a gross exaggeration. She'd been around him enough to see that while he liked desserts, he didn't overindulge.

"I read somewhere once that you get one hundred percent satisfaction from the first bite of something." Gabi kept her tone casual, hoping she didn't sound as though she was preaching. "When I'm tempted to eat too much I tell myself one bite is all I need. A bonus is fewer calories and minimal artery-clogging fat."

His gaze slid sideways. "You certainly don't have to worry about extra weight."

"Best to be proactive." Then, realizing how prim that sounded, she flashed a smile. "I bet you're sorry now that you didn't bring me candy. I'd have one bite and the rest would have been yours."

Jude snapped his fingers, shook his head. "Blew that one."

They exchanged a smile. Time seemed to stretch and extend. He took her hand. It was as if they were two young lovers out for an evening stroll without a care in the world.

"That wasn't even two blocks." A hint of regret filled her voice when the elaborate hand-painted sign came into view.

The Garden sat smack in the middle of a block of cute little shops. Couples dressed for a special evening lingered on the outside sidewalk. Gabi wondered if they'd have to wait, but when Jude gave the hostess his name, they were immediately escorted to a table.

"The power of a reservation," Jude quipped as he pulled out her chair with a flourish. The small zebrawood table by the window was adorned with a bud vase holding a deep red rose and sprigs of baby's breath.

"This is very nice." Gabi let her eyes linger on the interior of the trendy bistro. She admired the stained glass windows, the copper ceiling tiles and vintage Art Nouveau French crystal chandelier in the entryway.

She pulled her gaze from the cut-glass crystals. "I'm surprised you were able to get a reservation here on such short notice."

"Actually I called several weeks ago, not long after we first met." He took a seat opposite her. "I figured if you didn't want to come here, I'd cancel."

She picked up the menu. "Or ask someone else."

"Why would I do that? The only woman I want to spend time with is you." He appeared genuinely perplexed.

She started to chuckle, then realized he was serious. The knowledge alternately pleased and terrified her.

"Well, I appreciate the invitation." She politely took the wine list the waiter handed her, though she had no intention of drinking. "Especially since I discovered *green* Jell-O was on the rehab center menu tonight, not red."

"Yes, but they are showing *Live Free or Die Hard*."

"Sacrifices had to be made." Gabi tried to stay serious but ended up making a face, drawing a laugh from him.

Jude reached over and took her hand. "Seriously, thank you for spending the evening with me."

She lost herself in his clear blue eyes. Finally, reluctantly, she slipped her hand from his and focused on the menu. "What's good here?"

"From what I've heard—" Jude opened his menu "—you can't go wrong with anything on the menu."

After some serious flip-flopping—because everything sounded enticing—Jude ordered a steak and Gabi selected the teriyaki salmon.

The waiter took their menus then discreetly returned several minutes later with their drinks. As Gabi smiled at the server, her gaze was drawn to a young couple at a nearby table.

"Look to your right," she said in a tone barely above a whisper. "Five bucks says it's their first date."

Jude leaned back in his chair and casually cast a sideways glance. A slow smile spread over his lips at the sight of the early-twenty-something young man sitting rigidly straight, Adam's apple bobbing, while the woman across from him with the too-bright eyes laughed nervously.

"Ah." Jude's eyes held sympathy. "The getting acquainted phase. Glad we're past that point."

"I disagree." Gabi lifted her glass of club soda. "There's still so much about each other we don't know."

"Well, I'm an open book." Jude grinned. "So, Miss Mysterious, tell me something I don't know about you."

I've had a heart transplant.

For a moment Gabi feared she'd spoken aloud. But when Jude reached across the table and took her hand, smiling encouragingly, she released her breath.

"C'mon, Gabi," he prompted. "One little-known fact."

She opened her mouth, fully prepared to tell him she only liked books with happy endings.

"I'm strong," she said instead. "I have this inner strength. I firmly believe I have it in me to handle whatever life throws my way."

"Confidence is such an appealing character trait." Jude caressed her palm with his thumb. "And so incredibly sexy."

Gabi's heart thumped. "You think everything is sexy."

His gaze caught hers and held. "Everything that concerns you, anyway."

Though she changed the subject and kept it light until their meals arrived, the air between them sizzled. Gabi's gaze kept returning to Jude. Each time their eyes met, the temperature in the room jumped thirty degrees. She was in the midst of one of those spikes of heat when the jarring sound of a tinny calypso beat broke the spell.

"Sorry." Gabi huffed out a breath. "Incoming text."

She reached into her purse, pulled out her phone and quickly read the message.

"Is everything okay?" Concern filled Jude's eyes.

"I told my father you were taking me out for dinner, so I'm surprised he—" Gabi paused. "On second thought, I'm not surprised. He knew very well he'd be interrupting—"

She handed the phone to Jude. "With a totally unimportant update."

Jude scanned the text, handed back the phone, smiled.

"Sounds as if he's having a good evening. It was nice of Sawyer and Laurel to stop by to see him."

Gabi savored a bite of asparagus seasoned with basil and rosemary and tamped down her irritation. She would not let her father's meddling affect the evening. "I don't know if you realize it but the Mendozas and the Red Rock Fortunes have been close for generations."

"Really?"

Gabi continued to nibble on the asparagus. Nodded. "There have been three marriages between the families."

An amused smile hovered on the edges of Jude's lips. "Sounds like someone has done her research."

"Actually, my father was in an extremely talkative mood one morning—" Gabi stopped, realizing she'd once again brought her *father* into the conversation. Pretty soon, Jude would be suggesting they drive to Lubbock and visit him.

"Your dad always seems to have something to say."

Gabi grinned good-naturedly. "Here's what I know." She lifted a hand and raised one finger. "Roberto Mendoza is married to Frannie Fortune."

Jude's fork stopped just short of his mouth. He thought for a moment then nodded. "Okay."

Another finger popped up. "Roberto's cousin Isabel is married to J. R. Fortune."

Jude took a bite of baked potato, chewed, swallowed.

"Hmm" was all he said.

"Lastly." Gabi raised a third finger. "Wendy Fortune is married to Marcos Mendoza. This adds up to three marriages between the two families."

"Well done." Jude lifted his glass of wine in a type of salute. "I believe you know more about the Fortune family than I do."

Something in his tone caught her interest. While he appeared to get on well with his cousin Sawyer, Jude rarely spoke of his connection with the Fortunes of Red Rock.

In fact, she realized he rarely mentioned that branch of his family at all.

This was one area where Jude wasn't an open book. "I've never asked how you feel about being a Fortune."

Jude placed his wineglass on the table and shrugged. "It's simply a name. But family means a lot to my mom. That's why I went along with her request to take the Fortune name. Carrying it doesn't change a thing. I'm the same person I've always been—Deke Jones's son."

"Your father is a great guy." Gabi toyed with her fork. "It takes a special man to agree to let his children bear the Fortune name."

"I've said it before and I'll say it again, my dad would do anything for my mom." Jude's tone was matter-of-fact.

Gabi thought of her own parents. "My father was equally devoted to my mother."

Dear God, had she really brought up her *father* again?

"Was it hard for Orlando to leave Miami?"

"In some ways this was like coming home for him. Remember, he lived in Texas until he was ten. My brothers and I were sad to see him move, but we believed the change of pace and the chance to be more involved with flying would be good for him." Gabi's fingers tightened around her fork. "None of us could have predicted his move would result in a near-death experience."

She blinked away sudden tears.

Jude said nothing, only reached over and gave her hand a squeeze.

"The accident only reinforced that life is precious," she murmured, almost to herself. "We need to savor every moment."

That's what she'd do tonight, Gabi promised herself. She'd enjoy every second of the time she had left with Jude.

Music smooth as warm cream filled the air. Couples

rose and headed to a dance floor where cascades of shiny red foil hearts hung from the ceiling.

Jude pushed back his chair and held out his hand. "May I have this dance?"

"Since you ask so politely…" Gabi rose. When they reached the shiny wooden dance floor, Jude took her into his arms in a natural, experienced movement.

She fit perfectly against him and discovered there was something incredibly romantic about being dressed up with a real band playing in the background and shiny red hearts hanging overhead.

By the time the set ended and they returned to the table, the dishes had been cleared and the waiter appeared for their dessert order.

Gabi politely declined dessert and the waiter's offer of a postdinner coffee. Jude ordered both.

Once they were alone again, she turned to Jude. "Did I mention I spoke with Steve earlier today?"

Jude's blue eyes cooled. "I don't believe you did."

Gabi took a sip of water. "He called when I was getting ready for tonight. He said The Garden was an excellent choice for dinner."

"Glad to have his approval." Jude gave a sardonic smile. "What did he want?"

"Apparently there's a big animal extravaganza at the Civic Center in Lubbock on Sunday. He asked if I'd be interested in manning the shelter's booth in the afternoon. There will be several adoptable dogs in the booth with me."

Jude toyed with the stem of his wineglass. "What did you tell him?"

"I said yes, *we'd* be interested." She offered Jude a slow smile. "Not inviting you was, I'm sure, a simple oversight on his part. After all, we are going steady.…"

The lines between Jude's brows that had appeared at the mention of Steve's name eased. He grinned.

Before Jude could say anything, the waiter returned to set up a mini dessert station tableside. Gabi watched him expertly combine then cook brown sugar, cinnamon, butter and banana liqueur in a small pan over a medium flame. Bananas were added and once the waiter appeared satisfied they were properly tender, dark rum was added to the pan and ignited. The mixture was served over a scoop of ice cream.

"It looks delicious." Gabi smiled at the waiter when he placed the dessert in front of Jude.

Though she'd insisted she didn't want any dessert, Jude dipped a second spoon into the dish and handed it to her. "The first bite is yours."

Gabi didn't argue. She shut her eyes and let herself savor the perfect blending of flavors. When she opened her eyes, she found Jude staring.

She licked the last traces of sugar off her lips with the tip of her tongue. "It's superb. You're going to love it."

With his eyes firmly fixed on her, Jude took a bite. "It is good."

He dipped his spoon into the dish then held it out to her. She stared longingly but shook her head.

"You're right. This isn't what I'm hungry for, either." He lowered the spoon, stared into her eyes. "I want to make love with you, Gabi."

Her heart began to pound as the desire for him that she'd kept under tight control rose inside her like a tidal wave. Gabi held out a hand and let him draw her to her feet.

For tonight, he would be hers.

Chapter Twelve

The short drive to Horseback Hollow seemed to take an eternity. In the truck, Gabi sizzled with pent-up need and intense desire for the man beside her.

To distract herself, she attempted to make conversation, asking about the lights twinkling in the distance.

"There's a lot of building going on around Vicker's Corners," Jude explained. "New condominiums and luxury homes, designed to lure those who want country quiet but also to be near their jobs in Lubbock."

While he spoke, he took her hand, caressing the palm with his thumb. When silence fell again and the simmering heat in the truck reached low boil, he brought her fingers to his lips and kissed her knuckles. The warm, moist touch of his mouth against her skin had sensation licking up her arm, down her breasts and on down to pool between her thighs.

"I wish we were there now." Gabi squirmed in her seat as her blood beat a primal rhythm.

He slanted a sideways glance. "Things might progress more quickly once we get to the ranch, if we do some preplanning."

The tone of his voice implied what he had in mind was something she might really like.

Gabi didn't need to feign interest. "What did you have in mind?"

"For starters, shedding some clothes." The boyish smile he shot her held a roguish edge. "I'd gladly participate but I have to drive."

He wore her favorite cologne and, in the close confines of the truck cab, she could smell something else; soap and that indefinable warm male scent that made her want to throw herself at him and agree to anything he asked. "What are you suggesting I take off?"

"Your dress. Or a piece of underwear," he said with an innocent expression. "Completely up to you."

"I prefer not to get arrested for indecent exposure," she said in a haughty tone that somehow managed to sound provocative.

"Appears the choice is clear."

Gabi liked teasing with him about such things, liked the shivering, sliding feeling that ran down her spine. She liked the way her blood hummed at the mere thought of removing her panties while he sat behind the wheel less than two feet from her. Of course she wasn't going to take off her underwear. Though the thought was intriguing....

"I had a friend during my freshman year in college who used to leave off her underwear when going on a date. She said it made her feel sexy." Gabi gave a throaty laugh. "I thought she was crazy."

"Did you try it?"

"I never did." That had been shortly before she'd caught the virus. Her boyfriend had vanished, and it had been a long time before Gabi thought of anything other than doctor visits and antirejection regimens.

"Perhaps it's time to be adventurous and give it a try." His eyes looked as dark as hers in the dim light, his words practically daring her to step off the safe shores of what she'd always known into a place where she could be over her head in seconds.

"What do you have to lose?" Jude asked, his voice smooth and persuasive.

Gabi's heart stuttered. She liked to think of herself as the adventurous sort. Besides, if she did as he suggested, it wasn't as if he—or anyone else—could see there wasn't anything beneath her dress but bare skin.

Telling herself not to overthink, Gabi turned in her seat and wiggled out of the silky panties, giving Jude a flash of her upper thigh.

She dangled the black satin-and-lace thong between two fingers, waving them the way a bullfighter might toss a cape. "Voilà."

In an instant, Jude had snagged the tiny scrap of fabric from her hand, rolled down the window and her pretty underwear disappeared into the night.

"Hey." Her voice took on a clip of annoyance. "I liked those."

His smile was smug and unrepentant. "I'll buy you more."

The thought of Jude Fortune Jones walking into Victoria's Secret in cowboy boots and hat to buy lingerie had her irritation melting away. She chuckled. "I'm going to hold you to that promise."

"Darlin'," he said in a sexy drawl that wrapped itself around her spine and caused an inward shudder. "I wouldn't expect less."

For a moment they sat silently. Gabi made a great show of straightening her dress. She smiled at Jude. "I don't feel any different going commando."

The use of the phrase seemed to make him smile. He lifted a brow and shot her a look that clearly questioned her veracity.

Well, perhaps she did feel a teeny-weeny bit wicked. And, when he looked at her with that heat in his eyes, the knowledge that she was naked beneath the dress did cause some different and interesting sensations to course through her body. "Okay, a little different."

His smile widened.

By the time they reached his ranch, Gabi understood her college friend a whole lot better.

Of course Jude had only continued to fan the flames smoldering inside her. Every topic they discussed could have or did have something to do with sex.

He spoke of the fence they were replacing in the north pasture, which made her think of their trail ride. Then he mentioned his sisters had gone shopping in Lubbock, which brought to mind her missing panties. Then there was the new bull...

By the time Jude pulled the truck to a stop and got out, Gabi ached for him, wanted him with a desperate intensity she'd never experienced.

He obviously felt the same. They barely made it inside before his mouth was on hers, his hands groping her through the lacy fabric.

"Take this off," he said, tugging at the dress.

"Not here." She pushed his hands away, her breath coming in short puffs. "Not with your mom watching us from over there."

Startled, Jude jerked his head toward the fireplace then expelled a breath at the sight of the family portrait of his family smiling back at them.

"You're right," he agreed. "Not here."

Jude grabbed her hand and began to pull her toward the bedroom. Once they reached the hall, he jerked her back to him and began kissing her—urgent, fevered kisses that matched the wild beat in his blood.

Raw need urged him to take her now, against the wall, on the floor. But he resisted, telling himself she deserved better than a wild tumble.

They stumbled into the bedroom, bodies and mouths

melded together. Still pressed together, he reached over and flipped on the light.

She switched it off.

"In the dark," she insisted against his mouth. "Just the first time."

At that moment, she could have asked him to do it standing on his head and Jude would have done his best to comply.

The shades were drawn, which, considering the proximity to the neighboring house, was totally unnecessary. The room was pitch-black other than a distant glow from the light in the living room.

Though her passion appeared as ferocious as his, the way she'd blushed in the truck when he first suggested shedding her panties told him she didn't have a lot of experience.

Through the haze of mounting desire, Jude found himself glad of the fact and determined she wouldn't regret trusting him with her body and with her heart. While she'd never said she cared, he knew she'd never let him get this close if she didn't.

He tightened his hold on his control and forced himself to speak softly in the same tone he used with a skittish colt. "Let me undress you. There's no reason to rush."

"I don't want slow." Heat vibrated in her voice. "You're lucky to have made it through the front door without me knocking you down and having my way with you."

Jude laughed, pulled her face up for a long, hard kiss. "You're something special, Gabi Mendoza."

"Yes, I am." She tugged at his suit jacket. "And you have way too many clothes on. Strip."

"It'd be easier if I could see," Jude muttered as he fumbled with his belt. Yet, the urgent need for her propelled his movements and his clothes quickly found their way to the floor.

"Easier isn't better." She moved to him. "Neither is slower."

When Jude wrapped his arms around her and felt only warm, fragrant skin, he realized she was already naked. *Almost* naked. By her position in his arms, she was obviously still wearing her heels.

If he hadn't already been hard, the mental image of her nude except for high heels would have sent him careening wildly in that direction.

"This is my favorite dance so far." Torturing him with her nearness, Gabi hummed one of the songs they'd dipped and swayed to at The Garden, while her body rubbed sensuously against his in all the best places.

Jude slid his hand into her tangled mass of curls. "I want you."

"I hope so," she murmured, "or I lost a perfectly good pair of panties for no reason."

Gabi felt some of her nervousness fade at his quick laugh. The touch of his knuckles against her cheek was wildly erotic.

"Jude." She spoke his name, then paused, not sure what she wanted to say.

Love me as much as I love you?

Please don't love me because I can't bear the thought of hurting you?

"I want you," he repeated, his voice a husky caress. Not quite steady fingers touched the curve of her cheek, trailed along the line of her jaw.

"I want you more." It was the truth. Her need for him was a stark carnal hunger she hadn't known she was capable of feeling. She'd never wanted anything or anyone as much as she wanted Jude Fortune Jones.

He ran his palms up along her sides, skimming the curve of her breasts. Gabi arched back while his long fingers lifted and supported her yielding flesh as his thumbs brushed across the tight points of her nipples.

His stroking fingers sent shock waves of feeling through her body. The melody she'd been humming died away on a soft little whimper as her knees went weak.

Scooping her up in his arms he carried her to the bed then dropped down beside her.

"If you were tired, all you had to do was say so." Her voice sounded breathless even to her ears.

He chuckled. "I've learned that when knees go weak, it's best to be horizontal."

Before she had a chance to respond, he folded her more fully into his arms, anchoring her against his chest as his mouth covered hers in a deep, compelling kiss.

Then his palms were once again on the move, skimming the curve of her breasts before he allowed the tips of his fingers the barest of contact with her flesh.

Her nipples stiffened, straining toward the remembered delight of his touch even as the warmth in her lower belly turned fiery hot and became a pulsating need.

She longed to run her hands over his body, to feel the coiled strength of skin and muscle sliding under her fingers. She wanted him to touch her in the same way, wanted to feel the weight of his body on hers. Wanted to feel him inside her.

Gabi planted an urgent kiss at the base of his neck, his skin salty beneath her lips.

His hand flattened against her lower back, drawing her up against the length of his body.

"You are beautiful," he whispered into her ear right before he took the lobe between his teeth and nibbled.

Shivers rippled across her skin.

"You're soft," he continued as he kissed below her ear, then down her throat. One of his hands lightly stroked her belly.

His hand moved up, pausing when it encountered the raised ridge of her scar. She tensed, but then his mouth replaced his hand and he was kissing his way up, touching his tongue to the tip of her left breast.

It was dark and all she could see was the outline of his head. But the combination of seeing and feeling was the most erotic experience of her life. Gabi cried out in delight.

He circled her nipple then drew it fully into his mouth. The gentle sucking had her arching against him. At the same time, his hand dipped low, slipping through her curls and between her legs.

She parted for him, catching her breath as he rubbed against her slick center, then slipped one, then two fingers inside her. When he shifted slightly and found that single spot of pleasure, she nearly rose off the bed.

This was like before, when they'd been on the trail ride, but more intense. She couldn't bear herself enough to him. She wanted to be more naked, more exposed, more intimate.

"Don't stop," she breathed, her blood like a fever in her veins.

Thankfully, he didn't. He continued to touch her, stroking her, teasing, circling as he worshipped her breasts. The combination made her mind go blank, her breathing come in hard pants. "I want you inside me."

She didn't have to ask twice.

Gabi heard the rustle of a condom packet being torn open, or at least that's what she assumed it was, then he was inside her.

He was large and stretched her in the best way possible. She felt filled, yet the need for more grew.

He wrapped his arms around her, drawing her close so they pressed together everywhere. She clung to him, urging him deeper.

"More," she breathed as he withdrew only to fill her again.

The rhythmic thrusting made her pulse against him. She couldn't get enough. She strained toward him, needing, wanting. She dropped her hands to his hips to pull him closer.

She hadn't known that this much pleasure existed in the world. That she could feel so good, so right, so everything.

Her pulse throbbed hard and thick. Gabi tried to catch her breath then gave up air completely as her release claimed her.

The climax rippled through her and still he touched her, gentling the contact until the last breath had been wrung from her body. At the very end, when she was sure there couldn't be anything else, he shuddered in her embrace and called out her name.

If Gabi hadn't known, hadn't had all the tests reassuring her that her heart was good and strong, the rapid pounding in her chest would have worried her. Yet, despite the *thump, thump, thump,* languid warmth filled her limbs as she lay curled in Jude's arms.

"That was," she said as she kissed his neck, "quite spectacular."

"I aim to please."

In the darkness, she felt his smile against her cheek.

"Do you want to tell me about it?" His voice was as warm and soothing as his arms.

Still, Gabi stiffened. "About?"

"The scar." He shifted, gathered her closer, kissed her temple. "I've seen scars before, you know. You don't grow up with four brothers and not get them. We used to call them badges of honor."

She could hear the hint of laughter in his voice.

"Why badges of honor?"

"Because they signified that you'd forged ahead, given whatever you were tackling your all, even if what you were tackling was one of your brothers." This time he did release a chuckle as his hand gently stroked her back.

Badge of honor. She might have to think of her scar in those terms. God knows, when faced with the situation, she'd forged ahead, given it her all, and came out whole on the other side.

Between them the silence stretched and extended, but Gabi didn't feel any pressure. She sensed that Jude would give her all the time she needed. He was kind. A good man.

"I had to have heart surgery." Gabi closed her eyes, breathed deep. "When I was nineteen. It, ah, fixed the problem, but left me with quite a scar."

The gentle glide of his palm up and down her spine paused for a fraction of a second then continued. "You're okay now?"

"Like new." Gabi told herself it wasn't a lie. In a way, it was true.

He exhaled a breath, pulling her tight against him for a moment. "Good."

Gabi thought she could be content to lie here with his arms around her until, say, the next millennium.

"Can I see your scar?" he asked.

She knew he felt her tense; she wasn't a good enough actress to keep her emotions that hidden. It irritated her that she could feel so vulnerable just because of the incident at the pool party.

"Not your scar," he corrected. "Your badge of honor. If you show me yours, I'll show you mine."

"You have a scar?"

"Darlin', every Jones boy has scars." He kissed her hair. "I've got one from an emergency appendectomy when I was nine that will blow yours out of the water."

"We'll just have to see about that."

"Okay, then." Still, Jude made no move to get up. "Tell me why I mentioned turning on the lights, when I'm so nice and comfortable right where I am."

"It's your curious nature." Gabi trailed a fingertip up his arm. "Trust me, that'll kick you in the balls every time."

His eyes widened in mock surprise. He leaned back, holding her at arm's length. "Miss Mendoza, does your father know you use such language?"

Gabi liked this playful side of Jude. But then she liked his serious side, his sexy side... She forced her thoughts back to the question.

"Who do you think I first heard that from?" She grinned. "And don't even try to tell me Stacey and Delaney haven't picked up a few of those kernels of wisdom from your dad and brothers."

"Guilty." Jude gave her a quick pat on the bottom as he rose and crossed the room to the light switch.

She expected the room to be immediately flooded with stark white light. The kind she remembered from the O.R. suites. Instead, Jude must have had a dimmer switch because the room definitely lightened, but no more than 30 or 40 percent.

Gabi decided she must still be basking in the afterglow of lovemaking because the light reminded her of golden moonlight.

Jude returned to bed, crawling in beside her, pulling her close once again. His blond hair looked as if someone had raked their fingers through it. Gabi smiled, realizing that someone was her.

His cheeks were dark with a light scrabble of whiskers, but those blue eyes were clear and oh-so-blue when they latched on to hers. "Who goes first?"

"You," she said. "So you can revel in being the best for a few seconds until my scar—er, badge of honor—blows yours out of the water."

"Ah, more talk of scars." His eyes danced. "Stirs me up."

"Let's see it."

Jude glanced down. "It's a bit wilted at the moment but—"

"Not that," she said, swallowing a laugh. "Your appendectomy scar."

He exhaled an exaggerated sigh. "If that's what really interests you—"

"For the moment," she said. "But hold the other thought. We can revisit that in a moment."

He rolled to his back, the sheet riding low on his hips. There, slashing a raised pink swath down his right side was his badge of honor. "Pretty impressive."

Gabi leaned forward for a closer look, trailed a finger down the ridge of it. Then impulsively leaned close and pressed her lips over it. As she lifted her head, she felt tears sting her eyes. "You could have died. If they had to do emergency surgery it meant the appendix was ready to burst."

"It was," he agreed, wiping back the tears with the pads of his thumbs, his voice gentle. "But it didn't. The way I see it, we can't worry about what might have happened or what could happen. We have to take life one day at a time."

Feeling foolish, Gabi blinked back the tears.

"Hey." He cupped her face with his hand, his eyes boring into hers. "It means a lot to me that you care."

When she smiled, he put a serious expression on his face. "I've showed you mine. Now you show me yours."

Gabi loosened the death hold she had on the sheet she'd pulled to her neck the second the lights came on. She took a deep breath before ever-so-slowly lowering the sheet.

Jude's expression remained impassive as he took in the scar that started just a few inches below her throat and shot down between her breasts to a spot midabdomen. He cocked his head.

"Well, it is longer than mine. I'll give you that," he said finally. "But it's also thinner and not as ropy."

He lifted his gaze. "I think we have a draw."

"It doesn't disgust you?"

Surprise flickered across his face. "Disgust? Why would it disgust me?"

Gabi vividly recalled the pool party held at a coworker's home. When she'd taken off her cover-up, she'd been shocked at the horrified looks by several new staff members. Until that moment, she'd never thought of her scar as ugly. But she'd seen several eyes widen and had even heard someone gasp. When the guy she was with grimaced and told her it was a total turnoff, she'd wanted to sink into the ground. Instead she'd told him his attitude was a total turnoff and walked away.

"It's ugly," she said finally.

He lifted his hands, looking truly puzzled. "It's simply a scar. Actually, a mighty good-looking one."

The tight grip around her chest began to ease. Jude might be somewhat adept at hiding his emotions, but she'd have known if he'd been horrified by what he was viewing.

Simply a scar.

Relief flooded her. "Now that our contest is over, I suggest we return to more important matters."

His lazy smile did strange things to her insides. "What did you have in mind?"

Gabi slipped her hand beneath the sheet, closed around him, found him in…full bloom. "I think we're on the same wavelength."

His arms encircled her. "Darlin', we are and have been…from the second we met."

Chapter Thirteen

Sunday proved to be warm and sunny. Gabi stared into her closet pondering what to wear that afternoon to the Animal Extravaganza at the Lubbock Civic Center. Knowing she'd be around dogs all afternoon, she didn't want to get too dressed up. Yet, with Jude coming with her, she wanted to look nice.

No longer needing to hide her scar from him, Gabi chose a sage-colored top with a slightly scooped neck. The lightness of the fabric hinted at spring, but the three-quarter-length sleeves said the wearer understood the season hadn't yet arrived.

Gabi paired the top with a pair of jeans that made her waist look thin, her hips curved and her backside well toned—the perfect trifecta. Her only concession to style—and to the hope of spring—was a pair of strappy sandals with a touch of bling.

Pulling her hair back into a low ponytail, she studied her reflection then added a little lipstick.

Her mouth curved upward as she topped the color with some gloss. She didn't know why she bothered. Jude would have it all kissed off by the time they arrived at the Civic Center.

Man, did he like to kiss. And being the honest sort, Gabi had to admit she liked kissing him, too. They'd certainly done plenty of it in the past forty-eight hours.

When she wasn't with her father, she'd been with Jude. Last night, when the handsome cowboy who she'd begun to secretly think of as hers asked her to stay over, she'd told him yes.

Once her father was discharged and able to manage on his own, she'd be leaving Horseback Hollow. In the meantime, Gabi would cram in as much time with Jude as possible.

Take this morning. She'd sat with him in his family pew and had been seriously tempted when he'd invited her back to his parents' house for Sunday brunch.

In the end she'd begged off, telling him she had to call her brothers and update them on Orlando's progress. Though her father spoke—and texted—regularly with each of his sons, he didn't always give them a clear picture of his progress. The boys—er, men—depended on their little sister for unbiased, factual information.

After giving the same basic report and answering the same questions four different times, Gabi felt as if her day was finally ready to begin. She glanced at the clock on the wall and frowned. Jude was late.

Considering they still had to swing by the animal shelter and pick up the three dogs they'd be taking with them to the Civic Center then drive an hour to Lubbock, every minute counted if they wanted to be there when the Animal Extravaganza opened.

She pulled out her phone to text Jude but stopped when she heard his truck pull into the driveway. Through the front window she saw him get out, looking mouthwateringly handsome in jeans and a white polo, and quivered like a sixteen-year-old about to embark on a first date.

He took her hands and stepped back. "You look amazing."

Before she could respond, he leaned over and brought his lips to hers in a long, lingering kiss.

Stepping back, Jude stroked one hand up her arm as if he couldn't keep from touching her. "I've missed you."

"We just saw each other a couple hours ago," she said, even as she found herself linking her fingers with his.

"Feels like forever," he said, then kissed her again.

Warmth spread through Gabi's body, and she realized it was the same for her. How had he become so important in such a short time? All she thought about was him. Only when he was with her did her world feel in sync.

Better get used to it being out of sync, she scolded herself then grabbed a jacket. "We should get moving. We still have to stop by the shelter and—"

"All done." The eyes Jude fixed on her were curious and she worried they saw too much. "Dogs are in the truck."

"What? How?" Gabi asked then waved away the questions. "It doesn't matter."

Once outside, she hurried to the pickup. Jude had stowed the three carriers in the backseat of the truck's extended cab. Two held small dogs, while the other was in the medium to large size range. Or perhaps he just looked large, she thought, in comparison to the others.

"Is that a Shih Tzu?" She gestured to a black-and-white puffball calmly licking a paw.

"Yes." Jude paused, as if searching his memory. "That's Ernie. Nine-year-old male. The elderly woman who owned him died recently. Apparently none of the family could take him. He's got papers and everything."

Gabi let her gaze linger on the small dog with big brown eyes, who'd recently lost the person he loved most in the world. Soon, very soon, she'd be in the position of being separated from the one she loved. Although Jude would still be alive, he wouldn't be with her.

"I'll find you a good home, Ernie," she said with an intensity that made Jude look up from the carrier he was straightening. "I promise."

The dog's fluffy tail thumped against the bottom of the crate, his big eyes full of trust.

Gabi took a steadying breath and shifted her gaze to the large carrier, the one holding the bigger dog. His sleek black fur was laced with silver and his golden eyes shone sharp and assessing. The animal's penetrating gaze never wavered from her face. "Who is this?"

"Shug."

Tilting her head, Gabi frowned. "That's his name?"

"Yep." Jude lifted a shoulder. "It was on his collar. He was a stray. He's a blue heeler, also known as an Australian cattle dog."

"I'd think with all your cattle, you could use one of these around your place."

"We already have a couple of border collies." Jude's blue eyes were warm and reassuring as he reached over and squeezed her hand. "Don't worry. We won't have any trouble finding this fella a good home."

The blue heeler must have finished his assessment of Gabi because his tail began to move slowly side to side, although his yellow eyes remained watchful.

"Jude is right," she told the animal. "We'll find you a home on a ranch. You can run and do whatever it is that cattle dogs do."

A low whine drew Gabi's attention to the last crate. It held a scruffy dog with longish hair and an even longer body. He stood, pawing at the metal door to the carrier as if saying, *Let me out, let me out.*

Gabi put her hand to the wire door and the plume of a tail shifted into high gear even as the animal's tongue snaked out in welcome.

"This one is a real cutie." Gabi shifted her gaze back to Jude. "What's his story?"

"Apparently some girl got him from her boyfriend as a gift. The girl moved out of state and the mother didn't want him." Jude smiled as the dog's whole body began to vibrate. "Best guess is he's a mix between a wire-haired dachshund and a Yorkshire terrier. The volunteer at the shelter called him a dorkie."

Gabi wrinkled her nose. "Dorkie?"

"Dachshund, Yorkie…dorkie." Jude chuckled. "His name is Chico, which doesn't fit, either."

"You're right. It sounds more like a Chihuahua or a Mexican hairless."

At the sound of his name, the dog began to whine again, pressing his scruffy face against the wire.

Jude glanced at his watch. "We best get on the road. Parking can be an issue around the Civic Center."

When Gabi stepped back, Chico crouched down and began to whimper, his dark eyes pleading.

Impulsively, Gabi opened the cage door. The dog sprang into her arms, slathering her face with doggy kisses. Keeping a firm hold on his wiggling body, Gabi ignored Jude's amused chuckle and took Chico with her to the front.

After securing the other doors, Jude climbed in behind the wheel. "Do you plan to hold him all the way to Lubbock?"

Chico, now relaxed, lay on his back, eyes closed as she stroked his belly.

"Maybe." Gabi smiled down at the dog. "I guess that will depend on how he tolerates the ride."

"He's liking where he's at right now," Jude observed.

Gabi shot him a wink. "If you're a good boy, I may rub *your* belly tonight."

Jude backed the truck out of the driveway and grinned. "This day just keeps getting better."

Before their shift was half-over at the Civic Center, Jude and Gabi had a rancher interested in Shug and an older couple in Ernie. Both had filled out the paperwork and set up times on Monday to stop by the shelter.

Jude fully believed they could have found a home for Chico, too, if Gabi hadn't been so determined to keep him out of sight. After they'd secured homes for Shug and Ernie, he told Gabi they should put Chico out front in the booth, engage people in conversation, let the lovable nature of the "dorkie" shine through.

Shortly after he made his suggestion, Gabi decided to take Chico for a walk. Jude noticed she took off the dog's red Adopt Me vest before leaving the booth.

She wants him, he thought.

Jude could already picture the little terrier running across the pastures, chasing the cats that'd soon show him who was boss. Though they'd mostly had big dogs growing up, Jude figured he wouldn't mind a small one. Not if that made Gabi happy.

While she strolled the exhibition hall aisles, picking up small bags of food from pet food distributors and other samples, Jude kept busy. People stopped and added their email addresses to the shelter's electronic newsletter list. He talked up the fact they were a no-kill shelter and passed out flyers containing pictures and blurbs on the animals back at the shelter eager for a "forever home."

A forever home. That's what Jude wanted with Gabi. He thought about all those times he'd been convinced he was in love and realized whatever he'd felt for those women had been but a pale imitation of what he felt for her.

He could be himself with Gabi. There wasn't anything they couldn't talk about, anything they couldn't share, anything they couldn't work out. The incident with the scars was a perfect example of the level of trust that existed between them.

His jaw tightened as he remembered the flash of fear in her eyes when she slowly lowered the sheet. Someone in the past had made some nasty comment about the scar, he was sure of it. That incident had made her so self-conscious she hadn't wanted anyone to see it.

Yet, for the first time since they'd met, today she'd worn a shirt that didn't wrap around her neck. He'd wanted to cheer. He briefly considered making some teasing comment about how good it was to see the scar come out of the closet. After a second's hesitation, he'd kept his mouth shut. The last thing he wanted was for her to think the scar was the first thing anyone noticed.

No one had said anything to her today, he thought with a smile of satisfaction. He was sure most of them didn't even notice it. They were too focused on her irresistible smile and her enthusiasm for the animals.

Besides, he meant what he'd said the other night. It was a badge of honor. She'd fought heart disease and won.

"How's it going?"

Jude jerked his head up and saw Steve at the entrance to the booth. Instead of the jeans he and Gabi had worn, the bank executive wore a brown suit and looked ready to conduct a presentation to his board of directors. "It's going good. I didn't expect you so soon."

Steve ignored the comment and glanced around. "Where's Gabi?"

"She's checking out the exhibition area." As far as Jude was concerned, now that Steve was here, she could take her sweet time returning to the booth. "Until ten minutes ago we were swamped. Traffic is finally beginning to slow down."

"Did you generate any interest in the animals you brought?" Steve gestured with his head toward the two crates where Ernie and Shug slept.

"We found homes for both of them." Jude glanced to a manila folder on the counter. "Both prospective owners filled out the paperwork and plan to stop by the shelter to-morrow to complete the adoption process."

"I thought you were going to bring three." Steve leaned casually against the table.

"We've decided to adopt the dachshund-Yorkie mix," Jude said without thinking, then watched Steve's brows rise.

"We?"

"Gabi," Jude clarified in a matter-of-fact tone. "She wants him. But if her dad gives her grief, I have plenty of room at the ranch for the little guy."

"Appears things between you and the lovely Ms. Mendoza are heating up," Steve said with a slow, lazy smile. "My aunt Alma lives down the street from Gabi's father. She mentioned Gabi has recently started sleeping elsewhere."

Damn.

He should have thought things through, Jude thought, furious with himself. Horseback Hollow was a small town where neighbors watched out for each other. Of course they'd be keeping an eye on Orlando's house. Especially considering the man was in Lubbock and his daughter was in an unfamiliar town all alone.

Jude wondered how long it would take for someone to mention the overnight sleepovers to Gabi's dad.

"O worries about his daughter," Jude said, his gaze pointed. "I'd hate for him to get wind of anything that might upset him."

Steve shrugged. "Hey, there are no secrets in a small town."

"Hi, Steve." Gabi strolled up with Chico on a leash at her side. "We didn't expect you until five."

"It's a beautiful day." Steve shot Gabi a speculative glance. "I thought you and Jude might want to enjoy what's left of it."

"That's kind of you."

"Who's this little guy?" Steve crouched down, extended a hand to the scruffy dog, which the animal carefully sniffed.

"His name is Chico." Gabi began to stammer. "I forgot his Adopt Me sweater and came back for it."

"Wouldn't putting it on be false advertising?" Steve pulled to his feet.

"I don't know what you mean."

"Jude told me you're planning to adopt him."

Gabi's gaze darted to Jude.

"I said you wanted him," Jude explained. "If your father doesn't like the idea of a dog in his home, I'll take him."

"You'd do that?"

Jude wished Steve wasn't there, watching so intently and obviously listening to every word. If they were alone, he'd tell Gabi he'd do anything to make her happy. He settled for a simple, "Of course."

For a second, Jude thought Gabi was going to fling herself into his arms.

"Hear that, Chico?" Gabi scooped up the dog and hugged him instead. "You're my boy now."

"Take him home with you," Steve urged, waving a magnanimous hand. "You can complete all the paperwork later."

"It's official," Gabi told the dog, who immediately began slathering her with kisses. "I'm your new mama."

Watching her gentleness with the animal, Jude felt his heart stir. Gabi would make a good mother. Their children would never lack for love.

"I need to swing by the shelter on my way back." Steve gestured to the crates where Shug and Ernie slept. "I can take these other two with me and drop them off. Have they been out to the pet relief area recently?"

"Less than a half hour ago," Jude told him. The grassy

knoll out back of the exhibition hall had everything a dog could want—grass, trees, bushes and even a fake fire hydrant.

"Good. One more thing." Steve's phone beeped. Though he pulled it from his pocket, his eyes never left Gabi. "Our branch manager in Vicker's Corners told me today she's accepted a position in Dallas. I'd love to get someone with your credentials for that spot. If you decide to apply, let me know. I'll fast-track the application."

Gabi opened her mouth, then closed it and just smiled.

Gabi kept Chico on her lap during the drive back to Horseback Hollow. Apparently all the excitement of the day had tired him out. The dog slept, cuddled close to her.

Which is where he'd like to be, thought Jude. He liked the feel of Gabi's body against his, liked having her beside him when he woke in the morning. But for now, the overnight stays would have to end.

The last thing he wanted was for Gabi to be hurt by gossip. If word got back to Orlando that Gabi had been sleeping elsewhere while he was in rehab, there would be hell to pay.

Not that Jude could blame Orlando. If he had a daughter, he'd be protective, too. A sudden image of baby Piper flashed. Would Gabi and his child look like his niece? Or would their son or daughter inherit Gabi's beautiful brown eyes and thick dark hair?

"I'm not sure what my father is going to think when he hears I've brought a dog into his home."

Jude pulled his thoughts back to the present and slanted a sideways glance. Her hand continued to gently stroke the animal's wiry fur, and when the dog snorted in sleep, Gabi smiled.

"I'm sure he won't mind," Jude assured her. "After all, it's only temporary."

Temporary, because if Jude had his way, Gabi would soon be his wife. Once they were married, she and Chico would move into the ranch house.

"You're right." Her smile vanished. "Once my father comes home, I'll be back in Miami."

No, Jude thought, with a hint of panic. There was no reason for her to return to Miami when everything she needed was right here, including him.

"You've enjoyed your time in Horseback Hollow," he reminded her.

"I really have. I'd never been this far west before." She settled back against the leather seat. "I wasn't sure what to expect. I'd kept an open mind, but this—" she lifted a hand and swept the air "—was far different than what I imagined."

He waited for her to continue.

"The people are so friendly. They look you in the eye and smile when they pass you on the street." Gabi's voice grew more animated as she continued. "Though everyone dresses nicely, there isn't the emphasis on appearance and youth that I saw in Miami. At the bank where I work, women who weren't even forty were visiting cosmetic surgeons, worried about looking 'old.'"

"Unbelievable" was all he said.

"I know. It's insane." For a second she simply stared out the window. "While I love the ocean and the palms, I love the vastness of the terrain here. It will be hard to leave."

Just hearing her utter the words in such a matter-of-fact tone struck terror in Jude's heart. But he kept his voice calm. "Your father will miss you."

She sighed. "I know."

"My parents always encouraged us to find our own way." Jude slanted a sideways glance. "But they also showed us that at the end of the day it's not how much money you have or how big of a home you can afford to build—family is what matters."

"Do you think that's why your mother asked you to take on the Fortune name?" Gabi asked. "To show them that she values her connection with them? And, speaking of the Fortunes, has the NTSB determined yet if sabotage was involved in the crash?"

"To answer your first question, I believe the reason she wanted her children to incorporate the Fortune name was to show her acceptance of that connection. In terms of the second, the ruling on the crash is expected any day. But it's a government agency, so who really knows." Jude kept his impatience under wraps, wondering how the conversation had shifted from the importance of family and Horseback Hollow to the Fortunes.

Regardless, he was determined to get it back on track and make Gabi realize what was really important in life and all she'd be leaving behind.

Jude pulled into the driveway of her dad's home and cut the engine. Across the street, he caught sight of Alma standing in her yard pretending to inspect the branches of a bush that hadn't yet budded out. "Having you here matters to your father. Having you care enough to drop whatever else you were doing and come and be with him when he needed you, matters."

"I had to come." A look Jude couldn't quite decipher crossed her face. "He was there for me through my surgery and recovery. He's always been there for me. I wanted to be here for him."

Finally, Jude thought, the discussion was firmly back on track. Now all he had to do was get Gabi to realize that the connection with him also mattered. And, more importantly, to realize that he was someone she simply couldn't live without.

Chapter Fourteen

The next week passed quickly with Orlando gaining strength and Gabi drawing closer to her favorite cowboy. Jude told her about neighbor Alma Peatry's eagle eyes. That put an end to the sleepovers. Though Gabi no longer spent the night, she and Jude found late afternoon with sunlight streaming through partially drawn shades was a perfect time to make love.

The increasing closeness they shared wasn't only in the bedroom. Every evening they took Chico for a walk, holding hands as they strolled down the sidewalk. One night they went to a renovated movie theater in Lubbock and sat in the back row. Gabi discovered the fun of eating popcorn and kissing a guy you were crazy about in a darkened theater.

During these long walks and times together, Jude told her about his childhood—amusing little anecdotes about his parents and brothers and sisters. Stories that helped her understand how he'd grown into the fine man he was today.

She did her own sharing, regaling him with stories about how during her father's deployments, her mother had kept the family's spirits up by playing practical jokes on her children. Though Gabi had gotten good at spotting the pranks and preempting them, her brothers had continued to be snookered each and every time.

She and Jude talked about how hard it had been to leave

family and go off to college. As they spoke of those years away from home, Gabi found herself tempted to tell Jude about her transplant.

The fact that he was so honest with her only compounded her guilt over withholding the information from him.

In the end, it was fear that kept her lips sealed. Fear if she told him about her new heart, he wouldn't walk away. He'd stick.

The love she felt for him refused to let him make such a sacrifice. She wanted him happy. He'd get over her, she told herself, find someone to marry—

The mere thought of another woman with him was a dagger to her heart.

"Maybe I *could* stay," she told Chico, as she sat on the porch brushing his wiry hair.

She'd risen early, too restless to sleep, and decided to give the dorkie a bath and a good brushing before heading to Lubbock.

The dog looked up from his position on the step. She swore she saw the question in his eyes.

"Wherever I am, you'll be with me," she assured him. Gabi wasn't sure what her landlord would say. But her lease was up, so if she needed to move, this would be the time to do it. "But, darn it, Chico, I like it here. I think you feel the same."

The dog appeared to nod, although it may have been simply the pull of the brush against the top of his head.

"Jude is wonderful." Just saying his name made her heart stutter. "I've never known anyone like him. I'll never love anyone else."

A lump clogged her throat and tears filled her eyes. "I don't know how I can do without him, Chico."

At the sound of his name, the dog licked her hand, thumped his tail.

"You love him, too, don't you?"

A tear dribbled down her cheek. She hurriedly swiped it away. Alma continued to be a one-woman neighborhood watch. Gabi had no doubt she could spot reddened eyes from fifty yards.

"The thing is—" though there was no one but Chico around to hear, Gabi dropped her voice to a whisper "—I know he loves me, too."

While Jude may not have said the words, she saw the emotion each time she gazed into those oh-so-blue eyes.

"I was a fool," she told the dog, "to think I could have a simple fling with him."

She continued to brush the wiry coat while her mind replayed that first meeting with Jude. From the first instant, he'd charmed her. But it was the man beneath that charming exterior who'd captured her heart.

"The core problem remains." She expelled a heavy sigh. "I can't give him children. I can't guarantee I'll be around in another ten years."

Gabi knew the stats. Knew that less than 40 percent of heart transplant patients were alive twenty years post-transplant. Still, she'd been young and healthy when she'd gotten her heart and had already made it this far with no rejection. But then she thought of her friends and knew that was no guarantee.

Gabi could already envision what would happen if she attempted to sit down and explain why she couldn't be with him. He'd call her a worrywart. And, because he was the optimistic sort, he'd try to convince her she was overreacting, making a major decision about their future because of fear over something that might never occur.

He'd look up the statistics and quote them to illustrate he was correct in his optimism. Gabi knew those stats as well as she knew her own name.

The numbers could be considered encouraging. It was

also true some transplant patients fared better than others. Several points in her favor were she'd made it seven years without a setback and took excellent care of her body.

But statistics didn't tell the whole story. Gabi thought of Kate and Mary, a couple of women she'd met online after her surgery. They'd had heart transplants around the same time as her and had appeared to do everything right. But Kate's heart had showed signs of rejection on a recent cardiac biopsy, and Mary had passed away shortly before Gabi arrived in Horseback Hollow.

"I saw the pain my father went through when he lost my mother." At the words, Chico merely thumped his tail and gave her another lick. "How can I knowingly put Jude in a position of having to face something like that?"

She glanced around the neighborhood. At the trees with tiny buds that would soon become leaves, at the bold green tips of flowers she couldn't even identify peeking their way through the rich soil, and desperately wished things could be different.

Perhaps she could simply stay in Horseback Hollow. She loved it here. It already felt like home to her.

She and Jude could continue to date. They didn't have to get serious....

The second the thought entered her mind, she rejected it. Though she'd like to believe keeping the relationship casual was possible, things were already serious.

Perhaps, she thought, grasping at straws, having kids wasn't a big deal to him. If she kept herself in good physical shape, she could keep the odds in her favor. Perhaps...

Her phone dinged. Gabi glanced at the fourth text she'd received from her father just that morning.

"Apparently the doctor is coming at two to discuss discharge plans," she told the dog. "I have to be there."

After texting her father she'd join him for lunch and stay until the doctor arrived, Gabi laid down the brush and picked up the small dog, hugging him until he squirmed. Though she'd learned long ago that wishing for something didn't make it so, those days preceding her transplant had also shown her the importance of hope.

This afternoon, she'd focus on her father. Then she'd decide what to do about Jude.

The tight set to her father's mouth when she walked into the dining area a little over an hour later told her today hadn't been any better for him than yesterday. Ever since the doctor had started talking discharge plans, his therapy had kicked into high gear.

When she'd visited yesterday, her father had been in a funk. He told her the therapists and nurses had no idea how hard he was working and certainly had little sympathy for his pain.

Though Gabi understood these past few days had been trying, by the time she'd headed back to Horseback Hollow last night, she had a pounding headache and her sympathies were firmly with the staff.

"Your food is probably cold by now," Orlando said in lieu of a greeting, pointing to a plate covered by a silver dome. "It's been sitting there for almost a half hour."

The nurse in the hall who Gabi had passed on her way to the dining room had told her she'd just brought in the guest tray, so it should be good and hot.

"I'm sorry I wasn't here sooner." Gabi brushed a quick kiss on her father's cheek then settled into the chair opposite him. "I gave Chico a bath and was brushing him when you called. I lost track of the time."

"I don't understand why you got a dog." Her father forked off a bite of meat loaf, scowled. "You know your landlord won't let you keep him."

"My lease is up." Gabi held on to her rising temper with both hands. She removed the silver topper from her food and separated the paper napkin from the utensils. "If I have to, I'll find a new place to live."

"You're going back, then."

Gabi looked at him in surprise. Ever since she'd arrived in Horseback Hollow, her father had been telling her she needed to get back to Florida. To her job. To her life there. Not going back had never been on the table.

Now he acted as if her staying was a possibility she'd been considering all along.

"My job is there." She forced a little laugh. "If I want to eat, I have to work."

"I heard Steve Watkins has an opening for a bank manager." For the first time since she'd walked into the dining room, the lines around his mouth relaxed. "It'd be nice to have you close. If you want to stay, that is. You know me. I don't interfere in my children's lives."

Since when? Gabi wanted to ask, but pressed her lips together until the impulse passed. "How did you hear about the bank job in Vicker's Corners?"

"I've got my sources." Orlando stabbed a green bean. "By the way, your boyfriend stopped by earlier."

Gabi's fingers froze on the napkin she'd been placing on her lap. "Jude?"

Her father's brow lifted. "You have more than one boyfriend?"

"No. But I thought Jude was busy moving cattle today." Gabi flushed. "And to clarify, Jude Fortune Jones and I are just friends."

"Look at these lines." Orlando pointed with his fork to his handsome, weathered face. "I wasn't born yesterday."

Her father's voice suddenly sounded almost jovial. The scowl he'd greeted her with only moments earlier had vanished.

Gabi took a bite of meat loaf, put it in her mouth and chewed for a moment. Orlando's change in mood appeared tied to the possibility of her remaining in Horseback Hollow permanently. Had it been Jude who'd planted that seed?

"Did Jude make a special trip to Lubbock to see you?" Though she tried to keep her tone nonchalant, the question sounded more like she was interrogating her father rather than asking a simple question about an unimportant topic.

"He may have mentioned something about picking up supplies." Orlando took another bite of green beans, ignoring the pile of carrots on his plate.

Gabi sensed he was waiting for her to pepper him with questions. Instead she brought a couple of steamed baby carrots to her mouth then followed it with a sip of skim milk.

"He came up during my therapy," Orlando offered when she remained silent.

Gabi expelled the breath she didn't realize she'd been holding. Between her father's therapy and Jude's errands, it appeared there had been little time for the two men to do much more than exchange brief pleasantries.

Besides, even if they'd had more time, it wasn't as if Jude would have mentioned they were sleeping together. "Too bad he came when you were busy."

"He stayed and watched." Orlando's lips curved in a slight smile. "After observing the session, Jude agrees my therapist is a sadist."

It took a moment for the words to register. Gabi dropped her fork. "He did not say that."

Orlando shrugged. "He thought it. Know what else?"

Gabi was afraid to ask, but the way the conversation was going, she had the feeling her father would tell her anyway. She lifted her glass of milk. "What else?"

"The boy is in love with you, Gabriella."

The milk Gabi had been swallowing took a detour. She coughed, gasped, fought for breath. After a few seconds, she regained her composure. "Let me get this straight. He told you he loved me?"

"I have eyes," her father responded. "It'd be obvious to a blind man."

"Just like it was obvious he thinks your therapist is a sadist?"

"That's right."

"You're mistaken." Gabi could have cheered when this time her voice came out casual and offhand, just as she'd intended. "It's true we've become good friends, but nothing more."

A shiver of disloyalty rippled through her at the lie. Why did she feel as if she'd let Jude down by her response?

"Ah, *mija*." Her father expelled a heavy sigh. "Do you think I can't see what's in *your* eyes? On your face? It's clear what you feel for him."

Heat dotted Gabi's cheeks. Was she that transparent? Putting down her fork, she abandoned the pretense of eating. "If there is something between Jude and me—and I'm not saying there is—are you telling me you approve?"

"It depends." Orlando stabbed another bean, looked up. This time his gaze was serious, his lips unsmiling.

"On what?"

"On whether you're willing to be completely honest with him."

Gabi licked her lips. "I don't know what you mean."

"You haven't told him about your transplant."

Something in her father's voice sent a shuddering chill through Gabi. "You didn't tell him." She grabbed her father's arm, her gaze riveted to his. "Tell me you didn't do that."

"He needs to hear it from you," Orlando said mildly, lifting her fingers from his sleeve. "So, no, I didn't mention it."

Releasing a breath, Gabi sagged back in her chair.

"I've never known you to be a coward, Gabriella. I have to say I'm disappointed." Her father's expression might be impassive, but his words held the force of a hard slap.

"I'm not a coward." She lifted her chin. "Jude knows I've had heart surgery. I just haven't decided the best way to tell him what kind."

"Your prognosis is excellent. There's no reason to be afraid." Her father's eyes softened and he reached out to grip her hand. "The man is in love with you. He has a right to know something that's such an important part of your life. Not telling him is tantamount to lying."

"I—" Gabi hesitated.

"Tell him." Her father's tone brooked no argument. "Or I will."

Jude jumped out of his truck in front of Gabi's house, a bouquet of flowers in one hand, a package of steaks in the other and hope in his heart. When he'd visited Orlando earlier today, it sounded as if the man would be released any day. Which meant Jude had to step up his game.

Not that securing Gabi's love was a game. It was more of a mission. He loved her so much he couldn't imagine not having her in his life. He didn't want her for a day, or a week or a year. He wanted her to be his wife, to be the mother of his children, to be the woman he grew old with and loved for eternity.

One hurdle had been jumped when Jude had sat down with Orlando after his therapy session. Jude told him he loved Gabi and wanted to marry her. Because Jude suspected Gabi's father was a traditionalist, he'd asked for his blessing.

The older man had gazed into his eyes for a long moment, as if he could see all the way into Jude's soul. Jude had held steady and let him look. He had nothing to hide. His feelings for Gabi were strong and sincere.

In the end, Orlando had said marrying him would be up to his daughter. But if Gabi said yes, they would have his blessing. Jude had ridden a high the rest of the day.

Tonight, he and Gabi planned to grill steaks then take Chico for a long walk. Jude liked it that they didn't have to do something special to have a good time. Some of his favorite moments with her were when they simply sat on the living room sofa in front of a fire and talked. Or strolled hand in hand in the cool night air with a thousand stars twinkling overhead.

He loved it when she placed her hand in his as if trusting him to look out for her. She was his woman, and he would do everything he could to protect her. To make her happy. And he would love her with each breath until the day he died.

"Jude. Wait up."

He turned to see Alma Peatry striding down the sidewalk toward him, her perfectly groomed standard-size white poodle trotting beside her.

As the gray-haired woman drew close, Jude saw her pale blue eyes snap with undisguised interest. "Flowers and candy. You went all out tonight."

"Actually—" Jude shifted from one boot to the other and lifted the package wrapped in butcher's paper "—these are steaks, not candy."

Her wrinkled face brightened. "T-bones?"

"What else?"

"You devil." Alma's hot-pink painted lips widened. "You'll have the girl eating out of your hands."

"The girl" appeared on the front porch. Gabi's smile flickered for a second when she saw him speaking with Alma, but she hurried over to them. "Hello, Mrs. Peatry."

"It's Alma, dear. Just Alma."

"Taking Monique for a walk, I see." Gabi leaned over and patted the poodle's topknot, while inside the house

Chico yapped, obviously not pleased at being left out of the action.

"It's too beautiful of a day to stay inside." Alma glanced down at the poodle. "Ready to rock and roll, Monique?"

The dog gave a high-pitched bark and did a little shimmy. Alma chuckled. "That's affirmative."

Waving a hand carelessly in the air, the woman sauntered down the sidewalk.

"I come bearing three gifts." Jude held out the daisies. "These are for you."

"You brought me daisies the night we ate at The Grill." Pleasure lit Gabi's face. "Thank you. Very much."

"You're very welcome."

She glanced down at his other hand. "Is that my second gift?"

He nodded and held up the package. "Prime beef. Alma assured me steaks are better than candy."

"Definitely." She leaned forward and kissed him lightly on the mouth. "But being with you is the best gift of all."

Though Jude knew they'd agreed to limit public displays of affection, he couldn't resist drawing her to him for a long kiss. "We're on the same wavelength there."

She laughed, a little breathless now, and he followed her inside.

Chico sprang the instant Jude stepped across the threshold. As if on a trampoline, the dog bounced high in the air, making little yipping noises.

Jude grinned. "Looks like you're not the only one who's happy to see me."

"Believe me. You're definitely a bright spot in a dismal day."

Not just the words but something in her tone made Jude stop petting Chico and straighten.

"Papi—" Gabi stopped, shook her head. "Actually, although my father was in a foul mood when I got there, he'd mellowed considerably by the time I left."

Jude watched her intently, now seeing the emotion she'd done such a good job of hiding. He folded her into his arms, pressing her resistant body against him.

"Tell me why you're sad," he whispered against her hair.

She pushed back, raked fingers through her hair. "It's noth—"

"Don't say it's nothing." He kept his tone gentle but firm. "Tell me."

She drew in a deep breath then let it out slowly. "This afternoon I got a call from Rosemary. She's my assistant at the bank. She had distressing news."

"They fired you?"

"No." Gabi gave a nervous laugh. "Although I almost wish that was the news."

Jude took Gabi's ice-cold fingers in his hand and led her to the sofa.

"Rosemary called to tell me about Faith's husband—" Gabi spoke in a scratchy voice, thick with emotion.

While the names were unfamiliar to him, these were obviously people who meant a lot to her. "Faith is—"

"One of my best friends. We work together at the bank. She and Daniel just celebrated their third anniversary. I was maid of honor at their wedding." The words rushed out then abruptly stopped. She cleared her throat before continuing. "Now he's gone."

Gabi's face crumpled and tears welled in her eyes.

"He left her?"

"No. Dear God, no." Gabi wrapped her arms around herself as if freezing. "He was killed."

"What happened?" Jude kept his voice soft and low.

"I thought Faith would have called me, but Rosemary said she was a mess. They were so much in love." Gabi looked at him, her eyes bleak. "She hasn't even returned to work yet. I think Rose said she was coming back in the next few days."

Jude took her hand again, squeezed in a wordless gesture of support.

"Daniel was in Manhattan on business. Apparently he was distracted while crossing a street and didn't notice the light had changed." A shadow crossed her face. "A cab hit him. He—he never regained consciousness."

"Oh, baby." Jude wrapped his arms around her. "When's the funeral? I'll go with you."

The stricken look in her eyes ratcheted up his concern.

"It was weeks ago. He died not long after I left to come here." The words stumbled from her lips in little bursts. "Rosemary didn't want me to feel obligated to come."

"She kept it from you." Because this was her friend and he could see she was upset, Jude tried to keep the condemnation from his voice. It was hard. Her assistant had effectively taken the decision to attend the funeral out of her hands.

Gabi lifted her gaze, a look of bewilderment in her eyes. "Rose knew what Faith and Daniel meant to me. It's not right she took away my choice."

"No," he agreed. "It wasn't right."

"I wish I could have been there." Tears slipped down her cheeks. "I would have been there."

Jude tightened his hold on her, gently stroking her back as she cried. After a moment, she straightened with a sound that was half sob, half laugh.

Chico had climbed up onto the back of the sofa and was leaning over trying to kiss Gabi's tears away.

"Chico, down." He reached for the wiggling dog, who only skittered to the other side of the sofa with the agility of a circus performer.

"Let him be. He's just being my friend." Gabi sniffled

and swiped at the remnants of her tears with her fingers. "I'm sorry for unloading on you."

"Hey, goes with the territory." Jude deliberately lightened his tone. "I'm your steady guy, remember?"

A reluctant smile lifted her lips. "Yes, you are."

"That brings us to gift number three." He reached into his pocket then pressed a ring into her palm. "Now it's official. You and I are going steady."

When Gabi only stared, Jude's heartbeat galvanized. The words tumbled out. "My senior year in high school, our football team took the state championship in our division. First time ever. They had rings made for everyone on the team."

He kissed her forehead. *Keep it light,* he told himself, *Don't spook her.* "I'd like you to have it."

"I can't accept this." She attempted to push the ring into his hands, but Jude shook his head.

"Do you want to date anyone else?" he asked her.

"No, but—"

"I don't, either." He smiled, brushed a tear-soaked tendril of hair back from her cheek. "Jude and Gabi are going steady. She has his ring."

Saying the words in a singsong tone made him feel silly but had the desired effect of bringing a momentary smile back to her lips.

"I'll keep it," she said finally. "For now. But when I leave town, you're taking it back."

Jude wasn't worried. There was no way he was letting her go. And, by the time he got through romancing her, no way she'd want to leave.

"Understood." To seal the deal, Jude kissed her, softly and with great tenderness.

The fear that had been a tight fist around his heart eased. So far, so good.

He'd gotten her to accept one ring from him. Before long, she'd accept another.

Chapter Fifteen

Shortly before noon, Gabi pulled the Buick into the lane leading to Deke and Jeanne Marie's house. When Jude's mother learned Orlando had been discharged from the rehab center, she'd called and invited them both over for Sunday brunch.

Even though he hadn't been home twenty-four hours, Orlando was determined to attend, especially once he heard Sawyer and Laurel would be there.

"Are you sure you're up to this, Papi?" Gabi asked for what felt like the hundredth time. But, darn it, she didn't like seeing him push himself so soon after getting home.

"It's lunch," Orlando reminded her cheerfully. "Not a daylong party."

Since he seemed to have no qualms about his ability to handle the outing, Gabi decided to quit questioning the decision. She had to admit his spirits had improved since he'd gotten home. He hadn't voiced a single complaint.

Chico had welcomed him at the door. Despite Orlando's initial resistance, Gabi hadn't been surprised by how quickly he'd taken to the small dog.

The second Orlando had settled into his favorite recliner to watch a basketball game, Chico had jumped onto his lap. With brown eyes firmly fixed on the television, the dorkie had appeared as mesmerized by the action as her father.

With nothing better to do—she'd told Jude she couldn't

see him that evening—Gabi had taken a seat on the sofa, prepared to watch two NBA powerhouse teams duke it out on the court. But she found it difficult to focus. All she could think about was Jude and how her best-laid plans had gone awry.

After her conversation with her father at the rehab center on Friday, she'd planned to tell Jude about her transplant. A carefully prepared speech—complete with statistics—had been firmly fixed in her head. Then Rosemary had called.

Everything after that conversation was pretty much a blur. Jude had arrived. Somehow she'd ended up accepting a "going steady" ring from him. A ring that now hung on a chain around her neck.

A fact which made her feel like a lovestruck teen. But she wasn't ready to give it back. Not yet.

Easing the Buick to a stop in front of the house, Gabi's lips lifted in a rueful smile.

"There's the welcoming committee," her father announced.

Gabi glanced over and saw Jude step out of the house, looking yummy enough to eat in slim-cut wool pants, a checked shirt and tailored jacket. She suddenly felt like a country mouse in her chinos and spice-colored cardigan.

But when he smiled at her, every worry disappeared.

Stepping from the car, Gabi lifted a hand in a casual gesture of greeting. But she couldn't stop her smile from blossoming when he hurried toward her.

Orlando chuckled. "Someone is mighty eager to see you."

"I'm sure he just wants to make you feel welcome," Gabi said, even as she moved around the front of the car to close the distance between them.

"Yeah," she heard her father say, "I'm sure that's it."

"Hi," she said, feeling oddly breathless.

"You look beautiful." Jude surprised her by putting his

hands on her shoulders and kissing her softly on the lips. With one finger he stroked back a strand of hair that had fallen over her forehead. "I missed you, darlin'. A whole bunch."

"I missed you, too," she whispered back.

Gabi felt heat climb up her neck, knowing her father watched from the front seat. But she was glad Jude seemed to have missed her as much as she'd missed him. Twenty-four hours apart had felt like an eternity.

"I need to get the walker out of the trunk," she said, but couldn't bring herself to step away from him.

"I'll take care of it." With obvious reluctance, Jude dropped his hands from her shoulders. He opened her father's door as he made his way to the back of the car to retrieve the walker. "Good to see you, Mr. Mendoza."

"Call me Orlando." A half smile played at the corners of her father's lips. "After all, we're practically family."

Family? Gabi frowned. *Where had that come from?*

"How was your first night at home...Orlando?" Keeping a firm grip on her father's arm, Jude helped the older man to his feet.

Orlando steadied himself, which Gabi could see by the tension on his face was no easy task. "Nothing beats sleeping in your own bed. I expected you to stop by. Say hello."

Jude shot a glance at Gabi. "I thought you might need time to settle in."

"I was tired," Orlando admitted. "More than I thought I'd be. But my Gabriella is an angel. She made sure I had everything I needed."

"Oh, Papi," Gabi protested. "I didn't do anything."

"You made that delicious meal for supper," Orlando insisted. "What did you call it? Rush Hour Something?"

"Rush Hour Stew," Gabi murmured.

Jude's eyes met hers. He smiled. "I wish I'd been there. It's a favorite of mine."

"Next time." Orlando grunted and wheeled the walker up the walk, halting every few feet.

Gabi kept to the left side of her father while Jude took the right side as Orlando inched his way to the front door.

Even though spring hadn't fully arrived, large pots of flowers decorated the front of the house. When Jude opened the door, the delicious scent of sizzling bacon and sausage teased Gabi's nostrils while the din of conversation assailed her ears.

There were people everywhere. Adults laughed and talked in the parlor. Several children Gabi didn't recognize ran through the house. Jude's sister Stacey caught her eye and offered a friendly wave. The blonde stood, baby Piper in her arms, chatting animatedly with Sawyer and Laurel.

"Welcome. Welcome." Jeanne Marie appeared in the foyer, arms opened wide in greeting.

Jude's mother wore a long, flowing turquoise skirt and a blouse with turquoise and silver threads running through the fabric. Large dangly earrings with a Southwestern design hung from her ears, a matching necklace on her throat.

"Orlando, it's so good to see you up and walking." She led them to the parlor and motioned for her daughter Delaney to get up from where she was sitting. "I've just the spot for you."

"I don't want to take the young lady's chair," Orlando protested, shooting Delaney an apologetic look.

"You aren't, Mr. Mendoza," Delaney assured him, her pretty face earnest. "I need to help Mom get the food on the table."

"If you're sure," he said, even as he aimed the walker toward the chair.

"Positive." Delaney glanced at her mother. "I'll fill the water glasses with ice."

Jeanne Marie gave Delaney an approving smile. "Thanks, honey."

Once her father reached the chair, it took a little maneuvering to get him settled with his booted leg propped on an ottoman.

"Orlando." Sawyer's deep voice called out as he and his wife, Laurel, hurried over. "You look better every time I see you."

"That tells me I must have looked pretty bad before." Her father's words made Sawyer and Laurel laugh.

Gabi rolled her eyes even as contentment draped like a warm blanket around her shoulders. Papi had to be feeling good to joke.

While Orlando spoke with the couple about the NTSB investigation into the crash, Gabi caught Jeanne Marie's arm.

"Is there any way my father could be seated at the end of the table?" Gabi kept her voice low. "I'm sorry to make special demands when we're guests, but I think it would be easier—"

"Not a problem, my dear." Jeanne Marie gave Gabi's arm a reassuring squeeze. "I'm having the food set up buffet-style. Everyone can fill their plate and sit wherever they like. Your father won't need to move from where he is now. I have TV trays available for those eating in the parlor."

"We'll eat with Orlando," Jude told his mother, positioning himself next to Gabi. "I'm betting Sawyer and Laurel will, also."

It was an excellent solution. Gabi wondered if Jeanne Marie chose to serve lunch in this manner because of her father's limited mobility.

As if she could read her mind, Jude's mother put an arm around Gabi's shoulder. "In this community we take care of our own. Your father is one of us now."

"Thank you." Gabi swallowed hard past the sudden

lump in her throat. "Knowing he's among friends means so much."

Even as she fought for control, tears stung the backs of Gabi's eyes. Her father had hit the jackpot when he'd moved to this little town in Northern Texas. He had a job he loved and people who cared about him. The only thing that would make him happier was if his children all lived nearby.

"I'll be back in a few minutes." Jeanne Marie gave Gabi's arm a squeeze. "From the look I'm getting from my daughter, I'm needed in the kitchen."

"Your mother is nice," Gabi told Jude as Jeanne Marie scurried off.

"She likes you." His eyes were clear and very blue. "A lot."

Gabi looked at him doubtfully. "I wouldn't think she knows me well enough to form an opinion."

"She knows what I tell her." Jude's hand grazed the bare skin above her blouse. "It's all good."

The simple brush of his fingers against her neck sent a shiver of longing rushing through her.

His expression softened as he gazed down at her. For a second Gabi thought he might kiss her. Right there in the midst of all his family. And she might have let him. But when two of his brothers who were walking by stopped, Jude stepped back.

Though Chris stayed but a second, barely long enough to say hello, Liam appeared in no particular hurry. He settled his blue eyes on Gabi. "You've been keeping my little brother busy."

Gabi slanted a sideways glance at Jude and smiled. "You could say he's been my personal tour guide to all things Horseback Hollow."

"He's not going to know what to do with all his free time once you're gone," Liam joked.

"Shut up, Liam," Jude said mildly.

Liam grinned and ignored him, keeping his focus on Gabi. "Any idea when you'll head back to Miami?"

Sensing Jude's scrutiny, Gabi chose her words carefully. "I have a woman starting tomorrow who'll cook, clean and do laundry for my father. A physical therapist and home health nurse will also be stopping by regularly. I won't be leaving until I'm confident his needs are well covered."

Once Liam walked off, Jude turned to her. "I didn't realize you had all those plans in place."

"My father insisted we do a lot of preplanning. He's worried about my job." At least he had been, Gabi thought, before his recent change of heart. "Even though my leave was approved, he's convinced they're going to put someone else in my position and give me the boot."

"Would that be such a bad thing?"

Startled, she blinked.

"You could apply for the position Steve mentioned." Jude took her hand, linked her fingers with his. "That way you could be around to personally supervise your father's recovery."

"My life is in Miami," she murmured, her mouth suddenly dry as sand.

"It *was* in Miami." Jude brought her hand to his lips and pressed a kiss into the palm. "What I'm trying to say is—"

His head jerked up as the sound of loud voices coming from the foyer drew his attention.

"What do you mean you're moving to Red Rock?" Anger filled Deke's voice. "I was counting on you this spring. You know this is our busiest season."

"Calving. Branding. Putting up hay. Grunt work," Chris declared in a derisive tone. "I have a brain. I'd like to use it for a change. Working for the Fortunes will give me that opportunity."

"You think you're too good to work with your hands? Is that it?"

Gabi wasn't sure if everyone heard the faint undercurrent of hurt in Deke's voice, but she caught it. Perhaps it was because her headstrong father was a lot like Deke Jones. She'd witnessed the anger and the hurt feelings that resulted when he and her brothers had butted heads.

"Let's just say I'm too smart to continue wasting my life on some two-bit ranch." Chris spoke in that smart-alecky tone guaranteed to light a father's fuse.

The clack of boots on hardwood echoed as Deke followed Chris onto the porch. Now that they were outside, Gabi had a perfect view of the two men through the window.

Fortunately the raised voices couldn't be heard over the noisy conversations in the living room.

"Don't walk away from me, boy." Deke's voice lashed sharp as a whip.

Chris stopped, turned back toward his father. The set of his face was rigid, austere, as if it had been carved from granite. Except for the sneer on his lips, which made his handsome face ugly.

"Let's face it. You never understood me. And I sure as hell never understood you. Why anyone would want to waste his life tending cattle is beyond me." Chris gave a humorless laugh. "The Fortunes could buy everything you own, down to that prizewinning bull you're so proud of, out of petty cash."

The words shot from Chris's lips like bullets. Gabi had no doubt they were intended to wound the target. By the rage building on Deke's face, they'd hit the mark square on.

"They run big businesses," Chris continued. "Important businesses. They command power and respect."

"Good for them." Deke spat the words. "But you seem

to be forgetting one important fact. You're not a Fortune. You're Chris Jones."

"Christopher *Fortune* Jones," Chris responded with extra emphasis. "I'm going to make something of myself."

"This has gone on long enough." Jude's easy smile had disappeared. He was clenching his jaw tight, and his hands were now fisted at his sides. But when he started to move, his mother stepped forward and grabbed his arm.

"Let your father handle this," she told her son in a low tone. "This is between him and Chris. You don't need to be getting in the middle of it."

"He's gone too far this time," Jude argued. "Acting like Dad is nothing and the Fortunes—"

"Jude." His mother's grip tightened. "I said let your father handle this."

"—and I'm not coming back."

Gabi shifted her attention just in time to see Chris hop into a pickup, slam the door shut and tear off down the road in a cloud of dust.

Standing as tall and stiff as any statue, Deke watched him drive off.

"Reminds me of some of the arguments between my father and brothers." Gabi kept her tone light, hoping to defuse some of the tension.

"Chris and his daddy." Jeanne Marie gave a little laugh, though her eyes remained troubled. "Oil and water."

Before Gabi could even begin to formulate a response, Jeanne Marie turned toward the roomful of family and friends and clapped her hands. The chatter of voices immediately ceased.

"It's time to eat." The older woman's gaze shifted to Orlando. She smiled. "Before we start, I'd like a round of applause for our guest. Orlando Mendoza is back home and racing down the road to a full recovery. Orlando, we couldn't be happier."

Her father blushed as everyone applauded and cheered.

By the time Gabi got her food and settled down next to Jude on the sofa, her mind had already made several trips back to her earlier conversation with Jude. She had the feeling he'd been about to ask her to stay.

It was probably best he'd been interrupted by his brothers. She still had to tell him about the transplant. Lay it all out. The good. The bad. The ugly.

She'd thought she could just walk away. But her need for him, her *love* for him, was a powerful force, urging her to discuss the matter with him before making any decisions. Just in case she was wrong and having a family wasn't that important to him.

Yes, she would tell him. Then they would see.

The dishes had been cleared and she'd risen to grab some dessert for her father when a sweet-smelling baby in a candy-striped dress with a pink headband was thrust into her arms.

"Could you hold Piper a sec, Gabi?" Stacey danced from one foot to the other. "Delaney and I have been on this drinking-more-water kick. The downside is now I have to pee every five minutes."

"Sure."

The word had barely made it past Gabi's lips when Stacey dashed off, leaving a seven-month-old who smelled like talcum powder in her arms. Piper gazed up, her green eyes large and luminous. For a second, Gabi feared she'd cry, but then the baby's rosebud of a mouth blossomed into a smile.

"You're such a cutie," Gabi crooned. She felt a lovely ache that went all the way down to her soul when the baby gurgled and waved her plump arms. "And this pink headband with the bling is super stylish."

"Reminds me of her at that age," Gabi heard her father say. "Prettiest little thing you ever saw."

Gabi looked up and realized she had an audience.

Her dad's eyes were dark with memories that likely included her mother. But it was the expression of longing and love she saw on Jude's face that ripped her in two. She knew his face, understood in that moment he was seeing her holding his child, *their* child, and envisioning a long and happy life with her by his side.

Suddenly the baby felt unspeakably heavy in her arms and the ring she wore beneath her sweater hung like a millstone around her neck. Thankfully, Stacey soon breezed back into the room to take the child.

While her father and Jude enjoyed the dessert of peach cobbler, Gabi brooded. She should have stuck to her original plan and kept things easy-breezy between her and Jude. She never should have let herself fall in love with him.

At least she'd come to her senses in time. She couldn't guarantee Jude the babies he wanted or a long life with the woman he loved. No matter what he might say, he wanted those things. The truth had been in his eyes.

That's why as soon as Gabi saw her father settled, she would leave Horseback Hollow and Jude Fortune Jones. Because she loved him, because she wanted the best for him, she had no choice.

Chapter Sixteen

Jude hated that he felt resentful of Orlando's improved health, but it was hard not to, considering he'd barely had a second alone with Gabi since her father had been released from the rehab center.

After lunch on Sunday, he'd offered to ride home with Gabi and help Orlando get settled. But Gabi had put him off, telling him she wanted some dad-and-daughter time.

On Monday when he called she'd said the nurse, therapist, as well as Orlando's new health aide would be in and out all day so she didn't want more company.

Jude told her he understood, but he didn't. He wasn't *company*. But he hadn't argued. She'd sounded tired and stressed, and he'd begun to wonder if her father's care was turning out to be more than she'd anticipated. Perhaps more than she could handle.

Thankfully today had started on an upswing. Orlando had texted him at the crack of dawn, sounding upbeat and cheerful. Gabi had called and asked him to come over at four.

The invitation gave him hope things were leveling off and they were settling into a routine. Frankly, he'd been worried about her.

When she left the ranch house on Sunday, the lines of strain that had appeared on her face as the afternoon progressed had been the only reason he hadn't followed through with his plan of enticing her out to the pond and getting down on one knee.

As he parked his truck in front of Orlando's house, he saw Alma standing on her curb, sweeping the street. Monique sat like a princess in the yard, tall and regal, watching her mistress work.

Jude waved.

"It's good to have Orlando home," she called out.

He deserved an Academy Award for his enthusiastic agreement.

Gabi opened the door to his knock. "Jude."

"You remember my name," he said in a teasing tone, then gave her a quick kiss before pushing past her to step inside. "It's a good start."

Pulling the door shut behind him, she brought a hand to her lips, looking oddly flustered. She wore jeans, sneakers and a long-sleeved blue Henley. Her hair was pulled back in a low ponytail. The shadows under her eyes and her paleness were new and made him frown.

It wasn't simply the pallor that concerned him; it was the sadness in her eyes. But when he reached for her hand, she stepped away with a casualness that seemed too calculated to be anything but deliberate.

Unease slithered up his spine.

"Who is it?" Orlando yelled over the television noise.

"It's Jude," Gabi announced as she followed him into the room.

Orlando looked up from where he was positioned in front of a big screen tuned to a sitcom popular in the late eighties.

"Hey, Jude," her father said, then chuckled as if he'd made an original joke. "It's good to see you. Gabi mentioned you'd be dropping by."

"It's such a beautiful day, I thought I might entice your daughter to play hooky and take a short walk with me."

Jude shifted his gaze to Gabi, offered what he hoped was an engaging smile. "Chico, too."

The dog, currently sitting on Orlando's lap, lifted his head and began to whine softly.

"I don't think I should go that f—" Gabi began.

"There's a park just around the corner," Jude said before she could refuse. "With swings."

"Gabi loves to swing," Orlando said.

She cast her father a narrowed, glinting glance.

"Well, you do." The older man shrugged, a smile tipping his lips.

"It's settled." Jude gave a short whistle and Chico jumped down and came to him.

"I couldn't possibly leave my father alone." Gabi spoke so quickly she stumbled over the words. "He just got home a few days ago."

"I'm more than capable of watching television without a nursemaid hovering—" Orlando paused, reached over and took his daughter's hand at the stricken look on her face. "Don't get me wrong. I love having you with me, fussing and making sure I have what I need. But you and Chico should take a walk with Jude. It'll do you both good to get out of the house, breathe some fresh air."

"Okay," she said finally, reluctantly, then leaned over to kiss her father's cheek. "I won't be long."

"Take your time." Orlando waved his good hand in the air. "My show is just starting."

"Do you need anything before I go?" Gabi asked.

"I'm fine."

"Your cell phone is right there." Gabi pointed to a tray table next to her father's chair. "I'm taking mine with me. If you need anything, call."

"Go." Orlando waved her away without shifting his eyes from the screen.

Bright patches of pink stained Gabi's cheeks. She grabbed

a leash and clipped it onto Chico's collar. When she reached the door, Gabi hesitated once more. But after seeing her father's gaze still glued to the television, she stepped outside without another word.

Wanting to comfort, Jude placed a palm at the small of her back, but her instant recoil had him dropping his hand to his side.

As they walked, Chico trotted happily between them.

"Nice evening," Gabi said in the polite tone you'd use with a stranger.

"It is indeed." Jude turned at the corner in the direction of the small park.

He'd hoped she would voluntarily share what was troubling her. But when another block passed in silence, Jude decided to go with the direct approach. "Tell me what's going on, Gabi. I want to help."

A nervous laugh slipped past her lips. "I don't know what you mean."

"For starters, you've been freezing me out." He slanted a sideways glance. "Did I do something on Sunday to offend you? Is that why I've been banished to Siberia?"

"No," she said quickly. *Too quickly.* "Of course not."

Jude waited for her to continue.

"You didn't do anything other than maybe put the wrong spin on things." She licked her lips. "That's why I asked you to come over, to set things straight."

A knot twisted in the pit of his stomach.

"I mean, what we had was supposed to be fun, but that's all." She huffed out a breath. "On Sunday I got the feeling you wanted more."

He did want more. Marriage. Kids. As his father would say, the whole ball of wax. She wanted that, too.

Before he could respond, she pulled his championship ring out from beneath her shirt and jerked the chain up and over her head. When she pressed the ring into his hand, he took it only to casually cast it into the cavernous depths of the bag slung over her shoulder.

Her lips pressed together. "I don't want to go steady anymore."

"I don't, either."

The response, delivered in a matter-of-fact tone, caught her off guard.

"You don't?" For a second her eyes widened. "I mean that's good. We're in agreement. Let me give this back to—"

She started to reach into the bag, but Jude laid a restraining hand on her arm. "I don't want to go steady with you," he said softly. "I want to marry you."

Gabi yanked back with such force she'd have fallen if he hadn't reached out to steady her.

"You don't want to marry me," she insisted, panic in her voice.

"I do."

"You don't know me." Frustration ground through her words like shards of glass.

Something was going on. Jude was sure of it. And whatever it was didn't have a darn thing to do with her father. He wished he could simply kiss the problem away. But he had a feeling this one was like a splinter. It would need to be dug out before they could be done with it and move on.

"I do know you." He gentled his tone, recognizing her increasing distress even if he didn't understand the reason for it yet. "Quite well, in fact."

They reached the playground. While the newer section, with its play center of slides and decks was overrun with toddlers, the area holding the swings was deserted. Jude took a seat in one of the slings and motioned for Gabi to take the one beside him. Chico sprawled in the sand at her feet and stared longingly at the children playing.

"You *think* you know me, but you don't." She slipped the band from her head and gave her hair a toss.

"I know everything important."

"Did you know I had a heart transplant when I was nineteen?" Gabi knew she wasn't playing fair, but she saw no choice. His future happiness had to be her primary concern.

Jude brought his swing, which had been swaying ever-so-slightly, to an abrupt halt. "What?"

She met his startled gaze head-on. "I had a heart transplant. Seven years ago."

For a second Jude forgot how to breathe. "You said you had heart surgery."

"A heart transplant is heart surgery," she said in a disdainful tone.

Jude didn't know much about transplants other than they were a big deal. And usually, like Leslie, who was now recovering in Houston from a liver transplant, you had to be pretty ill before getting one. He leveled a long stare in her direction. "Why did you have one?"

Surprisingly, she gave him the details without much prompting. He listened as she recounted the bout of stomach flu, the shortness of breath, learning the virus from the gastroenteritis had attacked the heart and left it with irreversible damage.

His blood ran cold at the thought of how close she'd come to losing her life.

"That's why I'm so focused on eating healthy and exercising," she added.

"Makes sense," Jude said automatically, even though right now nothing was making sense.

He felt as if he'd plunged into an alternate world. The way Gabi was acting didn't make sense. The fact that she'd kept something that was such an important part of her life a secret from him sure as heck didn't make sense. "Why didn't you tell me before now?"

"Our relationship was supposed to be light—just fun and games." She lifted one shoulder in the type of irritating shrug his sisters often used. "Heart transplant stuff is heavy."

His head spun. Forget alternate world. He'd fallen headlong into an alternate universe. "Then *why* tell me now?"

"Because you seem to have gotten the mistaken impression there's more depth to our relationship than actually exists." Her tone was cool, distant. "I used the disclosure of the transplant to illustrate you don't know me as well as you think."

Jude fought his way through the fog shrouding his brain. "On Sunday, you told me how much you missed me." *That* he knew he hadn't misunderstood. In fact, his heart warmed now remembering her words and the intense emotion he'd seen in her eyes.

Gabi hesitated only a second.

"It was code." Her laugh reminded him of nails on a chalkboard. "I was telling you I missed having sex with you."

"You seriously expect me to believe I meant nothing to you? That what existed between us was only about good sex?"

Something flickered in those dark depths before a shutter dropped, hiding any emotion.

"That's exactly right." Hopping off her swing, Gabi tugged on Chico's leash then shot Jude a bright smile. "I should get back to my father. I'm glad we had a chance to clear this up before I left."

He pressed fingers against his temples, where a headache had begun to pound, making it difficult to think. "When are you leaving?"

"Does it matter?" She tilted her head, her brown eyes

unreadable. "With my dad home, there can't be any more between-the-sheets action."

Jude could only stare. Could he really have been so wrong about…everything?

The walk back from the park was a blur, and when they reached the house, Jude didn't come in. Gabi didn't really expect him to and told herself she was glad he'd gotten the message.

Keeping that phony smile on her face all the way home when all she wanted to do was dissolve into tears had taken all her energy. She wasn't sure how much longer she'd have been able to keep up the pretense he meant nothing to her.

She stepped inside the house, conscious of a truck door slamming shut, then seconds later, an engine roaring to life and tires squealing.

Still, Gabi didn't let her guard down until the front door was firmly shut behind her and locked. Only then did she allow the tears to fall.

"How was the walk?" her father called out. "Is Jude still with you?"

Gabi unclipped Chico's leash then hurriedly swiped the tears from her cheeks.

"He had to get back to the ranch." She forced a bright smile and strolled into the living room. "You were right. It was nice to get some fresh air. And Chico really enjoyed the park. There were a lot of kids there and he couldn't take his eyes off of them."

With sudden horror, Gabi realized she was babbling. She clamped her mouth shut. At least she'd done a stellar job of keeping her tone light, or so she thought, until her father's gaze latched on to hers.

"What's wrong?" he demanded.

You mean other than me decimating the man I love with a pack of lies?

"No-nothing."

Orlando's gaze narrowed. "Did that boy say something to upset you?"

"Actually, I believe I may have upset him." Gabi fought to project a cavalier tone. "I told him, because I'd soon be heading back to Miami, I didn't see any reason for us to continue our friendship."

"Friendship."

Gabi nodded. "That's right."

A watchful look filled her father's eyes. The same look she'd seen numerous times in high school when she slipped in past curfew and tried to fib about it the next morning.

He always seemed to be able to tell when she was stretching the truth. In fact, he'd once told her he could even tell when she was lying to herself.

Gabi settled herself on the sofa, forced herself to breathe past the tightness in her chest. "Oh, and you'll be happy to know, I told him about the transplant."

Orlando's dark eyes flickered but his expression remained impassive. "How did he react?"

"He asked why. I told him. He was surprised I hadn't told him before." Her tone turned clipped as she fought to keep her emotions under control. "Ah, well, it was fun while it lasted."

"He's in love with you."

Gabi started to deny it then shrugged. "Maybe."

"You're in love with him."

Gabi shifted her gaze to the silly sitcom playing on the television. The characters acted as if life was one big joke. Maybe it was for some, but not for her. Gabi jerked her head toward the screen. "Mind if I turn it off?"

Orlando picked up the remote, flicked off the television, then turned back to his daughter. "I can't believe Jude doesn't want to be with you because you've had a heart transplant."

Her father's voice was heavy with disappointment.

"It wasn't him. I'm the one who said it was over between us." Gabi paced a moment then returned to sit. "He wanted to get serious. Since I don't plan to marry, I didn't see the point in continuing a relationship with him."

"Even though you love him you don't want to marry him?" Now her father looked totally confused.

"I don't want to marry *anyone*. I saw what you went through with Mama." Gabi wiped her sweaty palms on her jeans and did her best to control the tremble that kept trying to creep into her voice. "I have a new heart, Papi. But we both know there are no guarantees I'll stay healthy. My body could reject it tomorrow."

Her father's eyes softened. "There are no guarantees with anything in life, *mija*."

"Some women are better bets than others." She rested her head against the back of the chair. "I won't put Jude through the pain of losing a wife. You, of all people, should understand that by walking away I'm giving him a gift."

"I understand love and wanting to protect." Orlando stared into her troubled face. "But every day I had with your mother was precious."

Gabi simply shrugged

"He won't give up," Orlando warned. "He loves you too much to just walk away."

"Then I'll just have to do or say whatever necessary to get him to stop loving me," she said in a weary voice. "I'm sure he's already rethinking how he feels about me after our conversation this afternoon."

As Orlando gazed at the face of his only daughter, he realized she needed time and distance to clearly consider all she was giving up by charting this course. She was smart, his Gabriella. He believed she'd soon see that Jude had a right to be a part of a decision that affected his future.

In the meantime, he couldn't sit by and let her destroy

Jude's love. Not when he knew the cowboy would make such a fine husband and son-in-law.

"Gabriella," he said, "I believe it's time for you to return to Miami."

"Soon," Gabi agreed. "After I make sure you have everything you need then—"

"Between the woman you've hired and my nurse and therapist, I'm covered. You need to get back to your job and your life in Miami." His tone brooked no argument.

"You're right." Gabi sighed and glanced at the dog on his lap. "But I'm going to need a favor. Could you possibly watch Chico until I find a place that allows dogs?"

Gabi shifted under the animal's unyielding stare and remembered promising him he'd always be with her. But it couldn't be helped. Just like walking away from Jude, that couldn't be helped, either.

"Of course he can stay with me." Orlando scrubbed the top of the dog's head with his knuckles. "I've grown fond of the little guy."

Gabi clumsily pulled herself upright. It felt as if everything was suddenly moving at warp speed. Which was good, she told herself. Once a decision was made, you went with it. "I'll have to start checking for flights—"

"I have a friend who's a bigwig at one of the airlines that fly out of Lubbock. I'll call him tonight. He owes me a favor. We may be able to work something out for tomorrow."

"Tomorrow?" Gabi gaped. "You must really want to get rid of me."

Though she tried to keep the hurt from her voice, she wasn't entirely successful.

"Ah, *mija*." He held out a hand to her, wrapping his fingers tightly around hers when she came to him. "I love you. While it's been wonderful having you here, it's time for you to go. Trust me, this is for the best."

His gaze dropped to their interlocked hands.

"I have to admit when you came I hoped you'd love it so much you'd want to make it your home, too," he said softly. "I'm sorry that didn't happen. Sorry things didn't work out."

She knew what he was saying. Her father had hoped she'd stay in Horseback Hollow and marry Jude. He liked her cowboy, she realized suddenly. Liked him a lot. Instead of comforting her, the knowledge only added to her pain.

"I'm sorry, too, Papi." She brought his hand to her cheek, resting the side of her face against his large workman's hands. "So very sorry."

Chapter Seventeen

Bright and early Wednesday morning, while the home health nurse was busy with her father, Gabi packed for her afternoon flight. She was headed to the kitchen for some Ziploc bags when the doorbell sounded.

"I'll get it," she called out, detouring to the front of the house.

Right before her hand closed over the knob, Gabi had a sudden image of Jude, standing on the porch, daisies in hand, begging her to stay.

When she opened the door it wasn't Jude but his mother who stood on the porch, a bakery box in one hand and a smile that reminded Gabi of the man she was trying so hard to forget.

"Jeanne Marie, how nice of you to drop by." Though seeing the woman tugged at her heartstrings, Gabi smiled warmly. "I'm afraid my father isn't available right now. The nurse just got here."

"Actually, it's you I came to see." Jeanne Marie raised the box. "Although I did bring enough scones for your father and his caregivers, as well."

"That's very kind." Gabi stepped back. "Would you like to come in? I can make coffee."

"I'd love a cup."

"I hope decaf is okay. It's all we have."

"It's perfect. While you get the coffee started, I can get

plates for the scones," Jeanne Marie offered when they reached the tiny kitchen.

"The dishes are in the cupboard to the right of the sink." Gabi started the coffee then set out skim milk and sugar.

The older woman pulled out two plates then placed a scone on each. She turned back to Gabi. "I hope you like cranberry-orange."

Gabi gave a little laugh. "I like them all."

While fruit scones tended to be higher in sugar than the plain kind, Gabi decided she'd make an exception this time and simply enjoy the treat.

"Was that a suitcase I saw in the hall?" Jeanne Marie asked moments later, lifting a mug of steaming coffee to her lips.

"It's mine." Gabi kept her tone matter-of-fact as she broke off a piece of quick bread. "Now that my father is on the mend, it's time for me to head home."

Jeanne Marie's eyes registered surprise. "This seems awfully sudden. You didn't mention anything about leaving when I saw you on Sunday."

Gabi popped a bite of scone into her mouth, forced herself to chew. "The bank will only hold my position for so long."

"Does Jude know you're leaving today?"

Gabi chose her words carefully. "He's aware I planned to return to Miami."

"No wonder he was distraught." Jeanne Marie spoke bluntly, a frown furrowing her brows. "You realize my son is in love with you?"

Gabi wasn't about to negotiate that minefield.

"Jude's been in love before." *Easy-breezy,* she told herself. "No doubt he will be again."

Yet the mere thought of him with another woman brought a searing pain to her chest.

Jeanne Marie snorted. "If you believe that, you're not as bright as I think you are."

Even though the scone had tasted like sawdust in her mouth, Gabi took another bite and kept her expression impassive. If Jeanne Marie hoped to goad her into a reaction, it wasn't happening.

The older woman fixed her steely-blue eyes on Gabi. "You'll break his heart if you leave."

I'll break it if I stay.

For a second Gabi feared she'd spoken her thoughts aloud. But when Jeanne Marie's expression didn't change, Gabi took another bite of scone and washed it down with a big gulp of coffee.

"Deke and I stopped by Jude's place last night." Jeanne Marie pursed her lips. "Even though he staunchly insisted nothing was wrong, I could tell he was lying. A mother knows such things."

Gabi squelched a nervous laugh. Shades of her father. Could it be parents were issued a built-in lie detector when children were born?

"Family means everything to Jude," Gabi said through lips that felt frozen. "And to you."

"We're a close-knit group." Jeanne Marie nodded as if the words required additional emphasis then added. "Most of us, anyway."

The older woman sighed and for a second, a look of profound sadness shadowed her eyes.

It was obvious Jeanne Marie was thinking of Deke and Chris. Though she hid it well, Gabi had seen on Sunday how much the argument between her husband and youngest son troubled her.

"Now you have even more family to love," Gabi pointed out, nudging the conversation in a different direction. "You're part of the Fortune family. Connected by blood."

Jeanne Marie's expression relaxed.

"Becoming acquainted with family I never knew existed has been wonderful. But I love and adore my adoptive parents even though we're not related by blood." Jeanne Marie inclined her head, a quizzical look on her face. "What's this about, Gabi?"

Gabi dropped her hands to her lap so Jeanne Marie wouldn't notice the trembling. "It's my rather awkward attempt to point out that Jude is surrounded by people who love him. And to assure you that you needn't worry. He'll do fine without me in his life."

Was it Jeanne Marie she was trying to assure of that fact? Gabi wondered. Or herself?

Jeanne Marie leaned forward, rested her elbows on the table. "My son is a good man—kind and loving. He'll make a wonderful husband."

The woman was like Chico with a bone. And, while Gabi knew it was unintentional, it felt as if Jeanne Marie had snatched up a butter knife and plunged it straight into her heart.

"I have no doubt Jude will be a good husband." Gabi smiled politely. "But not to me."

Color rose in Jeanne Marie's cheeks, and for the first time since she arrived she appeared embarrassed. "I'm not normally an interfering woman. I certainly wouldn't be one of those stick-my-nose-into-your-business mothers-in-law everyone jokes about. It's just that, though he's doing a good job of hiding it, my son is hurting."

Jeanne Marie brought a work-hardened hand to her floral blouse and placed it on her chest. "Seeing him suffer breaks my heart."

Genuine, loving concern radiated from every pore of the woman's body. For a second, Gabi was seized with the urge to fling herself into Jeanne Marie's arms and beg her to make it all better.

But Gabi wasn't a child. And Jeanne Marie would never

be her mother, not even by virtue of marriage. Yet, the desire to do something so radical told Gabi that her control over her emotions hung by a slender thread. If Jeanne Marie mentioned Jude's unhappiness one more time, Gabi might break down and sob.

"I'm sorry I have to cut this short, but I have a plane to catch." Gabi pushed back her chair and stood. "Your family has been so kind to me and my father. I appreciate you stopping by and giving me this opportunity to personally thank you for all you've done."

Jeanne Marie pulled to her feet. Her eyes seemed to soften as they surveyed Gabi's face.

"I'll see you again, my dear." The older woman placed her hand flat against Gabi's cheek. "Very soon."

Jude dropped down on a bench outside his barn and took a putty knife to his muddy boots. While he scraped, he brooded. Once he'd been able to factor out the emotion, he realized what Gabi had told him had been nothing but a huge scoop of bull.

She loved him. While she may not have said the words, he had eyes. He'd seen the emotion in that big, beautiful, brown-eyed gaze. Yet she'd felt the need to make him believe she didn't care. Why?

He had the feeling the reason had something to do with her heart transplant. It was a logical assumption, considering she'd deliberately withheld that bit of information from him, a fact which had initially pissed him off royally.

But he'd forced himself to put aside the anger and focus on discovering just what was going on in that head of hers. Despite spending much of last night researching heart transplants and hoping something would jump out at him, the root of her rejection remained as muddy as his boots.

He had lots of facts. But no answers.

"I thought you'd be out riding the range."

Jude glanced up to see Sawyer striding across the yard looking very much out of place in his suit and Italian loafers.

"What are you doing way out here?" Jude finished with one boot and began on the other. "I thought you'd be ten thousand feet in the wild blue teaching someone how to crash."

"It's 'how to fly' and that's on tap for later." Sawyer's face eased into a smile as he glanced at Jude's boots. "What did you do to those Tony Lama boots?"

"Cow decided to give birth to twins in the only muddy spot in the whole damn pasture." Jude's lips curved. "Had a little trouble, but Doc Green and I got her a happy ending."

"Congratulations." Sawyer lifted his briefcase. "I brought those papers you wanted. I can leave them in the house."

"I'd appreciate it." Jude rose to his feet. "I need to get some hay to the herd in the north pasture."

He walked with his cousin on his way toward the house.

"What'd you think of Gabi leaving so suddenly?" Sawyer asked casually just as Jude turned to get into his pickup.

When Jude had been nine, Liam had knocked him out of their tree house. He'd hit the ground with a solid thud, hard enough to knock the air from his lungs. Jude remembered how he felt that day. He felt the same way now.

"Left?" Jude was surprised at how rational he sounded with the chaos inside him. "Where'd she go?"

"Back to Miami." Sawyer shrugged. "Laurel gave her a lift into Lubbock. We were both surprised she was leaving so soon, but Gabi said there wasn't any reason for her to stay in Horseback Hollow any longer."

Jude's fingers tightened into fists. He focused on breathing. In. Out. In. Out. When he finally had his emotions under control, he smiled grimly. "Looks like I'll be taking a little trip to Florida."

"You're going after her?" There was surprise in Sawyer's voice.

"Damn straight." Jude spoke through gritted teeth. "Gabi and I can't get our...situation...resolved with a bunch of miles between us."

Sawyer stared at him thoughtfully. "But if she doesn't want you—"

"Damn it, Sawyer." Jude slammed his hand against the side of the truck, almost relishing the pain that shot up his arm. "She does want me. But something is causing her to back the hell away. I need to dig out what it is and make it right."

A ghost of a smile touched Sawyer's lips. "Well, since you put it that way...any ideas what the 'something' is?"

"No," Jude said immediately then paused as a sudden image of the longing on Gabi's face when she'd been holding Piper surfaced. "Maybe."

"Good luck." Sawyer clapped a hand on Jude's shoulder. "I hope it works out."

"It will," Jude said, because the only outcome he'd accept was he and Gabi together, forever.

Gabi arrived in Miami late Wednesday night and walked through the bank's employee entrance bright and early the next morning.

There was really no alternative. Unless she wanted to stay in her apartment—which was in the middle of being fumigated—and cry. No, it was best to jump back into her life with both feet.

The trouble was, it didn't feel like her life anymore. Battling the traffic on the drive to the bank made her long for the quiet roadways surrounding Horseback Hollow. Seeing the palm trees lining the boulevard felt...odd. And the humidity. Had it always been this oppressive?

Thankfully, her office was a cool oasis and the work

that had piled up in her absence kept her mind busy and off Jude. Or so she tried to convince herself. At two-thirty, she decided to stretch her legs and refill the mug of water she kept on her desk.

At this time of day the break room should be deserted, which was an added bonus. Gabi was sick to death of answering questions about Texas and her father. Her dad was doing well, she assured her coworkers. And she agreed that Texas was far different than Miami. Yes, she had seen cows and had even, gasp, ridden a horse.

The hardest was when they teased her about all the hunky cowboys. She pushed open the break room door, blinking back unexpected tears, reminding herself for the zillionth time that walking away from Jude had been for the best.

Gabi stepped back, startled, when she realized the room wasn't empty. But her disappointment turned to pleasure when she saw it was her friend Faith rising from the table.

"Rose told me you were at an outside meeting today." For the first time since setting foot on Florida soil, Gabi was glad she was back. Though she and Faith had spoken on the phone several times since she'd heard the news of Daniel's death, it wasn't the same as being here with her.

"I'm so glad to see you." Emotion clogged Gabi's throat as she crossed the room to embrace her friend.

"I've missed you." Faith hugged her tight and swiped at her eyes with the back of her hand. "You have to tell me all about Texas."

Gabi understood the code. Don't mention Daniel. Not at work.

It had been the same for her when her mother had been ill. Her emotions had run too close to the surface. Any questions, any well-meaning expressions of concern, could set off tears.

"Do you have time to chat for a second?" Faith motioned to the table where she'd been sitting only moments before.

"Absolutely." Gabi filled her cup with water then slipped into a chair opposite Faith.

"Now, tell me. How's your dad?"

"He's doing great."

Faith leaned forward, resting her arms on the table. "What did you think about Horseback Hill?"

"Horseback Hollow," Gabi gently corrected. "And it was great, too. A nice little town with a lot of wonderful people. Papi was so happy to have me there."

"I know you were always close." Faith reached over and covered Gabi's hand, gave it a squeeze. "Did Rosemary tell you we had an office pool on whether you'd come back? A lot of us—me included—thought you'd find a rugged cowboy and ride off into the sunset with him."

"There are definitely good-looking men in Texas." The lighthearted words were too close to the truth and emotion clogged her throat. Gabi took a sip of water to clear it. "But we both know finding the right one is hard."

A shadow slipped across Faith's face then disappeared. "I got lucky. Daniel was perfect for me."

By mentioning her husband's name, Faith had eased open the recently closed door. Gabi took a tentative step inside. "How are you doing?"

"I'm taking it a day at a time." Tears swam in Faith's eyes. "It's so surreal. I never imagined my life with him would be over so soon."

Would you do it again? Gabi wanted to ask. *Knowing what you know now, would you do it again?*

Faith gazed into her eyes and for a second it was as if her friend could read her thoughts.

"I loved Daniel. I will treasure every day we had together." Faith met Gabi's gaze. "If God had told me before we married that I could have him for only three years before he'd be called home, I'd still have walked down that aisle. I believe what a person should fear, even more than losing the one you love, is never loving at all."

When Faith left to return to her desk, Gabi remained seated. The doctors had told her she stood a good chance of living a long, healthy life, but she knew that was no guarantee. What she'd failed to consider was that no one's life came with a guarantee.

She'd been angry with Rosemary for not telling her about Daniel's death, for taking the decision to return to Miami for his funeral out of her hands. Granted, it would have been difficult to leave her father when he'd been so ill, but she deserved to be given the information so she could make the choice herself. She'd railed against the injustice. Yet, hadn't she done the same thing to Jude?

She never gave him a choice.

Gabi picked up her phone and stared at the screen. Booking a return ticket to Horseback Hollow so soon probably didn't make sense. Unless you were a woman with a strong, healthy heart who was willing to put that heart on the line for love.

She felt the warmth of the championship ring between her breasts as the airline website popped up and her fingers began to tap.

Chapter Eighteen

Gabi had always enjoyed the energy of Miami International Airport. But this morning she was preoccupied as she navigated a crowded security checkpoint.

Yesterday, after her conversation with Faith, she'd booked a one-way ticket to Horseback Hollow then resigned her position at the bank. Though being without a job was a bit scary, Gabi knew, regardless of what happened between her and Jude, Miami was no longer her home.

She gave her landlord thirty days' notice and made arrangements to have professional movers pack and ship those items she wanted to keep. Rosemary and Faith had assured her they'd take care of disposing of everything else.

Once those tasks were completed, she'd called her father.

Orlando had sounded thrilled to hear she was moving to Horseback Hollow. There had been a lilt in his voice when he informed her that he and Chico would keep the light on for her. Recalling the reference to a popular motel slogan made her smile even now.

Once her feet hit Texas soil, Gabi planned to call Jude and ask him to meet her at The Grill. She'd figure out exactly what she was going to say during the five-hour flight to Lubbock. But she already knew her confession would include a heartfelt, "I'm sorry I wasn't honest with you."

She'd just been cleared through gate security when her phone dinged, announcing a text. Gabi heaved a sigh. Her father had been on a texting marathon all morning.

It was as if she was a child flying alone for the first time. He was obsessed with tracking her every movement. She didn't have to read the latest text to know what it said.

Where R U?

Gabi eased out of the line of foot traffic. Dropping her carry-on to her feet, she relaxed against a wall and texted back.

At MIA. Just cleared security.

Then, because she knew he'd ask, she added,

Heading to Field of Greens for lunch.

Chili dog, fries and large shake?

Hahaha, she texted back.

Good luck.

Gabi pulled her brows together. What kind of response was that? Did he know something about Field of Greens she didn't? Or was he simply trying to be funny?

For a second she considered asking, but immediately banished the thought. A question like that was practically guaranteed to launch a slew of additional texts.

She wanted quiet. A moment to herself. Which was a joke considering Miami International was one of the busiest airports in the country. Yet, when Gabi picked up her bag and began walking in the direction of the café known for its healthy cuisine, the mass of humanity miraculously parted in front of her.

That's when Gabi saw him. That's when her heart stopped. Just. Stopped.

Striding toward her in jeans and white T-shirt with a familiar Stetson on his head was Jude. *Her* Jude.

She increased her pace, hurrying toward him until she was almost running. When she realized she was about to plow into him, she abruptly halted. Jude covered the last few feet to her.

"Hi." With sudden awkwardness, she shifted her bag from one hand to the other. "I didn't expect to see you in Miami."

He swiped the hat off his head, raked a hand through his dark blond hair. "I'm here on business."

Her heart dropped. "Oh."

Gabi told herself she was being foolish. After the way she'd treated him, could she really believe he'd fly all this way to see her? But what kind of business could he have in Miami?

Ignoring the grumbles and muttered curses from travelers forced to scoot around them, Jude hooked his thumbs in the pockets of his jeans and rocked back on his heels.

"How about a drink?" He gestured with a jerk of his head to a nearby bar designed to look like a Mexican cantina. "Can I buy you one?"

Gabi experienced a surge of hope. At least he wasn't in a hurry to rush off. While it might be simply wishful thinking, his eyes appeared more watchful than angry.

She offered him her best smile. "I'd love a ginger ale."

He put the strap of his duffel crosswise over his body then hefted her overnight bag from her hands. On the short walk to the bar, Gabi resisted the urge to fill the silence with nervous chatter. A hostess led them to a table overlooking the runway and a server quickly took their drink order.

Jude glanced at the bag he'd placed by her chair. "Going somewhere?"

Hoping to lighten the mood, Gabi playfully brought a finger to her lips. "Airport. Suitcase. What was your first clue?"

When that adorable grin of his flashed, the tightness gripping her chest eased.

"I'm on my way back to Texas. Horseback Hollow is going to be my home," Gabi announced. "Keep your fingers crossed the position at the Vicker's Corners bank is still open."

"Last I heard" was all he said.

Her nerves, which had started to calm, began to jitter. Gabi nodded her thanks as the server returned with their drinks as well as a bowl of tortilla chips and sauce. Without thinking, she grabbed a handful of red-and-black chips and popped a couple into her mouth.

Jude lifted the bottle of Corona to his lips. "I thought you didn't eat junk food."

She dropped her gaze to the single chip left in her hand and flushed.

"Because of your heart transplant," he said pointedly then took a long pull of beer.

Gabi lowered the chip, her mouth suddenly dry as dust. She'd planned to ease into the transplant talk, dip her toe into the water before starting to swim. Now she stood teetering on the edge of the deep end where she could be over her head in seconds.

Taking a breath, she plunged in. "I owe you an apology."

He popped a couple of chips into his mouth then washed them down with another pull of beer.

"I'm sorry. *Very* sorry. I should have told you about

the transplant from the beginning instead of keeping it a secret."

"Yes, you should have." Those brilliant blue eyes remained cool.

"I was convinced there could never be anything between us other than sex." She winced when his face went stony. "I was lying to myself. I was scared."

"Of what?" Confusion blanketed his face. "What were you afraid of? Be specific."

Gabi thought longingly of the flying time she'd counted on to organize her thoughts. But she didn't have the luxury of five hours in the air. Jude was sitting across from her now.

Folding her hands in her lap, Gabi cleared her throat. "When my mother was diagnosed with cancer and given a not-so-good prognosis, the knowledge that he might lose the woman he loved sliced my father in two. I saw a decorated air force officer, a man who'd flown in battle more times than I could count, break down and cry. When she passed away…"

Gabi closed her eyes for a second and willed herself to settle.

"They'd been together a long time," Jude commented.

"If you add in the time they dated, well over forty years." Gabi moistened her suddenly dry lips. "Seeing a strong man crumble had a profound impact on me. I started thinking that one in four heart transplant patients aren't alive in ten years. How could I get serious with any man, knowing what he could face?"

His gaze dragged slowly down to the tips of her hot-pink toenails in heeled sandals and back up again, lingering on the formfitting royal-blue cotton tee. "You look healthy to me."

"I've done well. My doctors call me their star patient." For the first time since she'd begun her explanation, Gabi smiled. "Not a single rejection episode. I let myself be encouraged by the fact I'd stayed healthy. But recently—"

At her hesitation, concern flashed across Jude's face like a bolt of lightning.

"Nothing with me," she quickly assured him. "But Mary, a woman who'd had a transplant around the same time as me, passed away before Christmas. She'd had some issues over the years, but none I saw as life-threatening. Then shortly before I came to Horseback Hollow, Kate—another fellow transplant recipient—called me, distraught. Although she had no symptoms, her annual cardiac biopsy showed evidence of rejection."

Out of the corner of her eye Gabi saw the waitress approach the table. Jude waved her off.

"Despite my reservations, I convinced myself we could make it work." Gabi closed her eyes for a second, breathed out. "Then I went to the luncheon at your mom's house."

"Piper" was all he said.

"Yes." Despite Gabi's efforts to control it, her voice turned wistful. "When I held her, when I saw the look on your face, I knew, *I knew,* you were picturing me with our child."

The look in his eyes told her she'd gotten it right.

"My cardiologist has discouraged me from getting pregnant. How could I possibly consider a future with you, knowing I couldn't give you a son or daughter of your own?"

"When you told me our relationship was only about sex, you spoke the truth." His voice was heavy with resignation.

"No." She expelled a shaky breath, gave a little laugh. "I broke my own rule. I fell in love with you."

With trembling fingers, Gabi lifted the ring hanging from a slender gold chain out from beneath her shirt. "I should have left this behind. I couldn't. In my mind, as long as I had it, the connection to you stayed intact. Even though we were apart, it was as if you were still with me."

Jude didn't say a word but she nearly wept when he reached across the small table and took her hand.

"I don't understand," he said slowly. "Why are you willing to consider a future with me now when you were so opposed before? What changed?"

"I realize life comes with no guarantees." Gabi quickly told him about her conversation with Faith. "I love you, Jude, and I really can't do without you. Just so we're clear, it was never just about the sex. Although I have to admit that was pretty spectacular."

His grin flashed.

"I just want to make sure you understand. Though my cardiologist may reconsider his stance, there's a very real possibility I might not be able to have a child." Gabi met his gaze. "I realize how important family is to you. You want children."

She said it as fact, instead of a question, knowing she spoke the truth. And if he denied it, he'd be not only lying to her but to himself.

"Of course I want kids. So do you."

Gabi slowly nodded.

"You don't have to give birth to them." His voice softened and he squeezed the hand he still held. "There are so many options nowadays. We could adopt, either a baby or an older child. We could use a surrogate. And if, when it's all said and done, it ends up just being the two of us, I'd be okay with that, too. What I'm not okay with is being without you."

Her heart hitched. Still, she refused to minimize what he might face in the future. "While I've done well since my transplant, something could go wrong without warning."

"Darlin'," he drawled, in a thick Texas accent that made blood slide like warm honey through her veins. "A horse could toss me tomorrow and I could break my neck. There are no guarantees for any of us."

"That's true. But just so you understand—"

"What I understand, what I insist on, is no more lies between us."

She swallowed hard, gave a jerky nod.

"One more thing." He paused. "I'd like my ring back."

Pain rose inside Gabi with a force so strong tears spurted to her eyes. Fumbling badly, she managed to pull the chain over her head then handed it to him with fingers that trembled.

With a careless gesture, he dropped the ring and chain to the table.

She'd given him the information. He'd made the decision to break their connection. The ground that had seemed so firm only seconds earlier was disintegrating beneath her feet. Jude clasped her hand in his for what she assumed was a final goodbye.

His choice, she reminded herself, blinking back tears.

"I remember the first time I saw you. It was like being kicked by a mule. I dated a lot of women in the past but never wanted to stick with any of them. Now I know why. I was waiting for you." His lips curved. "But I see now that starting off as friends gave our relationship a rock-solid foundation."

For a second his gaze dropped to the championship ring and chain lying on the table. Then he lifted his gaze and those eyes, clear and so very blue, pinned her. "Going steady was good. But not enough. Not nearly enough."

As she struggled to remember how to breathe, he continued, his voice deep and thick with emotion.

"I want more. I need more." Jude spread his hands in a helpless gesture. "I love you, Gabi. I can't imagine my life without you in it. Whether God gives us fifty days or fifty years, I want to spend them all with you."

Before she could comprehend what was happening, Jude dropped down on one knee and snapped open a small velvet box. A sparkling square-cut diamond flashed fire while love blazed strong in his eyes. "Gabriella Mendoza, will you do me the honor of becoming my wife?"

Tears streamed down Gabi's cheeks. Now that it was her time to speak, all she could do was nod. Oh, and hold out her hand for him to slide that gorgeous ring on her finger.

The bar, which had quieted during the proposal, erupted into cheers and applause.

"Way to go, cowboy," someone yelled.

Jude rose, tugged her up against him. "We're going to be so happy."

"Guaranteed," Gabi murmured as his lips closed over hers.

* * * * *

LASSOED
BY FORTUNE

BY
MARIE FERRARELLA

To
Susan Litman,
who somehow manages
the monumental task of
keeping all these stories
straight
while keeping us all
in line.

Chapter One

Liam Jones leaned back in his chair, nursing his beer and listening to two of his younger brothers, Jude and Toby, talking about a third younger brother, Christopher, who had recently picked up and moved to the nearby town of Red Rock.

As he listened, Liam's frown, already a fixture on his face from the beginning of this conversation, deepened, highlighting his increasing disapproval.

Christopher, apparently, at least in his eyes, had gone and sold his soul to the devil.

Liam's initial intent in coming to the bar at the Horseback Hollow Grill with two of his brothers was to unwind a little. Instead as he listened to Toby and Jude, he found himself getting progressively more and more annoyed. The current discussion was merely a theme and variation of the same old thing; a topic that had taken center stage in his family for months now: his mother's rediscovered wealthy siblings.

Liam had always known his mother, Jeanne Marie, had been adopted and, like her, he'd thought nothing of it. Countless people were adopted; it was no big thing. Just this past year his own brother Toby had taken in three foster children.

What made it such a big thing, not just in his eyes but in everyone else's, was that it turned out his mother had been given up for adoption, along with a sister she hadn't even known about until just recently, by none other than a member of the highly revered Fortune family.

And that little bit of news had turned all of their worlds upside down.

The ironic thing was that his mother might have very well gone to her grave not knowing a thing about her roots if her brother, James Marshall Fortune, hadn't come poking around, telling her that she was not only his sister but that she, he and the sister she had previously known nothing about—a British woman named Josephine May—were actually triplets.

The whole thing sounded like something out of a movie and if it had been a movie, he would have walked out on it right in the middle. Specifically around the part where this "long-lost brother" of hers gave her a whole wad of money. That had been James Marshall's way of "making it up to her" for having lived a life that hadn't been embedded in the lap of luxury.

As if money could fix everything and anything.

Liam found the whole money thing offensive and degrading. He resented the offering of a "consolation prize" to make up for the fact that his mother had lived a life that James Fortune obviously felt was beneath her.

When his mother gave Fortune back his money, Liam had never been prouder of her. But then she'd gone and spoiled it all by turning around and asking him and his siblings to not just recognize these interlopers as their blood relatives but to actually take on their surname.

Oh, they'd still be the Jones family, but now they'd all be known as the *Fortune* Joneses.

The hell they would, Liam thought angrily as he took another swig of his beer, which by now was decidedly no longer cold. But he hardly noticed.

In all honesty, he had expected his six siblings to feel *exactly* the way he did and was utterly stunned to discover that the whole thing didn't even *begin* to bother them as much as it did him.

In fact, it felt as if his brothers and sisters were dropping like flies around him, taking on the Fortune name and forgetting just who the hell they were to begin with: Deke Jones's offspring.

Granted, their father wasn't an emotional, verbally effusive man. But at the same time, he was a decent, hardworking man who had always made sure they had food in their bellies, a roof over their heads and more opportunity to make something of themselves than he had. Some men showed they cared by talking, others by doing. Deke Jones fell into the latter category.

Liam sensed that this rush to embrace the Fortune

name was a slap in the face for his father, even though Deke had said nothing about it either way.

But the look in his eyes certainly did.

As the conversation continued to revolve around Christopher and his drastic move out of town, Liam found that his temper had been brought dangerously close to the edge and was about to flare.

"You know, it's like he's not even the same person anymore," Toby observed about the absent member of their family. "When this whole thing started, Christopher hated the Fortunes as much as we did. Now he's run off to Red Rock to work for them. I just don't get it," Toby, who at twenty-eight was the youngest of the three of them, confessed, shaking his head.

Jude shrugged carelessly. "Oh, they're not so bad," he told Toby, defending this newly uncovered branch of the family. Blessed with a keen survival instinct, he deliberately avoided looking in Liam's direction. Jude *knew* what his thirty-two-year-old brother thought of all the Fortunes and the last thing he was looking for was a fight. He just wanted to impart the information he'd learned about these new relatives of theirs. After all, fair was fair.

"Gabriella knows them," Jude went on, referring to his fiancée, "and she said that they're good people who just got a raw deal, bad-mouthed by folks who're just jealous of their success and their money." He spared one quick, fleeting glance in Liam's direction to see how he was taking this and then just as quickly looked away. "You know how some people are. They try to drag down anyone who's doing better than they are, thinking that might somehow elevate them."

Liam had heard enough. Fed up, he slammed his beer mug down on the table with such force, the sound reverberated loudly enough to garner him a few curious looks from people seated at the nearby surrounding tables, not to mention the attention of several other patrons.

"Oh, come *on*." Liam ground the words out angrily. "Wake up and smell the coffee, guys. Anyone saying anything good about those people is just trying to cozy up to their fat bank accounts and their fancy circle of friends. The Fortunes *use* people. Anyone who thinks different is just fooling themselves."

Toby felt that his brother was forgetting a very important point in all this. "But Mom says—" he began.

Liam waved his hand at his younger brother before the latter could say anything further.

"I love Mom, but she's just being emotional right now and I don't fault her for that. But I'm a 'Jones' boy. Not 'Fortune Jones,' just plain old 'Jones' and I'm proud of it, proud of the old man, of having a father who worked hard to make a life for himself and his family. And I'm not about to change the way I feel just because some rich guy comes along and tells us we're the missing branch of his family. Who knows if he's even telling her the truth, anyway?"

"Why would he lie about something like that?" Toby wanted to know.

"Hell if I know," Liam answered with a shrug. "Who knows why people like that do anything? Maybe there's something in it for them that we don't know about yet."

Which, to him, was all the more reason why they should view the whole scenario suspiciously. That way, they wouldn't be wide open if something *did* happen.

Jude gave him a steely look. "You're reaching, Liam. It doesn't matter what you feel or don't feel. That doesn't change any of the facts—and the facts are you've got Fortune blood running through your veins. We all do. Face it, big brother, you're a Fortune."

Liam held up his hand, as if to physically stop the flow of words that could only lead to a knock-down, drag-out argument between them. Clearly nothing was going to be resolved here by talking about those people.

Deep down in his soul, he really felt that if by some wild chance he and his family welcomed these people with open arms, the Fortunes would only wind up infecting them with their greed.

With that in mind, it was best just to change the subject and talk about something else.

"How much longer are you planning on hanging on to those Hemings kids?" he asked Toby. "I mean, don't you think that five months is plenty?"

"Not really," Toby answered. "I haven't exactly figured out what I'm doing yet. But just so you know," he told Liam, "I *like* having those kids around. They make me see things differently."

Liam laughed shortly. That certainly wouldn't have been the way he would have felt about having three children infiltrating every corner of his life.

"To each his own, I guess," he told Toby. "As for

me, I don't like being responsible for anyone else but myself."

"Yeah, we already know that," Toby commented dryly. "That's not exactly a news flash."

"If I were you, I wouldn't go boasting about that too much," Jude warned Liam. "The gods have a way of taking you down a peg or two if they think you're being too happy—or too irreverent," Jude pointed out. And then, as if not to leave Toby out, he couldn't help commenting, "You know that being responsible for three kids can't be doing much for your social life."

"Why don't you let me worry about my social life," Toby told Jude in a laid-back tone.

Jude turned toward Liam. "Speaking of social life, how's yours been lately? You seem a little...I don't know, solitary these days," he said. "I can remember a time when you had to beat girls off with a stick."

"I do just fine, thanks, Jude." He grinned. "I've learned not to beat them off anymore."

Liam had always been devoted to working on his ranch from sunup to sundown—and then some.

"Just remember—both of you," Jude said, looking from one brother to the other. "Don't underestimate the value of having a good woman at your side."

Liam drained his mug, setting it down again. He had to be getting back soon. As always, there was work to be done.

But he wasn't ready to leave just yet. "God, Jude, ever since you got engaged to that little Mendoza girl, you're acting whipped."

"Don't let Gabriella hear you call her a little girl," Jude warned seriously. "She's certainly more woman than you ever went out with—except for maybe that Julia Tierney."

Something within Liam tensed at the mere mention of Julia's name. It always did. Everyone had at least one person they thought of as "the one that got away." Julia was his.

"He never went out with Julia," Toby told Jude.

Jude looked a little confused. "I thought Liam asked every girl in his senior class out," Jude said.

"He did ask," Toby answered, keeping a straight face. "But Julia was the only one with the good sense to turn him down." He turned his sharp blue eyes on Liam. "That wounded your fragile pride, didn't it, big brother?"

"Shut up, both of you," Liam ordered in a flat, emotionless voice. "And for the record, my pride's not fragile and it wasn't wounded. Not going out with me was Julia's loss, not the other way around," he informed his brothers in a no-nonsense voice.

He saw Toby's mouth drop open and wondered why since he hadn't exactly said anything earth-shattering or that novel for that matter. The next moment, both his brothers were scrambling to their feet, as if, belatedly, to show their respect.

"Funny, I remember it the other way around," a melodic female voice behind Liam's chair said.

Caught off guard, Liam swung around so fast he almost caused his chair to tilt and deposit him on the sawdust floor. He managed to steady the chair at the very last moment, preventing a spill and a great deal of embarrassment on his part.

The object of their conversation was smiling a greeting at his brothers.

Julia had stopped by the Horseback Hollow Grill with a definite agenda in mind. The Grill was the town's only restaurant and she had just happened upon a situation that could very well enable her to bring a second eatery to the small town.

She had been looking at The Grill with fresh eyes, as if she'd never seen the place before, when she'd heard Liam Jones making a commotion as he banged down his mug. Curiosity had prompted her to move closer to his table to find out what was going on. Ordinarily she would have kept to herself, but she was feeling hopeful about her future for the first time in a long time, so she'd decided to indulge herself and find out what the man was carrying on about.

He had certainly changed a lot since their high school days, she couldn't help thinking. His build had gotten way more muscular and his tan appeared to be permanent, no doubt from his days on the ranch. But what he had gained in looks, he had lost in temperament. From the little bit she had caught, he sounded as though he was well on his way to becoming a grumpy old man, not the exciting, wild-eyed bad boy she had known in high school.

"Hello, boys. How are you?" she asked, looking at Toby and Jude. Then, as they nodded, offering almost a

synchronized chorus of "Fine, how are you?" she looked
at Toby. Her blue eyes crinkled as she asked, "How are
the kids, Toby?"

"They're doing great, thanks for asking," Toby told
her, beaming.

She didn't leave it there, although she knew she
could have. But she was serious in asking after the
children Toby had selflessly taken in—surprising a
lot of people—and she wanted Toby to be aware of
something.

"You're doing a good thing, Toby, taking those children in like that," she said warmly. "Kids need to feel
wanted. It anchors them."

So now she was dispensing child-rearing advice?
Liam thought. Well that went with the territory, didn't
it? Julia had always acted as if she felt she was above
him and, by association, above his family, as well.

"Since when did you start dabbling in child psychology?" Liam asked, acutely aware that the one girl
in high school who had actually hurt his budding male
ego was still going out of her way to ignore him. And
even more acutely aware that no matter how much he
tried not to let it bother him—it did.

"That's not psychology, that's just common sense,
Jones—or should I say Fortune Jones?" she asked, the
corners of her mouth curving as she looked at him.

"Might just be wiser not to say anything at all," Liam
countered.

Jude and Toby exchanged looks and pushed their
chairs in against the table.

"I think that's our cue to leave," Jude said to his younger brother. He then tipped the rim of his hat to Julia. "Nice seeing you again, Julia."

"Yeah, see you around," Toby echoed his brother, tipping his own hat belatedly.

Liam waited until his brothers had walked out of the bar before he said, "If you're expecting to hear the same from me, you're going to have to wait until hell freezes over."

Rather than be affronted, Julia smiled up at Liam. "I've never expected anything from you, Liam, except exactly what you delivered. Which was nothing," she added after a beat in case there was any question as to her meaning.

He was *not* about to take the bait, he told himself. Instead he said mildly, "Been sharpening that tongue of yours, I see."

Julia inclined her head. "I guess you just bring out the worst in me, Jones."

He appeared unfazed by her assessment. "I didn't know there was anything else to bring out," he replied mildly.

"Is that why you asked me out that time in high school?" she questioned with a knowing smile. She had been more than a little attracted to him at the time, but he had always had all these simpering girls around him, ready to do anything he asked just to be with him. It had been enough to turn her completely off. There was absolutely no way she would have *ever* allowed herself to be part of an adoring crowd, a devoted groupie like the others. Liam had had a large enough ego back then without her adding to it.

"Anyone else would have realized that I'd asked you out because I didn't want you to feel left out and wonder if there was something wrong with you. I didn't want to hurt your feelings."

"There's a difference between being left out of a crowd and being superior to the crowd. You seemed to thrive on having all those girls fawn over you and, frankly, I never saw what all the attraction was so I never wanted to join that very limited club," she informed him. There was no way in heaven she'd admit to being attracted to him then—and she was even more unwilling to admit that the attraction had never really faded away.

His eyes narrowed, pinning her down. "For someone who didn't want to join the club, I sure caught you looking at me enough times," he recalled.

"Yes, I looked at you," she admitted. "But if you'd actually looked back at me, you would have realized that was pity in my eyes, not admiration." She shook her head, her long, straight hair moving like a mesmerizing red cloud as it framed her face. "But you just assumed that all the girls were so crazy about you."

This could go on for hours. Though he would have never admitted it out loud, they were pretty evenly matched and he wasn't about to get the best of her any time soon. She might not have anything else to do— since she was obviously not rushing back to the grocery store she managed for her ailing father—but he had a ranch to run.

"I don't have time for this," he declared abruptly.

"You never did have time for the truth," he heard her say as he turned his back on her and walked out of the bar.

It took Liam a while to cool down. Longer than the trip back to the ranch. Julia Tierney was the one person in town who could raise his blood pressure to dangerous heights with no effort at all.

She could also do the same thing to his body temperature.

Chapter Two

As was her custom six days a week, Julia came down from the small apartment above the store where she lived at exactly 7:00 a.m. to unlock the front door to the Horseback Hollow Superette, the town's only grocery store, which had been in her family for several generations. It was also the only grocery store for thirty miles.

The store served its customers from seven until seven Monday through Saturday. On Sundays, the hours were somewhat shorter. However, since Julia did live just above the grocery store, she could *always* be reached in case someone had a "food emergency" of some sort—such as relatives showing up for a forgotten dinner just when the cupboard was bare.

Running the family business had *not* been what she'd envisioned doing with her life when she had been a senior in high school, but this was—at least for now—the plan that *life* seemed to have in store for her.

Twelve years ago she had been all set to go away to an out-of-state college with an eye out to someday perhaps owning her own restaurant. She'd loved to cook ever since she could reach the top of the stove without the benefit of using a stool. She could still remember the very first thing she had prepared for her parents: cinnamon toast. At four she'd been proud enough to burst at what she'd viewed to be a major accomplishment: toast buttered on both sides with a dusting of cinnamon.

Her parents had been nothing but encouraging and supportive from the start, telling her there wasn't anything she couldn't do or become if she set her mind to it.

And then, just like that, her world had come crashing down all around her.

Right before she was to leave for her first semester at college, her father had had a heart attack. For a while it was touch and go and the doctors weren't sure if he would pull through. There was no way she could leave him or her mother at a time like that.

And even when her father began to come around, she found more than a ton of reasons that kept her right where she was. Between concern over her father's health and trying to keep up her mother's morale—not to mention because her parents needed the income to pay for her father's medical bills—there was no way she could find the time to go away to school. Her family needed her too much and she'd refused to leave them high and dry.

Though they always had part-time help at the Superette, there was really no one else to keep things going. Math had always been her mother's undoing.

So Julia had stayed on, putting her dream on hold— which sounded a good deal better to her than saying that she was giving up her dream—and doing what needed to be done.

Looking back now, that almost seemed like a lifetime ago to her.

With time, her father, Jack, had improved somewhat, although he was never again the hale-and-hearty man he'd been before the heart attack. And eventually, she'd seen the color come back into her mother's face to the point that Annie Tierney no longer looked as if she was auditioning for the part of a ghost.

As for herself, she'd gone from being a carefree, whimsical young girl to being a practical, pragmatic young woman with the weight of the world occasionally on her shoulders.

But she managed. She *always* managed.

Those years had also seen her married and then divorced, neither of which happened with a great deal of emotion or fanfare. Marrying Neal Baxter, a local boy who had just returned to Horseback Hollow to practice law after getting his degree, seemed like the right thing to do at the time. She and Neal were friends and Julia had honestly believed that having a friend to go through life with was a smart thing to do.

But a few years into the marriage, a marriage that seemed to be built on little more than mutual respect and a whole lot of boredom, she and Neal came to the conclusion that they really liked one another far too much to be trapped in something that promised no joy to either of them.

So an uncontested, amicable divorce settlement was quickly and quietly reached. They each came away with whatever they had brought into the marriage.

It was a case of no harm, no foul, except that Julia had learned that dreaming about things you couldn't have—such as a passionate marriage—really *did* hurt.

After that, the store became her haven, her home base. It was the one thing she could always depend on to be there. After a time her job became so ingrained she went about her day's work routine practically on autopilot.

Before unlocking the door, she first prepared the store for customers. Produce was put out and carefully arranged in the appropriate bins. The breads, pastries and especially the doughnuts were baked fresh every morning—she saw to that even though it meant she had to get up extremely early to get the goodies to the store in time to arrange the display. It was her one creative outlet and she looked forward to the scents of sugar and butter in her kitchen each morning.

Aside from that, there were always a hundred different little details to see to and Julia kept a running checklist in her head at all times, making sure she hadn't forgotten anything.

She did all this by herself and even, at times, found the solitude of the store comforting at that hour.

So when she saw her mother in the store, Julia was more than a little surprised. Her mother was sweeping the aisles, a chore Julia normally took care of just before opening, a full hour before she normally came in. Annie always arrived *after* having made breakfast for her husband.

Judging by her presence—not to mention the look on her mother's face—something was definitely up.

Julia approached the problem—because there *had* to be a problem—slowly by asking, "Mom, what are you doing here?"

Looking far from her normally sunny self, Annie answered, "It's my store. I work here. Or have you forgotten?"

"I *know* you work here, Mom," Julia said patiently, "but you don't come in until after eight. Everything okay with Dad?" she asked, suddenly concerned.

Julia realized that was the only thing that would make her mother break with her regular routine. Her mother was nothing if not a creature of habit. It was Annie who had taught her that a regular routine would give her life structure.

And she had been right.

If it hadn't been for her routine, Julia was certain that the act of setting her goals and dreams aside would have crushed her spirit so badly she wouldn't have been able to function and come through for her parents the way she had. She had taken everything over, becoming what her mother was quick to point out was not just her right hand, but her left one, as well.

Julia owed that to a well-instilled sense of structure, not to mention to a very keen sense of family loyalty.

"Your father," Annie said, answering her question, "is the same as he was yesterday and, God willing, the

same as he will be tomorrow. Well, but not perfect."
She paused to smile at her daughter. "But then, no man
is ever perfect."

It was a familiar mantra that her mother had uttered
more than a handful of times.

What was different this time was the sadness around
the edges of her smile. And the deeper sadness she
could see in her mother's eyes.

Taking the straw broom out of her mother's hands,
Julia leaned it against the closest wall. She then took
both of her mother's hands in hers and said, "Mom, if
your face was hanging down any lower, you wouldn't
need that broom to sweep up all that imaginary dust
you always see on the floor. You could use your chin.
Now come clean. What's wrong?"

Annie took a breath, apparently struggling to find
the right words.

"It's you."

Julia stared at her mother. Whatever she'd expected
to hear, it wasn't that.

"Me?" she cried incredulously.

Her mother's answer had succeeded in stunning her.
How could she possibly be responsible for that look of
utter devastation on her mother's remarkably unlined
face? Hadn't she all but lived and breathed family and
the business for twelve years now, leaving aside her
own hopes and dreams?

In her view, that would have been cause for her
mother to celebrate, not look as if someone precious
to her had just died.

"Mom, how can you say that? What more can I do?

I'm almost knocking myself out every day to make sure the store stays open and running," Julia pointed out.

Her mother shook her head, her expression telling her that she just didn't understand. "That's just it, Julia. You *shouldn't* have to be knocking yourself out. This is the time of your life that you should look back on fondly when you get to be my age. You shouldn't be forced to feel like you worked your life away."

"But I *don't* feel that way, Mom," Julia protested with feeling. Granted, there were times when she felt as if she did nothing *but* work, but for the most part, she did fine running the grocery store—not to mention putting out her baked goods in a little area that was set aside for the shopper who required a cup of coffee and a pastry to jump-start their morning.

Rather than look relieved, her mother looked as if she was growing agitated for her.

"Well, if you don't, you should," her mother insisted. "You should be resentful that your father and I stole twelve perfectly good years of your life away from you by allowing you to be here for us."

Still holding her mother's hands, Julia led her to a chair over in the corner, just behind the main counter, and knelt in front of her, looking directly into her mother's kind, warm eyes.

"Mom, what's this all about?" she asked gently.

"Maybe I'm seeing things clearly for the first time in years. This isn't fair to you, honey," she insisted, "making you work here day after day. You've sacrificed your education, your career, your marriage—"

"Hold it," Julia declared, holding up her hand. "Back

it up, Mom. First of all, I didn't sacrifice my education. I can always go back to college. It would take a little doing, but it's not impossible. Second, I do that. I can get a career going. And besides, the one I had my eye on back then didn't ultimately require having a college degree so much as it required dedication—it still does," she said, unlocking the front door, then walking back to her mother.

"And third, working here was not what killed my marriage. Mutual, soul-snuffing boredom did that." Julia sighed, feeling a wave of sadness taking root. She had never failed at anything before, but it was about time she accepted the fact that she'd failed at marriage. "Neal and I should have never gotten married in the first place."

"But Neal was such a nice boy," Annie pointed out, protesting the whole idea that their marriage had been a mistake from the beginning.

"Yes, he was and he still is," Julia readily agreed. "But we got married because it seemed like the right thing to do and *nobody* should get married thinking pragmatically like that. When Neal and I were married, there was no magic, no chemistry, no starbursts—and those are three *very* important qualities to have in the foundation of a marriage," Julia stressed.

Leaning in, Julia affectionately pressed a kiss to her mother's forehead. "So stop beating yourself up. I'm exactly where I'm supposed to be and when the time is right, I'll go on to another phase of my life. Until then," she said, rising to her feet again, "why don't you make sure all the eggs are out of the refrigerator in the storage room?"

The bell that hung over the entrance to the grocery store rang, signaling the arrival of the store's first customer of the day.

"You do that," she told her mother, "while I go see what this customer wants."

Turning from her mother, Julia found herself looking straight up at Liam Jones. She wasn't a short woman—five foot eight in her bare feet and her feet weren't bare—but at six foot three Liam literally seemed to tower over her. Especially, she noted, since he was wearing boots that added another inch and a half to his height.

Seeing him here surprised her—when was the last time he'd come to the grocery store?—but Julia managed to recover quickly enough.

"Wow, twice in one week," she joked, referring to seeing him. "Are the planets about to collide or something equally as dire?"

Liam was frowning. She was beginning to think that his face had set that way, like some grumpy old man who whiled away his days parked in a chair on a front porch, scowling at the world.

"I don't know about the planets, but we sure are," he told her darkly.

"And exactly what is *that* supposed to mean?" Julia wanted to know.

"I came to hear you say that it's not true."

"Okay," Julia said obligingly. "'It's not true.'" She

waited for him to say something. When he didn't, she gave in and asked, "What's not true?"

"The rumors I heard."

They were back to this again, she thought, frustrated. "Okay, I'll bite. *What* rumors?" she asked, gritting her teeth.

What was it about this pompous cowboy that set her so completely on edge every time they were within ten feet of each other?

She couldn't answer that, which only made the whole situation that much more frustrating for her.

"The rumors that say you're trying to convince those damn Fortunes to stick their noses where they don't belong and open up some high-falutin' restaurant in Horseback Hollow."

Now how did he know she'd been talking to the Mendozas?

"'Damn Fortunes'?" she echoed. "Correct me if I'm wrong, but aren't *you* a Fortune?" she challenged.

His sharp, penetrating blue eyes narrowed as he said, "Consider yourself corrected."

That caught her off guard for a second. Had the stories she'd heard been wrong? "So you're *not* a Fortune?"

"No." He all but spit the word out with all the contempt he could put into the two-letter word.

And then she remembered something else she'd heard. Something that completely negated what he'd just told her. "Funny, your mother was in here the other day and she seems to think that all of her children have now adopted the Fortune name." She had him there, Julia thought.

To her surprise, Liam didn't take back his statement. Instead he said, "My mother is too softhearted for her own good. She'll believe anyone. And don't try to turn this thing around so I lose track of the question. Are you or are you not trying to talk those people into bringing their tainted business into our town?"

She seized the word—but not the one he would have thought of.

"That's right, Liam. *Our* town. Not your town, but *our* town. That means I get a say in what happens here, too, not just you and your incredibly narrow vision." The man was practically medieval in his outlook. If it were up to him, everyone would still be living in the dark ages.

Liam looked at her coldly. "So it's true."

She might as well spell it out for him, otherwise she had a feeling that she would have no peace from this man. Why was he so against progress, anyway?

"If you mean am I trying to show Wendy and Marcos Mendoza that building another one of their restaurants here in Horseback Hollow is a very good idea, then yes, it's true." The restaurant would attract business and provide jobs. There was no downside to that.

He succeeded in taking her breath away with his very next question. "Why do you want to destroy the town, Julia?"

For a second she was so stunned she was speechless. And then she found her tongue. "Are you crazy? This wouldn't destroy the town. This would be an incredibly *good* thing for the town."

"Right," Liam sneered. "'A good thing,'" he echoed contemptuously. "And after they build this restaurant, what's next? Bring in chain retail stores? Or maybe a shopping mall? Don't forget, they bring in a chain store, that'll be the end of this little family store of yours, as well." He gestured around the store. "You and your parents will be out living on the street—and you'll have no one to blame but yourself."

How could he come up with all this and still keep a straight face? It was just beyond her. "You know," she told him, "you should really be a science-fiction writer with that imagination of yours."

Annie Tierney picked this moment to emerge out of the rear storeroom. Seeing Liam beside her daughter, the woman beamed and came forward.

"Hello, Liam," she greeted him. "Tell me, how is your mother feeling these days?"

Chapter Three

Annie Tierney's unannounced appearance caught Liam off guard.

He offered her a polite smile. "She's feeling fine, Mrs. Tierney."

Julia's mother laughed, the look on her face telling him that he had misunderstood her question. "I'm not asking after her health, dear. I'm asking how she feels about finding out that she's actually the long-lost daughter of such a very well-to-do, powerful family. The Fortunes," she added when Jeanne Marie's son didn't immediately respond. "Personally, I find it all very exciting," Annie went on to confide. "It certainly would be a load off my mind if I found out that I was related to them."

The older woman turned to look at her daughter.

There was unmistakable affection in her eyes. "The first thing I'd do is send my girl off to the very best college that money could buy instead of letting her slave her life away here."

"I'm not slaving, Mom," Julia reiterated the point she'd made before Liam had burst into her store with his annoying accusations. "And this is a conversation we can continue later, when we're *alone*." She deliberately emphasized, then looked directly at Liam. "Which will be soon because Liam's just leaving. Aren't you, Liam?" Julia asked, looking at him pointedly as she did her best to muster the semblance of a friendly smile, strictly for her mother's benefit.

"Yeah, I guess I am," he agreed, his eyes never leaving hers, "seeing as how I was never any good at banging my head against a brick wall."

"Oh, you poor dear," Annie declared, instantly sympathetic. As she spoke, Annie reached up to move Liam's light brown hair off his forehead so she could examine it, but he took a step back, preventing her.

"No, ma'am, don't worry. I didn't hit my head in your store."

When Annie looked at him quizzically, Liam knew she was waiting for him to explain his comment. He was forced to lie so that the woman wouldn't think he was being flippant about the Superette. He really liked Annie Tierney. She was friendly, always saw the good in everyone and had a kind soul. In his opinion, Julia could have stood to learn a few things from her mother.

"Then where did you hit your head?" Annie asked.

"At the ranch," he told her, trying to ease away from

the topic. "Last week," he added to forestall any further questions.

"Oh, well mind you watch yourself," Annie cautioned. "Head injuries aren't something to just be shrugged off." And then the serious look on her face vanished as she told him, "I just put on a kettle in the back. Would you care for some tea?"

"No, but thank you for the offer." Since he knew it seemed rather odd that he'd come into the grocery store without buying anything and was now leaving empty-handed, he told the older woman, "I just came by to have a word with your daughter."

"Oh." The thin face lit up, completely erasing the very few lines that were evident. "Well, then by all means, have words," Annie said encouragingly. "Don't mind me. I'll just be in the back, having my tea," she told them as she made her way out of the store and retreated to the storeroom again.

"She's a very nice lady," Liam commented to Julia, watching her mother leave.

Well, there at least he would get no disagreement from her, Julia thought. That was possibly the *only* area that they wouldn't clash over. For the most part, he had the very annoying ability of making her want to say "black" whenever he said "white."

"Yes, she is," Julia agreed quietly, deliberately avoiding making any eye contact with him.

Liam obviously had no such inclination. Instead he turned to look at her. Julia could tell by his expression that the temporary truce that had been silently called while her mother had been in the immediate vicinity was officially over.

"What would she say if she knew?" he suddenly challenged.

Okay, maybe she just wasn't sharp today, Julia thought shortly. What the hell was he talking about now?

"Knew about what?"

He looked at her as if she'd suddenly turned simple. She caught herself wanting to strangle him.

"That you're seriously thinking about trying to get the Fortunes to bring their big-city blight right here to Horseback Hollow."

"If you're still referring to my wanting to encourage Wendy and her husband to open up their second restaurant here, she would probably say, 'Go for it, Julia.'" She raised her chin like someone bracing for a grueling battle. "My mother has always been very supportive of my dreams and I've had this one for a very long time."

His eyes became blue laserlike slits as he regarded her. "So you're telling me that it's your dream to destroy Horseback Hollow?"

She wasn't saying any such thing and he knew it, Julia thought angrily. How could she have *ever* been attracted to this Neanderthal? She must have been out of her mind.

"No," Julia contradicted with feeling, struggling not to raise her voice and yell at him. The last thing she wanted to do was to have her mother overhear her giving Liam a piece of her mind—even if he did sorely need it. But she'd had just about all she could take of his holier-than-thou pontificating. "It's always been my dream to build the town up."

He laughed shortly. "Right now, that's the same thing from where I'm standing."

And just who had died and made him the reigning authority on things like this?

"Well, then, maybe you'd better move and get the sun out of your eyes because you certainly aren't seeing things clearly."

"The town's doing just fine as it is," he insisted. What was wrong with her? "Why can't you see how destructive it would be to allow outsiders' interests to take over Horseback Hollow? What do we need with another restaurant, anyway?" he challenged her.

Just how blind was he? she wondered, frustrated. "Does the term 'freedom of choice' *mean* anything to you?" she returned frostily.

His mouth curved in a humorless smile. "Only if it means I'm free to ignore you."

"Go right ahead," she declared, gesturing toward the door. "But you're going to have to do it outside my store."

The next moment she'd suddenly put her hands against his back and began to push him toward the door.

She managed to move Liam a few stumbling feet only because she'd caught him by surprise. But once he regained his balance, Liam employed his full weight as a counterforce and there was no way she could budge him more than a couple of shaky inches.

"I just want to say one more thing—" he began.

Exhausted by her effort to move him any farther

toward the door, Julia dropped her hands to her sides. "I'll hold you to that," she told him sharply.

"How are your folks going to feel when this store is forced to close down?" His tone was surprisingly mild as he put the question to her. He looked like a man who felt he'd scored his winning goal and was just waiting for the fact to sink in with the opposing team.

Julia, however, looked at him as if she thought he'd just lost his mind.

"Why would this store be forced to close down?" She wanted to know his rationale.

Like a parent introducing a new concept to a child, he began to patiently explain. "Hey, chain drugstores aren't going to be the only thing that'll be turning up here once you open the floodgates and start 'building the town up.' Big chain supermarkets will be horning their way in here, too." Liam paused to look around the grocery store that had remained relatively unchanged for most of his lifetime. He found that rather comfortingly reassuring. "And this store, with its neat little aisles and limited selections will be boarded up faster than you can say 'I told you so,'" he concluded.

"I wouldn't be saying 'I told you so.'" There were small, sharp daggers coming from her eyes, all aimed at his heart—if he actually *had* one. "That would be your line," she retorted.

"Yes," Liam agreed, grinning from ear to ear. "It would be."

The strange thing about that grin, Julia later recalled, was that it didn't seem to reach his eyes. In her experience, any smile or grin that was genuine in scope always included the eyes. Without the eyes being involved, the person who was smiling was only trying to fool people as to his mind-set.

Sometimes, she couldn't help thinking, they were out to fool themselves, as well. The first time she noticed the difference between real smiles and ones that were entrenched in deception, consciously or otherwise, was when she'd caught a glimpse of her own face in the mirror on her wedding day.

Her eyes hadn't been smiling then, either. At the time, she was doing what she felt was the "right thing." It had taken her three years before she'd admitted that to herself.

"Look," she told Liam, "either buy something or leave. I've got work to do and I don't have time to let you go on badgering me like this because you're so small-minded you can't see that you either progress or wither and die on the vine. And *you* might be content to let Horseback Hollow stagnate, but I want it to flourish."

He looked at her for a long moment, as if he was debating saying anything to her or not. Finally he said, "There's a third alternative in that multiple choice of yours."

She didn't see it and couldn't imagine what his point was. "Enlighten me," she told him.

He laughed at her choice of words. "That'll take a lot longer than I have right now. But let me just tell you what that third choice is…. It's maintaining the status quo."

That was just theme and variation of one of the two choices she'd presented to him.

"In other words, stagnating," she declared. But before he could say anything further to contradict what he'd just labeled his so-called "third" choice, Julia started talking rapidly to get her point across.

"Nothing ever remains the same, no matter how much you might want it to. Change is inevitable and you can't stop it or stand in its way. But you *can* guide it," she emphasized.

Liam frowned as he shook his head, the ultimate immovable object to her irresistible force. "Sorry, it's going to take a hell of a lot more than that to convince me to surrender to the boys with the deep pockets. I'd rather just go my own way."

"Why don't you?" she said encouragingly. The next moment she'd crossed the floor to the door and held it wide open for him, her meaning clear. "Nobody here will stop you, that's for damn sure."

Rather than do exactly that and just leave, Liam pulled himself up to his full height and seemed to just loom over her, his bearing fully emphasizing just how much taller than her he really was.

"No, but someone should really stop you," he told her in a voice that was completely devoid of any humor. "Before it's too late and we all wind up suffering the consequences."

Again Julia raised her chin defiantly, her eyes flashing as she barely managed to suppress her anger.

"It'll take a better man than you to do it," she informed him hotly.

"Maybe," Liam allowed, "but that doesn't mean I can't try."

Before Julia could ask him just what he intended to do, Liam did it.

Did something he hadn't even foreseen himself doing—at least not in the heat of this exchange. Although if he were being completely honest with himself, he would have had to admit that he *had* envisioned *exactly* this transpiring more than just once or twice in his head—as well as in his unguarded dreams.

One second they were exchanging glares and hot words, the next it was no longer just the words that were hot.

It was the two of them.

Liam had caught her by her shoulders and brought his mouth down on hers.

There was the argument that doing this was the *only* way to stop her from talking and, more importantly, from espousing the so-called cause she seemed so intent on pushing.

There was a whole host of arguments and half-truths he could have told himself about why he had done what he'd done. But deep in his soul, he knew that there was only one real reason he was doing this.

Because he wanted to.

Rather than embracing the cause that was so close to her heart, after a beat, to her dismay, Julia found herself embracing *him* instead. Found herself weaving her arms around Liam's neck as best she could, raising herself up on her tiptoes so that she could lean her body into his.

She *had* to have lost her mind; there was no other explanation for behaving this way.

Yet, as upset as doing this made her, Julia just could *not* make herself pull back or break away from Liam and his lethal lips.

Not even the tiniest bit.

Not when the very blood in her veins was rising to an alarming temperature and the room was spinning around her faster than Dorothy's house when it was snatched up by the twister that had sent it whisking off to Oz.

Julia realized that her heart rate had quickened to the point of doubling and the very air seemed to have disappeared right out of her lungs.

Heaven knew that she'd been kissed before, more times than she could possibly count. And of course she'd made love before, as well, but this… This was some kind of new, crazy sensation that she had never, *ever* encountered before and although she knew, *knew* in her heart, that whatever this was, was bad for her, she just couldn't make herself pull away and stop.

Not yet.

A few seconds from now, yes, but *not yet*.

Liam was completely convinced that he had succeeded in utterly losing his mind. There was no other reason for what was going on.

He wasn't that eighteen-year-old hotshot that he once been anymore, wasn't that cocky high school senior who reveled in the adulation he saw in every single high school girl's eyes when she looked at him.

Back then, he'd thrived on those looks and those girls.

But right now he would have been hard-pressed to remember *any* of their names. They all seemed like just so many interchangeable entities, feeding his fragile young ego and providing a release for all those wild, raging hormones that plagued so many boys at that age.

He'd eventually outgrown that stage, settled down in his thinking and while he did enjoy female companionship with a fair amount of regularity, he wasn't looking for anything permanent because he wasn't interested in settling down with any one woman.

Settling.

There wasn't really a single girl he'd gone out with, a single girl or woman in Horseback Hollow who turned up in his dreams at night, who gave him a reason to whistle tunelessly to himself as he looked forward to Saturday-night outings.

But this, whatever *this* was, was different. Different enough to put a fire in his belly and make him suddenly feel alive.

Finally pulling back—because Liam was afraid that if he didn't, he wouldn't be able to surface ever again—he looked at the woman who had just shaken up the foundations of his well-ordered world. Looked at her for a long, hard moment.

And when he spoke, the words could definitely not be viewed as romantic in any manner, shape or form.

"What the hell was that?" He wanted to know.

"I have no idea," Julia answered hoarsely, trying desperately to look angry, to *feel* angry, and completely unable to manage to do either. "But don't ever do it again."

"Don't worry, I won't," Liam replied in a voice that

was just as hoarse as hers, a fact that really annoyed him no end.

He said it because, at the time, he meant it.

Or at least he *thought* he did.

Chapter Four

Harlan Osgood wore not one but two hats in his everyday life.

First and foremost, like his father before him, Harlan was the town barber. He owned and ran The Cuttery, Horseback Hollow's only barbershop. Eventually he'd expanded the shop to include a hair salon, as well, for those ladies who were brave enough to cross the threshold and place the fate of their flowing tresses in Harlan's hands.

Almost everyone in town sat in one of his chairs at one time or another, most on a fairly regular basis. Interacting with these town residents gave Harlan some insight into the way the locals felt about all sorts of matters that concerned them. He was a good listener, always had been, and that, in turn, helped him make some of the decisions he needed to make when he donned his other hat, the one that figuratively belonged to the town mayor.

All things considered, the latter was almost an honorary position. For one thing, there was next to no monetary compensation for the job. Being elected mayor by the good people of Horseback Hollow fed his self-esteem rather than helped him put food on the table. That was what running the Cuttery was for.

Harlan had always been considered a decent, fair man by his friends and neighbors. He wasn't one to impose his will over the objection of others, didn't look for ways—devious or otherwise—to line his pockets or the pockets of his friends at the town's expense. What had put Harlan in office and kept him there election after election was his honest belief that in a town as small as Horseback Hollow, that everyone's voice really counted and was equal to everyone else's.

The way he saw it, one person was no better, no worse than another, and that included him.

Harlan first heard the rumor about the possibility of a new restaurant—funded by some of the Fortunes of Red Rock—coming here to Horseback Hollow the way he heard about almost everything else that came to his attention: from one of the customers sitting in his barber's chair.

In less than forty-eight hours, what began as a vague rumor quickly became the topic that was on *everyone's* lips. No matter who was doing the talking, it seemed that everyone, young or old, had an opinion on the subject of this new restaurant that might be coming.

Some spoke with feelings and passion about this restaurant that had yet to materialize. Others chose to feel *him* out first before stating how *they* felt on the matter.

"What do you think about that new place that's coming to Horseback?" Riley Johnson, one of his most regular customers, asked him.

The rancher, lean and rangy of build, came in for a haircut like clockwork every two weeks despite the fact that he had very little hair to speak of these days. He came, Harlan suspected, for the company and a chance for some male interaction. Riley owned a fairly small spread as far as ranches in the area went and he and his wife had been blessed with all girls. Riley spent most of his days feeling outnumbered.

The barbershop was a place to regroup.

Riley twisted around in his chair to look at the man he'd known going on five decades, waiting for the latter to answer.

"Well, it's not a done deal just yet, Riley," Harlan pointed out as he made rhythmic cuts to the hair that *was* there.

"I heard it's more done than not," Clyde Hanks, another regular, waiting for his turn with Harlan, spoke up.

"Well, you heard wrong," Harlan told him, keeping his eyes on his work and Riley's balding pate. "Nobody's put in any papers for it and nothing's crossed my desk yet. There's gotta be permits issued, land measured, all sorts of tedious things like that before anything gets started," Harlan said. "You boys know that."

Riley still looked a bit skeptical. "And you're not just holding out on us?"

"No reason not to tell you if it was happening," Harlan answered mildly.

"You ask me, it's not a good idea," Riley said.

"Bringing in new business is *always* a good idea," Clyde maintained.

Harlan could see both sides of the matter, the way he always did. The good *and* the bad. Which was why he decided that calling a town meeting to put the matter up for discussion and then eventually to a vote might just be the best way to handle this budding tempest in a teapot—before that teapot boiled over.

The meeting was set for Friday evening at seven.

As always, Harlan relied primarily on word of mouth to spread the news of the town meeting. To play it safe, he also had a couple of notices posted, one in the Superette because most of the town frequented the grocery store, and one in the town's only post office. To his way of thinking, this was as close to covering all bases as he could possibly get.

And then Harlan went back to business as usual, doing what needed to be done until the day of the meeting.

Julia glanced at her watch. It was almost time for the meeting. She was so preoccupied, going over what she wanted to say and trying very hard not to be nervous, that she didn't hear her father's soft footfalls until he was next to her. The once heavyset man had lost a great deal of weight, but he was on the mend and determined to get better with each passing day.

"Julia?"

"Oh, Dad, you scared me," she said, looking up, startled.

He smiled at her. "I just wanted to wish you luck tonight. Some of our friends and neighbors can be real stubborn about changing anything." His protective attitude toward her was out in full display as he said, "Maybe I should go with you."

He still thought of himself as being stronger than he was. She knew these baby steps toward full recovery were frustrating for him, but she didn't want him taking on more than he should. "No, you know excitement isn't good for you, Dad. You've more than done enough already," she told him with feeling. "Finding out about the Mendozas and how they were looking for a new location for a second restaurant, setting up my introduction to them... I'll take it from here."

"You know, I wanted this for you. Wanted to find some way to pay you back for what you gave up to stay here for me."

She didn't want him to feel obliged to her in any way. She'd stayed out of love, not because anyone had made her. "Dad—"

"Let me have my say, Julie. I didn't do all that much, just asked around to find out where you could get in contact with that Marcos Mendoza guy. Most of it was just a matter of luck, anyway, him being married to Wendy Fortune. They're looking to expand their business, so why shouldn't it be here? Especially since

James Fortune is so thrilled to finally make contact with his long-lost sister Jeanne Marie, and her living right here in Horseback Hollow. You might even call it fate. I just tugged a little on fate's hand, that's all. You did the rest. You wrote to them and laid it all out, nice and pretty, the way I knew you would, telling them about all the ways building their next restaurant right here was a good idea for them *and* for the town. You always did have a real good head on your shoulders, Julie. Almost as good as your heart," he said with barely contained emotion.

Moved, she hugged him. "I love you, Dad."

"Right back at you, baby. Now go knock 'em dead," he urged.

The meeting was held at the Two Moon Saloon. As usual, the bar was declared officially closed for the duration of the meeting. The establishment's tables were all pushed to the side, against the walls, and extra folding chairs had been brought in.

As always, there were more people than chairs, but that was just the way things were and no one seemed to mind all that much. Standing for the duration of the meeting seemed like a small price to pay for being included in the town's voting process.

At exactly the stroke of seven, Harlan began the meeting. "Thank you all for coming," he said, addressing people he considered to be his friends rather than his constituents. "I don't think many of you have to be told why we're here."

"I dunno about anyone else, but I'm here to get out of

doing more chores," a male voice at the back of the room piped up. A smattering of laughter followed the remark.

"Glad we could help you out, Zack," Harlan said, recognizing the speaker's voice. "All right, let's get started," he declared, bringing down his gavel and officially calling the meeting to order. "It's recently come to my attention that there's been some serious talk about some out-of-towners thinking of opening up a new restaurant right here in town."

"Why do we need another restaurant? What's wrong with The Grill, I'd like to know?" a woman on the left asked indignantly.

"Have you been there lately? It ain't exactly the Four Seasons," her neighbor, a woman with a rather heavy-set face, pointed out.

"Well, this ain't exactly New York now, is it?" the first woman countered.

"Ladies, ladies, you'll all get your chance to state your opinions," Harlan promised calmly. "That's why we're here. No need to try to shout one another down. We're not taking a final vote tonight. That's for the next meeting. Right now, we're just going to discuss it. All right, one at a time, please," he requested, looking out at the sea of faces before him. "Who wants to go first to make a case for or against a new restaurant opening up in Horseback Hollow?"

More than a few hands shot up. This certainly was a hot topic, Harlan thought. He fervently hoped that it wouldn't divide the town and put the residents at odds with one another. Something like that could turn ugly quickly.

Though he rarely expressed his own opinion on things, he felt strongly about one thing. He would not stand by and see the people who were his neighbors come to blows over this. He wouldn't allow the restaurant to be built here if it came down to that.

Though she was friendly on a one-to-one basis, especially with her store's customers, for the most part Julia considered herself to be rather on the shy side. She certainly didn't like to call attention to herself, and as a rule, didn't like speaking up in a crowded room. She always preferred to keep out of the spotlight.

Julia had attended more than one town meeting without saying a single word during the proceedings, only raising her hand those times when a vote had to be taken.

But this was different.

This—the restaurant that was under discussion—could very well mean the resurrection of her own dream, as well as representing some definite choices for the residents of Horseback Hollow.

Contemplating the restaurant's advent, Julia had already gone so far as to create whole menus in her head, menus that offered *so* much more than The Grill—the building next to the saloon—did. The latter only served burgers, hot dogs and a grilled-cheese sandwich, which served as the establishment's main and most popular meal. The selection at The Grill was so limited that it almost hurt.

So, after listening to one opinion being stated after another, with little being resolved—it was more like mundane bickering—Julia decided that maybe it was time for her to speak up on the side of the restaurant. She could see only pluses in having the business built here.

"Anyone else want to say something?" Harlan asked when the last speaker had finally and mercifully run out of steam and sat down. His eyes quickly swept the room.

When he saw the raised hand, he looked rather surprised to see who that hand belonged to.

"Julia?" he said uncertainly. "Would you like to say something?" Even as he asked, the mayor still expected to hear her say "No," that she hadn't really meant to raise her hand.

But she didn't.

"Yes, Mr. Mayor, I would," she said in a firm voice that gave no hint to the fact that her stomach had flipped over and was currently tied up in a very tight knot.

"Well, stand up and speak up," he said, gesturing for her to rise. "No use talking if nobody can hear you or see you."

"Might not be any use her talking even if we can," someone scoffed.

"Shut up, Silas, and let her say her piece."

The tersely worded command didn't come from the mayor, as Julia might have expected. It had come from Liam Jones.

Stunned, she looked over toward where the rancher was standing at the back of the room. He was indolently leaning against a wall, the expression on his face moderately contemptuous. Initially, she would have said the contempt was aimed at her. But now, with his becoming her unlikely defender, she really couldn't say *what* Liam was being so contemptuous of.

"Thank you," she mouthed.

Liam just nodded silently in response, indicated that she should get on with what she had to say.

Liam Jones was a hard man to read, Julia thought, turning her attention back to the subject that had brought her here.

In truth, Liam wasn't sure just what had prompted him to speak up just now to silence the would-be heckler. The man had only said aloud what he himself had been thinking. But the thought of someone trying to ridicule Julia into holding her peace had unexpectedly raised a fire in his belly.

If anyone was going to put her in her place, it was going to be *him,* not some half-wit who thought himself to be clever. And he definitely didn't want to hear her put in her place in front of a crowd where she could be publicly humiliated. There was no call for that sort of crude behavior.

Julia's soft, melodic voice broke into his train of thought. Liam turned his attention, albeit somewhat against his will, toward the redhead who had been haunting his thoughts ever since he'd kissed her and had messed up life as he knew it.

"Now I know that a lot of you think that things are going along just fine the way they are in Horseback Hollow—" A smattering of voices agreeing with her echoed around the room. "But they're not really," Julia insisted. The same voices now muttered protests.

Harlan raised his gavel in a warning gesture as he looked around the room, daring the mumblers to continue. The murmurings stopped.

Julia continued as if nothing had happened. "You can't tell me that things are so good, so perfect that we couldn't stand to have a little more revenue coming into the town."

"You mean like taxes?" someone asked, somewhat confused as to where she was going with this.

"No," Julia answered patiently. "I mean like people coming here from some of the nearby towns to eat at the new restaurant and spend their money."

"So the people who own the restaurant make money, what's that do for us?" Riley Johnson challenged. Julia could see by the man's expression that he was one of the ones she needed to convert to her way of thinking. The man could be very persuasive when he spoke.

"What it means to us is a great deal," Julia insisted, quickly explaining, "after all, the restaurant isn't going to run itself. It's going to need waitresses and busboys as well as people to do the cooking, to make sure there's enough food, enough coffee, tea and other beverages to drink. It takes a lot to run a decent-size restaurant.

"The restaurant's backers are going to be hiring local people, not busing in people regularly from Red Rock," she pointed out, effectively shooting down a rumor she'd heard making the rounds this morning. "And those customers who'll come to eat at the restaurant, they're not just all going to get back into their cars and drive away into the night," she said with a laugh. "Maybe they'll stay and look around, buy something before they go—"

"The town's only got a handful of shops," Riley pointed out, still not convinced that the good outweighed what he viewed as the bad in this case.

Julia approached the subject from another angle. "Maybe this'll encourage some of you to open up more stores. The way it is right now, we have to drive to other towns to get almost everything. For example, we could stand to have a full-size bakery right here in Horseback Hollow," she suggested.

Liam raised his voice above the voices of several other people, pointing out, "You've got a bakery in your store."

"What we've got are doughnuts and coffee," Julia corrected him, smiling amicably. "I'm talking about a *real* bakery, one that has proper cakes, pies, fresh-baked bread straight out of the oven on the premises, to name just a few things."

She looked around to see if she was getting through and to her surprise, she began to make out faces rather than just a sea of blurred features and hair all running together.

Some of those faces were smiling at her with encouragement. Julia took heart in that.

"I'm talking about building up a place that I am proud to call home. It is *not* going to be easy and it is not going to happen overnight. But it all starts with that first step," she said with sincerity because she really believed what she was telling the people at the meeting.

Unconsciously holding her breath, she looked around the room to see if she had managed to make her neighbors understand.

"Yeah, but that 'step' you're talking about involves inviting those Fortunes into our town," someone toward the back piped up. "Who knows, after they're finished, it might not even *be* our town any longer."

Where did they get these ideas? Julia couldn't help wondering. Even as she did, she caught herself slanting a look in Liam's direction.

Had *he* started that baseless rumor? She didn't want to think that and he *had* come to her defense when Silas Marshall had tried to heckle her, but Liam wasn't the kind of man who could be easily swayed with just a few well-placed words and a smile. The man was nothing if not frustratingly stubborn.

"Now listen," she said. "I've done some research on the subject of the Fortunes. I found out that this family *always* gives back to the community they're in, usually far more than they ever received. Why, they even built a medical clinic in Red Rock and started the Fortune Foundation."

"What's that?" Dinah Jackson queried.

"That's a nonprofit, charitable organization that helps take care of people in need," Julia answered, addressing her words to the woman directly. "People who might have fallen on hard times through no fault of their own."

"Oh, handouts," someone snorted contemptuously.

At times, these people had more pride than sense, Julia couldn't help thinking.

"No, a hand *up*." She put emphasis on the last word. There was a difference. "The foundation helps people stand up on their own two feet again. As far as I can see, there's nothing wrong with that."

A smattering of murmurings rose around the room again as people made comments to their neighbors, rendering their own opinions on what seemed to be the Fortunes' obviously selfless behavior.

There were a few in the gathering who required more convincing—Liam among them—but for the most part, Julia could see that she had managed get the wavering and undecided thinking about the benefits of having this new restaurant here.

The mayor scanned the room, took note of some of the expressions and made a judgment call.

"All right, I think that we've had a fair amount of pro and con debating on this subject for tonight. It's getting kind of late and we all have somewhere to be. If there are no objections, why don't we put the matter to a preliminary vote, see where we all stand on this issue right now? Remember," he warned, "no matter what the outcome of tonight's vote is, nothing's final. You all have time to think about this, do a little research before we take a final vote on the matter. As of right now, there've been no concrete bids made yet, no proposals about building this restaurant.

"As far as I know, this could just be one great big rumor with legs," Harlan told the people at the meeting, chuckling at the verbal image he had just created for them.

"If the preliminary vote turns out to be yes, then I will personally go to Marcos and Wendy Mendoza and convince them to build their second restaurant right here in the heart of Horseback Hollow," Julia promised.

The "heart" of Horseback, at the moment, only involved a two-block radius since that was all that actually comprised the little town.

"Mendoza?" Clyde Hanks echoed, confused. "I thought you said that the Fortunes were the ones who were behind this venture. Just who the heck are Marcos and Wendy Mendoza?" He, as did many others, wanted to know.

"Her name's Wendy *Fortune* Mendoza," Liam told the man tersely.

It felt as though everywhere he turned, he just couldn't get away and avoid those damn people, Liam thought darkly. They were trying to worm their way into his family and now into his town. Maybe the first was happening because they wanted the latter, he realized.

The Fortunes were like some biblical plague he couldn't outrun.

Chapter Five

"Bet you're pretty proud of yourself, aren't you?" Liam remarked, his tone of voice completely unreadable.

Coming out of the saloon at the end of the town meeting, Julia was utterly preoccupied, her mind rushing around here and there as she made plans to get in touch with the Mendozas first thing in the morning. Though nothing had been finalized between them, she was very hopeful that if and when the restaurant did come here, she could impress them enough with her skills to be hired as at least one of the chefs. To that end, she wanted to keep them abreast of what was happening as far as the town's considering the possibility of voting to have the restaurant built in Horseback Hollow.

The preliminary vote regarding the restaurant's construction on Horseback soil had been close, very close, but it looked as if more people were for it than against it. That, in turn, made Julia very excited. She intended to try to bring *everyone* around by the time the final vote was taken.

This was the beginning, she could *feel* it.

Lost in thought, she didn't see Liam standing adjacent to the saloon's entrance, leaning against the side of the building. Busy making plans, she wasn't aware of him at all until he spoke. She'd very nearly jumped out of her skin. She'd thought he'd be halfway home by now, especially since he'd walked out after the vote was tallied and it was obvious that the position he'd taken wasn't going to win. At least, not tonight.

To Liam, the fact that the vote had been so extremely close made the very real possibility of an ultimate loss all the more painful to him. It was one of those "so near and yet so far" moments.

Regaining her composure and managing to cover up the flustered feeling that had corkscrewed through her without warning at the sound of Liam's voice, Julia squared her shoulders as she resumed walking back to the Superette. The grocery store would be open for another half hour because of the meeting and she needed to get back. Tonight her mother was manning the register alone and she didn't want her to be too taxed.

"Yes, I am, actually," she said, responding to the flippant assumption he had tossed at her. She'd said it in as cheerful a tone as she could.

Because she had a natural tendency to want to see everyone happy, she decided to give raising Liam's spirits a shot. "The new restaurant is going to be a good thing for the town, you'll see," she promised him.

"Maybe you and I have a different definition of 'good thing,'" he pointed out with a trace of barely suppressed sarcasm.

"My definition involves prosperity," she replied succinctly.

They'd already gone all through this at the meeting. Hadn't he been paying attention? Why was he refusing to give the whole venture a chance? What was he *really* afraid of? she couldn't help wondering.

His eyes pinned her down, almost keeping her a prisoner as he stated his feelings about the fate of the town. "Mine has to do with the town keeping its individuality, in not turning its back on its roots just to put a few pieces of silver into a few people's pockets."

He made it sound as if she was trying to get the people of Horseback Hollow to sell out for her own private gain and she deeply resented his implication. Selling out had absolutely nothing to do with this.

"People don't deal in silver anymore, Liam," she informed him tersely. "It's the twenty-first century, not the 1850s."

He regarded her for a long, poignant moment, his thoughts utterly masked behind an expressionless face. "Maybe that's the problem," he told her.

She was *not* going to get sucked into playing any mind games. "Maybe the problem is that you're a dream killer," she accused angrily.

Couldn't he see past his own dislike of the Fortunes long enough to try to understand what the infusion of new blood, new places could do for the town, for its economy? How it could just lift up everyone's lifestyle at least a notch or two?

"The 'dream' is the simple life we have here and you're the one killing it because you're an opportunist," he accused, his temper suddenly flaring higher— more than the situation warranted. "Look, aside from all my other objections, I just don't think it's really smart to invite more of these people into Horseback Hollow. Just look what happened with that pilot, Orlando. You going to tell me what happened to him in his plane was just an accident? Not to mention that there've been a bunch of anonymous flyers showing up at the post office here, saying Fortunes Go Home! Can't be any clearer than that."

"Orlando's not a Fortune. He's a Mendoza," Julia began, but got no further.

"A Mendoza who was piloting a plane for Sawyer Fortune. He almost got killed when it malfunctioned. These people are bad news. I say pack it up and go back to where you came from, don't give them another reason to set up camp."

He could see that he just wasn't getting through to her and it exasperated him. They were standing all but toe-to-toe right now. "You think just because you kissed me the other day I'm going to wag my tail and meekly follow you no matter what?"

Her eyes widened in utter shock. How *could* he say that?

"Hold it, buster," she ordered angrily. "I think you

have your facts a little mixed up. *I* didn't kiss *you,*" Julia reminded him flatly. "*You* were the one who kissed *me.*"

Liam shrugged as if he hadn't really expected her to say anything else about the matter. Her denial left him completely unfazed. "If it makes you feel better to believe that, go right ahead," he told her in a disinterested voice.

She hated how he twisted things. "It's not a matter of 'believing' it, it's what happened," Julia insisted, her eyes narrowing as she silently dared him to actually deny it.

There went that chin of hers again, he noted, watching as it stuck up pugnaciously. The single action gave him such a tempting target that he found himself having a really hard time resisting it.

But a man never hit a lady—not unless he was fighting for his life and although that might be what was going on figuratively, in reality it was just a heated battle of words

And even though in their own way those words could deliver even heavier blows to the heart and psyche than fists could, he was *not* about to give Julia the satisfaction of glimpsing that tender region that belonged to him and him alone.

"Looks like we're not going to agree on that, either," he observed.

Had there not been the very real possibility that one of the people who had attended the meeting could stumble over them right now, he would have swept Julia into his arms and showed her what being kissed by him actually meant and felt like.

But, like his father, Liam had always been a very private man. He had absolutely no desire to become the focal point for local gossips. Since the possible construction of this outsider-backed restaurant had everyone stirred up, one way or another, this little drama currently unfolding between Julia and him would be like throwing kindling into a campfire that was already lit.

They would be irresistible fodder for the tongue-waggers of this town and beyond. He wanted no part of that.

So, throwing up his hands, Liam made an unintelligible sound and stormed away before he and Julia could get deeply embroiled in yet *another* argument.

Unlike Julia and more than half the people in that damn saloon who voted with her, Liam thought as he kept walking, he could *not* see anything good coming of this venture Julia was so hot about. What it was going to do was change life in Horseback Hollow as they all knew it. He would bet money on it—and *that* wasn't something he *ever* did lightly. He worked too hard for his money to ever waste it on anything other than what he felt was a *sure* thing.

But the majority—a rather damn *slim* majority at that—had voted to give the project a chance to prove itself as they all gave it a closer inspection. It was up to him to find a way to sink this project before it could actively move forward and become a reality. He needed to do something to get the town to vote against it when the final vote was taken.

At the moment, as he cast around, he was coming up empty.

However, he wouldn't have been his father's son, he thought with a hint of a smile curving his mouth, if he just gave up altogether. He was going to have to think on it awhile, like a dog gnawing on a bone. There *had* to be another way to make Julia see reason about this— and he had to find that way *before* the restaurant opened up and eventually ruined the face of the town.

Even if construction started—and no matter which way you sliced it, that was still a ways off—it could be stopped if enough people could be convinced that he was right and she was wrong.

It had come down to that, he thought. Him against her.

The best way for him to go about that, of course, was to convince *her* that she'd made a mistake. If he did that, the rest would fall neatly into place—and the town would be spared.

But what the hell could he do to make her see that what she was proposing wasn't just a restaurant, it was a whole new change of lifestyle for everyone who lived in and around Horseback Hollow?

So caught up in the dilemma ahead of him, Liam didn't see the tall, rangy rancher until he all but stumbled into him. Stopping short to keep from bodily colliding with the six-foot-tall man, there was an apology on his lips before his eyes and brain focused and engaged one another to identify just who it was that he'd almost walked straight into.

"Hey, sorry, I wasn't looking where I—" *Oh, damn,*

he silently cursed. This was the *last* person he wanted to run into right now.

Quinn Drummond had been at the meeting; he'd taken a seat all the way at the back so that he could observe everyone. Liam doubted the rancher had said two words during the meeting. *And* he had voted for the restaurant. Another reason to avoid the man until he came up with his strategy, Liam thought.

Quinn's solemn face gave way to a small smile. "Liam, just the guy I wanted to see. You got a minute?"

He doubted it was going to be this easy to disengage himself but he gave it a try anyway. "Actually, no, I don't. I was just on my way to see someone—"

"Good, I'll walk with you," Quinn offered, falling into step with him.

"I'm going to be *driving* to see this person. Driving *out of town*." Liam built his lie a piece at a time.

Quinn was nothing if not flexible and accommodating. "All right, I'll just walk you to your truck, then. That'll give me a chance to grab at least a couple of minutes of your time."

Liam was about to say that a couple of minutes wouldn't produce any sort of viable results, but Quinn didn't pause or stop talking long enough to allow him to get the legendary word in edgewise.

"Did you get a chance to find out anything at all about what the inside story on Amelia really is?"

Liam began to scowl. Ordinarily most people would back off at that, but Liam could tell Quinn was desperate. Amelia was obviously haunting the man—he needed *answers* and obviously didn't know where to get them.

"I know you're busy," Quinn continued, "but hell, man, she is part of your family and I thought that maybe you could ask someone who knows her just what—"

Liam abruptly stopped walking and sighed. He'd already tried to ignore the young rancher once before when he'd come at him with questions about the Fortunes. The *British* branch of the Fortune family, for God's sake. What was he supposed to know about any of them? He was trying to avoid them, not lobby for a position as the family's best friend.

Specifically, Quinn had questions concerning Amelia Fortune Chesterfield, whose recent engagement to some guy named James Bannings had been the subject matter of endless headlines, magazine covers and an incredible amount of media coverage that Liam found infinitely boring. There were enough speculations bouncing around about the duo to boggle the average intelligent mind.

In his opinion, the whole thing was just hogwash. Who gave a damn about two people getting married in England, anyway?

"Look, man," Liam began as evenly as he could manage, "I already told you. I don't know anything more than you do. Less probably."

Quinn couldn't bring himself to understand that. "But she's your cousin. Your mother and her mother are sisters—more than sisters," Quinn noted.

He didn't need to rehash what had already been all

but rammed down his throat, thanks to the newspapers, not to mention his own family.

"Something my mother and even this princess's mother didn't know about until like six months ago," Liam pointed out, cutting Quinn off before he got up a full head of steam on the subject and rambled on endlessly.

Nevertheless, Quinn didn't give up easily. "But still—"

"There is no 'still,'" Liam informed him. "Look, I don't know how to say this any clearer so that you can understand, but those people—all of them, British or otherwise—are *not* my family. They've never *been* my family and they're never going to *be* my family. Do I make myself clear?" he demanded.

Although he was looking into the face of anger, Quinn refused to be put off like that. "But your mother—"

"Is free to do whatever she wants and if she wants to acknowledge these people and pick up so-called 'family' ties, fine. So be it. But *I* don't and that's *my* choice. Sharing a name doesn't mean a damn thing to me," Liam insisted heatedly.

Who the hell did the Fortunes think they were, he wanted to know, barging into his life like that and thinking he and his siblings would just turn their backs on what they believed were their roots, to happily pick up the Fortune mantle? Well, not him, by God. Not him.

"It's more than a name," Quinn stubbornly insisted. "It's blood."

"Yeah, well, I don't believe it." Maybe there was

some underhanded reason that these people came crawling out of their fancy woodwork at this time. He hadn't figured that part out yet. All he knew was that he wanted to be left alone and not hounded about these damn people every which way he turned around.

"Look, Quinn, the bottom line is that I don't know anything about these people and I don't *want* to know anything about these people, so you're going to have to ask someone else about them." Normally not a curious person, curiosity got the better of him this time, thanks to Quinn's relentless persistence. "Considering that this princess you're asking about has her picture plastered all over the front pages, what are you trying to find out about her that hasn't already been covered a hundred times over in every means of communication available?"

Quinn sighed, running his hand through his rather longish brown hair. "I guess I'm just trying to find out if it's true."

Well, that didn't clear anything up. "If what's true?" Liam asked.

It pained Quinn to even frame the question. "If she's actually engaged to this guy Bannings."

He'd seen the headlines himself—and he hadn't particularly wanted to know anything at all about these people. "Well, if it's not true, there're going to be an awful lot of reporters and newshounds with egg on their collective faces."

The second the words were out of his mouth, Liam saw the look of absolute misery cross the other rancher's face. What the hell was *that* all about?

"You got a thing for this Princess Amelia or whatever she's calling herself?" Liam ventured.

Rather than answer the question, Quinn said, "She doesn't use any kind of a title.

"Calling her a princess might be something the tabloids enjoy doing, but when Amelia was out here for Sawyer's wedding at New Year's, she told me that she hated being related to the royal family. It meant that she was never alone, always in the public eye, always having her every movement—her every mistake— photographed and forever documented."

Liam shrugged even as an inkling of sympathy stirred within him. He knew that he would have lost his mind if he had these relentless reporters and photographers following him around like that, night and day.

"Yeah, well, the papers aren't paying attention to what she likes or doesn't like. They're doing what sells, which means they're going to go on calling her a princess."

In his heart, Quinn had thought of her as *his* princess, but that just showed him how naïve he could be. It irked him when he thought that she and that mealymouth James Bannings were together, maybe even having a good laugh over all this, over him, the hick rancher who'd been dumb enough to fall for her.

"I can't help you, Drummond," Liam was saying. "In fact, I don't think anyone can help you but yourself."

"Yeah, sorry to have bothered you," Quinn mumbled darkly, retreating.

The sight of the ordinarily easygoing rancher looking so dispirited as he began to walk away caused Liam to have some second thoughts on the matter. He didn't care to be related to those people, true, but his mother had embraced it. Maybe she knew more than he did. She sure couldn't know any less.

"Hey, Drummond."

Quinn stopped walking as Liam called his name.

"Yes?" The single word vibrated with unspoken hope.

"Why don't you go talk to my mother?" Liam suggested. "Chances are she probably doesn't know anything helpful, either," Liam warned the other man, not wanting him to get his hopes up too high. "But then, on the other hand, you never know."

He'd heard one of his brothers saying something about his mother staying in touch with this new sister she had suddenly become aware of. If that was true, then maybe she knew something about this Amelia person, who apparently had Drummond tied up in knots.

Quinn appeared to visibly brighten at the suggestion, flashing a wide, grateful smile. "Thanks, Liam," he called back.

"Yeah, well, good luck to you," he responded, turning away.

As for him and his own problem, Liam thought, he was going to need a lot more than just plain luck. He was going to need a miracle or two—or eight—because that snobbish Julia Tierney gave him the impression that when she latched on to something, it would take a stick of dynamite—if not more—to get her to let go and step back.

It was up to him, he thought, to find that so-called

dynamite stick so he could separate her from this "cause" she had taken up and get her to clear away the cobwebs from her eyes.

None so blind as those who refuse to see, he couldn't help thinking. He just needed to find a way to make her see.

Good luck to me with that, he thought as he got into his truck. He'd see what could be done tomorrow, he promised himself. As for now, what he needed was a good night's sleep, something that had been eluding him of late. He hoped he'd finally get it tonight.

Although he really had his doubts about that.

Chapter Six

The idea came to Liam the following morning.

He wasn't exactly sure when or how it had actually occurred to him, but out of the blue, the adage about a picture being worth a thousand words seemed to burst on his brain as he was having his first cup of eye-opening coffee before heading out to begin his morning chores on the ranch.

In this case, the so-called "picture" that rather nicely took the place of long-winded rhetoric was a restaurant in Vicker's Corners, a town that was located some twenty miles from Horseback Hollow.

Liam had had occasion to drive over to Vicker's Corners a month ago and he remembered thinking to himself as he passed it that the restaurant seemed just too fancy for him—he preferred The Grill. The Grill right here in town. It was more down-to-earth.

But the Vicker's Corners' restaurant seemed like just the kind of pretentious eatery that it looked like Julia was aiming for. The establishment was supposedly a good place for couples looking for a romantic atmosphere. To him that was just downright lazy. You created your own romantic atmosphere. You didn't expect someone else to do it for you. He sure hadn't had any trouble doing that back in high school, when things like that had been a priority for him.

He had become more serious and down-to-earth these days, but that kind of restaurant had to be what Julia had in mind, he thought. And seeing as how Vicker's Corners was a lot more crowded and noisy than his own Horseback Hollow was, Liam thought if she saw it, it might just prove his point to Julia: that building something like that was going to spoil life as everyone in Horseback knew it.

Making up his mind about the matter, Liam hurried through all the immediate chores he needed to do, left instructions with the part-time ranch hand he had working for him to take care of the rest and headed into town. The sooner he could put this fool notion of Julia's to bed, the better he'd feel.

It had become his personal crusade.

Liam felt certain that if Julia took away her support for the new restaurant, the whole project would just fall apart. She was acting as the Mendozas' go-between. He was fairly certain he had enough sway to get a majority of the town to agree with him if Julia wasn't there to gum up the works.

Now all he had to do, he thought, was to convince Julia to come see the place.

"Have you been to Vicker's Corners lately?" Liam asked her the second he came up behind Julia in the Superette.

She had her back to him—and the front door—as she was busy stocking the refrigerated section with the fresh milk that had come in earlier this morning. Liam's question, uttered in his low, baritone voice and coming from behind her had nearly made her drop the bottle she was holding. Regaining her composure, Julia turned around to look at him.

"And good morning to you, too, Liam," she said, forcing an obviously strained smile to her lips.

"Yeah, good morning," he muttered, brushing the greeting aside. "Well, have you?" he asked again, impatience marking his every syllable.

"Have I what?" she asked, not really sure what he was asking her.

Liam sighed. "You know, for the manager of a place like this, you sure don't act like you pay attention to people when they talk to you."

"People, yes," she corrected him. "You, not so much. Now, either say what you came to say outright or just go about your business, whatever that is, because I'm busy right now." She gestured around the store for emphasis. She had a lot of shelves to restock.

Liam could almost *feel* his temper rising. He was

pretty much of an easygoing guy but there was something about this woman that had him seeing red almost instantly.

For that matter, there always had been, he admitted to himself silently. But that wasn't something that he cared to advertise. It might give Julia the wrong idea about the kind of power she had over him.

"I asked you if you had been to Vicker's Corners lately."

"No," Julia told him. "No need to, really," she explained, reaching for another bottle of milk from the delivery crate her regular supplier had brought in for her.

She'd seen the restaurant that Wendy and her husband owned and ran. That had stolen her heart and she wanted to be in charge of the kitchen at a place just like that so that maybe someday she'd be able to own her own restaurant.

"So you *haven't* checked out that restaurant they've got there," Liam concluded.

Liam had piqued her interest. Why was he pushing this place on her, asking all these questions? "No, I haven't. Have you?"

"I've seen what it's done and is doing to the town," Liam said pointedly.

Julia noticed that he hadn't actually answered her question directly. From his tone, Julia had a feeling that any second now, the former big man on the high school campus was going to start going on and on about the evils of having anything in town but a down-to-earth, bare-bones eatery whose idea of a "selection" was having two things to choose from on the menu.

Instead he surprised her.

"Why don't I drive you down there so you can see what having a place like that in town is like firsthand?" He came around the side of the counter and took out the last two bottles of milk for her, putting them into the display refrigerator.

Julia looked around. There was the usual number of people in the store, so it wasn't particularly busy. But she did have shelves to restock. Her mother had seemed somewhat preoccupied this morning so she didn't want to ask her. That would only leave the part-time clerk who was helping out this morning if she took off.

Julia made up her mind. She was needed here, not running off to a neighboring town with Liam. "I'm afraid that I can't get away," she began.

"Sure you can," her mother insisted, coming up behind her. "Elliot and I can handle the customers," she assured her daughter, nodding toward the clerk. "It's not like we're having a run on the place. Go, take some time off. Enjoy yourselves," she encouraged. "Shoo," she added for good measure, gesturing both of them toward the door.

You'd think her mother would know better than to all but throw her into Liam's arms. "This is a scouting trip, Mother, not a getaway," Julia told her mother in all seriousness.

Annie patted her daughter's cheek. "Then *think* of it as a getaway, dear," she encouraged before looking pointedly at Liam. "See what you can do to loosen her up a little, Liam. She is just much too serious for a girl her age."

He smiled at the older woman, his expression softening his features and making him look every bit as roguishly attractive as he had looked in high school, when he was every girl's idea of the classic exciting bad boy.

"I'll do my best, ma'am," he promised.

Annie returned his wide smile. "That's all I can ask."

"I think I should warn you that I carry Mace in my purse," Julia told him as she walked by, lowering her voice so that only he could hear.

"Duly noted," he murmured without changing his expression or letting it betray him.

As Julia went to the back office to get her purse and shrug out of the oversize apron she always wore in the store, Liam turned toward her mother and said, "Don't worry, I'll have Julia back in the Superette in a couple of hours."

"That hardly seems like enough time, dear," Annie replied, shaking her head and obviously shooting down his initial agenda. "There's no rush to get back— really," Julia's mother insisted. "Julia doesn't take nearly enough time for herself. She's the most selfless girl I have ever known," Annie lamented. The older woman moved closer to him, straining to look up since Liam was a foot taller than she was. "Force her to have fun if you have to. Take the long way home. Enjoy the day, the evening," she elaborated, expanding on her initial instruction. "I was serious when I told you to loosen her up a little. Julia's going to be old someday without ever giving herself permission to be young."

"We're just checking out the restaurant there, Mother," Julia reminded her as she came back. Her purse strap was slung over her shoulder. "Not going for a hayride."

Annie heard what she wanted to hear. Her face brightened at the mention of a hayride. "Now, there's an idea," she declared.

"An idea that is going to lie exactly where it is, Mom." Julia brushed a kiss against her mother's cheek. "I'll be back *soon*." She put emphasis on the last word. "Hold down the fort until then."

"I was holding down the fort before you were born, my girl," her mother reminded her. "I won't have any trouble doing it again. And you, mind what I told you," Annie told her daughter.

Julia knew that her soft-spoken mother was every bit as stubborn as she was in her own way. This wasn't an argument that she was destined to win even if she stood here for the remainder of the day, so she appeared to silently surrender.

Not that she had any intentions of thinking that this excursion was anything except what it was: an exploratory excursion to check out what would eventually become her competition—*if* she ever got that restaurant built in Horseback.

Julia was aware that she was counting her chickens before the hen had even laid her eggs, but she was really excited about the prospect of this restaurant and what it would mean for her future, for the town's economy.

Julia realized that this was the most alive she'd felt in a long, long time.

Since even before her marriage to Neal.

"Okay, if we're going to go, then let's go," she told Liam.

Liam grinned, waved goodbye to her mother and fell into step beside Julia.

"I thought we'd take my truck, since I suggested the trip. Any objections?" he asked because, knowing Julia, there were *always* objections of some sort to anything he suggested.

"Not yet," she said glibly and then added, "You'll know when I have any."

"I have no doubts about that, Julia," he told her. "I have no doubts at all."

A retort rose to her lips, but she forced herself to swallow it. For now it just might be safer to let things like that just slide off her back. There was nothing to be gained but a headache from any kind of confrontation at the beginning of this trip.

She had no doubt that there'd be plenty of time for that on the way back.

The trip to Vicker's Corners went relatively quickly. The twenty miles between Horseback Hollow and the other town was rather desolate and the only traveling companions they encountered were close to the ground and seemed unfazed by their passage.

It wasn't until he got closer to Vicker's Corners that other trucks as well as a few cars could be seen in the vicinity of the town. Rather than the simple two streets with their quaint, weathered shops that were at the center of Horseback Hollow, Vicker's Corners had stores that he'd heard one of his sisters refer to as "charming." More than a couple of these "charming" stores lined Main Street, attracting a significant amount of vehicular traffic.

And just outside the town proper there was a tall, colorful sign that Liam made a point of calling her attention to.

"See there?" he asked, indicating the sign as if there was any way she could have missed seeing it. "It says they're going to be building condominiums outside of town. Condominiums and 'luxury estates,'" he quoted in disgust, whatever "luxury estates" was supposed to mean. "They're completely wiping out the honest, friendly country life folks around here grew up with, all so that someone can make an almighty dollar profit."

It was going to be an awful lot more than a dollar, she couldn't help thinking. But the idea didn't appall her the way it obviously did him.

"You've got something against earning a living?" she asked, really curious as to what his answer might be.

"I've got something against destroying a living," he countered. "And from what I hear, this all started with that fancy restaurant right there," he told her, gesturing toward the establishment they had come to view.

He made it sound as if the restaurant had some sort of evil powers. She refused to believe that *he* actually believed that.

"They built that place," he went on, "and then everything else you see kind of fell into place around it."

Liam clearly meant it as a criticism. "The shops. The traffic. The 'luxury estates…'" He all but sneered.

Liam obviously thought of it as some sort of pending doom.

She, however, saw what had been achieved as a model for her own goal. But rather than argue with Liam about it, which she knew would happen if she started trying to point out favorable things about the restaurant to him, she decided to try another, more practical approach to the problem in front of her.

"Have you ever been inside the restaurant, Liam?" she asked him.

He stared at her. The question had caught him off guard and he wasn't prepared for it. "Me?"

"Well, I don't see anyone else in the truck and I know I haven't been inside the restaurant. Have you ever eaten there?" she asked, phrasing her question another way.

He debated lying, then decided against it. He had a feeling that somehow she'd know and then she'd dismiss everything he had to say. So he went with the truth, which was a lot simpler to keep track of.

"No, I haven't," he admitted and then asked defensively, "What does that have to do with anything?"

He was kidding, right? The whole point of a restaurant was what was inside it, what it served, the kind of people doing the serving as well as the cooking, not the physical building itself.

"It *has* everything to do with it. Stop the truck. We're going to go in and eat there," she told him with finality, leaving no room for argument.

"Why, Julia Tierney, are you asking me out on a

date?" he asked, pretending to be shocked. He was clearly amused.

Julia felt as if she'd been blindsided.

Had he done this on purpose? Had he deliberately set her up?

Looking at him now, she couldn't decide whether he had, but they both needed to go inside the restaurant and sample the food—he more than she. But she also needed to set Liam straight right from the beginning. Otherwise, she had a feeling she was *never* going to live this down. Not that the idea of going out with him didn't appeal to her, but it would have to have been clear from the beginning—and he would have to have asked her out to begin with, not thrown out a vague suggestion. Otherwise, he would make it out as something she'd done, and there was no way she was going to ask him out on a date.

"No, this isn't a 'date,' this is just research. I wouldn't go out on a date with you," she informed him pointedly. "I wouldn't in high school and I won't now."

When she'd turned him down in high school—the only girl who had—it had stung his ego badly. He was surprised that the memory still bothered him a little.

The difference being that this time around, he knew how to cover things up a whole lot better.

"Don't knock it until you try it," he told her glibly. "There're a lot of women around in Horseback Hollow who can tell you that you're really missing out on something."

"What I'd be missing is my brain if I thought of

this as anything but what it is—research," she stressed with feeling.

The next moment, since he had stopped the truck as she'd asked, Julia got out on her side. Closing the door, she looked in at him. "Well, are you coming along? Or are you afraid that I'm right and you don't want to be forced to admit it?"

That did it for him. Liam was out of the truck in a second, locking it behind him.

"The day I'm afraid of anything that you might have to dish out is the day I pack it in and just give up altogether. You, missy, are wrong—on a lot of counts. And I'm going to take extreme pleasure in proving it to you and in hearing you say 'You were right, Liam' when this is all over."

He walked slightly ahead of her to the restaurant's double doors. The establishment's hours were posted to the right of them. Luckily, they had opened for lunch merely a half hour ago.

Which meant that they were free to go in.

He held the door open for her. "Let the adventure begin," he said.

She looked at him as she walked past Liam and went inside.

"My thoughts exactly," she informed him tersely.

Neither one of them had a clue what the other actually meant by that but there was no way either of them was about to admit that.

Chapter Seven

The atmosphere within the upscale restaurant seemed incredibly tranquil and soothing.

The words *soft* and *romantic* were the first two that sprang to mind when Julia looked around. Instrumental love songs drifted through the air, thanks to a better-than-average sound system. The music was just loud enough to be detected, yet quiet enough not to be obtrusive.

This was definitely a place, Julia concluded, designed for lovers and couples who wanted to become lovers.

She and Liam did not belong here, she thought. But to suddenly turn around and walk out of the restaurant at this point would only seem odd and attract unwanted attention. Not to mention some undoubtedly snappy, unwanted comments from Liam.

They were here so they might as well stick it out, Julia decided, scanning the immediate area for a second time. Maybe she'd learn something she could use when she talked to Wendy and Marcos about the design and theme of the restaurant they were looking to build in Horseback Hollow.

"First time here?" a tall, slender blonde asked them with an understanding smile. She was wearing a name tag and looked every inch the hostess as she indicated that they were to follow her into the dining room.

"How can you tell?" Julia asked. Did they look as if they were so out of place to this woman?

"It shows in your faces," the hostess answered. "I promise you'll be repeat customers soon enough." Her words were accompanied by a light laugh.

Even her laughter was soft, blending in delicately with the rest of the ongoing muted sounds in the restaurant.

As she followed behind the hostess and her eyes became accustomed to the dim lighting, Julia saw that the restaurant appeared to be full to capacity. By her calculation, it had only been open since twelve-thirty. Business was apparently *very* good.

"Is it always like this?" Julia asked the young woman walking ahead of them.

The slender blonde turned around. "No, it's usually a lot busier than this," she replied in all seriousness. "Standardly, we have a long waiting line out front. But if you're wondering, your privacy is guaranteed," she promised. "Will this booth be all right?" she asked, stopping at a booth for two.

The booth was part of several set up along the wall, each one cleverly arranged so that it gave the impression of being isolated from the others, even though it wasn't.

"The booth is fine," Julia replied. "But we really don't need to have our privacy guaranteed," she added.

"Speak for yourself. I don't want anyone to know I'm here," Liam said, waiting for Julia to slide into the booth first so that he could finally sit down himself. He had been hungry for more than the past half hour and his stomach was growling, more than a little impatient, waiting to be fed.

"I wouldn't worry if I were you, Jones," Julia told him shortly. "The kind of people you know wouldn't be found in a nice place like this." Her voice was distant, but that was his fault. He'd stung her pride with his dig about not wanting to be caught in a romantic restaurant with her.

"You two have been a couple for a while now, haven't you?" the hostess asked knowingly, handing each of them a menu.

"No," Liam declared, looking at the hostess as if she had a trifle too many birds perched on her antenna.

"Not even for a few seconds," Julia denied with feeling.

"Sorry, my mistake," the woman said, although she didn't sound as if she was really convinced that she had made one. She paused a moment longer to explain the possible misunderstanding. "It's just that the two of you sounded so intense, I just naturally assumed that you had been together a long time."

"We haven't been together at all," Julia told the hostess with feeling. "We just know each other from high school. Slightly," she underscored.

There was an enigmatic smile on the hostess's lips as she nodded and murmured, "I see." The smile crept into her eyes. "Your server will be here in a few minutes," she promised, then lowered her voice just a touch more before saying, "Enjoy your first time."

"She didn't say 'here,'" Julia said, her voice slightly agitated after the woman had retreated to the front of the restaurant.

Liam stared at her. Julia was babbling, he thought. "What?"

"'Here,'" Julia repeated. "That hostess should have said 'Enjoy your first time *here,*' but she left off the last word."

He didn't see what the big deal was. From where he was sitting, Julia was getting herself all worked up over nothing. "Maybe it was implied and she just forgot to say it."

Julia looked in the direction that the hostess had disappeared. She shook her head. "No, I really don't think so."

"Okay," Liam answered gamely—and then his voice dropped seductively. "So maybe she really meant for us to enjoy our first time."

Julia didn't have to ask him what he meant by that. There was what she could only refer to as a wicked smile curving Liam's rather full mouth and that, in turn, could only mean one thing.

Incensed, Julia raised her chin defiantly. "It would take a lot more than soft lighting and soft music to make that happen."

"Well, according to the hype, the soft lighting and soft music in this place are supposed to be the starting point. That's the purpose for all this, am I right?" he asked her pointedly.

How did she manage to get backed into a corner like this? "Much as I hate to say it, yes, you're probably right," she grudgingly admitted.

Liam leveled a look at her. Ordinarily he didn't mind matching wits and exchanging barbs, but somehow, it just didn't seem right in a place like this. Since they were here—and he was hungry—he made up his mind to make the best of the situation. But only if she wasn't going to be waspish.

He gave her a choice. "Look, you want to bicker or do you want to see what the food is like here?"

He was being reasonable, she realized—and worse, she wasn't. Who would have ever thought—?

"Sorry, you're right. We should order and see what's good." After all, that was why, at bottom, she had come here.

"Wow." He looked properly surprised just before he added, "Alert the media. We came to an agreement."

"So how about we strike a temporary truce?" she suggested.

"Absolutely," he told her with enthusiasm, putting out his hand across the table.

Julia hesitated for a moment, then slipping her hand into his, she shook it.

Their waiter, a tall young man with sandy-brown hair, perfect, chiseled features, gleaming white teeth and no hips to speak of, approached, greeted them unobtrusively and left them with a basket of warm, crisp bread, pats of butter wrapped in silver foil and the promise to return for their orders "soon."

"At least he didn't recite the specials of the day," Julia commented. That tradition, meant to be helpful, had for some reason always gotten on her nerves.

"Maybe they're all special," Liam quipped. He skimmed the two pages that made up the menu. The specials were listed at the top of the first page. "Or maybe he just assumes we know how to read."

Julia laughed at his comment. Liam could be amusing when he wanted to be, she grudgingly—and silently—admitted.

"What looks good to you?" she asked Liam, glancing over the two long, descriptive columns that comprised the restaurant's afternoon menu.

When Liam didn't answer, she raised her eyes from her menu and began to ask her question again, but the sentence remained stuck on her tongue, unable to move, to materialize. He was looking at her pointedly, answering her question without saying a word.

And just like that, she could feel the room around her growing warmer. Could feel heat creeping up the sides of her neck, threatening to turn everything in its path a unique shade of pink.

Julia's innocent question had instantly brought a single word to his mind as well as to his tongue.

You.

Mercifully, Liam managed to stop the word before it actually emerged and wound up embarrassing both of them. He was rather certain that he wouldn't have had a clue how to talk himself out of that one.

But the incriminating word hadn't been said aloud, so, for now he was safe and as long as he made no slips, everything was going to be all right.

After a beat Liam replied, "Not sure yet. There's a lot of flowery rhetoric to wade through. In my experience, good food speaks for itself. If it can't, it might mean it's not so good after all and it's just trying to pull the wool over your eyes with a lot of pretty ten-dollar adjectives." He decided to give her an example of the point he was making.

"I once bought a watch that was supposed to be waterproof. The ad claimed it 'laughed' at water. One day I accidentally spilled some water on it and not only didn't the watch 'laugh' at the water, it didn't even so much as chuckle. The damn thing died less than five minutes later, never to 'tick' again. The bottom line is if something's good, it doesn't have to convince you of the fact."

"You might have a point," she heard herself saying grudgingly. Maybe all the adjectives that went along with this place were overkill. She made a mental note to herself to be careful of overkill.

"Wow, you agreed with me twice in one day." He pretended to cover his heart to keep it from leaping out of his chest—or worse. "I'm going to get a swelled head."

"'Going to?'" she echoed, dryly questioning his last comment.

"And she's back." Liam couldn't resist mimicking the voice of a radio announcer making an introduction.

"I never left," she informed him dryly.

The waiter returned, looking from one to the other, a silent question in his soulful brown eyes. Julia ordered something referred to as Heaven's Promise, while Liam pointed to an item called Love At Last. The waiter pronounced them both excellent choices and promised to return within a few minutes with their meals.

"You know what you ordered?" Liam asked her after the waiter had left.

"Chicken—" The note of confidence left her voice after a beat. "I think, but I'm not sure."

Liam laughed, nodding his head. "Actually, I think we both did."

"Should be interesting," she ventured, looking forward to comparing the meals once they arrived.

"We'll see," he replied.

He noticed that she was scanning the area again, doing her best to take in the other booths. But they were, as the hostess had promised, arranged so as to maximize the occupants' privacy. He could either watch her, or make small talk. But he had no patience with either.

Instead he decided to ask out of the blue, "So what happened between you and the perfect husband?"

Her head whipped around. Julia looked at him, completely stunned. "What?"

"You and Neal," he elaborated. "Neal seemed like perfect husband material. He was a lawyer, faithful— He was faithful, right?" he asked, checking.

"Yes, he was faithful," she snapped. There was no way she wanted to chance Liam starting a rumor that Neal had fooled around. Neal was one of the good guys and deserved better. She wasn't about to see his reputation dragged through the mud just because Liam happened to have a fanciful mind.

"And he was good-looking—if you liked that all-American look," Liam qualified, making it sound like a minus instead of a plus. "On paper, you two sound perfect for each other. So what went wrong?"

She couldn't believe the nerve of this man. "And what makes you think that's any business of yours?" She really wanted to know.

"Well, we have to talk about something and talking about the weather gets boring fast. But we argue about everything else, so I thought this might be the one topic that was safe to talk about. If you don't want to," he continued gamely, "we could just stare at one another until the waiter comes back. Then we can pretend to be busy stuffing our faces, making it impossible to chew and talk at the same time—"

Julia sighed. He had a point, she admitted grudgingly. And she really didn't mind talking about Neal. She supposed this came under the heading of making the best of an uncomfortable situation.

"Nothing 'happened,'" she finally told Liam. "The marriage had just run out of steam."

That presupposed that there had been steam once

upon a time. He found that a little hard to believe. Neal
Baxter had as much vibrancy about him as a prescrip-
tion tranquilizer.

"Then there was steam to begin with?" Liam asked
her.

Ordinarily she would have indignantly replied that
of course there had been steam. Lots of it. But the
way Liam was looking at her—as if he could read her
thoughts—she had a feeling that he knew that "steam"
between Neal and her had never been part of the equa-
tion. Moreover, that he somehow knew that hers had
been just a marriage not of convenience, but a convenient marriage.

"Neal was a really nice guy and we were friends,"
she told him. "I think we both got married hoping that
what we had would grow. Instead, it just stagnated.
We were far better friends than lovers." The second
the words were out of her mouth, Julia was suddenly
stunned that she had actually said that. Flustered, she
attempted to cover it up. "What I mean—"

He could almost read her mind and feel her sudden panic—as well as know the reason for it. It wasn't
hard to guess.

"Don't worry, I'm not going to quote you anywhere.
It goes no further." He looked at her knowingly. "So
what you're saying is that there was no spark between
the two of you, no flash and fire." It wasn't a guess on
his part but a reaffirmation.

"What I'm saying," she told him with conviction, "is
that Neal deserves to be happy and I hope he is. Someone told me that he'd gotten engaged recently. If it's

true, I just hope the woman realizes that Neal is a very special man and that she's very lucky. I wish Neal and his future wife nothing but the very best."

Liam looked somewhat surprised by her good wishes for a man who had once shared her bed. And she meant that, he could tell by the look in her eyes. It was all too calm and genteel for him.

"You do?"

"Yes. Why?" Why did he look so surprised to hear her say that?

Liam shrugged. "Nothing. You just seem very complacent about all this and that wasn't what I'd heard through the grapevine," he told her.

The grapevine. Not exactly the most straightforward source of honest news, she thought. She didn't bother asking him what it was that he *had* heard. Lies didn't bear repeating, not even once.

"Well, people like to talk, it helps while away the time, I guess. And if the facts make something dull, well, can't have that, can we?" she asked sarcastically. She didn't care for gossip and it was all the worse when it was about her. "But if you want the truth, I really do wish him well."

"Well, my hat's off to you," Liam told her in all honesty. "And him, I guess."

She'd followed him up to a point, but now he'd veered off again. "What do you mean?"

"Well, I take it that you broke it off with him."

She did her best to keep a poker face. "Why would you say that?"

She actually had to ask him that? He found it amusing, but he played along, giving her a reason. "You never struck me as someone who just went along with things if she didn't like the way those things were going." She was nothing if not a scrapper. Maybe that was one of the things that he found attractive about her.

"Well, if you must know, yes, I broke it off with Neal, which is why I'm glad he found someone else." She didn't like having him on her conscience. She could still remember his expression—shock mingled with sorrow—when she'd finally gotten through to him.

"And he went quietly, huh?" Liam mused, seemingly marveled and clearly surprised by the man's behavior.

"Yes. Why?" It was her turn to push the question.

"Nothing." He shrugged carelessly again. "But if it was me and my woman had decided that it was over between us and told me she was taking off, well, I wouldn't just meekly lie there and take it. I'd do something about it. I'd do something about getting her back," he said with conviction. "And I'd do it fast, before she had time to get used to the situation."

"Oh, you mean like hog-tie her and leave her in the barn until she was going to come to her senses?" she scoffed, her voice a mixture between being flip and a tad contemptuous.

"Well, maybe not that—" he conceded, then tagged on, "unless it was a last resort." His reply was followed by a wide, amused grin.

She knew he was kidding, but there was something in his eyes, something about the way he was looking at her, that caused a little thrill to tango up her spine and back down again. For just a fraction of a second, she felt that he was talking about the two of them—even though logically, she silently insisted, he really couldn't possibly be. After all, there was nothing between them. They hadn't even gone out.

And yet...

They looked at one another for what seemed like one of the very longest moments on record, interrupted finally by someone clearing his throat. Belatedly, she looked over to see that their waiter had returned with their covered meals on a cart.

"I can come back later if you wish," he offered, ready to wheel the cart with their meals on it away for a little longer.

"No," she replied to the young man. "You came just in time."

She thought she heard Liam murmur, "Amen to that," but she wasn't sure it wasn't just her imagination giving voice to her own thoughts.

Chapter Eight

"So, what do you think?" Julia asked him as they walked out of the restaurant more than an hour later.

She did her best not to sound eager, not to sound as if his answer was as important to her as it was. They'd talked all through the meal, but he hadn't commented at all about the restaurant, even though she had given him ample opportunity to do so. And, after all, the only reason they were here was to check out the restaurant to see what it had to offer.

Liam was, she thought, a rather difficult nut to crack. During the course of the meal, he had managed to ask her a great many questions about herself while volunteering next to nothing about himself.

Then, again, she probably knew about as much about

him as there was to know. He'd been rather transparent in his dealings in high school.

Still, after the lunch they had just had, accompanied by his twenty questions, he owed her, she decided.

Liam was squinting, trying to acclimate himself to what seemed like intense sunlight at this point after having been inside the dim restaurant for so long. It was a little like emerging out of a cave after a very long, dark winter. "What I think is that it's too damn dark in that place."

She should have known he'd say something flippant like that. The man had a knack for dodging direct statements whenever it suited him.

"Besides that," she countered as they circled to the lot behind the restaurant, where he'd parked his truck. "What did you think of the food, the service, the selection on the menu?" she prompted since the man wasn't volunteering *anything* on his own. After all, that *was* supposed to be the reason they had come to Vicker's Corners in the first place.

Liam shrugged. "They were okay."

"Try not to burst a blood vessel in your enthusiasm," she said sarcastically.

He stopped walking, annoyed with her flippant remark and with the fact that she was trying to get him to agree with her. He'd thought that once she saw how the simple life seemed to be dying back in this town, she'd be willing to admit that he was right in voting against the new restaurant coming to Horseback.

The part that bothered him the most was that he

could see how a restaurant like the one they'd just left might appeal to some people back home.

Irritated, he demanded testily, "What is it you want me to say?"

If she told him what to say, it wouldn't count or carry any weight. "I can't put words in your mouth," she retorted, frustrated.

"Well, you sure don't like the ones that are coming out," he pointed out in frustration. "Look, the place was okay, but so's The Grill. The Grill doesn't try to put on airs. You want to know my requirements for a good restaurant?" It was a rhetorical question on his part because he didn't wait for her reply. He just went on to answer his own question. "Here're my requirements. I like my food to taste good, to be hot and to arrive in something under half an hour. The rest are just added frills. I don't need frills," he said flatly. He saw disappointment flash in her eyes. "Not what you wanted to hear, was it?" He realized that he took no particular pleasure in that.

That should have been his first warning sign.

No matter what, Julia had always tried to find at least one positive thing in any situation. It took some doing this time, but she did find one positive thing.

"I wanted you to be honest and you were honest." They resumed walking again. "Obviously," she continued philosophically, "you're not the target audience the people who own and run that restaurant were trying to reach." She looked around at both the number of vehicles in the parking lot and the people who were passing them, heading for the restaurant's front entrance. "Lucky for them, your reaction isn't typical."

"Never thought of myself as part of the herd," Liam told her, reaching his truck.

"That's good because you're not," she assured him with a small laugh. Julia waited for him to unlock his truck, then got in on her side.

"If you wanted a 'typical' reaction, as you call it, you should have brought your ex-husband here, not me," he told her with a trace of annoyance in his voice. From what he knew about the man, Neal Baxter was the poster boy for the word *typical*.

Glancing to see if she was strapped in, Liam started up the truck.

"Neal moved away, remember?" she said, raising her voice slightly as the engine rumbled to life. "He's not here and you are. Your opinion was the one I decided counted."

He laughed shortly as he drove away from the lot. "You mean mine is the opinion you want to change."

"That, too," she admitted. She gestured toward the sidewalk as they stopped at a light. "Look at all this foot traffic going on."

"I'm looking, all right." And he didn't like what he saw. There seemed to be too many people, in his opinion. Did they all live around Vicker's Corners, or were they just passing by, the way he and Julia were?

She could hear the hostility in Liam's voice and glossed right over it. She knew if she commented on it, she'd be sidetracked into an argument and that wasn't going to lead anywhere except to have her going around in an endless, frustrating circle.

Been there, done that.

"Having the restaurant here is good for everyone's business, not just the restaurant's," she pointed out adamantly.

He saw it differently. "If the people are here, in town, it means they're not working their ranches."

"Not everyone has a ranch," she reminded him.

Yeah, and there was a reason for that, he thought cryptically. "That's because they spent all that time, sitting in a dark restaurant," he told her.

Liam sped up to make the light—the last traffic light before he drove out of town. A minute later Vicker's Corners was behind him and he could feel a sense of relief washing over him.

Most likely just his imagination, he thought—but it still felt good to leave the place.

Julia bit off an inaudible, frustrated sound. "You are absolutely infuriating, do you know that?" she said, struggling not to shout at him.

"The way I see it…" he told her, speeding up just a touch because they were out on an open road, even though it was only two lanes wide. "I'm absolutely right. But have it your way. Which you are," he reminded her. "The preliminary vote went your way. There's no reason to believe that when the final votes are cast, the results will be any different. That means the town's going to let those people come in and build their damn restaurant anywhere you tell them to. Frankly," he said, sparing her a look, "what I don't get is why you're still trying to convince me that building that restaurant is the right thing to do."

She blew out a frustrated breath. She'd asked herself the same question. But even though the answer wasn't logical, it was important to her that he come around about this. "Because I want you to see the merits of having a business like this in town."

He slanted a quick glance toward her. "And if I don't, you'll stop building it?"

That wasn't the point she was trying to make. "No, of course not—"

He rested his case. "Like I said, there's no point or need to convince me."

She tried again. "Maybe I'd just like to have you on board with this."

She still hadn't given him an actual logical answer. "Why? You afraid I'm going to do something to sabotage this fancy eatery of yours?"

Was that it? Did she think him capable of doing something drastic?

As the thought sank in, he could feel himself growing insulted.

"No, of course not."

Although, Julia had to admit, albeit silently, the thought had crossed her mind a couple of times. Not that she believed Liam would actually attempt to destroy anything, but he was very capable of working on changing some of the people's minds about siding with progress in this case.

"Well, then, why is it so important to you that I see

your side of this and agree with you?" he repeated, wanting her to make him understand.

She wasn't about to admit that she *cared* what he thought. He'd just take it the wrong way—although she didn't know what other way he *could* take it.

Frustrated, Julia threw up her hands. "Never mind. Maybe I just need my head examined."

"Maybe," he affirmed matter-of-factly.

She had no idea why he'd said that, but she knew it *really* annoyed her. Annoyed her even more that they *weren't* on the same side of this issue. "You know, I could be gloating that the preliminary vote went my way and I'm not. Maybe you should chew on that for a while," she told him in mounting frustration.

Liam's profile was to her as he looked straight ahead, but she could see that the corner of his mouth was curving. He was *smiling* to himself, she realized angrily. At her expense?

"What?" she demanded.

"Nothing," he answered in a tone that told her that there indeed was something. And that something was a thought that her words had unearthed. Rather than the food for thought she'd believed she'd just given him, what he would rather "chew on," he realized, was her—starting from the toes on up.

There was no denying it. The woman definitely aroused him.

She was certainly not the kind of woman he was accustomed to. Julia was not as voluptuous as he liked them and certainly not as accommodating as he'd gotten used to, but there was just *something* about her.

That flash in her eyes, that mouth of hers that never seemed to stop moving… It just all went to stir him, stoke that fire in his belly that created a yearning for her within not just his loins, but more importantly, in his mind, as well.

That was the part that both intrigued him—and scared the hell out of him.

"Doesn't sound like 'nothing,'" she retorted. "What is it?" she persisted.

"Nothing," he repeated. "Just leave it alone." He issued the warning in a low, terse voice.

"Or what?" she challenged. When he didn't answer, she repeated, "Or what?" more loudly this time. If she did know what was good for her, she wasn't focusing on that now.

"You don't want to know," Liam told her, his tone almost growling the words out.

"I wouldn't have asked if I didn't want to know," she snapped. "I don't scare off easily, Jones. I'm not like those little harebrained groupies you used to surround yourself with in high school," she said, referring to the other girls contemptuously. "I don't hang on your every word but I do give you credit for having a mind and I just wanted to open your eyes and have you see what—"

"Damn it," Liam swore in utter frustration as he pulled over to the side of the deserted road. "Don't you ever shut up, woman?" he demanded.

He didn't leave her any room to answer—not that he actually even *wanted* an answer from her—because at the same time that he asked the question, he'd simultaneously pulled her to him as he managed to press the release button on her seat belt. And before Julia could even begin to express her surprise at both his question and his actions, his mouth was covering hers.

The second that it did, it seemed to open a floodgate of emotions within him. They were so powerful that he found he had to struggle to get the upper hand and not have them take charge of him or drag him under before he knew what was going on.

The only thing that he *did* know was that he wanted her.

Wanted her badly.

More than he had *ever* wanted anyone before—possibly more than he had ever wanted everyone *combined.* The dalliances, the interludes, the trysts he'd had before belonged to the boy he had been—his actual age didn't matter. What he was experiencing now belonged to the man he had just become.

He had a man's appetite and a man's desires.

And, heaven help him, they were all centered on Julia.

Liam had caught her completely and utterly off guard. She knew she should be horrified as well as furious. And scared.

Very, very scared.

Not of him, of course, but *herself.* She was scared of the intensity that had been aroused by this sudden contact, this sudden profusion of feelings—his and hers—that had washed over her.

And scared because she wanted to make love with him.

Make love to him here, on the side of the road, out in the open where anyone could unexpectedly drive by and see them.

This wasn't the kind of reaction she expected of herself and yet, at this isolated moment in time, Julia felt powerless to do anything about it, to cut this intense desire short, to call a halt to what was happening.

Instead she was *reveling* in what was happening because she wanted it so much, probably had subconsciously wanted it for a very long time.

She could feel her body heating with incredible longing.

Maybe this was why she and Neal had never really had a chance together, because there was something in her soul that had been waiting for this.

For *him*.

For Liam.

Somehow, though she wouldn't have been able to say how or why if her life depended on it, she had detected this, been waiting for this to find her. And now that it had, all she wanted to do was to wrap herself up in it and melt into it, become one with it.

And with him.

Damn it, what the hell are you thinking? an angry voice in Liam's head demanded. Where were his morals, his scruples? He was overwhelming Julia, taking advantage of her and this just wasn't right no matter *how* much he wanted her. If they *were* going to make love, the first time couldn't be out in the open like this, like two reckless teenagers without any restraint, grabbing any opportunity that came their way.

To mean something, the first time had to at least be civilized.

In order to mean something? that same voice in his head echoed, mystified. What the hell was that supposed to mean? Since when had he wanted lovemaking to *mean* anything but exquisite release? What the hell was going on with him?

Whatever it was, it had to do with her and the sooner he got himself away from her, the better off he'd be—at least until he could untangle all this and think clearly again.

So with what amounted to supreme effort, Liam forced himself to back away.

Taking hold of Julia's shoulders—feeling her shaking beneath his hands—he separated himself from her.

An incredible feeling of desolation and loss swirled through him so quickly, Liam thought he was hallucinating. Self-preservation had him instantly shutting down so that he would stop feeling altogether.

"Sorry," he said gruffly. "I shouldn't have done that. Won't happen again," he added stoically.

Buckling up again, he turned on the ignition. Then, staring straight ahead, he pulled his truck back onto the road and drove toward Horseback Hollow.

"You're 'sorry'?" she echoed, then repeated with both bewilderment and anger, demanding, "'*Sorry*'?"

"That's what I said," he answered in a voice so devoid of any feeling it could have easily belonged to a robot.

Julia sucked in a lungful of air. Liam had all but incinerated her world, stirred up longing and desire to a degree she had never even *dreamed* existed and he was *sorry?*

Just what was that supposed to mean?

And what had that just been? An exercise in mind control? In complete and utter disarmament of her body and soul?

She'd been all ready to make love with him and he—

He'd been what? Experimenting with her? Trifling with her?

"What the hell do you think you're doing?" she demanded just as the town began to come into view.

She realized that Liam had to have been doing ninety to get back as fast as he did. Maybe his goal was to somehow crack the time barrier and get back to Horseback Hollow before they had even left so that what had just happened could be wiped out.

So he didn't have to bear any responsibility for it.

"Making a big mistake, apparently," he told her, his voice just as dead and emotionless as before.

The answer couldn't have hurt any more than if he had stabbed her.

The second they reached the outskirts of town, she unbuckled her seat belt, opened the passenger door and jumped out as she angrily shouted, "I'll walk!" tossing the words over her shoulder.

Liam slammed on his brakes, afraid she'd really hurt herself. He reached to grab her but it was too late.

She was already out.

Landing on her feet, Julia ran home without looking back.

He watched her go, wishing with all his heart that he had never suggested going to see that damn restaurant in Vicker's Corners.

Because he had just opened a door to something that wasn't going to be easily shut again and more than likely, what was contained behind that door was going to lead to his undoing.

Chapter Nine

He'd lost sight of what was important.

He had allowed himself to get sidetracked without realizing it, Liam thought, more than a little annoyed with himself. What was important here was the ultimate fate of the town, not the fact that when he'd pulled off the road that day he and Julia had gone to Vicker's Corners and kissed her, his insides twisted up so badly a corkscrew would have looked completely straight by comparison.

The first couple of days after that, he had deliberately thrown himself into working on the ranch, going from first light to beyond sundown with hardly a letup. He thought if he worked hard enough and long enough, his mind would become blank, having no room for anything more than putting one foot in front of the other and simple, basic instructions.

He should have known better.

Exhausted, he'd fallen onto the first flat surface he came to within his house and slept—not the sleep of the just or even the sleep of the weary, too tired to even think. Instead he'd slept the sleep of the troubled—and dreamed.

Dreamed of a blue-eyed redhead and a desire that set fire to his very insides. And when he woke up, he wasn't rested; he was even more tired than when he'd fallen asleep.

At this rate, he'd burn himself out in a week and nothing would be accomplished. Avoiding all contact with Julia wasn't working. This was obviously not a matter of out of sight, out of mind. The only thing that was going out of his mind was him.

That's when the idea came to him. Rather than trying to deny what he was feeling—because that certainly wasn't working out—he made up his mind to *use* that very same intensity to gain the goal he was shooting for: stopping the restaurant from being built and keeping those Fortunes out of Horseback Hollow before they could get a toehold. And the way he was going to do that was to turn on the charm he'd relegated to the sidelines, pursue the woman who was currently haunting his thoughts and seduce her not just into sharing his bed but his philosophy about Horseback Hollow, as well.

The second he formed his plan, Liam smiled to himself. Smiled for the first time in almost a week.

This was going to work, he promised himself. And

maybe, just maybe, after this was over, after he'd bedded her, he'd be over Julia, as well, and could get back to life as he knew it.

It gave him hope.

Damn it, Julia upbraided herself. What was *wrong* with her?

Why did she keep looking at the door, hope springing up within her chest every time she heard that silly little bell go off, alerting her that another customer had walked in?

She knew why, Julia thought sullenly, because even after six days had gone by—six days without so much as a *single* word—she was *still* hoping to see that big, dumb lout walking into her store. She'd always known that Liam Jones was as shallow as a puddle, so why was her pulse doing these stupid, erratic things every time she thought he was walking into the Superette?

He probably had enough supplies up at that ranch of his to see him through six months without needing to restock—and when he ran out, most likely he'd send one of his brothers to buy supplies for him.

She was supposed to be smarter than this, Julia silently insisted. She'd always prided herself for having more brains than those worshipful groupies that had always clustered around Liam back when they were in high school. Why in heaven's name had she suddenly voluntarily joined their club?

"I haven't," she declared staunchly.

"You haven't what, dear?" her mother asked, turning from the magazine display she was rearranging.

"Um, I haven't a clue what I did with that inventory list from last week," Julia told her mother, silently congratulating herself on her quick thinking. She'd been so preoccupied thinking about that idiot that she hadn't even realized she had said anything out loud just then.

She was going to have to exercise a little more control over herself, she thought.

"It's on your desk in the office. I saw it there earlier." Her mother looked at her, concerned. "Are you sure you're feeling all right?"

Julia waved her mother's concern away, feeling slightly guilty about giving her mother something else to worry about. She'd remained here in Horseback Hollow all these years to *help* her mother, not give her more to worry about.

"I've just got a lot on my mind, Mom, that's all."

Annie shook her head. It was obvious that she was in agreement with her daughter.

"You take too much on yourself, Jules. Why don't we hire more help?" she suggested. They already had five part-time workers here at the store as well as two full-time employees. "We're doing well enough to afford it, honey," Annie pointed out.

Now her obsession with that jerk was going to cost them money? Not if she could help it, Julia silently promised.

"We'll talk about that tonight, Mom. With Dad," Julia added.

Annie smiled at her only child. "You're a good girl, Jules, to include your dad like that. After all the work you've put into keeping the Superette open and running, anyone else would have just shut him out."

"Hey, I want him to get well enough to run this place again with you," Julia told her mother, even though they both knew that was probably never going to happen. But for each other's sake—as well as for Jack's—they pretended that it would.

Annie squeezed her daughter's hand, mutely thanking her. When the bell over the door went off this time, Julia didn't bother turning around.

Not until she heard his voice.

"Good afternoon, Mrs. Tierney. Would you mind if I had a word with Julia alone?" Liam asked politely.

"Absolutely not," Annie told him, letting go of her daughter's hand and stepping back. She smiled warmly at Jeanne Marie's son. "She's all yours, Liam."

"I'd rather be staked out next to an anthill," Julia declared, her eyes shooting daggers at the man who had haunted her dreams *every single night* since she'd gotten back from Vicker's Corners.

He had his damn nerve, she fumed, first reducing her to a palpitating mass of desires and longings, then completely ignoring her for nearly a week only to waltz in here as if nothing had happened between them—as if the world hadn't been reduced to a pinprick when he'd kissed her like that.

"Choose it well," she told him as her mother went to wait on a customer at one of the checkout registers.

"Choose what well?" Liam asked, puzzled.

"The 'word' you want to say to me," Julia said to

refresh his memory, "because I've got a really good one for you—that can't be repeated in polite society."

He just bet she did, he thought, tickled despite himself.

The only way to deal with whatever insults and accusations Julia was going to heap on his head, he thought, was to head her off before she ever had a chance to say any of them.

"And it probably isn't even strong enough," he told her, doing his best to look contrite and remorseful. "I acted like a horse's ass," he readily admitted.

"Not even nearly that good," she returned. Her eyes narrowed to intense, accusing slits. "What are you doing here?"

He dug deep for his sincerest voice. "I came to apologize for the way I behaved—and to tell you that I'd like to start over."

Just what was his angle? she wondered. "Start *what* over?" she asked suspiciously.

"Us. You and me," he told her simply, his eyes meeting hers. He knew if he so much as looked away for a second, it was all over for any chance he had to get to her.

"There is no 'us,'" she informed him tersely. "There's not even a you and me. There's me and there's you. Separate," she pointed out.

"Look, whatever name you want to call me, whatever insult you want to hurl at me, I more than deserve. But I felt something back there that day on the side of the road," he told her in a low voice, taking care that it didn't carry to anyone. "I'd like to give it a chance to take root and grow."

"All the great plagues started that way," she reminded him contemptuously, "taking root and growing."

"This isn't like that," Liam protested.

Her eyes narrowed accusingly. "It's *exactly* like that. I don't know what your game is, Jones, but I'm not playing, so why don't you just pick up your marbles and go home?"

"No game," he told her, holding up his right hand as if he was taking an oath. Glancing to see where her mother was, he saw that Annie was busy. But any second now, the woman would turn around and see them, possibly even decide it was time to join them again. He didn't want to be interrupted until he was finished.

Taking her arm, he pulled Julia over to an alcove for more privacy. "You can't tell me that you didn't feel something back there on the side of the road that day."

She looked at him defiantly, echoing his words back to him. "I didn't feel something back there on the side of the road that day."

His eyes held hers. "I don't believe you."

"That is not my problem," she informed him, "and if you don't let go of me, you're going to find out what a problem really feels like."

Reluctantly, because he didn't want to attract any attention to what was going on, he released her arm. "I just wanted you to know that I've been thinking these past few days—"

"First time for everything," she quipped dismissively.

He ignored the dig and just forged on. "And I think

that you might be right about the restaurant. About it being a good thing for the town."

Surprised, Julia looked at him incredulously. "Nobody told me that hell was freezing over."

He smiled at that. He was making headway one small step at a time. "I thought that maybe we could talk about it some more over dinner."

"At The Grill?" she ventured, thinking that was what he had up his sleeve, to subtly show her how more than adequate that eatery was for the locals.

"No—" Liam started, but he didn't get a chance to tell her what he had in mind.

"You want to go back to Vicker's Corners?" she asked him, surprised.

"No," he said patiently, forging on this time. "I thought that I'd have you up to the ranch— I cook," he told her.

She didn't know whether to laugh out loud at the idea of Liam attempting to actually cook something edible, or to be concerned because he had apparently lost his mind. "You cook," Julia repeated.

"That's what I said," he confirmed, his voice unshakably confident about the ability he had just professed to possess.

"And have people eaten what you've cooked?" she asked. "Are they still alive so I can question them?"

"Every last one of them," he assured her. "I can print up a list of names for you if you'd like," he offered, taking what he assumed was a joke on her part and raising it to the next level.

"I'd like," she told him without so much as crack-ing a smile.

Well, that told him one thing, he thought—not that it was anything new on her part. But then, he'd known when he'd decided on this course of action that it wasn't going to be easy.

Nothing about Julia Tierney had ever been easy.

He supposed that was part of what he'd found so compelling about her—not that any of that mattered right now.

All that mattered was preserving Horseback Hol-low the way it was.

"You don't trust me," Liam said.

The old, polite Julia would have denied it, or tried to explain why she had reservations. The Julia who hadn't gotten a decent night's sleep in a week congratulated him on his insight.

"You're catching on."

"You're going to have to learn to trust me sooner or later," he predicted.

The hell she did, Julia thought. "Why?" she asked flatly. "Why do I have to learn to trust you sooner or later? Why do I have to trust you at all?"

"Because I can be a help with this restaurant thing. You still face having to get that final vote from the town at the mayor's next meeting and you still have to convince those friends of yours—the Mendozas, was it?—that Horseback Hollow is the right location for their new business."

Liam had done a complete about-face in six days. Something didn't feel right to her. "Why this sudden change of heart?" Wanting to know, she pinned him down with her eyes. Dared him to come up with something believable.

He plumbed the depth of his being for sincerity. "Because I realized that I was guilty of putting my own feelings about the Fortune family ahead of the town's welfare."

That sounded a great deal more noble than she thought that Liam could *ever* be.

"I thought you said you believed that having that sort of high-traffic restaurant here was going to be bad for the town's 'welfare,'" she reminded him.

He'd found that it was always best to keep his story and his answers simple. That allowed for fewer mistakes to be made. "I was wrong."

"Just like that?" she asked him skeptically. He was nothing if not stubborn. This just felt way too easy to Julia.

"Sometimes it happens that way," he told her innocently, shrugging his shoulders for emphasis and as a testimony to his own mystification. "Have dinner with me and I'll tell you about my ideas. You might find them helpful." He looked at her pointedly, his eyes all but delving into her very soul. "C'mon, say yes," he coaxed. "What have you got to lose?"

A great deal if I actually bought your story.

She continued to play along, but she was beginning to entertain the idea that whether he was serious about his conversion or not—and she had a hunch it was "not"—she could make him believe she was hanging on his words until she was ready to spring her own trap. A trap that would get him to do what *she* wanted rather than him having convinced her that his opposition to her plans was justified.

"I don't know," she replied honestly. "But I'm afraid I'm going to find out."

He couldn't put his plan into action unless he got her up to his ranch. He decided to take an even bigger risk than he was already undertaking and proposed a compromise.

"If it makes you feel any better, you can bring your mother with you, Julia—or anyone else for that matter. I just want a chance to talk to you away from the store and any distractions."

If it makes you feel any better.

Julia knew how that sounded. It sounded as if she was afraid of him and she wasn't. She'd known Liam Jones most of her life and in his own way, he was as honorable as they came. He never took a woman against her will—he just made her very, very willing.

She supposed that she could have dinner with him and hear him out. If he actually was on the level, she really *could* use him to convince the few diehards on the council who might make pushing this vote through difficult for her.

And if her plan worked, then she would *really* wind up turning Liam and bringing him into her camp.

She made up her mind.

"I don't need to bring anyone with me to act as a chaperone," she informed him.

He pretended to give her every chance to change her mind. "You're sure?" he pressed.

"I'm sure," she said firmly and then asked, "What time do you want me to come over?"

He was leaving nothing to chance. She could always change her mind at the last minute and not show up. "I'll pick you up," he told her.

She wouldn't have been Julia if she made this an easy win. "I know my way. I can drive up."

This was turning into a tug-of-war, but then, he would have expected nothing less of Julia. An easy win was a win he held suspect.

"A gentleman always picks up a lady," he told her simply.

She pretended to be surprised by his statement. "You're bringing a gentleman?"

"Very funny," he quipped. He also knew that if he pushed too hard, Julia would back away quickly. It was like a tango, two steps forward, one step back. "All right, suit yourself. Dinner's at seven."

Julia inclined her head. The first round was hers. "I'll be there," she promised.

And she fervently hoped it wasn't going to wind up being something that she would end up regretting.

It's up to you, a little voice in her head said, *to make sure that it won't be.*

She looked up at Liam and said, "And now, if there's nothing else, Jones, I have got to get back to work—or dinner's going to wind up being something I have to cancel."

He raised his hands in a universal sign that he was backing off. "Already gone," he assured her. "Tonight. Seven" were his parting words.

Chapter Ten

Driving to Liam's ranch that evening, Julia almost turned her car around twice.

She talked herself out of it the first time, but the second time she almost succeeded in talking herself into not going. She would have probably made it home if it wasn't for the fact that she *knew* Liam would say that she'd chickened out. The problem was that he would be right. That one small fact would wind up giving him power to lord it over her.

Power over her that she absolutely refused to allow him to have.

So she squared her shoulders, turned around one last time and headed for his ranch. She had to drive as if the devil himself was behind her to make it on time. She'd never been late for anything in her life and she wasn't about to let this be the first time.

Telling herself that she wasn't making a mistake she would wind up regretting, Julia walked confidently up to Liam's front door—in case he was watching—took in a long breath and knocked.

Liam opened the door before her knuckles had a chance to meet the dark wood twice. "You came."

She couldn't tell if he was more surprised than pleased or the other way around. The expression on his face was a combination of both.

"Didn't you think I would?" she asked him as she walked past him and into the front room of his home.

From what she could see, it was a small, sturdy ranch house, very masculine, very him. She remembered hearing somewhere that Liam and his brothers had built it together. They did good work, she couldn't help thinking in admiration.

"Let's just say I wasn't placing any bets on that one way or another," he told her as he closed the door behind her.

The sound reverberated in her chest but she congratulated herself on her poker face. "Since when did you become so cautious?" she asked, keeping her voice light, amused. "You used to be reckless."

He shrugged, leading the way into his kitchen. Intrigued by the hint of aroma she detected coming from that direction, Julia didn't need to be prodded to follow him.

"I grew up," Liam told her matter-of-factly.

"Oh. When? Sorry." Julia laughed dismissively in the

next breath. The jab she'd just taken at him wasn't really fair. "I just couldn't resist. You don't usually leave yourself that wide open."

Something on the grill in the center of his stove top was sizzling and Liam turned down the heat. "I'll be more careful next time. Are you hungry?"

She'd half expected the kitchen to look like a tornado had passed through it, leaving a fire in its wake. Instead everything appeared relatively neat, with several dishes of varying sizes drying on a rack next to the sink. In addition to the main course on the grill, she noticed that the oven was on. Was he baking something in addition to grilling?

"At the moment, I'm more curious than hungry," she confessed.

He switched off the oven. Whatever he had in there was done. "Curious about what?"

"About what you think passes for 'cooking.' The Superette has a fairly well-stocked frozen food section," she reminded him. Although, she had to admit she'd be hard-pressed to match frozen food to the aroma of what he was making on the grill. The oven was a different matter. Maybe Liam had made one thing himself and whatever was in the oven was his backup in case he messed up what he was cooking on the grill.

Liam looked amused by her implication. "Did you see me buying any frozen food?"

She was keenly aware of every time he came into the store—which definitely was *not* often. However, she was not one to give up easily. "No, but you have brothers and sisters who could do the buying for you," Julia pointed out.

"Were any of *them* in today—or yesterday for that matter?" he asked, glancing at her for a second.

Opening the oven door, Liam grabbed a towel in one hand and used it to extract the potatoes he had baking in the oven. He took them out one at a time and deposited them on the counter.

"No," she answered grudgingly. "But that still doesn't mean that you actually cooked the meal you're going to serve."

He took a chilled bowl from the refrigerator. As he put that on the counter, as well, she realized it was a bowl of salad. Nothing fancy; lettuce, quartered cherry tomatoes, diced-up peppers—green and red—and a host of bacon bits spread out in a layer across the top. She still couldn't picture him chopping and shredding, even though she basically had the evidence right there in front of her.

"If you're so skeptical that I can actually cook, you should have been here earlier so you could have watched me making the meal from scratch." He turned the heat beneath the main course off altogether and turned to look at her. The amused smile on his face widened. "Why is it so important that I'm the one cooking the meal, anyway?" His eyes teased hers.

"No reason. I would have just been impressed, that's all," she answered in a low voice that told him she already was impressed and it was killing her.

"And you don't want to be impressed by me, is that it?" he noted.

Fidgeting inside, Julia still didn't look away. She wouldn't allow herself to do that. When she was a kid, the first one to look away in a staring contest lost. Old habits died hard, she realized.

"I didn't realize that the predinner appetizer was going to be twenty questions," she said.

"Fair enough," Liam allowed, then told her, "Dinner's almost ready." The spareribs he'd been grilling were almost done. They just needed a couple more minutes to reach their full flavor. "Would you like a drink while we wait?"

She would have loved a drink to help calm the sudden flurry of butterflies that had come to life and were now circling around in her stomach, growing to the size of vultures.

But a drink would also loosen her up and loosened up was *not* the state she felt she should be in right now. Not when she was alone with Liam and he was looking far better than a man had a legal right to be.

"A glass of water will be fine," she told him.

Liam frowned. "Water is for swimming in. Don't you want something with taste to it?"

Julia thought for a minute, then told him, "Okay. "Orange juice."

"Orange juice it is," Liam replied, taking the bottle out and reaching for a glass. "You want a shot of anything with that?" He nodded toward the bottles of alcohol clustered in the see-through portion of one of the cabinets.

"Just straight-up juice is fine," she answered.

He filled the glass and then handed it to her. "Is it

that you don't drink alcohol or that you don't trust your-self once you've consumed some alcohol?" he asked.

"I have never not trusted myself," she informed him, "and I drink alcohol on occasion, but this isn't one of those occasions." A look of defiance entered her eyes. "I want a clear head when I'm sampling your culinary endeavors."

Replacing the bottle of juice back into the refrigerator, Liam shut the door. "Wouldn't have it any other way," he told her glibly.

"So, what are we having?" she asked, wanting the conversation to go into neutral territory.

"Besides a truce?" he asked her, the amusement back in his eyes. "We're having grilled spareribs—" he nodded at them, then at the counter "—a salad and baked potatoes. Simple," he proclaimed.

"Sounds good," she told him, although she was still having trouble seeing him as someone who could actually put together a meal that didn't involve removing it from a box and peeling back some plastic wrap.

"So," Julia began, taking a steadying breath, "what can I do?"

Liam looked at her, slightly confused. "What do you want to do?" For once, he hadn't meant it as a leading line—although once the words were out of his mouth, there was a wide, inviting grin punctuating the end of his sentence.

Julia tried again. "Let me rephrase that. What can I do to help with the meal?"

He was going to say "Nothing" since the meal was already done, but he could see she wanted to keep busy.

He could understand that. "Well, I haven't put the plates and other things out yet. You can do that if you want to. Dishes are over there." Liam nodded at the far cabinet. "Knives and forks are in the drawer directly below them. You can put them outside."

"Outside?" Julia questioned.

"Yeah, I thought we'd have dinner on the patio. It's a nice night," he told her needlessly. "Unless you'd rather eat in the kitchen. Choice is yours," he added, thinking she would feel more secure if she made some of the decisions herself. He didn't particularly care where they ate dinner as long as they ate it.

She supposed that having dinner outside might be a pleasant change of pace. "Outside is fine," she told him. Armed with plates and utensils, Julia opened one of the double doors that led outside.

Liam was right, she thought. It *was* a beautiful night. Possibly a tad *too* beautiful, she decided on closer scrutiny. A woman could lose her head, not to mention her heart, on a night like this.

She was just going to have to be on her guard, that was all, Julia warned herself.

But to come back inside and suggest that they stay indoors for dinner would make Liam think she was afraid to be alone with him on a moonlit night. The last thing she wanted was for him to think that. That she was some kind of pushover like the other women he was used to.

She knew she'd damaged his ego that time she'd turned him down for a date—her refusal was the only "black mark" on his so-called dating calendar. Every other girl in high school had all but fallen at his feet—

and a couple had, literally. These days, though, she knew Liam was too busy being a rancher to actively seek out the company of fawning women.

Maybe he *had* grown up, she thought.

Julia came back inside to get napkins and glasses, including hers, which was still more than half filled with orange juice.

As she reentered the kitchen, Liam looked up from what he was doing. "I was going to send out a search party. Thought you'd gotten lost."

She lifted a shoulder in an indifferent shrug. "Didn't know that there was a time limit for setting the table."

"There isn't. I just thought that maybe you had second thoughts about having dinner like this with me and circled out to the front of the house to where you parked your car."

She stared at him, insulted that he thought she was running away. "And what? Hightailed it home? You're not that frightening, Jones."

"Never thought I was," he told her mildly. Still, he was fairly certain it had crossed her mind. "Okay, dinner's ready," he announced as he picked up the serving platter. It was filled to overflowing with spareribs and she had to admit that the aroma was activating all sorts of salivary glands, making her mouth water.

Walking in front of him, Julia opened the door leading to the patio for him, then set down the glasses and napkins she'd brought.

"Looks good," she told him.

"Tastes better," he assured her.

Julia laughed, shaking her head. "Not much on modesty, are you?"

He looked surprised at her comment. "I thought you were the one who valued honesty."

"Touché," Julia replied, inclining her head and giving him the round.

Next he brought out the salad and the baked potatoes, carrying both items on a serving tray that, once emptied, he set on its side next to the door. He was going to need it when he took everything back inside after they'd finished eating.

"Okay—" Liam gestured toward the table "—don't stand on any formalities. Dig in," he urged her.

Despite what he'd just said about not standing on any formalities, Liam surprised her by waiting until she had taken a seat and then helping her move the chair in close to the table.

"All right, now I'm impressed," Julia told him honestly as he circled around to his own chair and sat down. "Cooking and manners—what other things have you got hidden up your sleeve?" she asked.

He gave her a look that was nothing if not the last word in innocence as he said, "Not a thing, Julia. Not a thing."

It was the innocent look that did it. She realized at that moment that she was in big trouble, but her stubbornness, not to mention her pride, kept her seated where she was, refusing to get up and flee.

But when she looked back later, reviewing everything, Julia knew that was exactly what she should have done: fled.

"Well?" Liam had done his best to be patient, but Julia had taken, by his count, five bites of her sparerib when by all rights, it should have taken just one bite for her to find out if she liked it or not.

Julia raised her eyes to his, doing her best to choose her words well, but her wonder and surprise got in her way.

"I'm speechless with amazement," Julia finally admitted. He watched with pleasure as a smile bloomed on her lips.

"So you think it's good," he concluded. It didn't hurt anything to get a real compliment out of her.

"No," Julia corrected, then paused just long enough to bedevil him before she added the kicker. "I think it's *better* than good. Who taught you how to cook?" Surprisingly, she wanted to know.

"Nobody," he replied honestly. "I watched my mother a few times and I guess it kind of stuck. It's a basically simple recipe," he went on to tell her, knowing she'd ask eventually. "I make this sauce, stick it and the spareribs into a plastic bag and let them stay in the refrigerator for twenty-four hours before I grill the ribs. No big deal, really."

"Hold it. Back up," Julia cried, all but holding her hand up like a traffic cop. "You *make* this sauce?"

He'd been cooking ever since he'd been on his own and didn't really see what the big deal was. "Yeah, that's what I said."

"Interesting. I just can't picture you like that," she told him in all honesty. She figured he deserved honesty from her after he'd gone to this sort of trouble, making the dinner. "Making trouble, yes. Making your own sauce, no. Who *are* you?" Julia asked him with a laugh as she leaned back in her chair as if to get a better, more critical view of the man who was seated at the table with her.

"Obviously not the person you thought I was," Liam answered glibly.

"Obviously," she agreed, echoing his intonation. "Do you have any other hidden talents?" she asked again, then instantly realized she'd set herself up by using that wording. "That it would be safe for me to know about?" she added.

He smiled at her over the glass of beer he had poured for himself. "I don't know. What's your definition of safe?" he asked.

The look in his eyes was pulling her in. She could all but literally *feel* the magnetism radiating from him.

Not you, she thought. *You are definitely not safe for me.*

"Not getting into a compromising situation with you," she said out loud.

It was supposed to come out sounding terse and offputting. Instead it almost sounded like a challenge, a dare issued with secret hopes that the challenge would be met and vanquished.

Hurriedly, she changed the subject. Or tried to. "Everything's very good," she admitted, the words all but sticking to her suddenly exceedingly dry mouth. "But maybe I'd better be getting back home," she told him. "I've got to open the store up early and—"

He didn't wait for her to finish making up the excuse she was giving him. "Julia, are you afraid of me?" he asked quietly.

"No!" In contrast, her voice was sharp and somewhat shrill as she answered sharply.

And it was the truth. She *wasn't* afraid of him.

What she was afraid of, again, was herself.

She didn't trust herself to stand fast and hang on to the principles that had seen her through high school—and stayed with her until she'd caught a glimpse of the new, improved Liam.

The problem was that with that torrid kiss she had also glimpsed what she'd been missing and, God help her, she didn't want to continue missing it anymore even though she knew that giving in was the fastest way to send a guy packing.

Especially a guy like Liam, whose longest relationship on record outside of with his own family was two and a half weeks.

"Good," he was saying to her, "because I wouldn't want you to be afraid of me."

Practicing the craft that was all but second nature to him, Liam took her hand gently in his as he looked into her eyes and promised, "I promise that I'll never do anything you don't want me to do."

Julia could feel everything within her tightening up. *Trying* to rally when she knew in her heart, *knew* that it was all but over as far as holding out went.

The problem with Liam's promise was that while he really wouldn't do anything she didn't want to do, at the same time he, just by his mere existence, by looking at her with his soulful eyes, made her want to do all sorts of things as long as those things were done with only him.

Chapter Eleven

Because she felt as if Liam was challenging her to remain, Julia stayed and finished her dinner.

And since prolonged silence would wind up creating a far too tense and pregnant battleground, Julia kept
up a steady stream of chatter, talking about whatever
came to mind.

They talked about his family, his siblings in general
and his mother more specifically. Julia had always liked
his mother and she asked him about Jeanne Marie's
reaction to discovering that she not only had family
outside of her husband and children, but that she was
actually one of triplets—and a Fortune to boot.

Little by little, Julia managed to draw Liam out on
the subject.

"I guess that for the first time," he said, nursing his

beer, "my mother felt as if she had roots that went back a ways, that she belonged to a family that had a history. Up until that point, she always wondered why she'd been given up. She didn't really talk about it, until she finally had some answers. Ma's like that," he attested. No one had realized how much knowing meant to her until that point.

"Did finding answers to her questions make her happy?" Julia asked.

He thought about the way his mother's face had lit up when the truth had finally come out. It wasn't even the money, which she'd promptly returned, it was the sense of belonging that had pleased her.

But all that was far too much to go into right now, so all Liam said in reply was, "Pretty much."

It was enough for Julia to work with. "Then why do *you* resent the Fortunes so much? Her brother, James Marshall, didn't have to come looking for her and he certainly didn't have to offer your mother her share of the Fortunes' fortune—no pun intended," she added. "Resenting them doesn't really sound reasonable, does it?"

He shrugged. In his heart, he supposed what she was saying was true, but he didn't want to admit it. "Feelings don't have to be reasonable," he told her. "That's what makes them feelings."

In a very odd, off-kilter way, she supposed Liam was right. When you came right down to it, a lot of feelings *weren't* reasonable. What she was feeling right now for him certainly wasn't reasonable.

What it felt like was that she was walking around

with some kind of a bomb inside her that was going to explode at any moment unless she found some way to defuse it.

And quickly.

If she listened closely, she could almost hear the seconds ticking away—synchronized with the beating of her heart.

"Yes, well, I guess that's something you're going to have to work out," she told him, trying to sound off-handed as she got to her feet. Rising from the table, she took a plate in each hand.

Liam rose to his feet, as well. "What are you doing?"

She thought that was pretty self-evident. "Cleaning up."

He put his hands over hers, trying to get her to set the plates down again. "Leave them. I'll take care of it later."

But Julia turned out to be stronger than she looked. And more stubborn, as well. She pulled her hands away, still holding on to the plates.

"No, you cooked, I'll clean. It's only fair," she insisted.

With that, she made her way back into the house and the kitchen.

Liam was quick to follow in her wake, catching up to her in the kitchen. "I never thought about dinner being a battleground for fair play," he told her.

She stopped by the sink, intending to wash off the plates and put them into the dishwasher.

"Just leave them in the sink, then," he urged. He was

behind her and he leaned over to turn on the faucet to rinse off the plates himself.

His goal was to get her to leave the dishes there until later. He had a feeling she was just going to take off if he let her and he didn't want the evening to end just yet. He found he liked talking to her if they weren't engaged in a game of one-upmanship.

And even if they were.

But Julia chose that moment, as he leaned over her, to turn around so that she could voice a protest over his instructions.

What happened next neither one of them consciously intended at all.

But it happened anyway.

Her body brushed up against his, the contact not leaving enough room for a whisper to slip through. She could feel her body temperature instantly rising and as she tried to speak, a single word—no more than a letter, really—got stuck in her throat.

"I—"

Liam couldn't help himself. He'd promised—no *sworn*—to himself that this wasn't going to happen a third time. He wasn't going to just snatch opportunity out of the air and act on it.

Wasn't going to kiss her even though every bone in his body begged him to.

But he discovered much to his surprise that the strength needed to resist Julia, to bank down the high wave of desire that she evoked within him, refused to materialize just when he needed it most.

So down he went for a third—possibly fatal—time…
and he kissed Julia.

Kissed her as if there was no tomorrow, no yesterday,
no future, no past. Only this moment—and he wanted
to make the very most of it that he could.

The instant that resolve echoed in his brain, Liam
gave himself up to the fire that was all but consum-
ing him. The fire that made him realize that tonight, it
wouldn't end with a flash of common sense that would
in turn cause him to pull away because this was, ultimately, all wrong.

This time it was going to end in an entirely different way—unless Julia protested or actually came out
and asked him to stop. She was her own best advocate
because he *knew* for a fact that he couldn't retreat on
his own anymore.

He wanted her that badly.

But she didn't say anything, didn't ask him to stop.
Didn't indicate in any way that she *wanted* him to stop.

And so, one kiss fed into another and another until
he'd lost count just how many there had been.

More than a little, less than enough.

Somehow they had managed to get from the kitchen
into the living room, a trail of hastily removed clothing
marking their path as they navigated the heady seas of
desires fueled with passions.

The more he kissed Julia, the more, he discovered,
he wanted her.

He could feel his body priming, yearning for her and
the mind-spinning feeling of fulfillment that waited just
beyond the torrid meeting of lips and limbs.

* * *

She couldn't think.

For perhaps the first time in her life, Julia couldn't think straight at all, couldn't put together a few coherent words into a sentence. Single words, all revolving around what has happening at this moment, were all that popped into her head.

And dominating them all was one three-letter word. *YES!*

This had to be, she thought, what jumping out of an aircraft was like, the air all but whisked out of her lungs, the ground coming up at her at an increasingly dizzying speed.

It was exhilarating and completely terrifying at the same time.

Terrifying because she had never felt like this before. Hadn't even *imagined* feeling like this before. The word *more* kept echoing in her head over and over again, coupled with an insatiable craving that seemed to have just taken over her entire being.

Arrows of heat shot through her body as Julia felt Liam press urgent kisses along her neck. Kisses that caused a quickening in her loins to such an extent, she was reaching peaks without even knowing she was climbing toward them.

Grasping Liam's shoulders, she dug her fingernails into his flesh, a cry of wonder and joy bursting from her.

Stunned, shaken, she looked at this tall, rugged rancher she'd known since childhood in abject wonder, almost unable to focus at all.

What was incredibly keen was this craving to have

those wild bursts that echoed throughout her body happen again—and again.

And they did.

She felt like sobbing.

She felt like cheering.

And each time another one of these thrilling explosions happened, Julia found herself being propelled just a little higher than she had gone a moment before.

This was something altogether new for her.

She'd had relations with Neal, perfectly good relations, she'd thought at the time, if a little lackluster. But anything that had happened between her ex-husband and herself paled in comparison to what she was experiencing this moment, here with Liam.

When he pressed her back against the deep cushions of his oversize sofa, she arched so that she could feel the hardness of his body against hers. Just the slightest contact was infinitely arousing to her.

When she heard the slight sound of pleasure escaping between his lips, she was empowered to continue, to go higher, because she sensed that while he was trying to be controlled in his responses, she'd tripped a wire within him that set all those sensations she was experiencing free within him, as well.

A sense of triumph echoed through her.

Further proof that what they were sharing was unraveling him, as well, came when she heard him groan, "What the hell are you doing to me?"

Joy cascaded through her because she had proof that this wasn't just one-sided, that she wasn't the only one in this swirling cauldron of wickedly delicious sensations that had so unexpectedly found her.

Julia wrapped her legs around his lower torso as she raised herself up against Liam, a silent invitation for them to become one, to join together and remain united for as long as they were physically able to do so.

If she was lucky, she thought, eternity would find her this way.

It made no sense and Julia didn't care. All she cared about was this exquisite lovemaking she had unwittingly stumbled across.

No wonder all the girls had flocked to him the way that they had. He was an incredible, natural lover. And tonight, he was hers.

Liam couldn't hold out any longer. Wanting to prolong their foreplay for as long as humanly possible for Julia's enjoyment as well as his own, he found he hadn't the power to resist going to the next level indefinitely.

The need within him to savor that final sensation was growing too great.

Gathering Julia to him, his heart racing enough to render him all but breathless, Liam finally entered her. Claiming what was already his from the very first moment that the world had been created.

She didn't think it could get any better.

She was wrong.

It got better.

Incredibly better.

She could feel herself rushing toward the top of the summit, to the farthest point on the star. And then, it happened, the anticipated explosion came and it was so much more than she had thought it would be.

Julia clung to him with the intensity she could have exerted if they were free-falling. Because, in a way, they were.

Slowly, the world came back into focus.

Reluctantly—that seemed to be such a key word in his life these days—the beat of her heart registered as it slowed to something less than the speed of light.

The magic dimmed a little.

Liam went on holding her, not knowing if she wanted him to, telling himself that if she didn't, she would have wedged her hands against his chest and tried to push them apart. He would have released her then, because she'd wanted him to.

But she gave no such indication, so he went on holding her to him. Went on inhaling the scent of her hair— vanilla mixed with lavender—went on savoring the pulses of heat as they went through his body, each a little smaller in magnitude than the one that had come before.

He stayed like that, holding her, until Julia's breathing returned to normal around the same time that his did.

"Was that dessert, or your closing argument?"

Her words, mingled with her breath, were warm against his chest, but he wasn't sure if he had made them out correctly.

If he had, he still had no idea what she was talking about. "What?"

Julia raised her head and looked at him, the ends of her red hair moving slowly and seductively along his flesh, arousing him all over again.

Arousing him almost as much as having her naked body pressed up against his was doing.

"Was that dessert—because we haven't had any—or your closing argument?" she asked again. Julia smiled when she saw the confusion on his face. "When you invited me to dinner on your ranch, I thought you wanted to corner me so you could make your argument against having that restaurant built here."

That had been his initial intention, but that wasn't something he wanted to admit to now, or even briefly touch upon. Not when she'd succeeded in knocking his entire world off-kilter the way she had.

When he had invited her over for dinner, he'd wanted to seduce her. Instead, somehow, though he wasn't sure just how, Julia had succeeded in seducing *him*.

"That would have been underhanded of me," he said, deftly not admitting or denying anything.

"I know." Her face flushed slightly, making him feel guilty over the lie—and attracted as hell to her all over again. "I'm sorry."

"Don't apologize," Liam told her, guilt getting the better of him. "I—"

Her mouth was so close to his, this time *she* was the one who gave in to impulse and lightly, teasingly brushed her lips against his.

It only made her want more, so there was a second pass in the wake of the first. This time she pressed her lips against his just a little harder.

Julia could feel him responding beneath her. Her eyes were laughing as she grinned wickedly. "I guess this is dessert, then," she murmured.

He was aching for her all over again. He couldn't remember *ever* responding so quickly after having just made love.

Nibbling along her lips he asked, "Would you rather have ice cream?"

Only if I could lick it off your body.

The thought, coming like a lightning bolt out of nowhere, startled her. And made her feel that much hotter.

"Nope," she said out loud, not brave enough yet to give voice to her wanton thoughts.

Liam laughed then, catching her up in his arms and rolling so that in one swift, single movement, their positions were reversed and he was back on top of Julia again.

"Me, neither," he told her.

Her heart began to race again as a fresh wave of anticipation washed over her. All she could think about was doing it again.

And again.

"I guess it's official, then. I've joined the crowd," she told him.

He knew she was thinking of the other women he'd been with, the others who had graced his bed or he theirs. But she wasn't just a warm body for the night—much as he wanted her to be.

She was more.

Much as he *didn't* want her to be.

Framing Julia's face with his hands so that all he

could see was her face without any other distraction—
a face that had its own beauty, both inner and outer—
he told her, "You could never be part of a crowd, Julia."

She liked hearing him say her name. It sent a small
shiver down her spine. She knew that some would view
that as an adolescent reaction, but she didn't care. She
still savored it.

"That's a lovely line. Practice it much?" she breathed,
her eyes teasing his, the rise and fall of her breasts
wreaking havoc on the rest of him as they brushed
rhythmically against his chest.

"No. Because it's not a line," he told her just before
he lowered his mouth to hers.

Because she desperately wanted to believe him, to
believe that for at least this small, isolated moment, on
this night, he meant what he said to her, Julia pretended
that it was true.

Tomorrow she could think about how foolish she
was being, to actually believe that she could be special
to him, a man who had had so many women, most far
more experienced than she would ever be.

But tonight, she told herself, she *was* special to him.

Almost as special as he was to her.

Chapter Twelve

Liam was in deep trouble and he knew it.

He had completely lost his edge, his clear perspective, and it was all Julia's fault. The indignation he'd been carrying around about the Fortunes intruding into his life, silently implying by their very existence—at least in his eyes—that he and his family, his *father,* weren't good enough, weren't important in the scheme of things unless they were Fortunes by birth, by marriage or by association, didn't seem to be nearly as explosive as it had been earlier.

He'd even begun to wonder if maybe he'd allowed unfounded anger to get the better of him, letting it dictate his reaction without any substantial evidence to back up his feelings.

After all, it wasn't as if he had been bullied by one

of the Fortunes, or humiliated by one of them, or any one of a number of embarrassing things that would have made him feel slighted.

He couldn't, in all honesty and with a clear conscience, point to a single incident that could be seen as a trigger that had created all this animosity within him.

He was being far too philosophical about this. What the hell was going on with him?

Had making love with Julia brainwashed him? Or had it somehow managed to clarify things for him?

He didn't know.

All he knew was that he was confused. That the anger he had felt about the Fortunes intruding into his and his family's way of life…well, that was gone.

Or maybe it had just gone into hiding.

He decided that if he talked to his father, listened to his father's take on all this—after all, it *was* his name that was being pushed aside to make room for the Fortune surname—he'd get some of his initial fire back.

Or make his peace with it being gone.

One way or another, talking with his father could very well resolve at least *some* things for him.

Leaving a few immediate instructions with his ranch hands that would sufficiently see them through the morning chores, Liam drove off to see his father.

The sooner he got this resolved, the better.

Tomorrow the town was taking a vote on the future of this restaurant that was so dear to Julia's heart. The townspeople had had a week to think about the matter. Any last-minute arguments, pro and con, were going to be made then. He knew he didn't have all that much time to make up his mind whether or not this was a fight he still wanted to have.

After the vote, the restaurant would be a reality or it wouldn't, depending on the outcome.

And the outcome, no matter what it turned out to be, was going to affect him more than he'd dreamed, because this issue had become very personal to him in ways he hadn't foreseen.

Deke Jones looked up when he heard his son's truck approaching.

Used to be, the man thought, that it was the sound of hoofbeats that would draw his attention. But he hardly heard those anymore, other than from the stock he was raising.

For the most part, the sound of hoofbeats only echoed when he was working with his horses, reminiscing about days gone by, or going places that a four-wheel drive vehicle couldn't go.

The tall, lean rancher was a basic, simple man who was satisfied with little, even though he'd always wanted his children to have more—but not *much* more, because that would make them soft and to survive in this world, a person had to be tough. The land was bountiful, but it was also harsh and only the tough managed to make it in Horseback Hollow.

When his second-born came driving up, Deke was busy cleaning the right rear hoof of his favorite horse, a palomino named Golden Lightning.

He'd broken in the horse himself. Broken the stallion in so that Lightning would accept him as his master, but Deke had taken great care not to break the horse's spirit. If he had done that, to his way of thinking it would have been a crime.

"What are you doing out here in the middle of the week, boy?" Deke asked after Liam had gotten out of his weathered vehicle. "Your ma call and ask you to come by?"

"No, I wanted to talk to you," Liam told his father. He leaned against the corral, watching his father patiently scrape away.

Deke went on working, removing debris that had gotten embedded around the horse's shoe. He'd noticed Lightning favoring that leg this morning. To his relief, Deke discovered that the problem was easily rectified. He'd been worried there for a bit that the problem might have been serious. Finding out otherwise put him in a basically good mood—although with Deke, as his wife readily pointed out, it was hard to tell his moods apart.

For the most part, Deke Jones kept everything to himself.

"So talk," he said without glancing up.

Now that he was here, Liam realized that he hadn't planned how he was going to phrase this. After he hesitated for a minute, he admitted, "This isn't easy to put into words."

"I suspect you'll find them if this means enough to you." Deke glanced up just for a second. "I'm not going anywhere."

He and his father had what Liam thought of as an "unspoken" relationship. They didn't talk all that much, but things were just understood. He'd never heard his father talk any more than was absolutely necessary to get his thoughts across—and only as a last resort.

But he needed to have this clarified for him, needed to know if he'd just assumed things and gone off half-cocked when he shouldn't have.

Or if his take on his father's reaction to having the Fortunes suddenly part of their lives was dead-on.

The only way to ask was to ask, right? he told himself just before forging ahead.

"How do you feel about Ma finding out that she's part of the Fortune family and her deciding to take their name and all?" Liam asked.

He knew he was stumbling through this, but it was the thought, not the poetry of the sentence, he was trying to get across. He was fairly confident that his father would know what he meant.

Deke went on working on the hoof and for a moment, Liam thought that his father either hadn't heard him or had decided to ignore the question.

Since it was important to him, Liam tried again. "Dad, how do you feel—?"

"I heard you the first time," Deke answered. Finished, he released the hoof he'd held nestled between his strong thighs while he'd worked.

Golden Lightning whinnied, tossed his mane and haughtily retreated to the other end of the corral, as if to say that he'd been patient long enough.

Brushing off his hands, Deke climbed over the slats of the corral fence and joined his son on the other side.

"How do I feel?" he repeated. "How do you think I

feel after years of breaking my back to put a roof over your heads and food in your bellies?"

It was a rhetorical question so Liam made no attempt to answer him. He waited for his father to continue. The wait wasn't long.

"I was mad, that's how I felt, thinking that maybe your ma didn't think I was good enough and that was why she took on that other name."

His sharp blue eyes narrowed for a moment, pinning Liam in place before he said another word. "Having Christopher take off like that, going to Red Rock to work for those people didn't help matters any." He had his own question and he put it to Liam now. "Did any of you kids feel like you were missing out on anything when you were growing up?"

Deke Jones hadn't been the warmest of fathers when they were kids, but Liam recalled that he had always felt safe, as if his home was his haven and his father was the sentry guarding the gate. Nothing could ever hurt him as long as his father was there. He knew the others had felt the same way.

"We had a great childhood, Dad."

The answer satisfied Deke. He wasn't the kind to milk it for more.

The wiry shoulders rose and fell in a careless shrug. "After I got over being mad, I started seeing things from your ma's point of view. She grew up thinking she was all alone, that whoever her mama was, she just gave her away like yesterday's hand-me-downs. It was nice for your ma to find out that she's got family that wants her.

Not everyone gets that." He let the words sink in and then leveled a look at his son. "Why are you asking?"

Liam was honest in his answer. His father would stand for nothing less. "I just wanted to know if you felt insulted."

Deke shrugged again. "It is what it is. I hear that the Fortunes are good people. That they don't just take without giving back and they don't act holier-than-thou, so unless I'm shown otherwise, that makes them all right in my book." Deke cocked his Stetson back on his head as he looked intently at his son. "We done here?" he queried. "Because I got work to do."

Liam grinned. This had to be the longest conversation he'd ever had with his father. "We're done," he answered. "I've got to be getting back, too."

Deke nodded. "I'll tell your ma you said hi," he said as he walked away.

"Well, you certainly have a spring in your step these past couple of days," Annie noted as she crossed the floor to reach her daughter. They spent a great deal more time together than the average mother and daughter did and Annie was keenly attuned to any changes in her daughter's behavior. "Anything that I should know about?" she asked, a warm, very amused smile curving her lips.

There was no way she was going to say anything about seeing Liam to her mother. Some things were best kept secret, Julia thought. Liam's reputation as a lady-killer had always been larger than life and things like that took a long time to die. She didn't want her mother worrying about her.

It was enough that she knew this was just an interlude and that it would be over soon enough. She was determined to enjoy it while it lasted.

Liam Jones wasn't the kind to settle down with one woman and as long as she didn't lose sight of that, didn't delude herself into thinking that she was unique enough to get him to change his ways, she'd be all right.

But her mother needed a reason for this upbeat swing in her personality, so Julia gave her one. That it also happened to be true was an added bonus.

"I'm just looking forward to the restaurant opening here in Horseback Hollow, Mom. I've been in touch with Wendy and Marcos Mendoza—they're the ones who are looking to expand—told them a couple of the ideas I had for the restaurant, and they really seemed to like what I had to say. I think they might offer me a job once the restaurant is up and running," she said with enthusiasm.

"A job? Why wouldn't they hire you to be the head chef, or the manager, for that matter?" Annie asked. "Why, if it wasn't for you, the council wouldn't even be thinking about this. And you're bright, enthusiastic—"

"One step at a time, Mom. I need some restaurant experience under my belt first." Marcos's explanation about that had made perfect sense to her. No one began at the top. "I *really* want this, Mom. I've always dreamed about being a chef and eventually having my own restaurant, and all this is going to be happening right here," she said, barely containing her joy. "I won't have to leave you or Dad," she added, pleased at the way things had turned out.

Annie had always been very supportive of Julia's dreams, but she didn't want her daughter getting all caught up in a dream before it was nailed down. "Has the final vote gone through?" she asked.

"No, not yet," Julia admitted, but that wasn't going to throw cold water on her plans. This was going to work, she just *knew* it. "But I've been talking to everyone who comes in and I think I've got them all convinced that having a restaurant, a real restaurant, not just a bar and grill, in Horseback Hollow could only benefit the town."

Annie squeezed her daughter's hand. "Don't go getting your heart set on that, honey. Maybe they were just being polite and didn't want to hurt your feelings."

She knew her mother meant well, but what she was suggesting wasn't the case here.

"Mom, I've known these people all my life. They love to argue. If they didn't agree with me, they'd definitely let me know it. No, I think this restaurant proposition is pretty much a sure thing."

Annie still held back. "What about Liam Jones?"

Why was her mother bringing Liam up? Did she suspect that she and Liam had something going on? That when she'd left the store those times, saying she was going back to Vicker's Corners to do further research into the way the restaurant was being operated, she was really going to Liam's ranch?

To Liam's arms?

"What about him?" Julia asked, trying her best to sound as if she was just being mildly curious why her mother would have brought his name up. Trying to act as if her heart hadn't just started beating rapidly at double time.

"Well, I heard him talking here to you that day. He really sounded as if he was dead set against having that restaurant built here and he might just find a way to keep that from happening. I just don't want to see you get hurt, honey."

"Liam Jones can't do anything single-handedly, Mom, and if the town votes to have it constructed—which I know they will—there's nothing much that he can do about it," Julia added.

Annie inclined her head. It *sounded* good. "Still, tomorrow, when the town votes on this at the meeting, I intend to be there. Another vote in favor can't hurt, right?"

Julia laughed. "Right, Mama," she agreed, resorting to the term of endearment she hardly ever used anymore. But this was a special time.

Bending over, she kissed her mother's cheek. "Another vote is always welcome. You realize that when this comes through, we're going to have to hire extra help for you here in the store. But then, I'll be bringing in more money, so we can easily pay for it."

"Whoa," Annie cautioned. "One step at a time. Get this voted in, then you can start thinking about hiring people. And don't worry about the Superette. It'll be hard, but we'll get along without you. We've taken up more than enough of your life as it is. Time you started carving out a life of your own."

The bell over the door announced the entrance of

another customer. Annie automatically looked toward the entrance.

"Right after you wait on this handsome gentleman," she told her daughter, smiling at Liam. "Hello, Liam, how are your parents these days?"

"They're fine, Mrs. Tierney," he replied politely. "Mind if I have a word with Julia?"

"Have as many words as you like, Liam. And while you're at it, why don't you take her off my hands for the rest of the afternoon?" Annie suggested impulsively, much to Julia's obvious surprise. "She hardly ever goes out of the store and she needs to get a little more color in her face."

Liam slanted a glance toward Annie's daughter. A rosy hue was inching its way up Julia's neck and onto her cheeks.

He wondered if Mrs. Tierney suspected that Julia and he were involved. He'd always regarded Julia's mother as a very sharp lady, despite her laid-back, unassuming manner.

For that matter, Liam couldn't help wondering if Julia suspected just how much she had managed to get to him in what seemed to be such an incredibly short amount of time.

"Well, I think she's getting some color in her cheeks right now, Mrs. Tierney," he pointed out, amused by the fact that Julia was actually blushing. "But I'd be happy to take her out for you right now."

"I'm right here, people," Julia said, speaking up as she raised her hand and waved it in front of her mother and Liam. "I can hear you, you know."

"Nice to know that there's nothing wrong with your hearing, dear," Annie said serenely. "Now go," she urged, all but shooing her daughter and Liam out the door. "Have an afternoon outside the store, outside of everything—like a young woman who's not perpetually trying to juggle too many things all at once."

Taking his cue from the older woman, Liam surprised Julia by suddenly going behind the counter and taking her hand.

Julia tried to pull it away and found that she couldn't. He was holding on to her hand rather tightly. "What are you doing?"

"Listening to your mother—like you should," Liam answered. Looking over his shoulder at Annie, he smiled. "See you later, Mrs. Tierney."

"Make it as 'later' as you like, Liam," Annie urged.

"Mother!" Julia cried. Okay, her mother *had* to know. But how? She hadn't said a word.

"She's stubborn," Annie told Liam as the rest of the customers in the store looked on in barely veiled amusement. "So you have your work cut out for you."

"I already know that, ma'am," Liam replied, ushering a protesting Julia out of the store.

The bell sounded, announcing their departure. Julia could have sworn she detected the faint sound of applause coming from the inside of the Superette and sending them on their way.

The color in her cheeks deepened.

Chapter Thirteen

Once they were outside and clear of the Superette, Julia slanted an uncomfortable glance toward Liam to try to guess his reaction to what had just transpired in the store.

"She knows," she said, referring to her mother.

She'd get no argument from him, Liam thought. "Your mother's a sharp lady. I suspect she probably does. Question is, how much does she know?"

Did the fact that her mother knew annoy him? Or did it just add notches to his figurative belt? Either way, she wanted Liam to know one thing. "I never said anything."

"I never said you did."

He didn't see her as the type who had to share every intimate detail with someone. He'd known more than

his share of *that* type, the ones who relived their relationships by going into great detail with every girlfriend they knew.

"But some mothers have a way of just looking at
you and intuiting things whether you want them to or
not. I've got a hunch that might describe your mother.
Is that a problem for you?" he asked. Unless he missed
his guess, Julia seemed to be rather upset or flustered
about the exchange that had just taken place with her
mother inside the store.

Julia shook her head. She wouldn't exactly call being
embarrassed by her mother a problem; she just didn't
know *what* to label it. "No."

"Oh." He wasn't 100 percent sure if he believed her.
"Because you look a little upset."

She supposed she did at that. "If I am, it's for you."

Why would she be upset for him? It didn't make
sense. "Now you lost me."

That'll happen all too soon, Julia couldn't help thinking.

Out loud she explained her reasoning to him. "I just
don't want my mother asking you a lot of questions,
that's all."

Was that all? Liam grinned. "Don't worry about that.
I can hold my own with your mother. Besides, she's a
nice lady."

Well, at least he didn't hold grudges, Julia thought
as she realized that she had gotten sidetracked by the
exchange between her mother and Liam.

"You said you wanted a word with me," she reminded
him. "About what?"

He looked at her for a long moment. The early afternoon sun wove its way through her hair, giving the red strands a golden sheen. He wondered if she realized that she was beautiful.

"I wanted to know if you wanted to see me tonight," he told her. Then, before Julia could answer him, he continued, "Because I want to see you."

Had she been slated to go out with some girlfriends, or attend a school reunion, she would have found a way to postpone it or beg off to go wherever he wanted her to go. Julia was well aware that it wasn't very independent of her, to be willing to rearrange her life because of a man, especially one with the sort of reputation that Liam had.

But frankly, she couldn't help herself. Being with him was like holding a bit of stardust in her hand. It was all magical and for as long as she could savor the experience, she intended to make the most of it. It would be over with soon enough and she didn't want to do anything that would hasten its demise or curtail its very short life expectancy.

She needed the memories to last her for the rest of her life because she instinctively knew that nothing, *nothing* was ever going to hold a candle to what she was experiencing with Liam.

"Is this the part where I'm supposed to be coy?" she asked when Liam paused, waiting for an answer.

He laughed. She was refreshingly devoid of any game playing. He liked that. "No, this is the part where you're supposed to say, 'Yes, Liam, I'd like to see you, too.'"

Julia grinned. "'Yes, Liam,'" she echoed, "'I'd like to see you, too.'"

His eyes were smiling as he regarded her. "Nice to know we're of like mind," he told her. And then a bemused expression came over his face as he cocked his head ever so slightly.

Was he waiting for something more? Or having second thoughts about what he'd just said? "What's wrong?" She wanted to know.

"Nothing's wrong," he told her. The grin was back and it grew wider. "I just never realized that you've got dimples. Two tiny ones," he went on. "Right there. And there." He lightly passed his forefinger along first one dimple, then the other, one at either corner of her mouth.

The moment his finger touched her skin, Julia could feel the longing beginning all over again, spreading a blanket of fire all along her body.

Abruptly he dropped his hand to his side.

When he saw her raise her eyebrow in a silent question, he explained, "I think I'd better stop touching you when we're out in public—because that might lead to kissing you and you wouldn't want people talking about you."

"I never cared about what people had to say," she told him honestly. There were people who were given to gossip and those who couldn't care less. Her friends wouldn't care and the others didn't matter.

"I do," he told her solemnly.

"Bad for your reputation?" she asked, curious.

He surprised her by saying, "No, bad for yours."

Julia blinked. "You're worried about my reputation?" she said incredulously.

He was accustomed to people talking about him because of his penchant to love 'em and leave 'em. Talking about Julia, though, was another thing entirely. He felt protective of her. Another new feeling for him. Being with Julia ushered in a series of "firsts," he couldn't help thinking.

"One of us should be."

Damn him, Julia thought.

Despite all of her silent lectures to herself, she could feel it happening. Could feel herself falling in love with Liam even though she knew there was no future for her in his life.

Falling for Liam was just about the worst possible mistake she could make.

And even though she knew that what he was saying to her was a line—he sounded so sincere, that just for a moment, she allowed herself to believe him.

He wanted to see her. She hugged that thought close to her heart.

"Why don't you come by my place tonight and I'll make you dinner?" she suggested.

Liam smiled and suddenly her immediate world seemed to light up. "I'd like that," he told her.

Not half as much as I will, Julia thought.

"I'd better be getting back," she told him. "Before my mother starts wondering what happened to me."

"If it came to that, I think she'd probably have a pretty good idea," Liam suggested. He turned his attention to what she'd said earlier. "What time tonight?"

"Eight?" It was more of a question than a statement. "It'll be after I close the store."

"Eight it is," he repeated with a nod. "Oh, and, Julia?" he called out just as she turned away.

She stopped and started to turn around to face him again. "Yes?"

Liam had crossed the short distance she'd managed to create between them and was right behind her as she turned, catching her off guard. The next moment he surprised her further by brushing his lips against hers.

Right where anyone could see them.

He grinned down into her face. "I figured it was okay," he teased, "since you don't care about people talking."

At this point, there *were* no other people in the world besides the two of them. For two cents she'd grab him by his shirtfront, pull him down to her level and kiss him long and hard.

She didn't do it. Not because of the people who were around, but because she knew that kissing him that way wouldn't satisfy her, it would just make her want even more. So she struggled to control herself as best she could.

"I don't," she murmured.

And then she was gone.

But as she hurried away, she could feel Liam's eyes on her.

Watching her.

Julia was grinning fit to kill by the time she walked back into the Superette.

* * *

The next afternoon found the Two Moon Saloon filled to capacity with people.

Unlike in some towns and larger cities, where meetings were conducted in auditoriums that echoed with apathy and little else, apathy did not have a seat here in the saloon in Horseback Hollow. Everyone prided themselves on taking a keen interest in civic affairs as well as in matters that affected the town's welfare. They'd come to realize that the concept of growth was more enticing than maintaining a status quo no matter how quaint that status quo might be in some people's eyes.

The meeting had been going for over an hour and when the mayor had thrown open the floor for a final discussion before the vote was taken, a number of people had come up to the makeshift podium in front of the bar to express their thoughts about the proposed restaurant.

Some spoke a little, others spoke more. And then the mayor turned toward Julia and asked if she had anything further to add.

She banked down her nervousness—this wasn't the time to indulge herself—and said that she did.

Coming up to the podium, she looked out at the sea of faces and told them what was in her heart.

"In this day and age," Julia said as she addressed the people at the meeting, "if a town doesn't grow, it shrinks and the outcome of that is obvious. Horseback Hollow means too much to all of us for us to watch it wither away on the vine.

"However, our choices have to be made carefully.

We can't just jump at the first offer that comes our way without examining all sides. Everything should always be examined and that includes weighing the pros and cons of inviting Wendy and Marcos Mendoza to bring their restaurant here to us.

"I know some of you are worried that we'd be sacrificing our way of life, become too 'citified' and so give up the warm, friendly atmosphere we all grew up with. That's exactly why we wouldn't bring in a chain discount store, or some big-name drugstore that cares more about profit than service. I can personally tell you that the Mendozas are good people and they're associated with good people. I'm referring to the Fortunes. The latter have no desire to use this town, pick it clean of its assets and then move on to do the same to another town." She paused for a moment to allow her words to sink in—and to take a breath.

"If we welcome them here, they will treat Horseback Hollow the way they treat Red Rock—like it was their home. And to insure that that is never lost sight of, they've asked me to be their assistant manager," she told the people she considered to be her friends and neighbors.

A murmur of approval went up.

As she spoke, Julia glanced more than once in Liam's direction. Each time she crossed her fingers behind the podium, hoping for a positive response.

To her relief, Liam appeared to be comfortable with what she was saying, unlike the first time when he'd walked out of the meeting when he saw that the preliminary vote was going her way.

When she was finished—having spoken longer than she'd intended—Julia left the floor open to any dissenters who wanted to air their last-minute thoughts. But there weren't any when the mayor called for any further comments or discussion before the vote.

"Well, if nobody else has anything further to say," he announced, "then I guess it's time to take the final vote. All in favor of the Mendozas' restaurant being built here in Horseback Hollow, raise your hands."

When a sea of hands went up, the mayor dutifully counted each and every one of them.

From the looks of it, it appeared that most of the people there welcomed the restaurant's construction. But bound by rules, the mayor called for a show of hands from those who opposed the restaurant being built in town.

"All opposed?" Several hands, totaling no more than nine, went up. He counted out each one.

"I guess it's settled then," the mayor told his constituents fairly confidently. "Looks like the ayes have it," he said to the people assembled in front of him. Then, raising his voice, he declared, "The measure to build a new restaurant here in Horseback Hollow is passed," and banged down the gavel to make it official.

"Meeting's adjourned," he announced needlessly since everyone was getting up anyway, talking to their neighbor, calling out across the aisles. It was obvious that despite the few dissenters, everyone appeared to have been won over by the idea of having a brand-new enterprise make a home in their town.

To a person, they looked forward to the pick up in

business that was sure to occur as a by-product of the restaurant's location.

Having taken a seat in the rear of the saloon so as not to call attention to himself, Liam had quietly taken in the proceedings as they'd unfolded. He knew that he'd surprised a few people by not speaking up when opposing viewpoints were requested.

Maybe he'd even surprised himself, as well.

The fire he'd felt initially in his belly concerning the matter eluded him now, having died out in the face of other things.

Talking to his father the other day had made him take a second look at his own feelings about being connected to the Fortunes. While he doubted that out-and-out jealousy had been behind his initial reaction to the discovery that his mother was one of them, he was willing to admit that he might have been more than a tad unreasonable, allowing his view of the situation to be tainted and made prejudicial by what he *thought* the Fortunes were like rather than finding out the truth of the matter for himself.

But he had to admit that the lion's share of what had actually changed his mind for him about the matter was Julia herself. If someone like Julia could be so in favor of an issue, then that issue deserved, at the very least, closer scrutiny.

With that in mind, he'd done a little research of his own into the matter by talking to Gabriella, Jude's fiancée. Gabriella, a Mendoza herself, had nothing but good things to tell him about the Fortunes, as well as her cousins. Julia was right.

The couple behind the new restaurant—not to mention the Fortunes themselves—*were* good people. And Wendy Fortune Mendoza was related to him and so she was family in the best possible sense of the word, he supposed.

Liam was *not* so naïve as to think that just because someone was family that automatically made them good people. He'd seen enough of the other side of that coin to know that was definitely *not* a given.

But these people liked to give back to any community they were part of and he liked that.

Ultimately he had a gut feeling that this restaurant that Julia was championing would be good for Horseback Hollow. Just as he had a gut feeling that Julia was the one woman he could see himself sharing forever with.

That had never been on his agenda. He'd just assumed that he would always remain free and untangled, able to go from woman to woman and dally for as long as it suited him, then just move on when the whim hit.

And now all he wanted was to be tangled up with her. Permanently.

Last night's lovemaking was still fresh in his mind. The mere thought of it sent his pulse up to a higher rate. But he didn't want to just look forward to their next evening together, the next time they made love together. He wanted to know that he could look forward to forever, that she would always be there whether he was thinking about the next evening, the next week, the next year or the next decade.

The more he reflected on it, the more he *knew* that she was the one for him.

He supposed, now that he thought about it, that this was what love, what *being* in love, felt like. Wanting one person to be part of your forever and wanting them to want you to be part of theirs.

Who would have ever thought he could feel this way? Liam marveled, swallowing a laugh that would only call unwanted attention his way. This was Julia's victory and she deserved to bask in it.

Flushed, thrilled, now that the meeting was adjourned and the vote was part of the town's history, Liam watched as Julia plowed her way through the milling bodies within the saloon to reach him.

She was positively glowing, he thought.

Liam slipped his arm around her the second she reached him. "Victory looks good on you," he told her, brushing his lips against her cheek. All he could think about was whiling away the night lost in her embrace and making love with her.

"You're not mad?" she asked, peering up into his face. She was surprised—not to mention relieved—that he was taking defeat so well.

"How can I be mad about something that makes you look so happy?"

But the din in the saloon had risen by several decibels as people were trying to out-shout each other. Unable to hear him because of the noise, Julia shook her head and pointed to her ear, indicating that she hadn't heard him.

Liam merely laughed, pulled her a little closer to

him. Bending over her ear, he said, "Let's get out of here."

That, she heard, as a wide grin blossomed over her lips. His suggestion was music to her ears. Julia was more than willing to follow him anywhere he wanted to go.

Chapter Fourteen

Julia felt as if she was literally walking on air and was seriously entertaining the idea of putting rocks in her pockets to keep from just floating away like a helium party balloon gliding on the wind.

It was the day after the vote and she was standing in front of what in a larger town would have been referred to as a vacant lot. At the very front of the lot was a sign driven into the ground by a wooden stake.

It was a large, no-frills sign that proclaimed the vacant lot to be only temporary because this site had been chosen as the "Future Home of The Hollows Brasserie."

I did it, Julia thought with no small enthusiasm or pride.

She had gotten everyone in town to come around and see how advantageous it was to have new business, new blood, come into Horseback Hollow. And because the restaurant was now destined to become a reality, she was going to finally—*finally*—realize her dream of running a restaurant and being, for all intents and purposes, in charge of its kitchen.

Granted, she wanted to run her *own* restaurant, but she knew that the path from here to there required a great deal of patience as well as baby steps. She was more than prepared to execute both, learning everything she could as she went. And this was really a very large step in the right direction.

That part of her future looked rosier than it ever had before.

As for the other part, well, Julia was fairly certain that the words to describe how happy she was hadn't been created yet.

She and Liam had gone to his ranch after the meeting last night and she'd cooked a meal for him—something she'd created on the spur of the moment out of things she found he had as leftovers in his refrigerator. She'd been inspired as she chopped and stirred and blended, but she really had no idea how her creation turned out because halfway through the preparations, she gave up trying to concentrate on what she was doing on the stove. Her mind kept insisting on wandering because of what Liam was doing to her with his hands and with his lips.

Between his caresses and his kisses, she'd gone from being a creative, independent young woman who had just experienced a major victory to a woman who had become all but completely liquefied.

Certainly unable to stand with any sort of demonstrable balance.

The only thought in her head at that point was that she wanted him. She gave up chopping, gave up stirring and blending and barely had the presence of mind to turn off the stove before she gave herself completely up to Liam and the magic that was him.

Last night it was as if they had both tapped into some secret source of energy because the lovemaking went on and on, encompassing the entire night.

Oh, there were breaks in between, but they were so small, they hardly counted.

What counted was that he wanted her as much as she did him. Even after having been with one another almost every night for two weeks, he hadn't grown tired of her, hadn't made love once or twice and then just rolled over to fall asleep. His energy seemed boundless, coaxing the same from her.

Consequently, as she stood admiring the sign that she assumed either Mayor Osgood or possibly even one of Marcos Mendoza's employees had put up, she felt both exhausted at the same time that she felt utterly exhilarated.

She had to be getting back to the Superette, Julia silently told herself. She wasn't the assistant manager of the still-to-be-constructed restaurant yet and until she was, her mother needed her to be working at the family business.

But Lord, Julia thought, sporting a huge smile, she did like looking at this pristine, sleek sign and its whispered promise of things to come in the very near future.

As she stood there, various people had passed by, taking note of it, marveling at how fast the sign had gone up and wondering out loud whether the restaurant would be built just as quickly.

Some sounded excited about the proposition, some seemed to be oblivious to its implications and still others were not overly ecstatic about the idea.

Such as the last duo she heard talking.

"'Future Home of The Hollows Brasserie,'" a low voice behind her read out loud to his companion. "What the hell is a Brass-y-yearie?" he mocked.

Julia was going to answer, but the man's friend did it for her.

"I think that's a restaurant where you don't have to order no food just to be able to order a drink."

"Huh," the first man snorted. "We already got that. It's called the saloon," the man said, referring to the Two Moon Saloon, where they had all voted yesterday. It was obvious by his tone of voice that he was not impressed and would rather the whole thing just go away.

That was his right, Julia thought, but she was very glad he and his friend were not in the majority.

"Guess the Two Moon ain't snooty enough for the Fortunes," the first man said. "And I bet that Liam was ticked off that his little plan didn't work."

"What plan?" the first man asked as they began to walk away.

"Well, he figured if he sweet-talked that gal who was pushing it—you know, the one who runs the Superette—and threw in a little loving to boot, she'd come around and see things his way. You *know* what that guy's like when he pours on the charm. Ain't a woman alive who can resist Liam Jones once he gets going."

"Well, looks like this Julia person did, though," his friend commented as their voices faded away.

Julia stood there, staring at the sign as the two men walked away. But this time, she really didn't even see it. Her vision was blurred with angry tears and she was unable to move—afraid to move because she felt physically sick and was afraid that one wrong step and she was going to throw up.

Literally.

Did everyone know about Liam's "plan"?

Was she the laughingstock of the town?

But she'd thought he loved her—

She'd thought—

Damn it, she *hadn't* thought and that was the problem, Julia upbraided herself. She'd gone leading with her heart, not her head in this.

More than that, she'd convinced herself that someone like Liam—the eternal "bad boy"—could have feelings, actual *feelings* for someone like her.

Just how stupid could she be?

Taking in a slow, deep breath and then releasing it, Julia did what she could to try to get hold of herself and her shattered ego. All she wanted to do was to crawl into a hole and die, but she couldn't indulge herself and just take off to cry this huge, searing, gaping pain away.

If she didn't turn up at the store soon, her mother would come looking for her and she couldn't have that sweet woman finding her like this.

Damn, but this hurt.

She'd remained in Horseback Hollow, giving up her dreams and her education, to provide support, someone to lean on, for her mother. In short, a solution to Mother's problem.

Solutions weren't supposed to generate their own set of problems.

At least, *she* wasn't going to create any problems, any waves. She was *not* going to let her mother see her cry or suspect that she'd just had her heart literally cut out of her chest.

All right, she'd survive this, she consoled herself, using the back of her hand to quickly wipe away the telltale tracks of her tears. Besides, she still had the restaurant to look forward to.

Somehow, that seemed like a very small consolation prize in comparison to what she'd *thought* she'd had in the palm of her hand just a few short minutes ago.

Served her right for believing that love actually conquered all. All it had conquered, to her huge regret, was her.

"I think you better get down there and exercise a little damage control—or maybe a lot," Toby told his brother without any preamble as he walked into Liam's stable looking for him.

Liam looked at him, surprised to see his brother here. They had no project set to do and as far as he knew, Toby was busy with work on his own place.

Obviously what he was talking about seemed important enough to Toby for him to come out here looking for him. He could have saved himself a trip.

"If you're talking about that restaurant coming here, I've decided not to fight it anymore." Liam grinned, thinking of last night and the way Julia had felt in his arms.

As though he had come home. Julia was his "home."

He finally, *finally* understood what it was that his brother Jude found so compelling about this thing called love, *real* love. The real thing—and this felt like it was—was absolutely, mind-blowingly wonderful. He was only sorry that it had taken him so long to find it—especially when it turned out to be right under his nose.

"No, I'm talking about your little plan coming to light," Toby stressed, disapproval imprinted on his handsome features.

Liam stopped mucking out the stall and stared at his younger brother. "What little plan? What are you talking about?"

Toby sighed. He didn't like to have to say this out loud. It seemed beneath Liam somehow—even though it sounded like the "old" Liam. "The plan to seduce Julia and get her to see things your way."

Liam frowned. He didn't bother saying he'd gotten caught in his own trap. That was self-evident to him and anyone in his life who mattered. Right now, there was something more important on the drawing board.

His eyes narrowed. "How do you know about that?" He wanted to know. While he'd initially intended to make Julia come around through unorthodox methods, he had never said a word about it to anyone that he knew of. If someone was shooting off their mouth about it, it had to be from pure conjecture, not something he'd actually said.

It pained Toby to have to say this to his brother. He'd seen a change in Liam these past two weeks. A change for the better. He was less caustic, far more cheerful. He'd actually caught Liam whistling a time or two. He didn't want this new, improved Liam to just disappear.

"Buck Holt was shooting off his mouth about your plans to 'seduce' Julia to one of his friends and you know how fast word spreads around here."

He could feel his heart quickening with anxiety. It didn't matter that he hadn't said anything to Buck. This was bad.

"You think Julia knows?"

"Unless she fell into a coma early this morning, yeah, I think she knows. What the hell were you thinking, trying to pull off something like that?"

"I wasn't thinking," he protested. "And I didn't try to pull it off. I abandoned that harebrained scheme before I ever tried to do anything with it."

Toby looked at him skeptically. "Before or after you slept with her?"

This was getting to be positively unnerving. Did *everybody* know everybody else's business? "How do you know about *that?*" Liam demanded.

He hadn't told *anyone* he'd slept with Julia. Had she confided in someone? It didn't seem likely, but right now, everything was in such a state of confusion for him—not to mention red alert—that he didn't know what was up and what was down.

"Wasn't exactly hard to figure out," Toby told him.

"She had that 'touched by Liam Jones' glow that three-quarters of the girls in the graduating senior class had. Don't forget, I was right behind you in high school," he reminded Liam.

To his surprise, Liam tossed aside the rake he was using and hurried out of the stable to where he had left his truck parked early this morning, after taking Julia back to her home.

"Hey, where are you going?" Toby called out, raising his voice.

"To see about that damage control you mentioned," Liam shouted over his shoulder.

Gunning the engine, Liam threw the transmission into overdrive and all but flew the entire distance from his ranch to Horseback Hollow and the Superette.

He had to make this right, he thought. This just couldn't end like this, here, today.

It *couldn't*.

This had to be what they meant by that saying about sins coming home to roost. Liam didn't consider himself a sinner per se, but he had pretty much taken what he wanted out of life and enjoyed all the advantage of being handsome coupled with an ability to say exactly what women wanted to hear.

Oh, he never lied, never made promises he had no intentions of keeping just to get what he wanted, but that didn't exactly make him noble, either. Everything had come easy to him because of his looks and his charm. And the irony of it was that the one woman he really, really wanted he was now in danger of losing because of his past behavior—and someone's big mouth.

Maybe not, he tried to console himself. Maybe it wasn't as bad as it seemed. Maybe Julia wouldn't believe that he had tried to get her to come around by seducing her—

Why not? a voice in his head asked.

Be honest. Hadn't that really been the plan to begin with? To get her to come around to his side using any means that he could?

It wouldn't matter that the moment he began to be around her, everything had drastically changed. Wouldn't matter that he'd gotten caught up in her, in wanting to *be* with her.

In wanting to see her happy.

The damage was done and that would be all that she'd see, all that she would focus on. She was, after all, only human, not a saint.

He should have leveled with her from the very start, Liam lectured himself. But he hadn't wanted to risk it. Instead he had hoped that if he'd let things ride, they would eventually go his way because everything else always had.

And since he had eventually found himself on the same side of the debate about the restaurant as she was, he felt that there was no point in letting Julia know that he had had less than honorable intentions when he'd undertaken this whole campaign.

The truth was highly overrated, he couldn't help thinking.

Look what the truth was about to do to him—it was going to torpedo the first real love he'd ever felt right out of the water.

Part of him wanted to lay low and wait for this to blow over. But that was the coward's way out and beneath him, he silently insisted as he watched his speedometer edge up to eighty.

It wasn't worthy of him—or of her.

He arrived in town faster than he'd thought possible. Drawing his courage to him, Liam parked his truck across the street from the Superette and got out. His knees shook as he walked toward the Superette, trying to figure out just how he was going to say what he needed to say to save what they had between them.

His mind temporarily went blank for ten terrifying seconds.

This had to work. Even if he had to get on his knees, this had to work. He couldn't think about it going the other way.

The bell tinkled, announcing his entrance. Julia automatically glanced toward the door.

Damn it, Julia thought, her heart wasn't supposed to leap up like that anymore at the sight of Liam, not when she knew what was behind that smile, behind those compelling blue eyes that had come close to being her undoing.

She had to remember that Liam didn't care about her. He'd probably spent the morning laughing about the way she'd become almost like the proverbial putty in his hands. He had tried to play her and he had almost made her into a laughingstock.

The thought stung something awful.

She wanted Liam to feel what she was feeling, to know the pain of hurt, the sting of humiliation.

At a loss how to begin to broach this smoothly, he just stumbled in with an apology. "Look, Julia, I didn't mean to—"

Her eyes were frosty as she looked at him. "If you're trying to apologize, there's no need to."

He wasn't going to take the easy way out. He could see that he'd hurt her and she was angry. "Yes, there is. I—"

"There's no need to," she repeated, continuing as if Liam hadn't tried to interrupt. "Because, obviously, what you were attempting to do didn't succeed. Not that it was a bad plan," she allowed loftily, totally confusing him given the expression on his face, "but you didn't count on the fact that two can play that game."

His confusion only intensified. It felt as if someone had taken his brain to use as a tennis ball and had just lobbed it far into the air.

"What are you talking about? What game?" he asked.

Because people were beginning to stare, she tugged Liam over to the side, away from prying eyes. "To keep it simple, we can call it 'victory by seduction.' I think that rather sums it up nicely, actually." Her eyes bored straight into him. "You think that you're the only one who uses seduction as a tool to persuade an unwitting person of something?"

He stared at her, dumbfounded. What was she saying?

He didn't have long to wait for an answer. "While you were trying to play me, I decided to turn the tables on you and seduce *you* into seeing things my way." Her smile was cool and never even came close to reaching her eyes. "And, seeing as how the vote went my way and the sign for the new restaurant went up this morning, I'd say I turned out to be better at this little 'persuasion' game than you were."

She pretended to laugh even though the sound tore at her throat.

"In all fairness, I guess you didn't realize that I had it in me—but I did," she told him. "So you see," Julia concluded, "there's no reason to apologize. What you did just activated what I had to do. And I did it. You didn't oppose me and now the restaurant's going to be built."

Was she being truthful? Had she really played him, gotten him to come around by playing up to him, by making him think of nothing else, *want* nothing else, but her?

Liam felt as if someone had rammed a knife into his gut and then twisted it. Hard.

"Congratulations," he rasped.

"Thank you," she replied in the same dead tone he'd just used.

She turned away, walking back to the register, pretending that she was needed back at work.

Julia didn't need to look over her shoulder to know that he was walking out. She heard the bell signal his departure. It almost sounded mournful to her.

Victory had never felt as hollow as it did this minute.

That was okay, she told herself. She'd get over this by and by.

In about fifty years or so.

Until then, she thought, squaring her shoulders and marching to the register, she had customers to wait on.

Chapter Fifteen

Five days went by. Five long, agonizing days that seemed to drag by in slow motion, leaving long, jagged, painful scars in their wake.

Julia found she had trouble concentrating. It wasn't that she would drift off; it was more a case of her mind going blank with nothing for her to catch hold of. That, at least, was more merciful than other moments when she would berate herself for being such a fool. For being so incredibly naïve.

She'd been smarter, she told herself as despair would start to fill every nook and cranny in her being, when she had been in high school than she was now. Back in high school, she'd made a point of deflecting Liam's attention that time it had been directed at her.

Granted, when he had asked her out, it hadn't really

come across as a full-fledged attack on her defenses, but at the time she'd been more than relatively inexperienced. And yet she'd been smart enough to say "No" to him when all the other girls in school had cried a breathless "Yes!"

She might secretly have been a little miffed when he didn't try to get her to change her mind and had just shrugged in response to her rejection, but she'd been proud of herself then. Proud of the fact that she hadn't just followed the crowd like some brainless lemming and gloried in whatever small crumb of attention Liam would have been willing to give her at the time.

The bottom line was that she'd been discerning and she had made her mark on him by being the only one who'd turned him down, the one who *hadn't* worshipped at his feet.

And where did that get her? Years of unconsciously wondering what it might have been like to be with him? Being ripe for his romantic advances when they finally materialized in full force? That didn't exactly seem like much of a triumph to her.

And now what?

Now that she felt like a hollowed-out shell of her former self, what exactly was she to do with herself? Now that she knew what it felt like to be on the receiving end of his touch, his kiss, his exquisite lovemaking, where did she go from here?

How did she go on knowing that the very best was behind her and that she had nothing but emptiness in front of her?

Frustrated, Julia wiped back one offending tear, silently forbidding herself from shedding any more.

A lot of good *that* did, she thought unhappily. She was just grateful they had closed for the evening and that there were no customers to witness her meltdown.

No one, that is, except for her mother.

Julia turned her head away, hoping her mother hadn't noticed the telltale tears before she had a chance to wipe them away.

But she should have known better. Her mother was one of those legendary eyes-in-the-back-of-her-head mothers and was almost always one step ahead of her.

"I hate seeing you like this," Annie told her, her voice throbbing with sympathy. She had given Julia five days to deal with whatever was going on in her life, but she couldn't bear it any longer and broke her silence as they closed up the store. "Maybe if you tried to talk to him——"

"No!" Julia snapped, then flushed. "Sorry, I didn't mean to yell at you," she said in apology. "But really, Mom, I'm fine."

"No," her mother replied quietly but firmly, "you're not." She pointed out the difference. "When your marriage to Neal ended, you were fine. A little sad, yes, but you mustered on just as I knew you would. You *didn't* look the way you do now——"

Carrying the dairy products to the refrigerator in the storeroom, Julia sighed. "Mother, you're exaggerating."

"No, I'm observing," Annie corrected. "And if anything, I'm understating the situation.

"You and Liam looked good together. *Were* good

together," her mother stressed. "Some mothers sense things like that," she explained, "and I sensed it about the two of you."

Yeah, well, it was an act, all an act, Julia thought. And she, and her mother apparently, had fallen for it.

"He fooled us all, Mother. Liam is a very good actor."

But Annie shook her head. Her still vibrant red hair was cut short and swished around her face as if to underscore the sentiment she expressed.

"Not that good, Julia. My vision isn't colored by a desire for you to marry well or to nab a wealthy husband. My only, *only* requirement was—and is—for you to follow your heart, which was why I wasn't all that overjoyed when you told me you were marrying Neal."

The corners of Julia's mouth curved sadly. She'd expected her mother to be overjoyed by the news that she was going to marry the affable lawyer. Seeing sadness in her mother's eyes had only confused her.

"I remember," Julia said quietly.

"I *liked* Neal," Annie insisted. "He was a nice boy and he was obviously taken with you, but I knew that while you might have even talked yourself into loving him, you weren't *in* love with him and that, my darling daughter, makes a world of difference." She looked up into her daughter's eyes, trying to make her understand. "Julia, I'm not the wisest woman in the world, but I could see that you were in love with Liam—and you still are."

Denial quickly rose up in her throat and was hot on her lips, but Julia gave up the lie before she ever uttered a word. She knew there was no point to it. So instead, she shrugged, silently acknowledging her mother's statement.

"I'll get over it."

"I don't want you to get over it," Annie insisted, closing the refrigerator door with a little too much force. "I want you to act on it. Love is *not* all that common. It doesn't happen to everyone. And if it happens to you, you should make the most of it. Grab it with both hands and hang on for dear life."

Julia sighed again, struggling hard to keep from crying. "Mom, it's over. If Liam felt anything remotely close to what you're describing, he'd be over here, banging on my door, demanding to talk to me, demanding we work things out."

She pressed her lips together before going on.

"If you listen closely, you'll see that there's no banging, no demanding going on. There's *nothing*. It was all a charade, an act. And now it's over. He's gone. And I have a life to live."

Pausing for a moment, she kissed her mother's cheek. "Thanks for worrying, Mom, but please stop. That chapter of my life is closed. Now, I need to get some rest because I'm meeting with Wendy and her husband tomorrow. They said they wanted to talk to me about managing their restaurant." This was supposed to be one of the best moments of her life, better than she'd initially hoped. But she felt dead inside. Julia forced a smile to her lips. It wasn't as easy as it should have been, she couldn't help thinking as she took her mother's hand. "This is my dream, Mom. It's everything I've ever wanted. Be happy for me."

Annie squeezed her daughter's hand. She knew better, but right now, there was no point in beating this dead horse. "If that's what you want, Julia, then yes, of course, I'm happy for you."

But it was a lie.

Neither one of them was really happy.

"You going to hide in here forever?" Toby chided as he walked into Liam's stable the next morning.

Toby and his brothers and sisters had all gotten together to discuss their concern about the state of Liam's surliness as well as his withdrawal from sight for almost a week. When it came to the topic of which of them would approach Liam about the matter, they decided to draw straws.

As luck—or lack thereof—would have it, Toby had gotten the short one. That meant that it was up to him to approach Liam about it as well as to try to get him to abandon this hermitlike existence and get back into the game of life.

"I'm not hiding," Liam retorted. He didn't spare his brother a single glance. Instead he just went on brushing his horse.

"Nobody's seen you since the day after the vote was taken at the meeting—the day that somebody ran off at the mouth and started that stupid rumor about you trying to get Julia to see your way by seducing her," Toby pointed out.

"It's called working, Toby," Liam snapped at his brother. "I've been working. You should try it sometime."

"I work plenty, Liam," Toby reminded him patiently. "I run my ranch and I'm taking care of three kids and once in a while, I get to sleep for an hour or two. But we're not talking about me, Sunshine," Toby said sarcastically, "we're talking about you. Everyone in the family is worried about you. Nobody's seen you at the saloon and Stacey said you blew her off when she suggested meeting her at The Grill two days ago. She left a message on your machine. You never called her back."

Liam shrugged off the accusation. "Like I said, I've got work."

From what Toby could see, Liam might have work, but he hadn't done any of it. Except for one thing. "From the looks of it, you've groomed your horse to death, but the rest of the place looks like it's going to seed."

"If you're here to nag me, I'd just as soon you save your breath, turn around and ride back," Liam told him with finality. He might as well have flashed a no-trespassing sign at his brother for all the friendliness in his tone.

"Can't," Toby replied flatly.

Liam stopped grooming his stallion and fixed his brother with a look. "Why not?"

"'Cause," Toby said very simply, "I drew the short straw."

Liam narrowed his eyes, fixing his younger brother with a penetrating look. "And what's that supposed to mean?"

Toby went for the literal interpretation. "It means that we all drew straws to see who was going to come out to talk to you and I got the short one."

Liam could only stare at him in disbelief. "You drew straws," he repeated incredulously.

"Yeah," Toby replied. "Nobody likes talking to you when you're like this."

"Like what?" Liam challenged darkly.

"Angrier than a wet hen trying to peck at his dinner using a rubber beak."

Despite himself, Liam laughed a beat before his scowl returned. "Now there's an image," he mused. Then he sobered and looked at Toby. "Well, you talked to me. So you can go home now."

It didn't work that way, even though Liam's suggestion was tempting. "I'm not supposed to just talk. I'm supposed to get through to you," Toby explained. "Not that that's easy to do, given your thick skull."

"And just what is it that you're trying to 'get through' my thick skull?" he demanded. "What bits of wisdom are you and the others in possession of that you think you need to 'share' with me?" His voice fairly dripped of sarcasm.

This was a different Liam than the one Toby had grown up with and he didn't much care for this version. "That you're behaving like a jackass."

Liam set his jaw hard before answering. "Great. You've delivered the message. Now go," he ordered, trying not to lose his temper.

Toby and the rest of his family had no idea what he was going through and he wanted to handle recovering from it in his own way, not submitting to being burned by their "good intentions."

Toby refused to give up—or leave. Besides, he wasn't

finished yet. "And that Julia Tierney's the best thing that ever happened to your sorry ass and if you don't do anything to get her back, you're even dumber than I thought you were."

Though he didn't want to, Liam had to grudgingly admit that Toby had good intentions, even if he had his signals crossed.

"Put down your arrows, Cupid, there's nothing to 'get back.' Julia was playing me, trying to keep me distracted so that the vote for her precious restaurant would go through." He shrugged, pretending that what he was saying no longer hurt. "The second it did, she dropped me like a hot potato."

Toby frowned. "That's not the way I heard it."

"Well, that's the way it was," Liam told him flatly. "She *told* me that she played me. There was no point in hanging around after that."

"And you believed her?" Toby questioned incredulously.

Liam narrowed his eyes angrily. "Why shouldn't I believe her? There was no point in her lying to me about that."

Toby stared at him. Was he serious? "Are you familiar with the concept of saving face?"

Liam's scowl deepened. "What's your point?"

Toby tried to explain it as simply as he could. "Rumors are bouncing around all over the place that you were looking to get her to see things your way and you weren't above seducing her to make that happen. She hears that and then you show up at her store, so she does what any normal human being would do to save face. She makes up a story about turning the tables on you so that she doesn't come off being the butt of every joke for the next six months."

It was a good enough explanation—but there was just one thing wrong with it. "But the vote went her way," Liam insisted.

Toby dismissed the point. "That doesn't mean that you didn't have that plan up your sleeve. And with the vote going her way, she had something to build her lie on." He could still see skepticism in Liam's eyes. "Now, if you can't see that, then you're not nearly as bright as I always gave you credit for being."

Toby addressed the last words to the back of Liam's head as his brother went back to grooming his horse for the umpteenth time.

Liam didn't bother commenting, or even grunting.

Toby stood there for another couple of minutes, waiting for some sort of a response, but Liam went on ignoring him.

Finally, Toby sighed.

"Well, I've got a life to get back to. I forgot how damn stubborn you could be when you put your mind to it. It's like trying to dent a brick wall with a marshmallow," he told Liam with disgust. "Just remember, when you wind up alone at the end of the day, you've only got yourself to blame. I tried."

Liam went on maintaining his silence, grooming his horse as if he and the animal were the only two occupants inside the stable.

And eventually they were.

* * *

"Julia, please, sit down," Marcos Mendoza requested, rising to his feet the moment Julia walked into the hotel suite.

Julia had driven to Vicker's Corners to meet with Marcos and his wife since, as of yet, Horseback Hollow didn't have its own hotel. But maybe it would, Julia thought, now that the first step toward expansion had been taken.

"I know you know Wendy, but you haven't met our daughter, Mary Anne," he said, gesturing toward the pretty little two-year-old with the animated face and lively dark eyes.

"Very pleased to meet you," Mary Anne said, smiling up at her.

"You've got a little heartbreaker there," Julia told the couple. There was a trace of longing in her voice. She had always loved children and try as she might, she didn't see any in her future. Ever.

"Thank you, we like her," Wendy said with a great deal of affection as her arms closed around the little girl who had climbed onto her lap.

"We can't tell you how pleased we are to be building our restaurant in your town," Marcos began. "And I know we have a great deal to talk about. So I thought that the most efficient way would be if I just came out and asked you for your input and suggestions right up front." He smiled at her, not bothering to ask if she had any. His instincts about the young woman told him that she did. So he urged her on by saying, "Go ahead, I'm listening."

For some reason, the moment he said that, Julia thought back to the two men she'd overheard talking the morning she'd stood staring at the sign announcing the site of the restaurant's future home. The ones who had blown up her world.

One useful thing had come out of that hurtful exchange between the two men. "I was wondering if you've given any thought to changing the restaurant's name."

"The name?" he questioned. "You don't like the way the Hollows Brasserie sounds?"

"Oh, I think it sounds lovely," she told him quickly because she didn't want to offend him and because she actually did like the name. "But the trouble is Horseback Hollow isn't as cosmopolitan as Red Rock. Some people don't know what the word means at all, or think it's…well, a little lofty-sounding," she said, substituting *lofty* for the word *pretentious* at the last minute, again in an effort not to offend the man. "I was thinking of perhaps calling it The Hollows Cantina, you know, in keeping with the local atmosphere."

She watched Marcos's face, holding her breath. After all, he was the boss and as such, had the final say in the restaurant's name.

To her relief, he grinned after a moment, nodding. "Cantina," he repeated. "I like it. Just proves that we were right in choosing you to work here. You know these people better than we do, obviously, and that can only work to all our advantages," Marcos said, beaming.

Julia let go of the breath she'd been holding. At least

some things were going her way, she thought with a touch of sadness.

And if her heart still felt as if there was a bullet hole smack in the center of it, well, she'd just go on ignoring that sensation until she finally stopped noticing it altogether.

Someday.

But not today.

Chapter Sixteen

He hadn't been in town since he and Julia had gone their separate ways and he had discovered what it felt like to have his heart burned out of his chest while he was still breathing.

Because he'd been holed up on his ranch, Liam hadn't seen the sign he was standing in front of. The sign proclaiming this piece of land to be the "Future Home of The Hollows Cantina."

Liam assumed that the word *Cantina* had to have been an afterthought since it was written just above the now crossed-out *Brasserie*. Apparently either Julia or the Mendozas had decided a more down-to-earth name for the restaurant was needed.

He supposed that was progress of a sort.

There were other things written in on the sign, things

that had been inserted after the sign had been completed because they were written in rather than painted on. Like the words *Grand Opening*.

From what he could see, it was scheduled for a date two months in the future. On the left side of the sign were the words *Now Hiring,* which had to be a welcome sight for a number of people. Those were the ones who knew that ranching was *not* their true calling, but they still wanted to live in Horseback Hollow and earn a living. Jobs that didn't involve ranching were scarce around here.

This new cantina would make them less so.

"Congratulations, Julia," Liam murmured under his breath to the sign. "You did it. You got your restaurant."

"You know, talking to yourself out in public might be viewed by some folks as a person losing his grip on reality."

Liam didn't have to turn around to know that his brother Jude was standing behind him. Seemed as if he couldn't make a move without tripping over a relative, he thought in resignation.

"And sneaking up behind people is one surefire way to get the living daylights beaten out of them," Liam commented as he slowly turned around to face Jude.

"Guess it's lucky for me that you're so even-tempered," Jude joked.

"Yeah, lucky," Liam repeated in a less than cheerful tone.

The next minute Jude was asking him eagerly, "Did you hear the news?"

He'd obviously heard it as well as seen it, given

that he was standing in front of the sign boasting of it. "Yeah, the restaurant's going up," he answered Jude dourly.

For a second Jude stared at him, confused. The restaurant was *not* what he was referring to. "Well, yeah, that's news, too," Jude agreed even as he shrugged it off, "but it's old news."

"And you have 'new' news?" Liam asked with a touch of sarcasm.

In all honesty, Liam really wasn't sure *what* he was doing here in town, or what he had hoped to accomplish by coming.

He supposed that, deep down, he was hoping to run into Julia and get a dialogue going between them. He missed her, damn it, missed the sound of her laughter, the way her eyes sparkled. The way her hair smelled.

It almost seemed impossible, given that they had only been anything remotely resembling "a couple" for little more than two weeks. And yet, when he was with her, he felt as if he had come home, that he was finally whole.

And without her, he wasn't.

It was as simple as that and he could either make his peace with being without her—or do something about getting her back.

The latter wasn't going to be easy and he knew it. For that reason, he secretly welcomed this unexpected distraction that Jude offered.

"Yeah, I do have 'new' news," Jude told him, pleased that he knew something that Liam didn't. "And it involves Toby."

"What about him?" Liam was curious. And if it involved his other brother, why hadn't Toby come over or called and told him about whatever it was himself? Liam could only think of one reason he hadn't seen Toby. "Is he okay?"

Jude grinned and succeeded in annoying him even more than he already had. "Oh, he's more than okay. He's pretty damn happy and more than a damn sight relieved."

Liam struggled to hold on to his patience. "Are you going to tell me what's going on in bits and pieces or are you going to just come out and say it like any normal adult?"

Jude looked just a little put off by his attitude. "Anyone ever tell you that you're no fun?"

"Yeah, lots of people," Liam assured him. "Now talk," he ordered, trying not to allow his concern to show through. "What's going on with Toby?"

Jude did what he could to maintain an air of mystery about what he was revealing, doing so a layer at a time. "Well, somebody slipped an envelope under his door yesterday. It was full of money. A whole bunch of money."

Liam stared at his brother, his expression becoming a deep frown. "From who?"

"That's just the thing," Jude told him, the excitement in his voice growing again. "There was a note but it wasn't signed. It just said the cash was to help take care of the Hemings kids."

"Had to be someone in town," Liam assumed.

But Jude shook his head. "Toby really doesn't think so."

"Why?" There was only one reason for that, he realized. "Just how much money are we talking about?" When Jude told him, it was all Liam could do to keep his jaw from dropping. "You're right," he agreed. "Nobody around here has that kind of money to give away, no matter how good their intentions."

"Nobody but the Fortunes," Jude reminded him.

Liam banked down his automatic desire to dismiss the family because he didn't think of them as altruistic. But of late he'd been learning more and more about the Fortunes and realizing that his preconceived notions regarding them were not just unfair, they were downright wrong.

"How does Toby feel about being on the receiving end of charity?" Liam asked. Toby had every bit as much pride as he did. He'd always liked earning his own way. "Is he resentful?"

"Resentful?" Jude repeated with a laugh. "Hell, no, he's downright grateful. It's for the kids, after all, not him. And Toby doesn't see it as being charity so much as he sees it as being charitable." Jude looked at him for a long moment.

Long enough for Liam to know that something was on Jude's mind that the latter was chewing on. "You have something more to say?" he asked Jude.

"Yeah," he said, picking out his words slowly, the way he might pick his path through a minefield. "Don't you think it's about time you got over your grudge—whatever started it—and accept Mom's family? You know that Mom has. And even Dad finally has, in a way. You're the family holdout."

Shoving his hands into his back pockets, Liam sighed. Ordinarily he wouldn't have cared about being the lone holdout. But he couldn't do it if he'd been wrong to begin with. "Yeah, I guess they really are good people, after all."

"So," Jude began, humor dancing in his eyes, "you don't want to tar and feather them and run them out of town anymore?"

Liam shrugged, doing his best to keep a straight face. "I guess we can hold off on that for a while, seeing as how they *are* family and all."

"There's that generous soul of yours, coming through again." Jude pretended to marvel as he slapped him on the back. "Well, I'll let Mom know. Your change of heart will make her very happy."

"You do that," Liam murmured. "There been any takers?" he asked his brother, switching gears out of the blue.

"What?" Jude stared at him in confusion. "What kind of takers?"

Liam nodded toward the sign. "You know if anyone's applied for a job yet?"

"Why, you looking to branch out?" Jude teased.

The scowl that came over Liam's face had his brother backing off. "Just wondering, that's all," Liam said flatly.

"Why don't you go and ask Julia about it?" Jude suggested innocently. "She'd be the one to know." His eyes narrowed as he looked at his brother intently. The truth came to him riding on a lightning bolt. "You haven't gone to see her yet, have you?"

"I've been busy," Liam answered, a vague, dismissive shrug punctuating his reply.

It was Jude's turn to shake his head in absolute wonder.

"You're my older brother, Liam, and I've always looked up to you. I know you don't exactly welcome advice, but you're selling yourself a bill of goods if you think you can use that excuse indefinitely."

"You're right." Liam turned to look at his younger brother. "I don't welcome advice."

And with that, he got into his truck and drove back to his ranch instead of toward the Superette the way he had initially intended when he had driven into town.

It wasn't that he had lost his nerve—exactly, he told himself—it was just that he realized he still hadn't found the right words to use in framing his apology. He didn't want to come across as either a sap or some gutless, spineless cowboy.

And even though he missed her like crazy, he wasn't about to go crawling to her, either. For one thing, she wouldn't respect him if he did. For another, he wouldn't respect himself, either, and once respect was gone, there was nothing left.

So he went home, to stare at his phone and mull over his situation.

When he did finally pick up the receiver, it wasn't Julia that he called but her future boss. Marcos Mendoza.

The latter was surprised to hear from Liam and even

more surprised to hear the reason for Liam's unexpected phone call.

"You want to reserve *two* tables for the restaurant's grand opening?" Marcos questioned as if he was fairly sure he hadn't heard correctly.

But he had.

"That's what I said. Two," Liam confirmed.

"You do know that we're not opening for another two months, right?" He obviously thought the reservations were a bit premature, since the building hadn't even gone up yet. But Liam always liked being two steps ahead of everything.

"Yeah, I know," Liam answered.

Marcos quoted a cover charge and Liam remained unfazed, saying that was fine with him.

"Okay, consider them reserved," Marcos assured him.

Liam gave him all the particulars Marcos required—phone number, name, etc.—and then hung up.

And crossed his fingers.

"Two tables?" Julia questioned when Marcos called her about the reservation a few minutes later. "You sure it was Liam and not one of his brothers?"

"I'm sure. I verified it twice," he added. "You're off to a really good start, Julia," Marcos told her. He was obviously very pleased. "I just wanted to let you know," he concluded.

Julia thanked him as she hung up, more than a little stunned.

Had she misjudged Liam, after all? She needed to untangle this before it made her crazy.

"Mom," she announced, taking her coverall apron off and leaving it bunched up beneath the counter. "I've got to take off for a couple of hours. Think you can cover for me?"

"If I can't, I'm gonna have to learn, sweetie," Annie told her, patting her daughter's face. "Go, do what you have to do," she told her, all but shooing her out of the store.

Julia was out of the Superette and in her SUV within five minutes of hanging up with Marcos. Her destination was Liam's ranch, to corner the lion in his den to find out what sort of games he was playing now. Or had he changed his mind, after all?

She knew what she wanted more than anything was for Liam to come around, to have him on her side and wishing her well in this brand-new, exciting venture she was undertaking. Because, despite the fact that this was what she really wanted to do, she couldn't pretend that she wasn't exceedingly nervous about undertaking this project. Assistant manager of the first real restaurant in Horseback Hollow was a huge amount of responsibility, no matter how clear-eyed she was about the benefits of the venture.

Her hands were damp as she clutched the steering wheel and drove a little faster than was her custom to Liam's ranch. She was going to have it out with him once and for all. One way or another, this was all going to get resolved.

Today.

Her heart was pounding madly by the time she pulled up in his driveway. The thought had also occurred to her less than five minutes ago that he might not even be at the house. After all, he could be breaking in a horse, repairing a length of fence—perhaps even out somewhere, finding a new companion for his bed.

The last thought succeeded in making her stomach flip over and churn wildly, which in turn made her nauseous.

This was *not* the way she wanted to feel when she finally saw Liam for the first time in more than a week.

Searching for courage, Julia raised her hand to knock on the door only to drop it before her knuckles touched the wood. Not once, but twice.

The third time, she succeeded in making contact with the door. There was no answer. Taking a deep breath, she knocked again, harder this time.

There was still no answer.

Frustrated, she tried again, all but pounding on the door.

"Maybe I'm not home."

Julia jumped, stifling a scream with her hands over her mouth as she swung around. That deep voice seemed to echo all around her.

"Liam!" she cried breathlessly, her heart leaping up into her throat. She dug her fingernails into her palms, trying to force herself to calm down.

Liam cocked his head and looked at her. "I take it that you weren't expecting me."

Chapter Seventeen

It took Julia another thirty seconds before she could finally think straight. Even so, about 90 percent of her brain was still shrouded in a fog, offering only shadows for her to work with.

She found herself torn between wanting to throw her arms around Liam—and wanting to pound on him for putting her through this hell she found herself in.

Get a grip, Jules. Remember why you're here.

"Yes, of course I expected to see you, just not standing behind me," she told him coolly. "But then, you were never exactly predictable, were you?" She couldn't help adding the small dig. Given what she'd been through, Julia thought, she could be forgiven for being a little testy.

"Guess not," Liam replied. Circling around her, he

opened the front door and then took a step back. "Why don't we go inside and you can tell me why you're here. Unless," he added as an afterthought, "you'd feel safer standing outside."

Liam looked at her, waiting for her to make her choice.

Julia raised her chin, braced for a fight. Was he hinting that she was afraid of him for some reason? That certainly wasn't the case. They were still the same people they'd always been—basically.

So, instead of taking the bait—if that was what he intended it to be, she thought—she merely breezed by Liam and walked inside his house.

A smile played on his lips as he followed her in. Maybe things were not quite as dire as he'd thought.

Liam mentally crossed his fingers.

Maybe, just maybe, there was a glimmer of light coming into the coffin before it was nailed shut. Enough light to detect life if there was any to be had. Because as far as he was concerned, there was a *great deal* of life left in the romance that she had pronounced dead.

He just needed to convince her of that.

"Can I offer you something to eat or to drink?" he asked, letting his voice trail off so that Julia felt free to make her own suggestion if she was so inclined.

She did.

"You can offer me an explanation," Julia told him.

Liam closed the door behind him and then turned to face her. "About?"

Liam struggled to keep his voice as cool and distant as hers, but it was taking everything he had not to just pull her into his arms and kiss her the way he'd been aching to do ever since he'd walked out on her at the Superette.

Pride had made him go. But pride was a pretty damn poor substitute for a living, breathing woman who had his heart shoved into her back pocket and probably didn't even know it. Pride couldn't keep him warm at night, or make him happy in any manner.

He'd come to realize in these past few days that pride was an empty, hollow thing that was liable to break at any moment and when it did, it would reveal a gaping hole inside his chest and nothing more.

"Marcos called and told me that you reserved two tables for the Cantina's grand opening. Did you?" she asked.

His eyes met hers. There had to be more, he told himself. But for now, he'd answer Julia's question. "I did."

"That doesn't make any sense. You were completely against the restaurant being built here in Horseback Hollow. Are you planning on burning the place down on opening night?" she asked him point-blank.

Try as she might, she couldn't think of a single reason why Liam would have reserved one table, much less two, in a restaurant he had been so determined to sabotage in the first place.

What was he up to?

"No, Julia," Liam told her calmly. "I'm planning on eating."

Yeah, right. Julia regarded him suspiciously. "And you need two tables for that?"

Her gaze was meant to nail him to the wall. He never flinched. "I'm not planning on eating alone."

"Oh. I see," she said slowly, her mind casting around for a viable scenario. She saw the first thing that occurred to her. "Is this going to be some kind of a reunion of your last dozen or so girlfriends?" she asked coolly.

"No, it's not," he answered, never missing a beat. "I was thinking of having my family accompany me. You know, Jude and Gabi, Toby and those kids, my sisters and even my parents. I thought it might make a nice event for my family," Liam concluded, leaving her completely dumbfounded.

Julia shook her head. "I don't understand. You were so dead set against having this…*invasion,* I believe was the word you used—having this invasion coming into the town just a few weeks ago. Now you want to bring your family on opening night?" she questioned.

Liam took a deep breath, swallowed the last of his pride and told her, "I was wrong."

Julia blinked. Had she not been looking at his mouth as he'd said it, she would have sworn she was hearing things. But he had actually said that.

Still, she had to make sure she wasn't suddenly hallucinating. "You're admitting that."

His eyes never left hers. This was for all the marbles, he thought. The old Liam would have never gone this far. But he'd already lost everything. This was his only chance to gain it back and he knew it.

"Yeah."

Julia blew out a breath. "Okay, what's the catch?" She wanted to know.

There had to be a catch. Much as she wanted to believe Liam, much as she wanted to trust him, a part of her held back, afraid of being proved wrong yet again. She'd barely survived—if you could call it that—once. Twice would kill her.

"There isn't one. I'm telling you the truth," he swore. He *had* to make her believe him. "I've made more than my share of mistakes, Julia, and I don't want to make any more. And while I'm at it, here's another 'truth' for you—"

Julia braced herself, expecting the worst.

"You were right. I did start out romancing you to get you to change your mind about backing the restaurant." His eyes on hers, he prayed what he was about to say wasn't a mistake. But if he was to win her back, there had to be nothing but honesty between them. "I thought if I could get you into my bed, I could make you forget all about your project. Instead, *I* was the one who forgot all about it. The first time we made love, I realized that the only thing that really mattered to me was you—and," he admitted, "that pretty much scared the hell out of me."

She knew it took a lot for him to admit that. What she couldn't understand was why something as special as what they'd had would scare him. "Why?"

"Because I couldn't seem to control the feelings I had for you. Instead they were controlling me. So when you broke things off, telling me you had done the same thing that I had set out to do, part of me thought, okay, maybe it was better this way. I thought I could get over you."

"Like a cold," she concluded with finality. She tried

to appear indifferent to what he was saying, but the thought hurt.

He laughed shortly. He could see why she'd say that. Liam shook his head. "People get over colds," he replied. And he had certainly *not* gotten over her. "You're more like a fever of the blood."

"People get over fevers, too," she pointed out in a low voice, doing her best to contain her feelings.

Was it too late? she wondered, the thought all but squeezing the air out of her lungs. Was Liam telling her that he was "over" her?

"I haven't," he told her. "And here's another truth for you. I don't think I'm going to. Ever."

She took in a long, shaky breath. She knew how hard that had been for him. The least she could do was come clean herself.

"All right," she began, "since we're telling the truth, I might as well tell you that I lied, too."

"You?" he asked. He braced himself for anything. "About what?"

She would rather not look him in the eye when she said this. But to look anywhere else would have been cowardly. "About seducing you."

"But you did seduce me," he reminded her. And with no effort at all, she'd held him in the palm of her small hand.

"If I did, it wasn't to get you to forget about convincing people to vote against the proposal." She could feel her cheeks growing warm as they turned a shade of pink, but she pushed on. "My only ulterior motive was to get you to want me for a while longer."

Relief swept through him. He smiled at her then, his eyes caressing her, making love to her even though his hands remained at his sides. For now.

"You succeeded beyond your wildest dreams," he told her. "Because I do."

"You want me?" she asked uncertainly, afraid to hope. "After everything that happened?"

"More than I ever did," he admitted freely. "I want you now. I'll want you tomorrow and all the tomorrows for the rest of my life."

She looked at him, afraid that she was hearing what she wanted to hear and not what Liam was really saying. So, at the risk of looking like an idiot to him, she asked, "What are you saying, Liam?"

He'd never tripped over his tongue before. Words had come so easily to him because they'd required no thought and had no heart behind them. But everything was different now. His heart—and the rest of his life— were on the line.

"I guess, what I'm saying—awkwardly—is that I want you to marry me."

Julia's mouth suddenly went dry as she stared at him. It was as close to dumbfounded as she'd ever been. "You're proposing." It was half a statement, half a mystified question.

"I did mention that I was saying it awkwardly," he reminded her.

Her eyes smiled and then the corners of her mouth began to curve ever so slightly. "You want me to be your wife?"

"I could act it out with hand puppets if you'd like," he offered.

"What I would like," she told him, still careful to keep any emotion out of her voice, "is to have you make me understand why you're asking me to marry you."

He could see why she would be skeptical. He wasn't doing this very well. But then, he'd never done this before and in all honesty, had never thought he would. "Because I've seen what living without you after having you in my life is like and I hate it. I don't *want* to live without you anymore and I'll do whatever I have to, to get you to say yes."

He took a breath, then, carefully taking her hands in his, he looked into her eyes and said, "I love you, Julia. I've never said that to another woman—other than my mother and I think I was five at the time. Point is, I'll never say that again to any other woman. I don't want anyone else. I want you."

Julia was silent for a long moment, and when she finally spoke, she uttered a single word.

"Wow."

It wasn't the word he was hoping for.

Liam looked at her uncertainly. "Is that a yes? Because if it's not, I intend not to give up until it is. Just tell me what I have to do to get you to say yes and I'll do it," he promised. "Because—"

She put her fingers on his lips to still them. "You can shut up and kiss me," she told him. "And make love with me." Because as far as she was concerned, way too much time had passed since he had.

The grin that took possession of his mouth was almost blinding. He took her into his arms, pulling her closer. "I can do that."

And he did.

* * * * *